Also by Robinson & Kovite

War of the Encyclopaedists (Scribner, 2015)

To Max!
You rock!
Thanks for reading
& for your own brain power
spent imagining the
future!

DELIVER US

A NOVEL

Christopher Robinson
and
Gavin Kovite

Alephactory Press
Seattle

Alephactory Press
325 23rd Avenue East
Seattle, WA 98112

www.alephactory.com

First Alephactory hardcover edition April 2018.

ALEPHACTORY and design are registered trademarks of Alephactory LLC, the publisher of this work.

Interior Design by C.G.R.

Library of Congress Control Number: 2017916090

ISBN 978-0-9994774-0-3
ISBN 978-0-9994774-1-0 (ebook)

For Amanda Knox and Molly Kovite

"I know this looks like science fiction. It's not."
— Jeff Bezos

DELIVER US

I

The city rises—up here, birds and smoke and clang, belched from below: the largest foundry in the world, where eighty-five thousand move in muscular rhythm, pockets fat with five dollar bills, black men firing the furnaces, dunking red-hot coil springs in quench tanks, and the Irish, Italian, and Polish—before they were white—cutting glass, fitting trim and cushion, miles of thick vinyl, black, tan, burgundy —a dream of steel and glass, a dream on wheels that rolls out the River Rouge plant by the minute—up here, the past becomes future, Model-As become Bs become Thunderbirds, Mustangs, men become hydraulic arms—up here, the drab and silent River Rouge, rolling out its F-150s, its crew at shift change, pallid and paunchy in cargo shorts and Tigers hats, sucking down Marb lights as they stare toward the riverfront, once an industrial preserve for the American Midwest junkie, now a pristine promenade for stroller-jockeys licking balsamic strawberry ice cream in the shadow of the RenCen rising up in its sterile mediocrity to GM headquarters, looking down on the immovable Joe Louis Fist that never quite smashed Jim Crow—

Luther Prince, ten years into his Ford retirement, stood on his sagging porch with a cordless phone. He had just called 9-11 about the fire licking up one of the vacant houses down the block. Arson, most likely. And there was a red truck coming down the street, but it wasn't no fire truck. It was a red pickup—one of those city contractors: a water shut-off truck. It rolled to a stop in front of his house. A man in blue coveralls hopped out, looked over at the fire, then walked up to his porch.

"Mr. Prince?"

"I sent in the check."

"Our records show an account outstanding of over a thousand dollars."

"No, I made the payment."

"I'm sorry, sir, but I've got to shut off your water unless you can confirm payment now."

"Hold on, hold on." He dialed up the Detroit Water and Sewerage Department and put the phone on speaker. Hold music blared out. The contractor flipped through his paperwork, tapping his clipboard with the pen affixed to it by a chain.

The Ford pension should have been enough to last Luther and Grace until the Lord called them both to His bosom. But Grace got sick. And then Nia, his eldest granddaughter, got sick. And not the kind of sick you recover from. They both hung on long enough that Luther had to take his pension as a lump sum; most of that went to the medical bills. And that *most* could still turn into *all* if his disputes with UnitedHealthcare went the wrong way. At least he still owned his own house. The cruelest irony was that Nia had been protesting these water shut-offs, chaining herself to fences even. And now that she was gone, they'd finally come to wrench him dry.

"Detroit Water and Sewerage Department. Are you calling to make a payment?"

"I'm calling to check on a payment. Gentleman here come to shut off my water, but I mailed a check out on Friday."

"I'm transferring you to Account Services, please hold."

"No wai—"

Up here, the glass and granite of One Campus Martius where billionaire Dan Gilbert swims inside a vault of mortgage loans, his pizza-faced bankers with their sport coats and kung-fu hair knots sipping lattes in the park below, eating kimchi tacos in a plot of artificial beach, an old black man banging out a Joplin number on a painted street piano, soundtrack for the dance of urban decay renewing itself— the Broderick Tower, once a wreck, strewn with dusty dentist chairs, graffitied walls gouged for their copper pipe, now refurbed for tech sophisticates with their miniature dogs, the Book Tower with its green copper roof, a mausoleum yes, but beachhead, too, for a newcomer from Seattle, ten floors crunching data, designing the future in a city whose arteries spread like a hand, the strangely vacant roads built for an empire that stepped out for cigarettes and never came home, rays stretching out through a sea of frame and brick houses—

The dog next door started barking up a frenzy. He could hear it before Luther, that noise, like a band saw cutting pipe, then, as it got closer, the bass thrum of the rotor blades bouncing off the concrete. The dog absolutely lost it, jumping at the fence like it was making Play of the Week pop fly catches. It wasn't usually a barker, but the one thing that invariably drove it wild was these buzzing drone helicopters that kept flying incessantly, for whatever reason, over Clarion street from the direction of City Airport, or what *used* to be City Airport until Amazon bought it. They weren't even making deliveries yet, far as Luther knew. The drone banked over his yard to avoid the smoke from the house fire.

Through the barking, and the rotor noise, Luther thought he heard, no, *definitely* heard the line pick up and the hold music give way to a tired call center employee. He started to shout *hello?* into the phone, but by the time the drone had passed, and the dog had quieted down to take a few breaths, the voice on the other end was gone, and the calming grooves of the hold music again prevailed.

"*Damn it!*" Luther barked at the phone, actually waving his fist, realizing that the gesture was almost parodic.

"Sir, I'm gonna have to shut you off now. They can get you started up again when you reach the call center and make a payment."

"I *already* made the payment!" Didn't he? He distinctly remembered sealing up the check for $459.84 into the plastic-windowed return envelope to be sent to Lansing. What if he hadn't mailed it? What if he was thinking of last month? No, he remembered mailing it. But the nagging doubt was raising his blood pressure. Wisps of black smoke were floating over his yard now. Luther glanced at the doomed building and saw some teenage kid with a bicycle on the sidewalk, watching the blaze. Fifty-fifty, he was the arsonist.

Luther gritted his teeth and went inside. He opened the hallway closet. There it was, leaning in the corner: his old single barrel, pump-action Remington shotgun, a budget duck hunter, and there, under an old Ford hat on the shelf, a cardboard box of shells.

Up here, Michigan Avenue is a lifeline shooting west, past Coney Island joints, police HQ, the MGM Grand, and Corktown with its brawling Irish buried in the brickwork now housing craft cocktails for kids with kitsch tattoos—up here, Grand River Avenue is a summer creek, nearly dry, flowing out past Northwestern High where the murder rate refuses to drop, out to Brightmoor, all shadow and loss, where the grass is colonizing the charred shells of houses, where windows are made of plywood and garbage is a weed that seems to sprout from the concrete, where people still live and tireless demo crews chip away at derelict housing stock, where hood rats roll blunts in rusty cars with expired tabs on polished wheels, bumping Danny Brown outside the party store stocking liquor and lotto behind level III ballistic glass—up here, Woodward Avenue is a length of tape measuring decay, stretching up the Cass Corridor, where once two kids got shot over an 8-Ball jacket long before the fusion restaurants arrived, north past the lone Whole Foods to the only English Gothic homeless shelter: the Woodward

Presbyterian Church with its octagonal lantern dome which offered respite from the summer of '67, the pounding heat urging throw something, break something, as police busted a black speakeasy blocks away and thousands tore through stores like fire, sparing those marked soul brother with lamb's blood—up here, Woodward measures out to Menjo's on McNichols where the men flex pecs and sing Madonna, north to Eight Mile, where the city ends and the white people begin, in Ferndale, Royal Oak, where the fire trucks arrive on time, north to West Bloomfield where the wine cellars outnumber negroes—

The hold music was still playing from the cordless when he took the shotgun back to the porch, set it on the railing next to the box of shells, flipped it over, and started plunking in the red plastic cartridges, one after another, glancing back down the street every few seconds to scope out the kid on the bike. Luther wasn't about to start shooting off, but he could at least give the little thug a good scare before the fire trucks came, if they ever came. He wanted to call dispatch again, but he was still on hold with the Water Department, whose funky hold-music jams were starting to get on his nerves, the jagged compound annoyance throbbing in the back of his head with every satisfying click of the shotgun's chamber. The contractor looked over, alarmed, and said, "Whoa now," but he was savvy enough not to overreact.

Truth be told, Luther had nearly forgotten about the contractor in all the excitement of the fire, the drone, and the hold music. Almost thirty years at Ford, married for twenty-five of them, owned this same house for twenty-two, and now here he was, a widower whose pension had been cashed out and spent, on a block where half the houses were vacant and collapsing, inviting playpens for teenage firebugs and flophouses for junkies and scrappers. Luther used to think of them as them and him as him, one of the upright citizens, a solid working man with a code of conduct and old country discipline. Now he mostly sat around alone, watching television, not

working, taking meds for back pain, and watching some white guy from Warren or Southfield shut off the water to his house. What would he tell Piper, his remaining granddaughter? Where was she going to take showers? Would they be able to use the toilets? Luther's squinty eyes fixed on that shifty teenage fire-starter.

Up here, I-75 is a steel beam dropped on Paradise Valley where black horns and drums and dice spilled out into the streets from the doorways of shabby buildings that looked like prophecy to nervous whites worried about the colored problem as realtors paid black children to walk their neighborhoods and scare them into selling, as they burned the trashcans of the black family who crossed the red line, as they picketed outside Sojourner Truth in '42—up here, Gratiot Avenue is a whip unfurling from Eastern Market where throngs of homemakers once procured produce and meat wrapped up in acres of butcher paper, where white kids from Chicago and Bushwick now weld cargo bicycles and hand-carve sunglasses out of fir, east to the Dequindre Cut, that lost rail trench, where young graf writers learned to bomb with a three-prong grip on a can of Krylon, past churches, a lot of them, in the sides of strip malls and one-story shops—Moses Emmanuel Baptist, Free Indeed Ministries, Jubilee House, Union Liquor, Sunset Liquor, so many different migrations—

The hold music cut.

"*We have received your last payment as of yesterday, so you are under the minimum balance and your next payment is due August tenth.*"

Luther yelled for the contractor. He yelled back that he'd already shut the water off, but he came to the porch to talk with the call center lady, seeming to be somewhat open to popping that water on again and letting Luther go another day without having to admit to Piper that he was on the edge of bankruptcy, just like the city.

And then the dog started up again, jumping up and down and

getting all crazy. That whine. Another one of the damned things, just five minutes on the heels of the last…

Up here, the city airport looks inviting, the new fulfillment center and factory hum along, but a pillar of smoke occludes, rising from the firewood of someone's house off Gratiot and Georgia, no fire truck in sight, a pillar bending sideways in the wind of prime air space above a trench of sagging houses, then everything gray, grayer, black, blacker, blind, a tumbling down below the smoke, ground rushing up—

The drone flew right through the house fire's black plume, and then flipped and dropped, banking over Luther's yard, drunkenly hitting a tree branch, sending a puff of rotor-shredded leaves in the air. It caught itself and wobbled back to a hover just a few feet off of his porch, the noise unbelievably loud and grating, the contractor with his fingers in his ears turning to walk back to the meter, the dog leaping against its chain, and the kid on the bike riding off, and the call center lady was just barely audible, inquiring, Are you still there, sir? You're breaking up. "Oh, shit."

Leveling now, fighting gravity, as a wizened black man with glasses bigger than his face hobbles off his porch with a shotgun, the mutt next door lunging at the fence, the old man sighting right down the barrel, fairly steady for a guy his age, then—flipping, spinning, falling, rising, thud.

1

"Wait wait wait, what happened? Did it just fall out of the sky?"

Jamal Dent, Chief Pilot for Amazon.Detroit, removed his video goggles and rubbed the bridge of his nose. Annika Dahl hovered over him, her Bluetooth headset blinking next to his face. Jamal cued up the video on his monitor and ran it back to just before impact, then paused at the old crank with the shotgun in the corner of the frame. "We got our first shoot-down," he said.

"Why were you flying so low?"

"Wasn't trying to. That smoke, I think it screwed with the accelerometer. She went into a spin and hit a tree branch on the way down—knocked out one of the rotors. I leveled her off over that guy's yard, and then, well…boom."

"Wow, okay, there we go." Annika sucked her cheek in and bounced on the balls of her feet—a nervous tic her ex had called *the stair-master*.

"Well, let's call in the response team," Jamal said.

Annika paced the windowed perimeter of the cramped pentagonal room—the Bird's Nest, what had been the control tower for Coleman Young Municipal Airport. Amazon had bought the rust-bucket property for its new UAV factory and fulfillment center. Jamal had insisted on setting up his piloting station here, four stories above the industrial campus.

"We should call in the response team," Jamal said again.

Annika drummed her fingers on the windowsill. She could see all the way to downtown, over six miles of residential blight, to the Book Tower, which housed Amazon's new Detroit office. Her boss, Davit Jasper, was there right now, somewhere on the 35th floor, swishing about in his velour tracksuit. He was not going to be happy about this.

"Why don't we just call in—"

"Response teams won't be up until we go live with deliveries," Annika said.

"Damn."

In the dog bed at his feet, Jamal's English Bulldog, Barry Sanders, lifted a leaden eyelid and snorted.

"I know. Annoying. I'll call the police," Annika said.

"The cops? Who knows what they'll do to that guy."

"What, you think they'll shoot him?"

Jamal had grown up in Detroit, and though his lust for comic books and model airplanes had kept him out of trouble, he knew plenty of other black kids who learned early on that the cops often made things worse. "Probably not, but…"

"We don't have a ton of options here," Annika said. They had two months to convince the FAA and the public that UAV delivery was workable. That would never happen if they let nutballs shoot the damn things out of the sky. "We have to set a—" She clutched her nose, some Midwest allergen playing kickball with her sinuses. Jamal offered her a tissue. The sneeze stood at the threshold, peering in, and then sulked off. "—set a precedent."

"But the whole point of the response teams was to keep any UAV crashes on the DL."

"Complaining is not a strategy," she said, reciting a common Jeffism.

Barry hoisted himself up, a string of drool stretching down to the crusty flannel of his dog bed. Jamal wiped Barry's jowls with the Detroit Lions quarterback towel clipped to his collar. Annika shuddered at the sight.

"Just saying," Jamal said. "You want Detroit to like us, right?"

How she'd make that happen was a complicated question. After six years at Amazon, her big promotion two weeks ago had landed her in the Motor City, with the fuzzy job title of "Prime Air Ambassador," and responsibilities that lay somewhere at the confluence of operations and PR, the latter of which was not on her resume. But Bezos promoted potential, not experience. He wanted managerial "athletes" who could take charge of anything, thinking outside boxes, then smashing those boxes to pieces. Now here she was, a Level 7, reporting to the S-Team, responsible for selling the city of Detroit on the idea of Amazon.

"DIAL 9-11," Annika said, and her phone vibrated inside the pencil case she carried with her at all times.

"Cops take forever on the east side," Jamal said.

"But we pay their overtime, plus this guy just fired a shotgun!"

"Nik, people pop off guns all the damn time in this city. You gotta call 9-11 like a week in advance."

"Fine. END CALL. You'll have to go recover it."

"I've got more mapping to—"

"Jamal...principle number two..." She leaned over him with a smile.

The scent of female-type shampoo drifted into his airspace. In the two years since his divorce, he had regressed to the undersexed teenage version of himself, where a woman's touch or smell fuzzed out his avionics. Jamal sighed. *"Never say that's not my job."*

He twisted in his chair to stretch out his back—all this office work was starting to make him feel like a fat, old man, even at thirty-two. He stood and clipped his phone to his belt.

Annika had thought of advising him against the clip-on phone thing. He already dressed poorly—his clothes too tight for his paunch—and the clip gave him the unfortunate vibe of an assistant scoutmaster who specialized in pinewood derby. But he was so terribly sweet, chivalrous in an old-fashioned way. Maybe it was his military background. And though she was a rung above him on the corporate ladder, she wasn't his direct boss; she needed him to like her. As a local, Jamal was her best window into this strangely foreign city in the heart of her own country. "Hey, dork," she said. "Thanks."

Jamal nodded. "Barry, let's go, buddy," he said, and the two them, man and dog, hustled out the door with the same awkward gait, working out the ache of prolonged sitting with every step.

Jamal sped south on Gratiot, windows down, Barry's cheeks flapping in the wind and his towel fanning out like a terrycloth cape. He swung onto Clarion Street, past a few boarded-up vacants being overtaken by jungle. Most of the houses at the end of the block were still inhabited, some dog-eared ramblers with collapsing porches, but a few with fresh paint and chain-link. The burning house on the corner was still spewing smoke into the sky, scenting the sweet July air with notes of carbon. The UAV lay belly-up on the sidewalk. There were half a dozen models in the Amazon fleet, including a few fixed-wings the size of Smart Cars for heavier payloads. This poor girl was an Amazon A-4 "Skeeter," the short-range octocopter that would handle most urban Prime Air deliveries: small black frame, yellow Amazon swoop, eight rotors, four stilt legs, and clamps to secure a Prime Air delivery box or, in this case, a gimbal for a quality camera. Jamal shook his head and chuckled. After thirty months of combat flight time in southwest Asia, his first shoot-down had been in Detroit, about a mile from his childhood home, by some eastside NIMBY who was just now opening his front door.

"That thing yours?" asked the old man. He wore a herringbone flat cap and light jacket, though it was nearly eighty degrees. His glasses were so big they magnified the entire swath of face between his upper lip and eyebrows.

This was awkward. "It's not mine. It's Amazon's," Jamal said. "I'm just the pilot."

"I oughta slap you upside the head," the old man said, stepping off his porch and approaching with what smelled like a grape-fla-vored cigarillo in his leathery hand. "That thing came buzzing down here, driving the dog next door out of its mind, scaring me to death."

"We're mapping the neighborhood for our delivery service."

"Y'all need to ask first. People still live here, you know."

Jamal plucked at his sweat-damp shirt. "You can't just shoot these things. They're private property."

"Let me tell you son, this here's *my* private property, so don't you be telling me about no private property when you're buzzing over my house. It happens again, I do it again."

Barry gave a huffy quasi-bark from the car. The old man eye-balled the dog, then gazed down the street to where a fire truck was finally pulling up to the burning house. Jamal wanted to yell back at the old man, but what would be the point? The guy wanted to fight off a future that had already arrived at his doorstep. It was sad.

"You should come to our press conference on the fourth," Jamal said. "You know, people in your neighborhood could really benefit from—"

"I'm seventy-one years old. I worked all my life—this ain't no welfare house. Bad enough I gotta watch out it don't get burned down by some punk cause a can of gas is cheaper than a damn movie. Amazon gon do something about that?" The old man turned and shuffled inside. The deadbolt clunked into place like the house itself was snorting with indignation.

Jamal laid the Skeeter in his trunk and gave an affectionate twirl to one of its bent rotors. His phone rang—Detroit number.

"Jamal Dent."

"*J-dogg, what up doe! It's Ellis, yo!*"

"Yo, Ellis? Ellis Wallace?"

"*Hell yeah, nigga, I heard you back in the D!*"

The phone looked dainty in the fist of Ellis Wallace, who wore his muscles like something he'd thrown on without much thought. He was tall, tattooed, and bald—intentionally so. The phone was bolted to a concrete wall. He'd seen on Facebook that Jamal was back in town, with a new job, a new house in Brush Park. "Well," Ellis said, "short of it is, I got in on some dumb shit, and I'm in county right now—"

"*Whoa what, county jail?*" Jamal said.

"Yeah…was bouncing over at The Sting, you know The Sting?"

"*The strip joint?*"

"Yeah, nigga, you remember." He laughed. "I was working the door, and niggas started acting foolish, we got into a tussle, kinda like I'm supposed to if I'm bouncing, and, well, looks like they might charge me. I don't know."

"*You hurt somebody?*"

"You know I ain't the one getting hurt."

"*Wait, hold up…you're calling me to bail your ass out?*"

"Nah, I'm calling you cause you my boy and I want to get a drink and find out what the fuck you been up to…but, yeah, real talk, I can't exactly do that if I don't make bail. It's just five hundred." The line went silent. Ellis held his breath. He hadn't seen this dude since that house party after high school graduation, where Jamal finally popped his cherry with that slam poetry chick who turned out to be Trey's mom's landlord. But he had no one else to ask. Most of his friends couldn't scrape up fifty bucks on short notice. And he didn't want his mom pawning her TV like last time.

"*Five hundred bucks?*" Jamal said.

"Yeah," Ellis said.

"*Alright…Be there in twenty.*"

Jamal ran his hand over Barry's furrowed head. Ellis Wallace. That idiot. It would be good to see him. They'd lived on the same block as kids and Jamal's parents had sprung for uniforms and pads so they could play Pop Warner football together, something most city kids never got to do. Jamal absorbed hits on the O-line with his fish-fry physique; Ellis was a running back. By high school, the social caste demarcations should have been clear. Ellis, the young pimp and four-year starter, should have left Aspergery Jamal at the comic shop, but that never quite happened. Yes, Ellis was always getting invited to parties which might as well have had signs reading, "No Jamals Allowed." Yes, he was getting booty while Jamal was booting Linux. And yes, he cribbed off Jamal's homework, but he stayed buddies with Jamal right until the end, even trying to set him up with some second-tier girls. But they all just wanted Ellis, of course, and when they realized he'd put them in the same date-class as his loser fat friend, they took it out on Jamal, spitting in his orange juice, spreading a rumor that he jerked it to Disney movies. Jamal had plenty of reason to hate Ellis, but the thing about Ellis was, he was just so damn friendly and happy. You couldn't hate him.

Jamal had wanted to leave Pershing high school as much as Ellis wanted to stay. When graduation rolled around, he bolted for Michigan State. By the time he'd moved to Seattle, after four years in the Air Force, it seemed pretty clear that he'd never see Ellis Wallace again.

Piper Prince parked her grandfather's '79 Granada at the corner of Grand River and Rosa Parks, next to the ivy-covered castle that had been vacant for years, but now, apparently, was housing yuppie douceholes in its stone turrets. An old bearded dude with a topknot was leaning against a telephone pole, smoking a cigarette, staring across the street at the brick wall Piper had come to see. Her friend had texted her an hour ago: that old MSK piece had been buffed by none other than Otto Slice, Detroit's Banksy. No one knew much about him, except that he'd been deep in the Detroit graffiti scene for years, and lately he'd been throwing up anti-corporate pieces jabbing at the local robber baron, Quicken billionaire Dan Gilbert. He'd even wheat-pasted the side of Gilbert's Z parking garage with the image of a small house underwater and a little fish swimming by, saying, *U mad bro*?

Piper jammed her hands into the back pockets of her jeans and took in the new piece: over a swirling abstract background of rubble and prairie, a huge, cheery lowercase **a** with a phallic yellow arrow swooping out and penetrating a Tigers' Old-English 𝕯, which was doubled over, taking it right up the ass. The 𝕯's Mickey Mouse arms were pressed to the hood of a rusty Ford Probe with grass growing out its windows. A curled-up sheet of paper near its tires read: consent. Piper laughed out loud. It was perfect. It was Otto Slice and the paint was so wet she could smell the aerosol silk of brain cell death.

She snapped a photo with her Nebula 6, then posted it to RNKR, the new app which had exploded the concept of "liking" into a hundred rankable specificities, from *Le sigh* to *Nazi* to *Boner*, limiting all comments to emoji. She'd seen the wave before it hit and migrated her social media from her AsFuck.tumblr page to RNKR, where she was now known as *Neptune Frost*, a name she'd lifted from a black revolutionary war soldier buried in a Boston cemetery. After a year of relentless pics and vids of fashion, graffiti, hip-hop, Detroit glitter and grime, she had close to 100,000 followers, without ever posting a photo of herself. A feat of restraint, considering she never left the house without a fresh pair of Jordans and some thick, precise eyeliner to make her eyes pop. Her bulging follower count was due in large part to the Otto Slice murals she'd been posting for the last few months. With Amazon moving into their city, Detroiters were hungry for this shit. The new photo was already racking up dozens of *Dope* and *LOL* ranks, but with that many followers, she was bound to get at least a few *Yucks* and *Snoozes*, too.

She turned and nearly bumped into the old dude. He smoked his cigarette down to its filter while looking her over. She could see his eyes linger on her crisp braids, the shaved side of her head, her iridescent moth's wing earrings. It was plenty light out, and they were in plain sight of the traffic on Grand River, and the guy looked more kooky than threatening, but still…

"On a personal health and safety tip," she said, "you might wanna back the fuck off." Piper was five foot three and 115 pounds. She was a stick; she'd learned to sharpen herself.

He laughed. "Neptune Frost," he said. "Nice shot." He held up his phone—there was the photo she'd just posted. "Still learning to use this thing. What shall I rank it? *Purty, birdflipping, Wu-Tang?*"

Piper untensed and cocked her hip to the side. This old dude followed her on RNKR? "You know Otto Slice?" she asked.

"Of course I know him. He's me."

"Don't even be acting like you Otto Slice, though."

The old man shrugged.

Piper glanced at his hands. They were speckled with paint. So was the Malcolm X T-shirt stretched over his Buddha belly. "I heard he was like a six-foot black dude with dreads."

"I heard that, too." He nodded back at the wall. "You like it?"

She looked back at the piece. It wasn't as crisp as Malt's spray-paint teratomas of feather and beak, it didn't have the hopeful sci-fi scope of Fel3000ft, but this Otto Slice piece was fucking funny, and sad, and instantly iconic.

"This shit right here, though," she said. "Basically…dope."

He gave a child-like smile, exposing a row of tobacco-stained teeth.

"But why'd you buff that MSK piece? Y'all got beef?"

"These MSK kids broke the old rules. They came in from LA and all they saw was a shitty tag on that wall—you can definitely buff a tag with a piece, but not if it was Prikle's last tag before he died. A goddamn Detroit legend. You gotta know what you're covering up."

"And now you just gon chill at the scene of the crime?"

"Look at me. You ever suspect an old fart like me? Plus, nowadays, getting busted for writing gets you gallery cred. I just linger to see if it's working."

"Is it working?"

"Well, it brought you here, and you just sent it out to the world for me."

Had he been waiting here knowing she'd show? "You gon say thanks?"

He laughed. "You know, I like fly sneakers and break dance videos much as the next guy, but you got reach now, you got people paying attention. Maybe you should use that."

"I'm just posting what people want to see."

"You could be posting what people *need* to see. We're at war. Don't think we're not."

Piper scoffed.

"All I'm saying is, think about the story you're telling. Hearts and minds."

"Whatever. You corny as hell. But you can fucking paint. Anyway, deuces," she said, chucking up a peace sign. She pictured him watching her strut back to the Granada, the evening sun soft on its Landau roof. The swaggery feeling evaporated as the starter whinnied, struggling to turn over. It choked to life and she drove off, glancing back at the undercover graf king. He popped a casual salute.

Ellis stepped out of the jailhouse doors in sweats and a sleeveless hoodie. He was shredded like some prizefighter with a tattoo problem: barbed wire (of course), some Chinese shit, and on his bulging shoulder, a Ninja Turtle jumping with nunchucks in one hand, pizza slice in the other. Ellis approached with a grin that could swallow a fist.

"What up doe!" he said, giving Jamal dap and pulling him in for a hug that turned into a brief, jokey headlock. He pulled back and took in his childhood friend. "You looking all professional, nigga."

"You, too, man. Not professional, but you know…shit, how long has it been?"

"It's been a minute. I mean a *minute*."

"Hey. Thanks, dog," Ellis said, as they walked to Jamal's car. "I owe you. I mean, I'll pay you back soon as I can, but let me buy you a beer at least. Where you want to go?"

"Man, I don't know even what's still around."

"You want good beer or shit beer?"

"Pssh. Good beer."

"Alright then, nigga, let's go see some white people shit!"

They rolled north in Jamal's electric Mazda, passing the M-1 rail, which had opened a week ago. It could only go thirty-five miles per hour, and it had to stop at traffic lights just like cars. On Detroit's wide-open streets, it was faster to drive—if you could afford it. A few lonely passengers stared from the train as they passed it. Barry stared back, leaning out the back window, panting in the heat. Jamal relaxed into his leather seat, a single wrist draped over the wheel, the way Ellis used to when Jamal was the one bumming a ride. He'd probably never see that five hundred dollars again, but it didn't matter. He had it together in a way that Ellis never would.

Ellis dialed up WJLB—

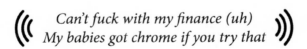

Can't fuck with my finance (uh)
My babies got chrome if you try that

"I heard that nigga's gay," he said. "Calls all his homies *babies* and *dolls*."

"Who?"

"Goldman Stackz. You ain't know this song?" Ellis bumped the volume and the bass frittzed out the speakers. "We gotta get you some subs."

They cruised up Woodward and took a left at the Whitney, an old timber baron's mansion turned restaurant. A clutch of bridesmaids was jumping in unison for a mid-air photo on the lawn.

"A wedding in Cass Corridor?" Jamal said. He pulled over, touched an icon on the dashboard, and the car silently parallel-parked itself.

"They calling it Midtown now," Ellis said, hunting for the recessed door handle. "Shinola's just down the block."

"Used to be, you didn't come here alone, remember that?"

"You didn't." Ellis cracked his neck like a rimshot.

"Wasn't it like a block away where you got caught with that Explorer?"

"Shit, was it?"

It was, and Ellis knew it. He'd done ninety days in juvie for that. He and Vince Chambers had killed a bottle of E&J, then *borrowed* a '99 Ford Explorer that some dumbass had left unlocked outside the Mickey D's. But it was a fucking stick-shift. Cops pulled them over as they grinded and lurched down Woodward. Vince bolted. Ellis never ratted him out. He barely graduated high school after that.

Ellis led Jamal to a joint with white siding like some house in the burbs. A sign above the door, lettered out in burnt orange shag carpet, read: "Latch Key." Jamal tied Barry up at a parking meter, rubbed his noggin, and gave him a treat.

The inside of the restaurant was tricked out like an old living room from 1990: popcorn ceilings, crappy watercolors on the walls. Behind the off-white linoleum bar, a dozen varieties of craft beer. Behind the tables, a few varieties of white people—hipster, collegiate, and young professional.

It was fairly quiet, but you could tell it would be packed and loud if it weren't a Sunday evening. Jamal scoped out the menu.

LATCH KEY
Gourmet Comfort Food for the Grown-up Kid

~

Fish Sticks
*Fresh Atlantic cod, breaded and fried with a mixture
of sesame and canola oils, served with pepper aioli,
$12.99*

Hamburger Helper
*Green Leaf Farms free-range beef, with fresh maca-
roni elbows and Asiago, $14.99*

Etc.

The waitress came by and took their orders for IPAs and Prosciutto Bagel Bites.

"Welcome to the new Detroit," Ellis said. "I ain't mad at it. There's a lot more of that..." He leaned to the side and impregnated the waitress with his eyes.

Jamal laughed. "You always had a thing for white girls."

"They had a thing for me."

When the food came, Jamal dipped a bagel bite in puttanesca, and held it up for consideration. "Man, I ate so many of these shitty delicious things back in high school. Now they're like...what? Soul food for white people?" He popped it in his mouth, made an "mmm" noise, and gestured for Ellis to partake.

"I'm good. Had my cheat day already this week."

Jamal had been reaching for another bagel bite, but stopped. He could feel his gut hanging over his belt. "You been lifting a lot, huh?"

"Never stopped. But now I'm on some Krav Maga."

"Israeli martial arts."

"That's right, dictionary-boy. Some train to kill shit, you know?"

"Level up from football."

"Yeah...that shit goes away when school goes away, so, I don't know, you find new shit."

"You working?"

"Was with a demo company for a minute. They had me going

around shutting off people's water. Shit was depressing. Mostly I been bouncing here and there. Working the door at The Sting. Well, was working at The Sting."

"So what, you Krav Maga some guy's ass?"

"Ah ha ha. Uh, yeah, basically."

"Shit, man, what happened?"

Ellis raised an eyebrow: *You ready for this*? "Alright, so. These three eastside niggas from Ravendale roll through, and one of em's thirsty for Ms. Berry, one of the girls, the hot one. This nigga starts making it rain with a hundred-stack of ones, right? So when she's done on the pole, she swipes the cash into a bag, like you do, then she goes over and gives him a dance. But he's crossing the line, she keeps knocking his hand away, and he keeps trying to slip her a finger and shit. So they call me in. I walk these niggas outside and tell em to have a smoke and get their shit together—manager hates to straight-up boot niggas with paper. So they're smoking, talking shit, kind of swaying back and forth. And this, like, subtle summertime breeze picks up. A car in the parking lot is bumping Parliament. *Chocolate City*."

"Alright, come on, come on," Jamal said.

Ellis took a long, slow, gulp of his beer, clearly for dramatic effect. "So, of course, who walks out? Ms. Berry. She's got her little stick arm around DJ Mad Thick, our regular guy. They're going out to his truck to hit a blunt or something, but when she passes this dude, she's like, *yeah whatever, scrub-ass nigga, do something*, and there's this moment when that nigga's eyes get all wide, like, it takes him a second to get it, that she's basically daring him to throw down with Mad Thick. It's like he can't believe she could possibly have that attitude, which makes sense since Berry is the kind of fine-ass girl that's solid gold at clubs cause she don't *look* like no stripper, more like she just wandered out of church and found herself in a g-string."

"Right."

"And plus these niggas is *faded*, you feel me? All three of em got they eyes open so wide and they hold em open so long it's like they eyeballs is fucking drying out, right?"

Jamal snorted his IPA.

"And so these niggas' eyeballs is dry as fuck, and they just keep blinking. Mad Thick is doing it too, he's looking at these bitches looking at Berry, and then just looking at me, like *oh, shit*, right? So this thirsty nigga throws down his cigarette and lunges at Berry like he's about to Ray Rice the bitch. Mad Thick steps in front of her, and these ho-ass niggas is shoving and smacking at him, so I just bum rush—it's like they don't even see me or something."

"Fog of battle."

"Yeah, or fog of vodka. So I clock the first nigga and knock his ass out, then pop the other one and he goes down, then I'm squaring off with the last one, but nigga on the ground starts grabbing my legs and punching me, like he's trying to punch me in the dick, right?"

"Alright, so..."

"So I stomped his ass into the pavement."

"Oh, shit."

"Yeah, like, that's a thing from Krav Maga, right? There's multiple attackers, you gotta take em out, put em down one by one by one before they kill your ass. So I stomped this nigga, and turned around and that last fool swinging at me basically ran away, at that point."

"What, then the cops showed up?"

"Yeah and the nigga was bleeding and shit. Just a concussion, I didn't crack his skull or nothing, but it looked bad. I told the cops, like, *Yo, three drunk assholes against one professional bouncer, and they were literally attacking one of the dancers, like what am I supposed to do, Officer? Like what am I getting paid for?* Anyway, anyway. What up with you? I mean, where you been?"

Jamal stuffed a bagel bite in his maw and chewed slowly. It would be weird to tell Ellis that he just got promoted and he was making more money than he could spend, that he'd bought an old Victorian house in Brush Park. And after hearing Ellis recount what landed him in jail, Jamal's own life seemed so...so boring.

"In Seattle or some shit, right?"

"Hold up, is that a 2008 Lions tattoo?" Jamal said.

Ellis held out his forearm: the team's heraldic blue lion rampant, with *2008* above it and *0-16* below it.

"You got a tattoo commemorating the worst season any team ever had in the history of football?"

"This Detroit, nigga. You don't love the city when it sucks, you don't love this city."

That was the thing about Detroit: while other rust-belt cities were still in denial, Detroit had moved through acceptance all the way to some kind of perverse celebration. Jamal had missed that attitude. He held his beer up for a clink.

"For real, though," Ellis said. "What up with you? How's the fam?" Then he remembered—he'd seen on Facebook, Jamal's wife had moved back a few years ago. Were they divorced?

Jamal sipped his IPA. He used to hate the stuff, too thick and bitter, but that's all anyone drank in Seattle and he'd developed a taste for it. "I don't know if you heard. Me and Sandra split up a few years ago."

"Shit, man. Sorry."

"Yeah, I see the girls on weekends though. She's right up on Six Mile."

"Wanna talk about it?" Ellis said.

Jamal had met Sandra at Michigan State. She was one of those hard-studying types that disdained the thug shit. He'd been running a lot to make tape for a ROTC scholarship and finally had clothes that fit. They went for a coffee on their first date, a drink on their second, and on their third, Jamal made her dinner in his dorm room: grilled cheese and tomato soup, the only thing he knew how to cook. Sandra chewed with her mouth closed and laid a paper towel on her lap. She was classy and warm, and she found his nerd obsessions endearing. He would sometimes stare at her smiling face until she said, *What are you thinking?* but he was never able to give words to the awe he felt over the simple fact that she had chosen him. They dated till the end of college, then he put a ring on her, got commissioned, and made pilot.

At first, he was flying C-17s, the transport fatsos, but then he was transferred to Creech Air Force Base in Nevada and he strapped his flight suit to a desk and started flying close air support with UAVs all the way over in Afghanistan. That's when the problems with Sandra really started: a couple of rough pregnancies, post-partum weight issues, living out in butt-fuck nowhere and him working really long, really weird hours. He'd pilot all day, then land the Reaper at Bagram

Airfield, unhook, climb into his Suburban, and drive a few miles down the road to their rambler, where she'd be waiting with the girls, looking a little heavier and more hollow-eyed every night.

The Air Force hammers in to all the spouses that they're the bedrock of the force, the nation depends on them, etc. And if Jamal had been overseas it might have been different. But Sandra just couldn't take having to deal with the home front alone, while her husband was "in combat" at a desk, just ten minutes away, but gone all day and night. She hung grimly on for almost three years until he was out of the Air Force and they left for Seattle—Amazon often recruited from the military, as they prized logistical know-how and a bias for action. But the light between them had gone out in Nevada and it couldn't be relit in the Seattle rain. Within a year, she asked him for a divorce. She wanted to start over, back home in Detroit, where her mother could help with the girls. Jamal was crushed, but he didn't fight. He even granted her sole custody, trusting her promise to bring the girls out to Seattle for summers when they were old enough.

"It's just one of those things," Jamal said. "The military stuff was hard, Nevada was hard, and I couldn't be there much. I was flying all these missions."

"Oh, they send you to Afghanistan?"

"Yeah, well, no, I was flying combat missions there, but remotely. I worked at a base outside Vegas."

"Shut the fuck up, serious? That's some Robocop shit. Wow."

"For real. People think it's weird. Normal for us though."

"And now what, you're flying planes for Amazon?"

"UAVs…you know, drones."

"Drones! That's money."

Jamal did his best to conjure up a smile. He'd done well at Prime Air, getting promoted over two years up to Senior Engineer. When the Detroit plan was announced, he jumped at the opportunity to return home. After Sandra left, his life outside of work had become little more than frozen meals, internet porn, and Netflix. They promoted him to Chief Pilot, a nominal title his coworkers bristled at, wondering if it was because he was black and from Detroit. Jamal trusted his own abilities, and he trusted that his bosses recognized his talent, but he could see the symbolic benefit of having a black Detroiter at the head of the UAV program. He had no desire to represent his race or his city in any public capacity, but those concerns paled next to the chance to be back in Detroit, near his baby girls, Nina and Eve.

"You know, the new fulfillment center's hiring," he said. "They got this program where they train you to become a UAV factory tech. I think the money's pretty decent."

"Shit, man, I got a record. Plus, I don't know. I ain't smart like you. I mean, I ain't dumb, but, you know."

"Hey, you're smart. You're not a *genius* like me…but you're smart enough."

Ellis laughed and slapped the table. "I don't think I ever heard you say that, not ever!"

"Well you—"

"Calling yourself a genius! That's some swagger. I like it."

Jamal *had* felt a bit swaggery, until now. Somehow, Ellis' well-intentioned props—and they really were well-intentioned—always felt slightly condescending to Jamal. "I mean it though," Jamal said. "You could work in the factory, easy. I'll put in a word."

"Yeah? I appreciate that, man. I know it's been a minute, and you don't owe me nothing."

"Forget about it."

"And I'm a get you that five hundred. I will."

"Don't sweat it."

"I'm a get you that five hundred. And shit man, you trying to get Sandra back, I know. I can help you with that, homes. We gonna make you a game plan."

Jamal rolled his eyes.

"But, hey, uh…could you spot me on this beer?"

Piper sat down to Sunday dinner with her Grandpa Luther. She'd bailed on a shift at *Capers Steak by the Ounce* to be here, even though her ass was broke. Her RNKR popularity was netting her free clothes and jewelry, but no cash, not yet. Family time meant a lot to Gramps, though, and it was the least she could do, living under his roof, driving his car.

"No sense of history, these kids. The civil war, the race riots. *Before my time*, they say, as if that means it don't affect em. It ain't before your time, it's history!"

He'd grown increasingly crankadelic since Piper's sister Nia had died last year, but he seemed especially so tonight. "What kids? You don't know any kids," Piper said.

"There's kids at church. You'd know if you'd gone this morning. Not enough of em, but some. Problem is, they don't use their heads for more than separating their ears." He took a slow bite of his peas and carrots, which Piper had thawed in the microwave and doused with Lawry's—the extent of her cooking skills. A single pea tripped off his spoon and landed on one of the tablecloth's pastel flowers.

"You get your walk in, today?" Piper asked.

Luther shook his head.

"You know you can't be sitting in front the TV all day. How many times you tell me to get outside when I was little?"

Outside, a hundred yards away, a squad car turned onto Clarion Street past the smoking remnants of the house the fire department had doused just an hour ago. Officer Cross, face like a bullet, was at the wheel; Shepard sat in a cloud of perfume in the passenger seat, filling out the report for their last call. Some punk had robbed the Sunoco at Van Dyke and Grinnell, making off with candy and pop—that's it—but the idiot had flashed a gun, bumping petty theft up to armed robbery. They'd found him booking it towards the sewage plant and Cross had wanted to run him down and pursue on foot if necessary. That's what he and Mack, his normal partner, would have done—they got after it, they put bad guys away. But aside from DPD, Mack was National Guard, and he'd just deployed to Florida for hurricane relief. Lieutenant had stuck Cross with Shepard, who fought crime like she was knitting a sweater. She had three years on him, though, and she'd pulled rank with that robbery punk. They called backup and headed him off at Huber. Routine, boring. Wendell and Riggs took him in. Shepard volunteered to write it up.

Cross slowed, and they inched down Clarion, drawing cold stares from porch-dwellers.

"This is it," Shepard said, without looking up from her clipboard. "8975 Clarion." It was creepy the way she did that. They walked up the drive in that slow, deliberate cop walk.

"Didn't have to tell your sister," Luther said. "Your sister knew a thing a two."

It was hot, the fans were on, and flies were buzzing through the house, which, aside from Piper's room, hadn't much changed since the 90s, when Piper and Nia had come to live with their grandparents, their mom taking off for Arizona with some guy named Ron. Her gramps was right, Nia was smart. She'd gone to Wayne State and got heavy into activism, black economic development, water rights. She'd been arrested time and again on poor folks' overgrown lawns, yelling at city contractors come to shut the water off. She went deep into all that African heritage shit—draping herself in colorful dashikis and beads. Piper never really got that; they grew up in Detroit, not Africa. Still, she'd always looked up to Nia. For a brief moment, Piper was drawn back to her younger self at Crockett High, where everyone had called her "Itty." Now that Nia was gone, oddly, she felt like a much bigger presence in Piper's life.

(((*KNOCK KNOCK KNOCK KNOCK KNOCK*)))

Piper left Gramps at the table, opened the door, and met eyes with two police officers. One white, mid-twenties, sharp nose, face exploding with freckles. He looked like he'd come to kick over her sand castle. The other cop was a black lady, early thirties maybe. Hair straightened and in a ponytail. Full cheeks. Subtle lip-gloss on a friendly smile. But she was still a cop. Piper said nothing, waiting for them to speak, the *aint's* and *nigga's* sinking to the back of her mind as a more formal dialect floated to the surface—college talk, TV news talk, questioned-by-the-police talk.

"Is this the residence of Luther Prince?" the white cop asked. His nameplate said: Cross.

"What's this about?" Piper said.

"May we enter the house, miss?" Cross said.

Luther had struggled up from the table and was shuffling across the linoleum. "Let em in," he said. "I got something to report. Disturbing the peace." Piper stepped aside.

"Sir," Officer Shepard said, "is that your shotgun?" Cross's head darted around bird-like looking for the weapon. Without breaking eye contact with the old man, Shepard pointed at the top of a bookcase to her left.

"Course it is, it's in my damn house," Luther said.

"And do you know anything about a drone that crashed on this street about four hours ago?"

"No, I don't know nothing about it, except it had no business being here. You want to ask if I shot the damn thing out the sky, then ask."

"Sir, did you—" Cross began.

"Yes, I shot the damn thing," Luther said.

Piper's eyes widened. "He's confused," she stammered. "He hasn't touched that thing in—"

"Hell if I'm confused," Luther said.

"That drone was the property of Amazon, and was licensed to fly by the city of Detroit and the Federal Aviation Administration." Shepard recited the phrase handed down from the Lieutenant. Since Amazon started paying their overtime, department priorities had shifted. They'd been briefed on responding to drone shootings—no pencil whipping, take it seriously. "I understand you're angry, sir, but—"

"You think I hate this Beezos fool," Luther said, "but I ain't got the energy to hate somebody I don't even like! He's a businessman and I don't begrudge him trying to do business. But have a little respect! These things been flying down my street for a week, riling up the dogs, and this one came down just floating over my lawn while I'm trying to deal with the water company, and kids setting fire to vacants—you seen the house on the corner. Believe it or not, this used to be a nice neighborhood."

Cross popped a pair of handcuffs from his belt.

"No, no no no," Piper said. "He's seventy years old, you can't arrest him. He'll have a heart attack!"

"Willful and malicious destruction of property," Cross said, "Reckless and negligent discharge of a firearm."

"Discharge of a firearm? Really? So where were you yesterday, and the day before? I hear gunshots every single day!"

"Not our decision," Shepard said. "Please put your hands out, sir, you'll have to come with us."

Luther shook his head and snorted. "In the middle of Sunday dinner..." He stuck his wrists forward defiantly. Cross' eyes lit with a tense glee as he slapped one cuff on, then Piper reached forward and batted her grandfather's other hand away. "You can't do this!" she yelled.

"Don't make us arrest you, too," Cross said. He stepped forward, and she stepped back, then whipped out her phone and began recording.

"That's not gonna help," Cross said. He slapped the other cuff on Luther's wrist.

Piper followed them out to the squad car, holding her phone out like a crucifix. "This is fucked, I'm getting a lawyer!" she yelled, knowing as she said it that she didn't know any lawyers and had no idea what her grandfather's rights really were. But what the fuck else could she say? "You wouldn't be arresting no white man over this bullshit! You gon regret this, you think you slick though, you gon be working at Metro PCS next week! Tell Jeff Bezos he can suck my dick soon as you're done sucking his!"

Cross shot her a smirk as they shut her gramps in the back. He looked at her softly through those huge glasses of his. Then the squad car drove off. Piper jumped in the Granada and followed, beating her fist against the stained ceiling, screaming through the windshield at the cops who'd taken the only family she had left.

2

Annika Dahl awoke in a ball of Egyptian cotton, hit snooze on the digital bird-song, then curled up face-down, half yoga pose, half cat stretch. She stuck a bare arm out of the blanket ball to grope for the A/C remote—it clattered to the oak floor.

Big day today. Wayne State University speech. Reporters, Representative Ingalls, probably angry luddites in the audience. The whole thing would end up on YouTube. She had four hours to go over her slides, make tweaks to the presentation, and rehearse. The bird-song began its slow crescendo—five minutes already?—but was cut short by the ringer. Davit Jasper, her boss.

Annika flipped onto her side and thought about leaving the room, then remembered: she was in Detroit, and sleeping alone now. She cocooned herself further into the comforter, leaving a small opening for the phone.

"Morning, Davit." Jasper was a total Jeff-bot. He'd shadowed Bezos for two years before Bezos put him in charge of Amazon. Detroit. Like Bezos, he saw any kind of communication as a sign of dysfunction. If things were running smoothly, there was nothing to say.

"*They did a head transplant,*" Jasper said.

"What?"

"The Chinese, Nik. They sewed a chimp's head onto another chimp's body. It's alive and showing nerve connectivity. Jeff can't shut up about it! Anyway, have you seen the news?"

Annika flipped the sheets back and made the run to the wall, clicking the A/C off. She flung open the curtains and the morning sun filled her 30th floor penthouse. She put the phone on speaker and started to get dressed. She was on a showering-at-night schedule.

"About the chimp?"

"No, our UAV that got shot down. That old crank we had arrested…"

"Right." Annika rummaged through a wicker bin for a bra and a pair of socks.

"The Free Press put out a story this morning. Eddie Noble, you know him? Guy wears a leather jacket and cowboy boots. You can almost smell the cigarette smoke and bourbon just reading the piece. It's not good, Nik. The shooter's seventy-one, a former Ford auto plant worker. He's a widower. And one of his granddaughters died last year."

"Great."

"So how are you going to deal with it?"

Annika went with a grey skirt-suit from H&M that she'd bought in Seattle a few weeks ago. Spencer had been with her, waiting outside the dressing room. That was one of the last days before the break-up. She'd wanted him to propose, to move with her to Detroit. He did neither. They'd parted on friendly if melancholic terms, and hadn't spoken since. She shut all thoughts of him into her mind-cabinet reserved for ex-lovers.

"We knew this would happen eventually," she said. "We'll just bring out our talking points a little early, say it's reckless to be firing guns in neighborhoods, and that shooting it down is like shooting at UPS trucks because they drive past your house, which is so obviously insane that no one—"

"Well, but this is an old black man, not some punk kid with a pistol…"

"Being old or black isn't a license to break the law. We focus on the crime, not the criminal."

"Okay, that's what I'll tell the boss. Fair warning, he may want to hear your speech ahead of time."

"The whole thing?"

"*Probably just the talking points, but you never know. I'd have the speech by heart if I were you. Soon. He may call. And I'd have explanations or justifications ready for anything in the speech. If, IF, you have that, that's a layer of armor that'll keep him from tearing you apart in the first few minutes, but after five or ten, he'll chew through the armor and find major issues with what you've got. Legitimate issues. Real insights. He's not human, Nik. He's more like a hyper-intelligent being that amuses himself by meddling in human affairs.*"

Once Jasper hung up, she threw on some Taylor Swift, slammed a Keurig cup into her coffee maker, shoved a toothbrush in her mouth, and set a timer on her phone—three hours and fifty-six minutes till show time.

Piper's eyes opened, and the buzzing fluorescent lights stabbed that tender and treacherous part of her brain that knocked her flat with migraines about once a month. She could feel a dull pressure building in her left temple, like a growing tumor behind her eye. She popped an Imitrex and willed it to start taking effect before the sound of the ticking wall clock began bludgeoning the inside of her skull and the smell of floor wax dredged the muddy bottom of her gut and hauled it out her mouth. She'd been in and out of sleep all night, slumped on a bench in the lobby of the Wayne County Jail. Her neck was a knot of rebar. She checked her phone: 10:05.

Her gramps had been put in some holding cell while they drew up the charges. Every time she'd asked to see him, they'd deflected. *Can't rush justice.* Not for a black girl anyway. During the night, she'd watched the video she'd taken of his arrest a dozen times and very nearly posted it to RNKR. It was the kind of video that could really go viral, but she was hesitant to throw her gramps into the spotlight. An officer she'd spoken to earlier walked back into the room. "Excuse me," she said. "Hello?"

He sighed, and looked at her like she was spilled coffee he'd have to clean up.

"Can I see him yet?"

"I'll check," he said, the way you'd say it if you weren't gonna check.

$((\; bzzzzz \;))$

A text from Aaron Farmboy:

> when do I get to see you again
> pretty lady?

She'd met Aaron Thistle a month ago by following the smell of shit. She'd been wrinkling her nose for weeks, and when she finally resolved to go investigate, she tracked the smell a block over to Armour Street and found the source. Next to a half-way decent house with a sign that read, *Detroit Art Farm*, there was an empty lot with rows of vegetables and a big pile of manure from the Detroit Zoo. A tall, handsome white boy in dirt-caked blue jeans came out and introduced himself, then gave her the tour. He'd bought the house six months back, and after three months of fixing it up, he'd invited artists and writers from all over the country to come stay for a few weeks at a time in exchange for a little urban farm work. He didn't own the lot next door, but no one seemed to care. He straight up asked her out while they were standing next to the shit pile. "Have dinner with me," he said. She laughed in his face and said, "No."

"But you're so hot, and we're so different," he said.

"Different? Really?" she said. "Are you sure?"

"We should all be expanding our cultural horizons. Don't you think?" he said.

She imagined slapping him, like he'd asked if her nipples were black. But he hadn't said that. And his smile was so genuine. He gave her his number and she put it in her phone as "Aaron Farmboy," planning to write it on a bathroom wall next to *I LICK ASS* or *FREE TAX PREPRATION*. But when she told her friend Tasha that weekend, she found herself lingering on her description of him, wondering out loud where he grew up, what led him to Detroit, and Tasha picked up on it. "Oh my god, you like him!" she said.

Piper denied it, but that night she gave him a call. A week later, they had dinner at the Art Farm, and she met some of the weirdos: a girl from Nebraska who made shadow art, an origami artist who only folded with defunct Soviet-era currency, and some kid from London who was writing an epic poem set to techno music. They had dinner again the next week, then she fucked him. It was all right—he was a bit too gentle. *Is this okay, that okay?* But he was nice, had a good body, and knew what he wanted. Lying in his bed, he'd told her all about Max Weber's critique of capitalism and modernity, the inversion of means and ends, where man exists for the purpose of his enterprise and not, as it should be, the reverse. She called bullshit. Diabetes sucks, but that doesn't make sugar evil. She liked the fact that if she was willing to buy a dope necklace, that meant there was incentive for someone else to make that necklace. How cool was that? How beautiful? How elegant? There was something deeply pleasurable about transforming your own energy, your work, into a fundamentally immaterial thing, money, then turning it back into something physical that you could never make yourself. It was a kind of magic. You just had to be careful not to lose control of it.

> got some shit I gotta take care of

> Tomorrow then. There's a stand-up comedy night at New Way in Ferndale.

The officer returned and grabbed a sheet of paper from a desk. Piper looked at him expectantly. "Maybe an hour," he said, "maybe more." He left again. Motherfuck. Piper stared back at Aaron's text. He wanted to take her out to Ferndale? This boy had no idea who she was.

> For real? You think I want to see some corny white boys telling jokes?

> What, you don't like jokes?

You're a joke. What do you u think?

I think you like jokes.

Sometimes

So I'll see you tomorrow then.

I'll think about it

The Danto Engineering Development Center at Wayne State University was all angles, planes, curving glass and metal—tasteful Euclidian porn. Inside, Annika stood at the front of the auditorium, facing over a hundred students, journalists, employment seekers, and curious grandmothers who sat in swiveling black chairs behind tiers of long gray desks. The can lights overhead were spaced perfectly, each cone of light overlapping the others, creating a matrix of shadows for every object in the room. It was an engineer's auditorium.

Bezos had never called. His silence felt oddly like scrutiny. She had never given a talk to this many people. She had never been accountable in public to the operations of a massive and complex entity like Amazon. She was coming up on her final slide, running on adrenaline, hyper aware. The guy in the third row with the trim mustache, biker jacket, and notepad had to be Eddie Noble, the *Detroit Free Press* reporter. Of even greater concern was Congresswoman Ingalls (D-MI), squinting at her from the back row.

People thought the Prime Air deal was a Trump Administration "Make America Great Again" thing, but it had been Ingalls who pitched the Detroit idea first. She chaired the Aviation Subcommittee of the Transportation and Infrastructure Committee of the 115th Congress, which oversaw the FAA. Ingalls' brilliant move was to realize that her district was the perfect cradle for the UAV revolution.

Other cities had expensive real-estate and ever-growing thickets of aviation regs pushed by grumpy technophobes annoyed at the rising tide of multi-copters crashing their wedding receptions and scenic lookouts. Detroit, on the other hand, was cheap and desperate, and Amazon had what it needed: tech cred, business cred, jobs. Ingalls had brokered the deal with the FAA and Mayor Duggan, who was up for reelection in November. Amazon laid out nearly a billion dollars on a new UAV factory, a massive fulfillment center, and on educational grants for the Mayor to brag about. All the government had to do was get out of the way.

"It's an ambitious vision—we're the first to admit that," Annika said, "which is why we need the ingenuity, intelligence, drive, and support of Detroit's best to fill the hundreds of new skilled manufacturing positions. To that end, Amazon has invested over twenty million dollars into Wayne State for a two-year pilot program to train workers on our manufacturing process. The certificate course will be free to qualified applicants, and priority will be given to those working at our new fulfillment center, which already has over seven hundred employees, eighty percent of whom are from Detroit."

The crowd wasn't fully with her. Half of them were flipping through their stapled packets—Amazon wouldn't spring for anything fancier—which covered the logistics of Prime Air delivery: under thirty minutes in a ten-mile radius for items less than five pounds; demarcated airspace for high-speed UAV traffic from two hundred to four hundred feet. She had to reach them emotionally. Hopefully, this final slide—a short video clip—would do the trick.

> An aerial view of Detroit, a slow fly-by of its art-deco skyscrapers...

"This is a new phase in the history of world-wide industry," Annika said.

> Descending now over the Detroit Institute of Arts...

"And Detroit is where it will all happen. Over a hundred years ago, Henry Ford's vision and new manufacturing process helped make this city the world capital of industry in what would become the century of the automobile."

Now swooping down even further, just east of the DIA, towards a two-story brick house with a manicured lawn...

"But it was never quite *auto*, was it? How could it be when we had to drive!"

The UAV lifting off, a woman opening her package, pulling out a box of pastel birthday candles...

"We are excited to be here to witness the birth of a new age: the age of automation."

Mom sticking the candles in a cake...

"Freeing us to focus on what really matters."

Wavering candle flames, the enormous eyes and lit-up face of the five-year-old birthday girl, the video fading out to the Amazon Prime Air logo.

Congresswoman Ingalls started clapping loudly, big bracelets jangling. The crowd joined in. Annika smiled as her stomach unclenched. Then she saw Jasper walk in at the back of the auditorium. He was wearing his maroon tracksuit—he always wore track suits, like some kind of corporate Armenian gangster. He stopped in an aisle near the front, leaned against the wall, and held aloft a tablet. There was the face of God: Bezos had come to witness her

Q&A. Annika's scalp caught fire. The applause died, and she became acutely aware of the sounds of a hundred people breathing and chewing pens and shifting their weight between butt cheeks.

Eddie Noble's hand shot up. It would be suicide to let him set the tone. She called on a young white woman with cat-eye glasses and a pinched face that would serve her well in a casting call for the role of militant vegetarian.

"I heard that Amazon may be selling drones to the government," she said. "Given that drones have killed thousands of civilians in Syria and Afghanistan in just the last year, how can Amazon, in good conscience, join the military-industrial complex by manufacturing drones?"

"At this time," Annika said, "Amazon has no arrangement with any government or corporation to sell unmanned aerial vehicles, and though we have spoken with certain parties about licensing navigation and sense-and-avoid software, we are not ourselves developing any software or hardware for military applications." She glanced at Jamal, who sat in the front row, and his face reminded her of the language she needed, something he'd said to her in a conversation weeks ago. "I would also note that civilian casualties abroad are the result of the US military target list. Whether they're carried out by manned or unmanned aircraft is irrelevant."

Annika glanced at Bezos. He remained attentive, but impassive, his right eye, as always, a bit squinched and off-center. She couldn't think of it as a lazy eye—if anyone could look at two things at once, it was Bezos.

"What will you do if people shoot down your drones en masse?" asked a guy who looked like a Mexican Justin Bieber. "You can't just have them all arrested."

Eddie Noble nodded in approval.

"We don't believe that will happen, which is why we are putting our trust in the citizens of Detroit to be responsible and law-abiding."

Eddie Noble clicked his pen. Jasper looked impressed. On the tablet in Jasper's hands, Bezos' face loomed larger, as if he'd leaned closer to the camera. Annika called on a put-together black woman in a pantsuit. A professor at the university?

"Your new factory and fulfillment center will create how many new jobs?"

"One thousand, in the fulfillment center alone," Annika said. "Once it reaches full capacity. And an additional five hundred in the UAV factory."

"Even so," the woman said, "There are still over fifty thousand unemployed Detroiters. And what happens when you automate away the very jobs you just created? Isn't that the plan? What measureable effect does Amazon really expect to have on the future of this city?"

Annika glanced at Bezos. His face was even bigger! The woman had a point: the deal wouldn't exactly usher in a new golden age of blue collar American Dreams. But it would provide inroads for Detroiters into the field of tech manufacturing. Was that enough? Quicken Loans was the big, flashy company that got there first, and Gilbert and Co. had brushed the cobwebs off downtown so Amazon wouldn't have to move into a war zone. But unlike Quicken, *Amazon made new stuff.*

"Amazon can't solve all of Detroit's problems," Annika said. "What we can do is show the world that this is a city where people still build things. A city that will invent the future, not predict it." That line was a Jeffism, almost verbatim. She glanced at him—only his eyes were visible…was he smiling?

"One last question," she said. She called on Eddie Noble. Couldn't ignore him forever.

He smirked, rapped his pen against the desk, and cleared his throat. "How can you possibly expect people to adapt to this idea, of drones flying through their neighborhoods?"

Annika swallowed and shut away all thoughts of Bezos watching, of Congressman Ingalls watching, even of Eddie Noble himself; she shut them all into a mind-cabinet. She felt her nose starting to itch—Detroit's floating dandelion seed about to break through her over-the-counter defenses. "Every day…" she said, then yanked her head away and sneezed into her shoulder. "Every day, there are close to one hundred thousand commercial and military flights in the United States and in the next ten years, that number will look tiny compared to how many short-distance unmanned aerial flights happen each day and this change will no doubt require a paradigm shift in both our regulatory system and in our relationship with technology, but we're not afraid of this and neither should you be because—" *SLOW DOWN, breathe,* she told herself. "Consider: only twenty years ago, it was unthinkable to even enter your credit card number into a website. Amazon has always asked radical things of its customers. We have faith they'll join us in creating the future. That's all I have time for. Thank you."

Her heart rate settled as Jamal sauntered up to the podium, slouched over it, and went over the specifics of the A-4 Skeeter and the A-9 Stork, which would handle heavier longer-range aerial deliveries. He was usually an awkward speaker at work meetings, but he was doing pretty well here. Maybe it was the hometown crowd. He answered a few questions about the UAVs' automated air traffic control and sense-and-avoid technology, most of them from a nerdy black teen named Darnell, who seemed to Annika like a younger version of Jamal, with his *Star Wars* t-shirt and the patchy beginnings of a beard.

As they left, Jamal pulled her aside to ask a favor.

"He's a good guy. Known him forever. Think you could put in a word?"

Annika whipped out her phone and shot off an e-mail to the head of HR for Amazon.Detroit. "Done," she said. "You owe me."

"Oh…I mean, thanks."

"I'm kidding, Jamal. But not really. You owe me."

Luther was limping on a crutch when they finally brought him out.

"Oh my god, what happened?" Piper asked. Her grandfather's shoe was off, and his ankle was wrapped and swollen.

"How they treat an old man," Luther said.

"He fell in the holding cell and sprained his ankle," said the officer, a portly black man with a silver, wire-brush mustache. He looked like he'd been working a desk for decades.

Piper shook her head. She wanted to say something mean, but it wouldn't come.

"I'm escorting him across the street for his arraignment," the officer said. "It's an open court—you can sit in."

The harried prosecutor opened a manila folder and read through the police report and transcripts of Luther's statements.

"What are the charges?" the Judge asked.

"The people charge the defendant Luther Prince with a misdemeanor count of Reckless, Wanton use or Negligent Discharge of Firearm under section 752.863a of the Michigan Penal Code, punishable by up to one year in prison and a fine of one thousand dollars, and with a Felony count of Willful and Malicious Destruction of Property under section 750.377a of the Michigan Penal Code, carrying a maximum penalty of five years in prison and a fine of not more than ten thousand dollars."

Piper's jaw dropped. Felony charges? Five years in prison? That was insane.

"Do you understand the charges against you, Mr. Prince?" The judge said.

Luther Prince had clambered up the ladder at Ford for thirty years while the rungs gave way beneath him, clattering onto the heads of the unemployed black masses below, as plant after plant fled Detroit. The city had become a hotbed of militant unionism, where postwar wildcat strikes shut down plants as fast as racist hate-strikes had before. Luther moved from union to management in the last ten years of his working life and had retired with a white collar. Never in his life had he imagined being charged with a felony. He shouldn't have shot the damn thing out of the sky, he knew that, but he'd been overwhelmed and angry, angry in a way that would have been rare for him just a few years ago, before his wife…before Nia…before it was just him and Piper.

Luther sighed and nodded. The judge set the trial for September 9th—more than two months off. The arraignment was over in five minutes.

As they escorted her grandfather back to the holding cell, Piper ran to an ATM and withdrew fifty dollars, bringing her balance down to $15. She paid the bail bond at Goldfarb Bonding a block away.

It was late afternoon when they finally released Luther. She helped him limp out to the car.

They drove in silence, until Piper said, "Fuck."

"I didn't teach you to talk like that."

"It's just—what are we gonna do?"

"Pray on it," Luther said.

They fell silent again, listening to the hum of the Granada, an old man's scratch in its throat.

Piper sighed. "Shit," she said.

"Yeah…shit," Luther said.

She slowed up to a red light at Gratiot and Mack and stared at the empty intersection. A long art-deco building, like some department store from the twenties, terra cotta with plywood windows, vacant. Store-front church. Liquor store. She heard a high-pitched whine and looked up. There above, zipping over Gratiot, heading northeast, another dog-sized metal insect. Another reason to be angry, as if Detroit didn't generate enough of those on its own.

3

Up in the Bird's Nest, four stories above the old airfield, Jamal stared at a monitor, banging his brain against a block of code, trying to fix the problem that had led to their first UAV shoot-down. On the other side of the pentagonal room, ten feet behind Jamal, Bud was at another console, piloting a Skeeter down Woodward for their final mapping runs.

Bud had been at Amazon for years, and he was the Senior Flight Programmer. With his Ben Franklin hair, Santa beard, and glasses, he fit the fat-guy programmer archetype; the only unexpected element: he always wore pastel t-shirts, the one deliberate signal he was gay. Jamal had been working under Bud for two years when, to his and Bud's surprise, Jamal was the one promoted to Senior UAV Development Manager, putting him in charge of Bud and the other team members working in the design lab below. No one said it, but they were all thinking it, even Jamal: Amazon was bringing UAVs to Detroit, and they wanted a local, a black local, in charge. Jamal had more flight time than anyone, but his coding game was weak by comparison. Bud had been programming since Jamal was slurping Gerbers. But Jamal wanted to prove to himself, and to Bud, who'd written most of this code, that he was up to the task.

Jamal had diagnosed the problem. The stabilization system

took its cues not just from gravity and acceleration, but also from ambient temperature. Not usually an issue, but the air above that structure fire he'd flown over had been super-heated. He'd checked the logs after the crash: the temperature jumped twelve degrees in a half-second. When he'd tried to bank left out of the smoke, the Skeeter flipped. Jamal had managed to level it before it hit the ground, but by then, it was too late—the old man had blasted it with his shotgun. He needed the accelerometers to respond to temperature changes in real time. The problem was, doing so would also cause them to recalibrate with respect to gravity, and doing *that* while airborne would make the UAV highly unstable. Prime Air went live tomorrow. He needed Bud's help.

Jamal noticed he'd been drumming his fingers rather loudly on his desk and stopped. He bent down and gave Barry a scratch on the head and a wipe with the QB towel, then walked over to Bud.

"How's it going?" he asked.

"Haven't been shot down yet," Bud said. He sipped from a can of Diet Grape Faygo.

"Yeah, well. There's gonna be more of that shit. This is Detroit."

"Can you stop doing that?"

"What?"

"That thing where you make Detroit seem super hard-core. Like it's the world's biggest hell-hole and if you're from there then you must be a badass."

"If you think this isn't going to happen again, you're nuts," Jamal said. "You'll see tomorrow. Detroiters don't give a fuck when it comes to popping off guns at night, especially on holidays."

"You worried about guns? They can only hurt your meatsack, my friend. We're all gonna upload soon and the whole gun debate will be moot!"

"Right…"

"Didn't you hear about Kurzweil? He was pronounced dead this morning at this cryo facility, here in Michigan—which I keep forgetting we're in Michigan. But he'd already installed his own server farm there, with the OpenAI team. I mean, he *must* have uploaded himself, or at least tried. I'm telling you, the transhuman race will look back millennia from now and today will be the origin date."

"Yeah, well, whatever quadrant of the future datasphere corresponds to Brightmoor, I wouldn't go there on the fourth of July either."

"Do you need something?" Bud said.

Jamal held his breath for a second, then said, "Yeah. Hit a roadblock with this accelerometer problem. Can you take a look?"

"Pretty busy, here, kiddo." A note of amusement had crept into his voice. "This Skeeter won't fly itself."

It would, actually, but someone had to oversee the route mapping. Bud was going to make him work for it. "I'll take over the mapping," Jamal said. "I've got the flight control code pulled up over there. You'll see what I'm talking about."

"Hmmm," Bud said, turning the Skeeter west, now heading down Six Mile. "You really want to risk another shoot-down?"

"Funny," Jamal said.

"You do have the all-time shoot-down record here." Bud tossed his empty Faygo over his shoulder. It clattered perfectly into the recycle bin.

"At one, yeah."

"What, you never got shot down in the Air Force?"

Jamal's mind flashed back to Panjwai. He'd been called in to support some troops in contact. The Royal Air Force was still twenty minutes away, and three of the Special Forces team were bleeding out in the saddle below the Taliban's firing position. Jamal was out of hellfire missiles. His eyes dry and heart pumping Redbull, he brought the Reaper in low to buzz the enemy, hoping they would squirt off the ridge and give some space for the Medevac to get those guys to surgery, but the Taliban held their positions and perforated his wings with AK fire, which never happens. The bullet holes in the Reaper got patched up within a week, and he was flying again. The soldiers went home in boxes.

"Shot at, not shot down," Jamal said.

"Kids," Bud said.

"What?"

"Sour Patch Kids. Five-pound bag."

Jamal sucked in his breath. "Yeah, sure," he said.

Bud popped up—more sprightly than he looked—skipped across

the room, and plunked himself in front of the other computer. Jamal sat down at the UAV controls. What a relief to be back in the pilot's seat.

"Ah, this is tricky," Bud said. "Reminds me of…"

Jamal piloted the Skeeter west on Six Mile, ignoring Bud, who tended to think out loud when he was tackling difficult problems. The churches and party stores whipped by, past Woodward, University of Detroit, Mercy. He was flying fairly close to—should he?

"…a separate calibration module would…"

Jamal steered the Skeeter south of the university to a leafy little street where the houses were all standing, almost none of them boarded up—

No sign of her and the kids. He hovered a hundred feet up.

> A black man watering his lawn, a young white woman out for a jog. Down the street to one particular house: the red Ford Focus wagon parked right there in the driveway.

"…there you are, you little null pointer bitch…"

Sandra's parents had been solid black middle class, even upper class, in the old Boston-Edison hood, Berry Gordy's neighbors. That was a big key to her whole personality and outlook: going straight to a four-year college without question, getting married to a nerd with a job, house, and car, moving away. How could she have expected this? To be a single mother, back in Detroit, two kids, living off a data entry job at GM and the child support Jamal sent each month.

"…into an infinite loop, oh yes, your conditions need a little makeover…"

> The front door opens, and there she is: pulling Nina and Eve out the house, hefting the folded-up stroller and a couple of ponderous looking bags into the car, then herding the girls into the back seat.

Jamal felt a sadness at the scene, at his own absence from it—the mundane task of carrying that crap, quieting the kids, driving around in a station wagon, all of it would have been easier with Jamal there. And he knew she knew it. It was the Air Force life—that's why she'd left him. There had been a flood of warm feelings after Nina was born, a sense of being chosen together for some sacred mission. All that oxytocin coursing through them. But a few months after the new-parent glow wore off, they were back where they were, only with less sleep and more responsibilities.

"…pretty, pretty, pretty module, but not where you belong…"

The problem was associative. All those bad old days in Vegas and then Seattle had been with Jamal. The kids, whom they both loved, but which had been the ruination of her normal life, that, too, had been with Jamal. Plus, she was just so goddamn stubborn. But these were conquerable obstacles. He'd break her down, now that he was back. It just didn't make any sense for him to be here in Detroit—with his new Victorian house in Brush Park, with all this money from Amazon—for him to be so close, and yet not be a father to his kids, a husband to his wife. It made no damn sense at all.

"Gotcha!" Bud declared. "Compiling now—and make it name-brand Kids, none of that Kirkland Signature Sour Youths bullshit."

"Put it on speaker," Piper whispered.

Luther waved her off. She leaned forward and made puppy eyes at him, then extended a finger and hit the button. The lawyer's voice erupted into the kitchen.

"…*because every charge on that sheet, they'd have to prove beyond a reasonable doubt, and even with a case like this, they'd rather it plea out.*"

"Okay, Mr. Benson, you're on speaker phone right now, and my granddaughter's listening in."

"*Not a problem. How are you, miss?*"

"I'm good, thanks."

"*I was just telling your grandfather the prosecutor is offering a plea deal. It's a fine of five thousand dollars and ninety days in jail in exchange for pleading guilty to a misdemeanor count of Willful and Malicious Destruction of Property and Negligent Discharge of Firearm."*

"Three months in jail?" Piper said. "No. And that drone ain't worth five thousand dollars!"

"This is not the bill to Amazon, you understand. This is a criminal fine imposed by the state."

Then Piper saw it—the envelope with some law firm letterhead lying next to the phone. Her hand flashed across the table for it. Luther leaned back and glared at her.

Dear Mr. Luther Prince,

This law firm represents Amazon concerning its civil claim against you in connection with an incident on Clarion Street, on July 1.

Upon reasonable cause, notice is given of Amazon's demand for payment of damages in the amount of $3,452.87 arising out of your alleged malicious destruction of an Amazon Prime Air unmanned aerial vehicle (Model A-4 — SN A4-00-52) which was authorized by the City of Detroit and the Federal Aviation Administration to fly within Detroit city limits.

You are further notified that if the above-stated amount is not paid, or a written agreement to its payment is not reached, within thirty days of the date you receive this letter, Amazon may bring an action against you for such amount, plus attorney's fees, plus court costs, and such other relief as the law provides.

Piper stared at the letter as the lawyer droned on. It was so... bloodless. Was there really another human behind those words? Or was it some Amazon legal bot that churned out lawsuit letters? Dear _____, you owe _____ for destroying _____.

"The statute specifies a fine of triple the damages," the lawyer said. *"That would have been about ten thousand, but I was able to bargain it down to five. And you will recall, this was initially charged as a felony with up to five years in prison. We're now looking at two misdemeanors and a mere ninety days, Mr. Prince."*

"Why not just take em to court?" Piper said. "You think a Detroit jury's gonna convict a sweet, old black man—you know he goes to church every Sunday."

"Miss, unfortunately, I must disagree with that assessment. The prosecutor has an easy case here, since your grandfather confessed to the police. All they have to do is put the officers on the stand and get his confession in, and they can prove the felony count. Now, the jury might indeed take mercy on him and only convict on misdemeanors, but then we're back to what we were offered in the plea deal."

"Well, Mr. Benson, I don't exactly have five thousand dollars sitting in my sock drawer."

"Sir, this is really the best I can get you. Another problem here is attorney's fees. Trials are a lot of work. I'll have to charge you for my time, and the legal fees alone would very likely put you over that five thousand dollars. And then you're rolling the dice on a felony conviction and jail time."

"He ain't going to jail," Piper said, "That's it, no way in—"

Luther Prince held up a gnarled hand and gave Piper the look. "That's enough, Itty." Luther rubbed the bridge of his nose. "Mr. Benson, if I took the deal, I'd need a bit of time to pay this fine. We've had some medical expenses in the last few years." An understatement, Piper knew. Her grandfather had spent his whole pension during his wife's final months and Nia's sickness and eventual death. He would never tell her, but she figured his savings account was close to empty.

"I can't promise you anything, Mr. Prince, but hopefully we can work out a six- or twelve-month repayment plan with the Judge and the prosecutor. Should I tell them you accept?"

Piper gritted her teeth and shook her head. Luther sighed.

"May I have some time to consider, Mr. Benson?"

"I'll talk to the prosecutor," he said. *"I imagine they'd give you a week, maybe two."*

Luther thanked the lawyer, said goodbye, then replaced the phone in its handset. A dial tone buzzed from the speaker. Piper clicked the speaker button to silence it, then glared at her grandfather.

"Piper…what do you think, I'm gon Rosa Parks this? Spend all this money I don't even got to wind up in jail anyway?"

"This is *bullshit*, though. You know how much money Amazon

has? Have you *seen* their new buildings at the airport? So how they gon come get you for three grand, five grand? It's bullshit!"

"I did shoot their gizmo. The lawyer says it's fair and square."

"You know it's not."

"Were you listening at all? Cause if you was—"

"Nia wouldn't stand for this shit."

"Nia is *gone!*" he shouted, pounding the table with his fist.

Piper's blood stopped moving through her veins—it had been years since her gramps had yelled at her, not since she'd graduated from high school and Nia had started to get sick. All those years she'd been carrying the virus and didn't even know until the pneumonia, until it was too late. In some deep part of Piper's brain, her child's mind awoke, scared. She crossed her arms and looked away from her gramps towards the muted TV, where bulky men in suits were laughing at some quip on ESPN. Her shoulders began shaking, and she started to cry.

"Okay child, I didn't mean that. I didn't mean to yell at you."

"I hate this," she said.

"I know, baby."

"We have to fight this," she said. "We'll figure it out."

Luther just shook his head.

"I wish she was here," Piper said.

"I know, I know."

Ellis Wallace ripped into the heavy bag—left, right, left-hook, body-hook—his coiled torso driving his fists—left, left, right elbow, bob, left—his right leg arcing up in a roundkick, again and again, touch and go, his foot tapping the ground then whipping up, rib height, kick, crunch, again, sweat rivering down his scalp, smack, crack, whack of bruising muscles, bruising pad, then swapping stance, and one final chest-collapsing switchkick—left foot, lower shin slicing air, a baseball bat to a flower—

The bag slipped off its chain and thudded to the floor. Ellis pulled his shirt up to wipe off his face.

David, the head instructor, came out from the office.

"God almighty, Ell, some girl break your heart?"

"Naw, it's just—" Ellis thought about telling him. Maybe David would have some advice or even—"Sometimes you gotta hit harder than you think you can hit, you know?"

David examined the bag. "This link keeps bending out," he said. "I'll get the stepladder and some pliers."

He popped into the storeroom and started digging around. David was a nice guy, short, Jewish, ripped as all hell. Ellis had impressed him when he came in to train last year, and he'd eventually offered to hire Ellis as a part-time instructor. That lasted all of two months. His life had always been disorganized, and he could never find a way to remember that Tuesday's class was at seven, Wednesday's at four, Thursdays at seven again, or was it Level Two at seven and Level One at six? David had said it wasn't working out, but he'd offered him a generous deal: If he subbed in once in a while to teach intro classes, he could use the gym whenever he wanted.

It was just after nine. There'd been a dozen Level Ones in class tonight, all white, late twenties or thirties, a variety of backgrounds: a cop, a Quicken dude, a lawyer. Mostly chicks, which suited Ellis just fine. He stuck around after class to work some things out. Seeing Jamal had stirred up a lot shit in the back of his head. And getting fired from The Sting, well, he was unemployed now.

David returned with the stepladder and pliers. Ellis helped him hoist the bag up, then David started bending the link back into place. Maybe David would give him another shot. Could he ask?

There was always the Centerfold Lounge up near Eight Mile. He knew one of the girls there. The two of them had been a thing for about three weeks, two years ago, back when he was still in the bad habit of dating strippers. It never worked out. She could probably get him a door job there. But the Centerfold was right up the street from his mom's house in Grixdale, same house he grew up in. And that was just weird.

"A little higher," David said. "Almost got it."

Ellis hoisted the heavy bag up another inch—his muscles shaking with fatigue. There was the Pantheion Club out in Dearborn, but did he really want to be working the door at another shitty strip club? That's not a life.

"Got it," David said. Ellis let go, and the chain held. David slapped him on the shoulder. "Thanks, buddy."

"Hey," Ellis said.

David turned.

"Ah, nothing. Forget it."

As Ellis showered, he thought about his overdrawn checking account, about the eighth of a tank left in his Charger. He thought about his sister, putting in long hours as an orderly at Detroit Mercy. He thought of Jamal, sitting at a desk with an Xbox controller, bombing terrorists.

When he got home—a shabby, under-the-table apartment in the crumbling Leland Hotel—he looked in his empty fridge. It smelled like old Tupperware. He fell back on his unmade bed. A quick search on his phone landed him at Amazon.com/jobs.

Piper had agreed out of a need for escape more than anything else. Aaron Thistle, farmboy from California, had picked her up in his rusty Toyota pickup. Somehow, with his blue jeans and white t-shirt, his three-day scruff, the truck was just another nod to not-giving-a-fuck. It was sexy. Bringing her to a stand-up show in the suburbs was not sexy. But it was intriguing. And it was so distant from the overwhelming frustrations of her grandfather's arrest, and her own impotence to do anything about it.

The New Way had a popcorn machine and a good selection of draft beer, but the crowd—mostly white—was drinking PBR.

They sat at a table halfway back from the stage. Aaron put his arm around her. Piper decided to let him.

The host was a Middle Eastern guy who was loud and trying his best to walk that line of being just offensive enough. "So we're about a year and a half into the Trump presidency," he said. "What do you guys think? This impeachment is taking forever! The wall's going up—keep out those lazy Mexicans. Guns for everybody! We got Donaldcare now. ISIS took over Gaza and we're allied with Iran! I mean, America's ratings are way up!"—laughter—"I wonder what they'll do for the finale. Ooh, maybe they'll bring slavery back!"

Aaron glanced at Piper to check her reaction. "You can laugh," she said. "You don't need my permission."

The host brought up the next comedian, one of two black guys in the crowd. He told a joke about his white ex-girlfriend whom he'd dumped after she said *n-word, you crazy*. Piper thought that was hilarious, until she realized that his ex had actually said *nigga, you crazy*. It was the comedian, the black guy, who had self-censored for this white crowd.

The next guy up was Danny Mikos: skinny, dark eyebrows, like a Greek version of James Franco with a 5 o'clock shadow that looked like it had been tattooed on. He grabbed the mic and said, "Dude, you can say that word. I can't say it. You get to. It's like the one privilege you have as a black dude, you gotta use that, nigga."

Piper laughed, but no one else did. People were glancing awkwardly at the black comic, checking his reaction. "He doesn't think I'm funny," Mikos said. "He's like, *n-word please*." That got laughs all around.

"You guys excited about this Amazon drone shit, or what? They're launching the program tomorrow. It's called Amazon Prime Target Practice."

The joke caught Piper off-guard. It both rekindled the rage at her gramps' arrest and gave her a glimmer of release. She smiled.

"Think about it—this is the beginning of the end of delivery guys. That's terrible. Not because of the jobs, or whatever. I don't give a shit about jobs—I'm a comedian—but it's gonna eliminate a whole category of porn! Guy with a *package* knocks on door, woman in lingerie opens up. That scenario got me through high school! Now what, I gotta imagine myself as a drone? Woman opens door, BZZZZZZZZ."

Huge laughs. Danny Mikos was killing.

"I don't want to be too hard on Amazon. They're doing some great things! They got this new service called Amazon Black Detroit. It's completely free. At any time of day, without you even having to request it, Amazon will fly a drone right over the hood on its way to downtown. That's a free aerial show!"

"I love this kid," Piper whispered to Aaron. He went for the uncomfortable jokes, he was willing to take his own shame and turn it inside out.

At the break, she went to find Danny Mikos and Aaron followed her. Aaron didn't seem at all jealous. She liked that.

"That was dope," Piper said to Mikos.

"Hey, thanks!"

"That Amazon shit, and *n-word, please!* You a funny motherfucker."

"Don't talk about my moms, yo!"

Piper laughed. Aaron leaned in with a solemn look. "Do a lot of comics around here deal with racial tension?" he asked.

"You kinda have to, right?" Mikos said. "It's just everywhere and obvious in Detroit. If you don't, it's almost like you're lying."

"Don't you think all that race tribalism shit is stupid, though?" Aaron said.

"I don't know if it's stupid. I know it's funny!"

Before they left, Danny Mikos said, "Hey, you guys on RNKR? You should follow me."

"Nigga, please," Piper said. "You should follow *me*."

On the drive home, Piper sidled up next to Aaron on the bench seat, but when she saw a cop drive past them, she tensed.

"What's wrong?" Aaron asked.

"Nothing."

"What is it?"

"It's fine. You're faded, and you got a headlight out. But…you know."

"What, because I'm white?"

"Uh, yeah."

"No, I'm privileged, I get it. But not because I'm—"

"Don't even say some shit about class."

"I'm just saying, that identity politics shit just gets in the way, it stalls progress."

"So what, I should just forget I'm black?"

"No, that's not what I mean. How do I say this?" He stared out at the road for a moment. "Okay, I went to Deep Springs, you know it? It's an alternative college. All about agricultural labor and self-suffi-ciency. I mean, we kept a cattle herd. It's weird, I know. Pretty much everyone there becomes a stoic. Then I spent four years after college WWOOFing."

"The fuck is Woofing?"

"World Wide Opportunities on Organic Farms."

Piper laughed and cocked an eyebrow.

"What?"

"Nothing. You just got this, I don't know, corny swag."

"You know it. Is that a compliment?" Aaron swung right off Eight Mile, heading south on Outer Drive E. People were already popping off fireworks. The streets would be exploding tomorrow.

"Keep talking."

"So I traveled around like South America and Eastern Europe and did farm work for room and board. You do that long enough, you start to see how superficial most relationships are. You know about the Dunbar number? It's like, well if you look at early humans or tribal societies, you don't see large groups. Basically, the size of our neo—(*hic!*)—neocortex limits how many in-depth social relationships we can maintain, right? Chimps can get up to about fifty, I think. Humans, it's like one-fifty. We evolved to work with our hands in small groups, not sit around at desk jobs and buy shit online! So there's got to be a cost, right, to living in these dense urban environments, depending on thousands of superficial relationships, like your relationship with the bus driver. The cost is like this spiritual—(*hic!*)—poisoning."

"That's your explanation for racism?"

Outer Drive turned into Connor street, which ran right along the old City Airport where Amazon had set up shop. *Drone City.* Piper stared out the window at the gray factory buildings.

"Well…yeah. If you can only conceive of a hundred and fifty people as real humans, then how do you treat people outside your own group? And what determines your group? Skin pigment and hair and all that, it's the easiest way to draw a line between us and them."

"That's bullshit, though," Piper said. "It takes away responsibility from racists for being fucking racist. Just cause you can't maintain a deep relationship with the bus driver don't mean you throw rocks at his house when he moves into a white neighborhood. That shit wasn't even that long ago. It's that, but it's also systemic shit that people ignore, and you know what, the fucking Dunbar number ain't no excuse for ignoring that shit."

"Sorry," Aaron said. "I'm not explaining this well."

"I ain't mad at you. Don't worry. I just…"

Aaron turned off Gratiot and onto Georgia. He slowed as they approached his street. "You want to kick it at my place? I got some moonshine one of the artists left."

Piper didn't answer, figuring he'd take her silence as assent, and head to his house. But Aaron drove on to Clarion, and stopped in front of her porch. He was so oddly…polite. They sat in silence for a moment. If Piper told him about all the trouble with her grandfather, she'd be inviting him in to a more private circle of her life. And maybe that would just provide more opportunities for him to say something stupid. Or prove he wasn't…

"My gramps got arrested," she said. "Few days ago. For shooting down a drone."

"Whoa, shit!"

"Yeah, it's actually kinda baller. But stupid, you know? He spent a night in jail and now he's got felony charges. He could go to fucking prison. Like minimum ninety days, but maybe years. *And* he's gotta pay a fine, at least five grand. And on top of that shit, Amazon wants three grand for the fucking drone. Plus lawyer fees…I don't even know. It's fucked, though."

"Shit."

"Yeah. I took a video of the popo cuffing him at least. Thought maybe I should post it, just as a fuck you to Amazon, but it would embarrass the hell out my gramps."

"Would he even know?"

"I got a lot of followers. He'd find out."

Aaron looked skeptical.

"Like a hundred thousand."

"Shit! Serious? Why don't you ask them?"

"Huh?"

"Ask your followers for help. With the fines. That's something at least."

"Just ask for money?"

"Why not?"

"Cause it's weak."

"What's—(*hic!*)—what's weak is being afraid to ask."

"I don't know. I gotta think about it." She stared at her house, her grandfather's house, the sagging porch, the peeling paint, the only sound the rough idle of Aaron's truck. When she finally turned back to him, he was staring at her softly, patiently.

"I had fun tonight," she said.

He smiled.

She kissed him.

4

The Book Tower, the home of Amazon's Detroit headquarters, was beautiful in its excess—the product of a demented cake decorator on a slow day with a full stock of icings, squeezers, mini-figurines, and sugarballs, dipping into little brother's Adderall prescription, intent on populating every inch of surface with Italian Renaissance flourish. Built just before the crash of '29, it was as classy an address as a business could have downtown, up until about 1975, when tenants started going bust, the owners stopped cleaning the Corinthian columns and nude statuary, and the copper roof rusted green. By the late '80s, the opulent cake had turned stale and gross. In '88, the owners defaulted on the mortgage, bringing twenty-five years of near-total vacancy and disrepair, until 2015 when Dan Gilbert bought the place for a cool thirty mil. Two years later, Amazon moved in, leasing ten renovated floors from the Quicken billionaire.

Annika Dahl was pumping her legs in the elevator as her phone pinged. A Google alert. Some RNKR video mentioning Amazon. Should she log it now? No time; she'd let Seattle know about this one after the meeting. The elevator doors opened.

Annika stepped out into a large, open office floor. Dead quiet. Empty. Except for some Hefty bags full of old drywall, a sledge hammer, assorted construction materials. Big chunks of carpet

were torn up, revealing old corkboard and two-by-fours underneath—the material of choice for twentieth century office towers?
At the far end of the room, a broken window, chunks of plate glass
clinging to its sides, a wide beam of sunshine plunging happily into
the office, a warm summer breeze with the scent of fresh-cut urban
prairie.

She'd gotten off on the wrong floor, that was all. The Book Tower
was still being renovated.

She found Jamal in the conference room on the 35th floor at
one end of an otherwise empty table. She joined him as an A/V guy
was cueing up the video feed from Seattle. It was the Fourth of July.
Not one of them questioned being in the office.

"I've never actually been in a meeting with this dude," Jamal said
quietly. Bezos had flown in last night and was due any minute.

"Don't worry, it doesn't get easier," Annika said.

The first time she'd met Bezos, she'd shown up uninvited at a
meeting for Prime Now, Amazon's one-hour booze and take-out
delivery service. She'd realized that customers mostly used the service for last minute party supplies, and that "one hour" translated
into "forever" when you were fiending for a re-up. Her solution:
have the drivers carry, always, a bottle of red, a bottle of white, and
a twelve-pack of beer—a limited selection, but available in fifteen
minutes. Bezos had yelled at her: "Selection is everything! Anything
less destroys our reputation. Stop wasting my life!" But he'd called
for her the next week, impressed with her creativity and backbone.
She was promoted a month later.

The screen blinked to life and there was the S-Team, the senior
leaders of Amazon, oligarchs of the tech nerd industrial complex,
sipping their morning Soylent, looking like a group of 19th level
wizards waiting for their Dungeon Master to walk in with a bag of
polyhedral dice.

A second later, the door behind Annika opened, and in walked
Davit Jasper and the man himself.

"Hello everybody," Bezos said, nodding towards the screen, then
to Annika and Jamal. Jasper sat down; Bezos remained standing.

Annika had been sweating about tonight's launch for weeks.

Bezos would give his speech, they'd roll the video, Jamal would cover tech specs, Bezos would close. She took a deep breath and organized her mind-cabinets.

"First thing's first," Bezos said. He clicked a remote, and Annika's heart sank. There on a second screen, an image of a brick wall with a graffiti mural: the Detroit 𝔇, bent over a junky car, getting fudrucked by a priapic Amazon **a**.

"So. Nik. Have you seen this before?"

"No," she said.

"Good. Because if you had, and I didn't know about it, you'd be fired. So tell me: why is it I had to learn about this from somebody else?"

"You're right, and that's my fault, and clearly I should be spending more time scanning social media for—"

"You know who brought this to my attention? Dan Gilbert. This makes me question how in touch our Detroit team is with what's actually going on in this city. So why is this happening? And what are we going to do about it? Anyone?"

Annika glanced at the flat screen—the S-Team was silent. She was going to have to answer. Why would someone paint…no, why would people *appreciate* such a mural? Perhaps they liked to view themselves as the little guy struggling against big evil? Or maybe the world just wasn't working out for them, and they had to pretend it was for some reason other than their own bad luck, laziness, and relative stupidity?

"This was bound to happen," she said. "Especially here in Detroit where there's a ton of street art, and given that we're high profile and the locals have had an…intense experience, historically, when it comes to the effect of large corporations on city life—"

"So what are you going to do about it?"

"I think, given that analysis, we should remain aware of it, but stick to talking points, rather than react publicly."

"Fair enough. Let's table this barring further developments. Now: tonight's press conference. I had a thought about the video. I'd like to see if any of you have the same thought. Can we roll the clip?"

> The Amazon logo dissolves into blue sky and clouds. An A-4 Skeeter rises from a fulfillment center. "Imagine," says a voiceover. "Emergency supplies, minutes away, no matter where you are." A car flashes its hazards on the side of a snowy road. A Skeeter touches down, the driver opens the box: thank God, tire chains. "Imagine...relaxation, a click away." A sun-bathing beauty bakes on a beach towel as a Skeeter lands beside her. From the blue box: a tube of sunscreen and a hardcover novel, *War of the Encyclopaedists*. "Imagine, your loved ones closer than ever before." A cozy cottage, crackling fire. Grandma at the computer. She clicks "Place your order."

"Stop, that's enough," Bezos said. "Anyone else thinking what I'm thinking?"

Annika steeled herself for humiliation. Her heart was pumping every last ounce of blood up to her face. She tried her best to look like she was thinking hard.

"This video is useless," Bezos said. "Wrong. Stupid."

"We put a lot of effort into—" Annika began.

"Sunk cost fallacy," Bezos barked. "I mean, *Imagine*? We don't want them to imagine. *Imagine* isn't going to cut it. I know that's how we launched Kindle and Fresh and pretty much everything else. But this is different. We're dealing with embedded hostility. We need to counter the negatives. So, what are the negatives?" Bezos looked to Jamal.

Damn. Bezos couldn't be any harsher to *him* than he'd just been to Nik, could he? "Safety," Jamal said. "Privacy. The annoying sound."

"You know a god damn tornado would do wonders for us right now! Do they have those in Detroit? If people saw UAVs providing disaster relief—"

"We can't control the weather, Jeff," said an S-Team member whose large head balanced on her neck like a pumpkin on a chopstick.

"Yet," said another.

"We've talked about this," said a third. "We still have time before competitor research starts biting into our ROI."

"I've been getting information about Google's progress on weather control and I think we need to move that decision point up or risk ceding initial market share."

"There isn't going to be any market. The government won't allow it because the people will freak out."

"The government has been imploding ever since Trump got elected. By the time this rolls around, Congress just won't be able to make itself work. If we don't hit Go on this tomorrow we're selling our intellectual property to Google for pennies on the dollar."

"Or to China," said Bezos. "Okay, we'll go for a vote this coming Monday, the thirteenth. Jasper, send out initial study packets. In the meantime, let's get back to UAVs. We're working on the annoying sound. How about we show them a live delivery? If they see a UAV flying at high speed over a main thoroughfare, it will be pretty damn obvious that it's not peeping through windows."

"We could stream the live feed," Jamal said. "Easy."

"Great. And I've got the perfect idea for that inaugural delivery. But what about safety. Safety's the main concern, is it not?"

The members of the S-Team nodded like dashboard bobble-heads on a gravel road.

"And are the UAVs safe?" Bezos looked to Jamal again.

"Of course," he said. "Very safe."

"So why don't people know that?"

"They've only seen UAVs in a military context."

"So let's give them a demonstration."

"We can't exactly fly UAVs in the auditorium, though," Jamal said.

"We can move the press conference outside," said Annika. "Have it on the airfield."

"Great idea. We'll show off the fleet. First a delivery, then an airshow. Make our little guys like the Blue Angels. Can we do that?"

Jamal nodded. "We…can do that, yes."

"You sound hesitant."

"I mean, it's going to be a long day for me."

Bezos tipped his head back and laughed again. "You didn't tell me this guy was so funny. Anything else?"

"Well, without the video," Annika said, "I'm worried about tone, and you know, a demonstration is great, but we don't want this to seem cold and robotic, so let's make it fun!" Bezos looked on in anticipation. "Maybe we cater the event, free hotdogs, or what are those gross Detroit chili dogs called?"

"Coneys," Jamal said.

Bezos rolled his eyes.

"Frugality, I know," Annika said. "But it's the Fourth of July and do you want people to show up? Because they'll be skipping out on barbecues to—"

"Got it. Convinced. Arrange it." Bezos checked his watch. "I've got a conference call with Domino's. Jasper, with me."

Annika and Jamal each let out a pent up breath as Bezos and Jasper walked towards the door.

"How's Shu-Yen doing?" Bezos said.

"Still alive!" Jasper said. "They're getting some nerve responses from the body, but no motor control yet. Main thing is, the body hasn't rejected the head."

Bezos' voice echoed from down the hall: "But would it be the body rejecting the head, or the head rejecting the body, Batman?"

Piper's phone was blowing up.

Last night, before going to bed, she posted the video of Gramps to RNKR, along with two photos: one of Luther staring out the window, pensive, his wrapped foot elevated on a pillow; The other a close-up of the letter from Amazon, demanding $3452.87 to replace the damaged drone. She'd written a single emoji sentence to explain:

She'd fallen asleep without plugging her phone in. When she woke around ten and powered it up, so many notifications poured in from RNKR that her phone was a buzzing unresponsive brick for ten minutes. Her follower count had doubled to just over 200,000. How could that be? She dug through the upranks and…*that was why*—Big Sean, who had nearly ten million followers, had *shined* her—a RNKR feature that let top-tier users spotlight lower-tier users, displaying them in everyone's feeds, way beyond their own follower base. The photo of Gramps had thousands of *raincloud* ranks and the arrest video was raking in *boos* and *grrs*—she could actually watch the count rise by the second. But she'd also been tagged in a post by someone named CaptainCrunk: a photo of a *Detroit Free Press* article about her gramps' arrest which was linked to a GoFundMe page: "Free Luther Prince." It had already surpassed the $3,452 goal, and was nearing $6,000. Holy shit. She had to tell Aaron about this.

Piper dressed as quickly as she could—which meant fifteen min-utes—putting her braids up in a knot, selecting some whale-bone earrings, and the right pair of bright red Nike high tops to go with her drop-crotch overalls—a gift from CrookedCrown, after she'd posted a vid of her friend Tasha pop-locking in a pair of CC jeans. She found Aaron Thistle crouching in a row of vegetables. She wasn't about to walk into the dirt in her crispy kicks. He stood with a freshly picked tomato, wiped it on his shirt—revealing his happy trail—then took a bite, all while looking at her. He walked up and offered it to her. She shook her head.

"You've never had a tomato this good. Try it."

Piper took a bite and the earthy liquid of the tomato flesh burst into her mouth. Aaron was right. It was amazing. And she didn't even like tomatoes. Maybe she was high on good news. She took out her phone and showed him the RNKR post.

"Whoa, that's incredible."

"Right?"

The door to Aaron's house opened, and a guy wearing a black body suit covered in hundreds of mirror shards walked out filming himself with a selfie stick.

"What…is that?" Piper said.

"That's Hans," Aaron said. "Visiting from Munich. He's a film-maker…sort of. He's on his way to the big press conference at City Airport. Bezos is speaking, I guess, launching the drone program."

"Let's go," Piper said. "I want see his face."

Jeff Bezos mounted the outdoor platform, his chrome-dome gleaming in the mid-summer sun, a mic clipped near his unbut-toned collar. Behind him, a large screen, and behind that, the gray hulking UAV factory. A crowd of hundreds stood on the airfield facing him: techies and finance bros, TV crews, Corktown hipsters, a few older black folks, and the caterers in back, scooping chili onto dogs, their grills adding to the cloud of Independence Day cookout smoke suffusing the entire city. Red, white, and blue banners fes-tooned the stage. An Amazon A-4 Skeeter waited patiently at the billionaire's feet.

"I'd like to tell you about the greatest start-up in the world," he said, speaking slowly, clearly, his arms hanging at his sides as he paced. "Its founders were young, ambitious, audacious—they imagined a world better than the one they were born into. They were risk-takers. They succeeded by inspiring millions to believe in their vision. You know this start-up. It's called the United States of America."

A few random woos erupted from the crowd, dripping coneys held aloft.

"Look back to 1776, the Founding Fathers. How do you see them? Are they wise, prudent men? Let me tell you something. They had *no idea* whether their grand experiment would work." Here, where one might expect his voice to crescendo, it remained, as it always did in presentation mode: calm, even, confident.

"Everyone assured them it would fail. *Nothing* like it had ever been done before. And they were young. Thomas Jefferson was thirty-three when he wrote the Declaration of Independence. James Madison was twenty-five. Alexander Hamilton was nineteen. They had three critical insights that have defined the United States ever since: *we must create the future we want to live in. Innovation requires risk.* And,"—a long pause—"*a government is useless if it doesn't serve the people.* Amazon lives and breathes these principles. We have always looked ahead. We have always taken risks. We have built our entire enterprise to serve the customer. That's the American spirit. And its heart is right here, in the city of Detroit, the city that imagined the automobile, a city built on innovation and risk, a city that made the rest of American industry possible."

"He thinks we're stupid," Piper said, peering at Bezos from the back of the crowd.

"That's kind of his thing," Aaron said.

With his selfie stick, Hans filmed the splintered crowd reflecting off his own body.

"*I love America, so I guess I love Amazon, too,*" Piper said. "*Thanks Jeff Bezos for showing me the light!*...Like, who does that shit work on?"

"Too many people," Aaron said. "Way too many."

"This city has had some hard times," Bezos said. "But it also has an indomitable spirit. It's bred people who refuse to give up on it. Dan Gilbert is one of those of people. His efforts to revitalize downtown have opened doors. Talent, energy, and capital are flowing back into this city. We'd like to recognize that fact by making our inaugural Prime Air delivery to Mr. Gilbert himself. Ladies and gentlemen: the Amazon Prime Air A-4 Skeeter."

That was Jamal's cue. He sat behind a partition off-stage with a tablet networked to the control center in the Bird's Nest. An Xbox-style controller was connected to Jamal's tablet, on the off-chance that manual piloting was necessary. The route was already inputted and set. Jamal hit the "engage" button, and the Skeeter on stage spun up its rotors and lifted off with its blue cardboard delivery box clamped below it.

The screen behind Bezos flashed to life with footage from the Skeeter's camera as it rose above the crowd. They watched themselves for a moment, until the Skeeter turned and whizzed southwest over Gratiot.

"It's six miles to One Campus Martius, as the crow flies. Travelling at fifty miles per hour, the Skeeter will arrive at Quicken Loans headquarters in 7.2 minutes."

All eyes watched the screen, the city whipping by:

> car wash, check cashing, vacant pavement, strip mall, smashed windows and tattered awnings, Family Dollar, gas station, grassy lot, Prince Liquor, gas station, downtown looming in the distance, wobbling left, just a bit, wobbling right…

Damn. Not good. Jamal pulled up *Locutus*—the Amazon internal chat program—to message Bud, but the tubby programmer was already bounding towards him from the base of the Bird's Nest.

"We got a problem," Bud said, panting. "Accelerometers are recalibrating to gravity, mid-flight! That's going to compound the roll-axis error every ten seconds!"

"Shit, you said you fixed it!"

"I…" Bud stuttered. "I fucked up. Missed a close-paren when I was updating the flight control code."

They looked back to the tablet. The footage from the Skeeter tilting slightly right, slightly left. The thing was going to overcorrect back and forth until it flipped!

"Even now," Bezos said, "I know many of you are skeptical. You're thinking: it will never work. Too expensive, unsafe, obtrusive. Let me tell you something. That very skepticism is how we know we're headed in the right direction. Where does innovation happen? It happens at the borders of the possible." He spoke deliberately, not a single *uh* or *uhm*, following the teleprompter in his head, Gratiot Avenue flitting past on the screen behind him.

> ...liquor and lotto, church, vacant bus stop, grassy lot after shuttered building after grassy lot—the city repeating itself like a scrolling backdrop of blight...

Annika was standing off to the side of the stage, both glad it was Bezos up there instead of her, and annoyed that he seemed better at her job than she was. Jamal tugged her sleeve, and she dipped behind the partition.

"Problem," Jamal said. "The Skeeter's accelerometers are off. It's going to crash before it reaches downtown."

Annika's eyes threatened to pop out of her skull. Jasper...she had to tell Jasper. She peeked back around the curtain and saw him standing with Congresswoman Ingalls and Mayor Duggan. Not a chance.

"Can't you fly it manual?" she asked Jamal.

"I can. I can manually compensate for the roll-axis errors, but it will get exponentially more difficult to fly the longer it's up."

"So get exponentially better at flying it!" she whisper-yelled.

"I'd like to read you a quote," Bezos said. He clicked the remote and a text box appeared on the screen, the Skeeter footage still streaming behind it. He read aloud:

> "What could be more palpably absurd than the elusive flying machine, requiring materials unimagined and machinery that defies the very laws of nature as we know them?"

He gave his short rhythmic laugh again, his face slipping into, then immediately out of, a smile. "That was October, 1903. Two months later the Wright brothers achieved their first flights at Kitty Hawk. By 1915, pilots were having dogfights over the trenches in France."

"It's too hard to anticipate," Jamal said, hands on the controller, eyes locked on the tablet. "I need a live read on the roll error."

"On it," Bud said, his fingers battering a drum solo on his laptop keyboard.

"Let me ask you this," Bezos said. "What's the most important thing Amazon has done in the last thirty years? The *Kindle? Amazon Prime? Amazon Fresh?* How about *Amazon Web Services*, which now runs seventy percent of the global cloud with over two-million servers?"

> the spire of St. Josephs, four and five story buildings now, windows instead of plywood, a/c units, a grassy lot, actually mowed in fresh alternating lines…

Piper spotted Otto Slice near the sound booth, hand on his hip, smoking a cigarette, sporting a derisive smile.

"No, the most important thing we've done," Bezos said, "is earn the trust of our customers. Now how do you earn trust? Well, I can tell you how you don't do it. You don't ask for it. That never works. Here's the recipe for trust. *One: Do hard things well. Two: Repeat.*"

> …Ford Field on the right, the forever unfinished jail, in the midst of skyscrapers now, tilted, then wobbling left—

Annika ducked behind the partition and glared at Jamal. "What is taking so—"

"There," Bud said.

The roll-axis error data popped onto Jamal's tablet. Four degrees left, eight degrees right, twelve degrees left. His back was tensing up, and he unconsciously twisted from side to side to relieve the ache. Anticipating the tilt now, he fought against the compounding accelerometer error, slowing it, but not reversing it. They were almost there.

"This is why we've been number one in the *Bigby Reputation Quotient* study for six years now," Bezos said.

Back near the grills, Danny Mikos, high as fuck, began choking with laughter, the coney he'd shoved in his mouth dribbling onto his Chuck Taylors.

Finally: One Campus Martius, a crowd on the rooftop, tilting
right, left, right—

Jamal pulled hard left at the controls and the Skeeter flipped!
The streaming footage did a full 360, and the vehicle landed, a little
rough, but upright.

Jamal angled the camera up. Bezos turned to face the screen.

Big shouldered, well-coiffed Dan Gilbert opening the box.
Inside: a mint-condition 1996 Captain Jean Luc Picard action
figure, complete with Type I phaser and tricorder. Gilbert
holding it aloft. For a split second his face betraying…
annoyance?

Bezos caught that moment and a thin smile slipped onto his face.
An instant later, Gilbert's own CEO grin flashed. "Perfect! Thanks
Jeff!" Gilbert and crew waved.

"Ladies and gentlemen," Bezos said, "You've witnessed the first
ever Amazon Prime Air delivery."

Gilbert faded out. Mild clapping from the crowd.

Annika ducked back to Jamal. "Glad I don't have to yell at you."

"Yeah, thanks. Goddamn," Jamal said. He wiped his sweaty brow
with his sleeve and gave his back a big stretch and pop.

"Are we set for the big finale?"

"Wha—Nik, are you nuts? Did you see what almost happened?
We gotta eighty-six that! It's gonna to be a disaster. That accelerometer error is still—"

"What if we keep it short?"

"Twenty-four Skeeters up at once? They're all going to flip and
splash into the crowd!"

"Jamal. I know you can do this, and you've got about a minute,
so tell me you can do this, because if this doesn't come off, then Jeff
is going to kill me, and I mean he will put my head in a vice and
slowly turn the crank, smiling, as my brains leak—"

"Okay, alright, damn. I'll try."

Annika held in a violent exclamation.

"Do or do not," Bud said. "There is no try."

"I can manually correct each Skeeter if you can cycle me through the channels," Jamal said. "How fast can we do that?"

"About once a second," Bud said.

"Think that's enough?"

"Don't know. Let's try."

"The world of unmanned aerial delivery is a world no one has seen before," Bezos said. "Above all, the question is: *Is it safe?* A single UAV in the sky is one thing, but the future we're inventing will be humming with UAVs. You don't have to imagine it. You can see it for yourself."

Bezos stood stock-still. Nothing happened. He glanced at Annika with a terrifying and subtle grin. She poked her head behind the partition.

"Almost ready," Jamal said.

She spoke through clenched teeth: "Now!"

Two dozen Amazon A-4 Skeeters buzzed out of the drone factory bay and circled a hundred feet above the crowd, their aggregate rotor sound phasing and shifting as they moved in and out of formations: a square, a diamond, a box. They swirled into the shape of a large lowercase a, then…they began wobbling, visibly wobbling.

"Next," Jamal said.

Bud flipped the channel. Jamal read the roll-axis error and manually adjusted the Skeeter's flight.

"Next." Flip. Adjust. "Next." Flip. Adjust. Two John Henry's racing the steam engine.

The face of Congresswoman Ingalls was growing increasingly squinched. Bezos eye-slapped Annika. The telepathic message came through loud and clear: distract Ingalls. Annika snatched a fresh unbitten coney from someone's hand, strode over to Ingalls, and proffered the hotdog in her face. "Hungry?" she said. Ingalls was confused, but she'd stopped looking skyward, where here and there drones began dipping down, flipping, righting themselves and ascending, dipping down and buzzing low over people's heads. The crowd *oohed* at what they presumed to be aerial acrobatics.

"It's compounding too fast," Jamal said. "I can't keep up."

Officers Cross and Shepard stood at the periphery of the crowd. Cross was eyeing the short-shorts on a girl he hoped was eighteen. Shepard's spidey sense was tingling. Were the drones flying out of control? She put her hand on her billy club. All hell was about to break loose.

Jam-packed in the middle of the crowd, reporter Eddie Noble stopped scribbling. Were the drones…malfunctioning?

Piper stared upwards with excitement. Something was about to happen. Something that would be glorious.

"We've got another twenty seconds until lawsuit," Bud said. "Let's shut it down."

"No, wait," Jamal said. "Switch my input to control all twenty-four."

"The accelerometer errors are random, they're all different. You can't level them all at once!"

"I know. But I can send them all at high speed to the same coordinates…"

Bud looked up, and they met eyes. "The sense-and-avoid will kick in and…"

"Do it," Jamal said. "Now!"

Bud channeled all twenty-four UAV feeds into Jamal's tablet simultaneously. Jamal set the coordinates: a single point one hundred feet above the crowd. Full speed. *Engage.*

The Skeeters careened toward each other, wobbling bottle rockets.

"The LEDs!" Bud said. A quick keyboard clatter.

Bent necks all around, no one breathing, the Skeeters lit up, and bolted towards each other—hands covered heads, preparing for debris—then as they approached that central point, encroaching on each other's airspace, their sense-and-avoid programming kicked in, and they rocketed past each other in every direction, some shooting down, some straight up, a blooming of spinning blades lit by LEDs in red and white and blue, spreading out in a massive sphere.

In his easy chair at home, Luther Prince watched the drones burst like fireworks, shaking his head for no one's benefit but his own, thinking back to when Piper and Nia were kids, running around with sparklers on Belle Isle.

Ellis Wallace sat in his mom's kitchen, watching the TV, as she prepped a Hormel Brown Sugar Dinner Ham. He set his beer down as the drone fleet blossomed above the crowd. Was that Jamal showing off?

Sandra Dent's daughters had been begging her to change the channel, until now. They stared in amazement as the drones painted the sky above the airfield. Eve clapped. "Did daddy do that?" Nina asked.

"We've got thirty seconds," Jamal said. Triggering the sense-and-avoid had put the Skeeter's into emergency mode, limiting their speed to ten mph and allowing the visual input from the cameras to override the gravitational offsets of the accelerometers. They would remain stable just long enough to get back to the hangar. Jamal set the coordinates, and the Skeeters swooped down and filed away, out of sight. Jamal flopped back in his chair like a marionette. Disaster averted. "You owe *me* a bag of Sour Patch Kids," Jamal said to Bud.

Annika watched the crowd erupt in cheers.

"Welcome to the future," Bezos said. "This is day one. It's always day one. What could be more exciting?"

As the crowd began filing out, Piper continued staring up into the sky, the image of those illuminated drones still circling in her mind. It was an impressive finale, intentional or not. But she was already imagining something even grander, something that would put this little fireworks show to shame. She heard music in the back of her head, a break-beat punctuated with shotgun blasts, drones falling out of the sky, a hail of metal thudding to the earth with every gut-vibrating thump of the bass.

Chihuahua / Dachshund Mix (male) 4.5 lbs

★★★☆☆ **Buggy Eyes**

By Burt Stuhrling on July 05

Verified Purchase

My wife ordered this dog for me for my birthday. She did not order it Prime Air, and did not expect it to come by drone, but Amazon told her it would come by drone. When we opened up the box, the dog was vibrating and its eyes were open extremely wide. We thought that would change but it didn't. Dog doesn't blink enough. After a little while, we started using eyedrops on the dog (wife has an MMJ Rx so we have visine everywhere in the house). We wanted a Chihuahua / Dachsund mix because we wanted a dog that was a little less high strung than a full Chihuahua but I think drone delivery changed the dogs personality so that she is more of a full Chihuahua. The dog's name is Peppermint.

1 Comment | Was this review helpful? | Yes | No | Report Abuse

Sour Patch Kids 5lb

★★★★★ **Sour Savings**

By Dwayne Biggs on July 08

Verified Purchase

I eat kids when I go to see films. 3.5oz cost $4.99 at my theater (Royal Oak). These bags are 80oz each, so that's 22.857 x 4.99 is $114, versus $19.29. Only issue is it's bulk, you provide the discipline. Mouth pain sets in @ about 16oz, give or take, depending on whether you run your tongue over the sour bumps. Stomach pain @ 22oz, but it's on a delay so you don't feel it until after the film. I bought them last minute and the drone dropped the bag off to me in the parking lot of the theater. Landed right on top of my car. Amazing.

2 Comments | Was this review helpful? | Yes | No | Report Abuse

Pillsbury Grands Original Flaky Layer Biscuit, 16.3 oz

★★★★★ **Aerial Breakfast**

By Janice Martone on July 08

Verified Purchase

Biscuits...$1.68, air shipping...$4.99, insta-biscuit breakfast when there's no food in the house and boy has the car...priceless.

3 Comments | Was this review helpful? | Yes | No | Report Abuse

Secrets of Dance Floor Seduction

★★★★☆ **Up Your Game**

By MangoJuice on July 08

Format: Paperback | Verified Purchase

Frist time ordering through drone delivery. Was panicking as a friend had invited me to go out cruising for girls and am just getting back into the dating game after the brutal end of a 10-year marriage. I'm a speed reader, through, and when I stumbled on this book, I thought it was just the thing to give me some confidence before going out on the town. Drone arrived in twenty minutes and I started reading right away. The author provides realistic step-by-step examples that help you approach women in clubs, even when they're packed tight in a chick "knuckle," by breaking down angles of approach, timing, etc. Fold out cheat-sheets with body-language openers, plus pointers on vibe, charts on which type of women respond best to which vibe/outfit/verbel openers. I was able to open a "knuckled up" set of HB8s. Set included two male orbiters (spergy author types) but I was able to AMOG them and hoook one of the girls. While she was in the bathroom, I ordered condoms via Prime Air and found the box in my driveway when I pulled up. Girl saw the book on my coffee table though and that was a set-back. Minus 1 star.

1 Comment | Was this review helpful? | Yes | No | Report Abuse

Remee REM Lucid Dreaming Sleep Mask (Yellow)

★★★★★ **Endless Time Quasars**

By Bruce Billford on July 08

Verified Purchase

I'd just flown back from a business trip in Seoul. Sleep schedule whacked, so I was primed for some crazy lucid dreaming. I'd herad about these masks but didn't think to order until I'd already popped 1.5 ambiens, so it was a race against time. The drone came in 25 minutes. I was holding my eyelids open and wiggling my toes to stay awake. The mask detects when you're in REM and then gives you an LED light show to tether you to the waking world. I dreamed I was the God Emperor of Dune.

0 Comments | Was this review helpful? | Yes | No | Report Abuse

Necco Assorted Original Candy Wafers 24-2.02 oz rolls

★★☆☆☆ **Rude**

By Ethel Bronson on July 08

MY HUSBAND RUDY USED TO GO THROUGH 2 PACKS OF NECCO WAFERS EVERY WEEK HE LOVED THEM SO MUCH AND HES GONE NOW BUT I STILL BUY THEM BECAUASE THATS WHAT HE WOLD WANT EXCEPT ITS BEEN HARD TO FIND THEM IN MY NEIGHBORHOOD SINCE ALL THE GROCERY STORES LEFT SO I HAVE TO DRIVE OUT TO FERNDALE TO FIND THEM AND I DONT DRIVE SO WELL ANYMORE. SO WHEN MY GRANDSON MICHAEL TOLD ME I COULD USE THE COMPUTER TO HAVE A ROBOT BRING THE NECCO WAFERS RIGHT TO ME I THOUGHT HE WAS JOKING ROBOTS! BUT YOU CANT STOP THE FUTURE FROM KNOCKING ON YOUR DOOR. SO THE ROBOT FLEW DOWN JUST LIKE MY GRANDSON MICHAEL SAID IT WOULD AND IT DROPPED OFF THE NECCO WAFERS AND I TRIED TO SAY THANK YOU BUT IT JUST FLEW OFF! I WOULD HAVE OFFERED IT A GLASS OF I DONT KNOW WHAT EXACTLY. OIL? SOMEONE OUGHT TO TRAIN THESE ROBOTS TO HAVE SOME MANNERS. BUT I DID GET THE NECCO WAFERS WHICH IS WHAT MATTERS. THE CLOSET IS GETTING FULL NOW THOUGH. MICHAEL CAN I ASK THE ROBOT TO BRING ME SOME KIND OF STORAGE BINS?

4 Comments | Was this review helpful? [Yes] [No] Report Abuse

II

5

The woman's cheeks were red, eyes welling up, and—oh no, no, don't. This is why you don't ask people if they're okay. "What happened?" Annika said. The woman, an Amazon Web Services Sales Rep, worked on the same floor. What the hell was her name? Jess?

"Some asshole stole my Fire tablet!" she said. "He asked for money, and I said 'no,' and then he reached for my tablet—I had it out cause I was reading emails on the way in, and the guy ripped it away and pushed me and knocked me down, and I just, I—" She broke into tears again.

Annika checked her watch. The meeting was starting. "That's just terrible," she said. "Did you call the police? No? You need to report this." She gave the woman a quick hug, then pulled back. "I have to—look, you'll be fine, trust me, okay?...I gotta run." Annika slipped past her and into the conference room.

Jasper was sitting in his velour tracksuit at the end of the table, his fingers steepled. "There you are," he said. "We can get started." On the teleconference screen, Bezos, now back in Seattle, paced around the S-Team. Annika could see the large picture windows in the background, the marine blue sky over Lake Union, the air probably warm but mercifully dry and breezy, the subtle notes of saltwater, evergreen, and snowline floating through the nostrils.

"Thad Burrows is in the lobby," Jasper said. Burrows was the FAA regulator who would be observing Amazon's Detroit operations for the next two months. "We've hit our ten-day mark on UAV delivery and he'll be giving us the initial assessment—I know you're all eager to hear how close we are to getting shut down!"

Only Bezos laughed at that.

"I'll have him sent in."

"No," said Bezos. "I want to cover sales and incidents first."

"We did say ten o'clock. He's out there waiting."

"He can keep waiting. Tell him we're looking into a mechanical issue, but he's first in line for takeoff!" The S-Team laughed.

Through the windows of the conference room, Annika saw the woman talking to someone else now, wiping her eyes with tissues. How could she be so fragile? Annika pictured a homeless man running up on her with a knife. Prickles on her neck. It was an uncomfortable thought.

"Hello, Nik? Did the audio cut out?" Bezos loomed closer to the camera and his face filled the screen.

"Sorry, yes, I heard you. Incidents. Two UAV shootings so far. The first near Puritan and Livernois where the shooter missed and the second on the East side, where a rotor was hit, but the UAV was able to land in safe house #27 at the old Kettering high school."

Bezos maintained eye contact, waiting for the rest. He wasn't going to like what he heard. She'd just have to spit it out.

"With package theft, we've had twelve incidents, which is just over once a day, but more importantly, with the cases downtown, Quicken security saw the crimes on their surveillance cameras and notified the police for us, while in the neighborhood deliveries, our own cameras were able to ID the thieves in three out of five incidents, which I'd say is pretty good, considering."

"I'd say it's pathetic," Bezos said.

That's what he always thinks, Annika told herself. Relax.

"But we'll get to that in a minute," Bezos said. "Jasper: Sales, go."

"We've seen moderate and climbing sales in all the areas where we anticipated early adopters," Jasper said. "Downtown, of course, Corktown, Midtown. And out in Ferndale, Royal Oak, and Grosse Pointe. Also a few unexpected clusters in Eastern Market and

Hamtramck. Hipster enclaves, judging by the top sellers: açai berry powder and gray hair dye. That's the good news."

Jasper paused for what seemed like forever. It couldn't be that bad, could it?

"So, the bad news: outside of a two-mile radius from downtown, the numbers drop off almost completely. We've got just a handful of deliveries in the east side neighborhoods of Grixdale, Conant Gardens, Kettering—south of Hamtramck, and out near us, in Ravendale and Lasalle College Park. It's just as bad on the west side in Burbank and Dexter-Linwood. And not even one delivery in Brightmoor."

Bezos was shaking his head. Annika had to jump in now.

"This shouldn't be that surprising," Annika said. "These are predominantly black, lower-class neighborhoods with high crime and poverty, where people are getting their water shut off because they can't pay their utility bills, and some of these places, like Brightmoor, have vacancy rates as high as fifty percent—you can't sell to people who aren't there, and for the people who are there, how many of them do you think have internet access, smart phones, credit cards or even bank accounts?"

"Wrong," Bezos said. "Fifty-five percent of American households below the poverty line have smart phones. Only twenty-four percent are without a bank account. And I'd be willing to bet that twenty-four percent overlaps with the forty-five percent who *don't* have smart phones."

Shut up, really? He had all these statistics memorized?

"Anyone know what percent of Detroit's population is below the poverty line?" he asked.

"Forty percent," said the S-Team member who never seemed to blink.

"That's about 270,000 people," said another.

"Projecting from the latest census data."

"If half of them have smart phones," Bezos said, "that's at least 135,000 people who ought to be buying everything a UAV can carry from us. If they are not, that would seem to be a failure of marketing and PR, wouldn't it? What's the status on that, Nik?"

"We're talking about people without much disposable income," she said.

"Should Amazon be disposable? We're talking about necessities. These people should be buying toilet paper, toothpaste, school supplies. Right now, there's a negative feedback loop in these neighborhoods—they stay poor and dilapidated because they don't attract people, and they don't attract people because they don't offer services. No libraries, bookstores, no toy stores or clothing boutiques, just gas stations and liquor stores." He walked around the table, the heads of the S-Team tracking him like dogs staring at a lasered red dot. "UAV delivery changes that. We can reverse that feedback loop, people. These neighborhoods shouldn't be vacant, they should be filled with customers, millions of them. You know you could fit San Francisco, Boston, and Manhattan inside Detroit City Limits? I'm not just talking about Detroit. I'm talking about Chicago, Baltimore, Pittsburgh." Bezos approached the camera, his face growing huge. "Urban decline is bad for business because population density drives down delivery costs. This is win-win for us. If we can gain customers in poverty-level areas—a largely ignored market—we'll not only boost sales, but we'll help make those areas more habitable, contributing to urban density which will lower our overhead. You've got to be thinking in terms of the flywheel, always." His face filled the entire screen now. "Are you hearing me, Nik?"

Annika stuttered. The man was planning Amazon's future in relation to huge demographic changes that would happen slowly over decades. Who thought that long-term? But that was Bezos. He was also building spaceships.

"I want to see deliveries in Brightmoor, in Kettering," he said. "Be brilliant, come up with something I haven't thought of. Is that really too much to ask?"

The conference table intercom beeped. Jasper hit a button, and voice said, "Mr. Burrows is getting a little…impatient."

"Send him in," Bezos said.

Thad Burrows, bespectacled, wiry, and just over fifty, bounded into the room like a rodent sentry on high alert. He smelled like shoe polish.

"You know Thad's also a commercial pilot," Jasper said. "And a seaplane enthusiast."

Burrows smiled at the S-Team as Jasper clapped him on the back. "And you should see the arms on this guy. I wouldn't mess with him—ah I'm just kidding." Jasper was really working this guy. "Actually, do we have time? We have time. Thad, could you do it, like you did at that party in DC?"

Thad Burrows swiveled his head at Jasper, his bushy eyebrows raised. "What, a, a desk handstand? You want me to do one right here in the meeting?"

"Yeah, why not?" Jasper held his hands out to the teleconference audience.

Annika observed carefully. Jasper was deft at these sorts of mind-games. What was the point of this one? Get Burrows used to the idea of giving in to Amazon's requests?

Burrows was either savvy enough to know how to play this or clueless enough that he didn't have to: he smiled, jumped up on his chair, flattened his hands out on the desk, and rolled up into a hand stand, his legs perfectly straight, his slacks falling down around his ankles, revealing socks with cartoon jumbo-jet airplanes, then he lowered his face toward the table—a hand-stand push up—down, then back up, his body shaking a little, Jasper moving his coffee out of the way.

The S-Team applauded as Burrows gracefully alighted onto his chair, and Bezos filled the room with his laugh. Annika gave her own little clap.

Burrows took his glasses off and cleaned them with a handkerchief.

"Incredible," Jasper said. "Wish I could do that." He clapped Burrows on the back again and said, "Shall we get down to business?"

Burrows nodded. "As you know," he said, "UAV flight clearance here is probationary and will be reviewed by the FAA and by the House transportation committee at the two-month mark. However, the FAA has the right to revoke clearance at any time if the threshold of major or minor incidents is exceeded. Can we have those slides up?"

A wave of shock rippled through the S-Team, seeing such a flagrant violation of Bezosian commandments: a PowerPoint slide that was *full of words*, a header with bullet points of incomplete sentencing—a masterclass on government inefficiency. You could almost hear the eyeballs rolling toward Bezos, who smiled serenely and winked at them. They could all be in on the joke, provided they kowtowed to this federal mandarin until the deal was done. It would be a long two months.

"The thresholds for revocation of flight clearance are as follows," Burrows said. "Either ten minor events, e.g. mid-air malfunctions that carry low risk to persons or infrastructure, or two major events, meaning harm or high risk of harm to persons, or property damage exceeding one-thousand dollars. For reference, the July first downing of a UAV in the airport neighborhood will count as a minor event. You have nine left."

"Let me stop you right there," Bezos said. "That incident was a crime—isn't that right, Nik?"

"Yes," Annika said—Bezos was giving her a chance. "An elderly man shot down our UAV with a shotgun, which is a criminal act, and Amazon was the *victim*. So, I think what Jeff is getting at is: Why would this be a strike against us?"

"The purpose of our oversight is to determine if commercial UAVs will cause undue risk or disruption to everyday life," Burrows said. "Fault is irrelevant."

Annika looked to Bezos, expecting him to flip and call out Burrows on the insanity of this policy—but Bezos gave a grim smile, a commando telling his squad that they were surrounded, and to fix bayonets. He was going to play nice. "Understood," he said. "If a UAV goes down, that's a mark against our program. So our job is simply to make sure that UAVs don't go down. *Zero accidents.* Zero close calls."

Burrows went through a few more dense slides, covering the byzantine requirements for filing of paperwork and access to flight data. Once he'd finished, Bezos thanked him and Jasper escorted Burrows out.

"There you have it, everybody," Bezos said. "If you enjoyed that experience, I'm sure The Donald has some desk jockey positions open in the other Washington. Moving on. Status update on UAV footage requests and the Department of Justice?" Bezos said.

"They've finally sent a heads-up letter; they consider it regulable."

"Which statute?"

"Electronic Communications Privacy Act of 1986."

"That's bullshit. We should go ahead and litigate it."

"I think that's going off half-cocked. If we lose on a facial challenge, we set some precedent," said the stick bug. "Why not wait until a particular incident and ensuing data request?"

"You know these federal court timelines."

"Most of it is just fighting off the injunctions until the tech moves on," sniffed the S-Team member who most closely resembled a small, overcooked cabbage.

"Question," Annika said. If she wanted to make it to the S-Team herself one day, she had to take every opportunity to be useful. "The success of Prime Air depends, partly, on providing peace of mind to our customers about surveillance worries, so wouldn't it be a non-issue if we simply didn't store the footage from the UAVs?"

"One," said the stick bug, "That would just pass the buck."

"Then we'd end up in court over whether we're required to store the footage."

"And two, we want to keep the footage!"

"There's a ton of data there!"

"Useful data!" said the cabbage.

"For the predictive marketing algorithms?"

"We could've been more explicit in the narrative."

Annika's face flushed. So it was…implied in the narrative? She wanted to re-read it now, but she could barely keep the thread of this conversation. She had to stop responding to problems and start anticipating them. What she needed was an in to the community. Jamal.

"See, King Nebuchadnezzar was a mighty king, a *powerful* king. He ruled over all Babylon. And he was straight balling. He had swag like you wouldn't believe. Gold chains, gold rings, gold teeth. He *loved* gold. And you know what you do when you love gold, when you need gold, when you spend your time thinking about gold? Well, you start to *worship* gold. That's just what he did. He made a golden idol, a statue of his own self, three score cubits high and six cubits wide—ninety feet tall!—and he commanded the people of Babylon: Respect the swag, or I will burn you down!"

Piper sat next to her grandfather in the third pew. He'd found out that she'd posted the video of his arrest, and as she'd expected, he'd been embarrassed. She'd tried to explain, she'd tried to apologize, but he didn't want to hear it. Joining him at church was something at least. On the screen behind Pastor Edwards: an image of clip-art flames and the title of his sermon, written in Comic Sans:

Who Got Swag?

(Part 3)

The pastor was trying to connect with the younger crowd, funny considering most of the congregation had gray hair: old black women in their Sunday best, fanning themselves, frail men in pinstripe suits, like her grandfather. The air smelled of potpourri, mothballs, and cocoa butter. Someone should have told Pastor Edwards that the teens didn't even say 'swag' anymore.

((*bzzzzz*))

Piper took a quick peek at her phone:

> I know you got them flowers girl

Oh god, really? It was her ex-boyfriend, Curtis Washington.

> How you gon send me flowers when we been broken up like a year?

"And everyone bowed down, everyone but three men, who refused, they *refused* to fall on their knees before the false god. And King Nebuchadnezzar was furious!" Pastor Edwards raised his fist, the microphone on his lectern picking up the swishing sound of his shiny brown suit. "But *these* men, and their names were Shadrach, Meshach, and Abednego, *these* men were *god-fearing* men. They believed, and they followed the Ten Commandments. *Thou shalt have no other GOD before me.* They were *firm* in their convictions."

"Amen!" a woman called.

"Yes, Lord," Luther said.

Whenever the congregation called out, Piper couldn't help but think of the vocal adlibs in rap songs—*yeah, what, uh huh, c'mon!*

> had 2 wait 2 know if it was real

> If what was?

And so the king cast them *down* into the *pit*. He bound their hands and robes with rope, and cast them into the *fiery burning furnace.*" Pastor Edwards took a breath and surveyed his congregation.

> Missing u girl

> Every nite u in my dreams

Her grandfather gave her a side-long glance.

"Now, friends, do you ever get the feeling, some people out there, they want you to worship something other than GOD? They say, wouldn't you *love* to have these shoes? What about that jacket?

They think they got swag, but you know what? They're bowing to that false god."

"God is good!"

"All the time!"

"Amen!"

> you don't miss me. Your dick's just lonely.

"And that false god is Mammon, it's money, it's shopping. It goes by the name of Nike, by the name of Mercedes-Benz, by the name of *Amazon*. And it's telling you that you should need and want *stuff*, and if you *don't* want stuff, then they try and cast you into the pit, just like old Nebuchadnezzar done cast Shadrach, Meshach, and Abednego into the furnace, those three God-fearing men, into the furnace. You think GOD forgot about them? Do you think GOD *abandoned* them?"

"Lord no!"

"MM-mmm"

> I wanna hit it I aint gon lie

> u 2 smart for that

> I wanna see you work dat ASS girl

"King Nebuchadnezzar looked down into the pit and was *astonished*. Because there they were, the three believers, walking right through the flames. Not a single scorch mark on them. Because they had faith, because they did not bow to the false idol, the Lord *saved* them from the fire. Who got swag now? GOD got swag."

"Amen!"

"Tell it!"

"Mmmm-hmm"

> I'm in church!

Pastor Edwards' head began to shake as the spirit possessed him, sweat pouring down his face, dripping off his mustache. Nearly all two hundred in the congregation rose to their feet, hands held high, feeling the spirit. The organist, recognizing the moment was at hand, struck a chord, another, rising, thickening the sound of the Pastor's relentless voice, the congregation's shouts of affirmation, everything building, building—

"That's right, GOD got swag. And when one of our own refuses to worship the *false* god of material things, the *false* god of shopping, the *false* god of convenience, thirty-minute delivery to your doorstep, when one of our own refuses the call to *buy buy buy* and is cast into the flames, GOD will not abandon him, GAAWD will reach down through us, through *family*, through *community*, and we will pull our brother out of the flames in His name, because the real swag, the only swag, GOD'S swag…is *love!*"

He fell silent. The entire congregation fell silent.

$$(\!(\ bzzzzz\ )\!)$$

> but jus cuz I wanna unh wicha dont mean I dont respect u as a individual

> on the contrary u got some magic girl

Pastor Edwards was sweating all the way through his shiny brown suit jacket, catching his breath, bathing in the collective gaze of his flock—he'd come a long way to be up here at the lectern. Edwards was fifty-five now, but he'd been an entrepreneur from the age of seven, when he'd started selling fruit and peanuts on a cart—you could do that kind of thing back in the 70s—it wasn't Eden, but you didn't have to worry so much about getting jacked. During the oil crisis, he sold bicycles in front of closed down pumps. He must have started ten different businesses before he was eighteen, each one failing just slowly enough to get him to the next. In the mid-eighties, he created his own board game—a Monopoly rip-off called Reaganomics—and very nearly sold it to a toy company in New York City. When personal computers came around, he jumped in early, selling IBM PCs to black businesses—but most of them would just listen to his pitch, then buy a computer from a white company. It wasn't until his early forties that God called him to the ministry. And what venture could be grander and more rewarding than starting a church? It had taken all his savings and a few loans to buy the old Episcopal church on St. Clair Street, which had sat vacant for two decades—an old yellow-brick building shaded by oaks, in seeing distance of vacant lots and fire-trap drug dens. He mowed the lots next door, installed a handicap ramp, and spruced the place up. It was a plot of hope in a bleak neighborhood. He called it A New Hope Missionary Baptist. Luther had been one of his first congregants—they were third cousins.

He looked directly at Luther now. "Before we end," he said, "I'd like to ask you all a favor."

> the way u lite people up with those eyes

> how u call niggas out on they bullshit

Edwards cared deeply about the community, and had been struggling to get the young men—the dealers and bangers—off the streets and into church. "Give me a thousand saved men," he was fond of saying, "and we can turn this city around." But he was also doing well for himself. He drove a Lincoln Navigator and lived north of Eight Mile where insurance premiums were so low, relative to Detroit proper, that fifteen of his relatives were using his address on their insurance forms.

"Many of you know Luther Prince."

The folks in the surrounding pews smiled and nodded toward Luther.

> I need that

> I need u

"Luther's lived in this city his whole life. And he could teach all of us a thing or two, believe me. He went to Korea with the Air Force, wasn't it?"

Luther nodded.

"And he came back trained as an engineer, worked for Ford for fifty years. Did just about everything, assembly line to management. For a while there, he was a micro-welder—they say he could weld two hairs together. Well, Luther's had some trouble lately. For standing up to protect the peaceful atmosphere of his neighborhood against these incessant drones flying every which way."

And here Edwards summarized Luther's legal difficulties, the felony charges hanging over him, the mounting lawyer fees. "I ask you all to pray for Luther and his granddaughter Piper that God will lead them from these dark woods and back into the light. We'll also be taking donations to help with his legal fees." The congregation turned and acknowledged them.

Piper squeezed her grandfather's hand. She hadn't yet told him about the money from the GoFundMe page—mostly because it still didn't seem real, just some number on a website—no money had actually transferred to her bank account yet. But if the church could cover his legal fees…

The choir closed the service. They were a little rhythmically challenged, working out some kinks still, or forever—but that didn't matter so much. Their hearts were in it, same as the old women clapping and swaying in the pews. You could go on counting all day what they didn't have, but they had love.

Up on Eight Mile, past the All Star Gentleman's Club, past the liquor stores and beauty supply shops, past boarded-up buildings spray-painted with phone numbers no one's calling, heading west towards the Lodge freeway, lies the glorious Hot Wheel City. It sells what it advertises, hot wheels—hundreds and hundreds of blinged-out rims: blades, pinwheels, flat black solids, Dubs, Lexanis, Borghinis, from 18s to 32s, which you couldn't even install without jacking your frame up. By day, the store was merely gaudy. By night, it was transcendent, a vision of the unattainable, humming with powerful neon lights, alternating red and blue, bathing the wheels stacked in the windows and painting a strip of Eight Mile road in warm purple light.

Curtis Washington could appreciate that shit. He stood behind the counter at the front of the store, wearing a twenty-four inch gold plated Cuban link chain he'd bought on Flossboss.com for $19.95, plus shipping. He was reading *The Five Love Languages: How to Express Heartfelt Commitment to Your Mate,* and thinking about the one and only bitch—woman rather—that he'd ever truly loved: his ex, Piper Prince. On the wall behind him was a poster for Rucci Forged rims with some white bikini models, a small cross, a security camera, and a sign that read, "No Credit Needed." The whole place smelled like new rubber and upholstery shampoo.

This was his first steady job in a while. It didn't pay much, but it did have the perk of being undemanding, and it gave him an employee discount—he'd put black and chrome Dub X-30s on the 2012 Chrysler 300 he was leasing. Plus, the clientele was chill—either niggas with good jobs who could finally afford dope rims, or mid-level dealers, like he himself used to be. Well, barely mid-level.

Curtis didn't fuck with that shit too much anymore, except on some weed and coke hand-offs to niggas he'd been slanging to for a while, and who didn't seem too tweaky. He was doing what smart, put-together dealers did in their late twenties: slowly cutting back on the risk while keeping a steady income stream to avoid spooking your connect. Getting out the game overnight was a sign of heat from the cops. You couldn't just ghost and then show up three months later asking for a re-up. That type of shit would get you strip-searched and stomped.

The door jingled, and in walked three young'uns who grew up down the street from him: Sean, Clevester, and Demetreus. He hid his book behind the counter and sneered as they sauntered in. They'd be high school seniors in the fall, getting ready to graduate or drop the fuck out, which is what he'd put his money on. They were all G'd up—long white tees, sagging pants, Tiger fitteds—dressed for the back of a squad car.

"Yo, Chips, what up doe," said Sean, posting up for a dap. Chips was the name he'd used when running his crew. He was having trouble phasing it out, in part because he didn't really want to see it go. He gave Sean a lazy double tap, then went around the horn to the rest of these jits.

"What up doe. Y'all niggas need rims for the school bus?"

"Pshh. We got plans, nigga. Been wanting to ax you sumpin."

Curtis pursed his lips and gave a shady look to either side of the shop floor. "Aiight, out back."

Curtis led them outside to where they swapped out wheels. The traffic on Eight Mile kicked old plastic bags into the summer air. "So why y'all coming round here? You know I ain't slinging like that no more."

Curtis had seen too many niggas get locked up for federal type shit—crack, molly, guns. He'd been lucky—never got caught with anything hard—only once slinging dimes at school. His record got sealed after he turned eighteen. He wasn't about to fuck that up.

"I feel you, nigga, we on some other shit," Sean said.

"Yo, we trying to get paid, son," added Demetreus. "We strapped," he said, and he started lifting his shirt.

Sean smacked him on the shoulder. "Yo, stupid, quit flashing it."

"Might as well say it, is what I'm saying," said D. "This motherfucker's robbed some niggas before."

"Back in the day, maybe," Curtis said. "I ain't looking for no encore, though."

"I'm saying," Sean said. "We just trying to peep some knowledge, since you done this shit."

"Yeah nigga, we know you rolled some party stores," Clevester said. "Errbody know that shit."

"Maybe I don't want everybody knowing that shit."

The young'uns looked at each other, deciding whether to press on.

"C'mon, yo," Sean said, "these niggas at Denby talking all types of shit, but they ain't done nothing. You gotta drop that knowledge, yo."

"Y'all niggas trying so hard to get booked."

"Come on, nigga, we gon do it anyway."

"Yeah, we doing that shit anyway, Chips. Hook us up, yo. Eastside."

Curtis snorted and looked around. "Aiight. I think it's a bad idea, I think it's fucking stupid. But if you gon rob some niggas, y'all better do it right. You know if you breathe a goddamn word that you was even talking to me, I'm a fuck your world, right?"

"We ain't no motherfucking snitches, yo."

"I'm saying. You breathe a word to ya little homies at Denby that you was even getting this OG knowledge from me, bond, nigga, I will reach down with my fucking tentacles. You try impressing some little hos that you running with Chips, I'm a know about it. Y'all hearing me?" It was so easy for Curtis to slip back into that mode. It was so hard not to when these kids were sweating out respect.

They nodded, eyes wide.

"Aiight. All these niggas run up in them party stores, right? What's good is party stores get rolled on the reg, and clerks don't want to catch one, so they give up the cash. Bad thing is, they expecting it and they got cameras. And you ain't gon get much, cause they never got much. They truck it out like twice a day. Right?"

"Yeah, we know," Clevester said, making it pretty fucking clear that they hadn't known until just now.

"So if you ain't rolling a party store, what you rolling?"

Three wrinkled brows.

Curtis sighed. "Bars, nigga. Gon be a lot of money in bars, especially on a good night. But, on a good night, you got a grip of people in there, right? Some gon be faded, some try to be heroes, filming you with they phones and shit. You gotta be on that, and it's gon be confusing. Plus, a lot of witnesses, like a ton of witnesses. So if y'all run up in there like bitches, then everybody gon be singing to the cops cause they think you ain't gon do shit. And they might just crack you in the domepiece and hold onto they money. Right?"

More nodding. A couple Harleys thundered past down Eight Mile.

"Now, you run up in there sticking guns to niggas' heads, cops be rolling hard on that. And if y'all end up pistol-whipping some nigga's moms, nigga be coming back on y'all next week. Right? I'm saying, there's considerations to be made. First, don't shit where you eat. Y'all live eastside, roll something westside. And y'all gotta case the joint. You going in hard or soft? Mask or no mask? I say, always do masks. Actually, you know what?"

Curtis paused. A sound was growing in volume behind them, like a swarm of killer bees coming out the city's grates and around Hot Wheel City. The group swiveled and saw it—the drone coming down Eight Mile, a hundred feet up, zipping through the hazy brown-ish blue sky. Curtis flipped it off.

"Yeah, actually, my advice is fuck this stick-up shit and go stock shelves at the Meijer. Or you know what? Just fucking go to school and graduate and move the fuck outta here. You niggas ever think of that?"

Clevester looked at D, unsure of whether to smile. They both looked to Sean. Sean gave a snort and grinned. "Yeah, right after you, nigga."

A few blocks north of the stadiums, between the Fisher freeway and Mack Avenue, sits Brush Park, a neighborhood once filled with Victorian mansions laid with Italian stone—pre-automobile houses, built by shipping magnates and dry-goods retailers, men who had supplied textiles to the Union Army in the Civil War, even some old furrier money. In the 1870s, these mansions were a quick carriage ride from downtown, but when the 20th century steamrolled in, they began to choke on the noise and soot and smell of industry. Soon after Ford started cranking out his Model Ts, the rich and fashionable began decamping for the burbs. By the Depression, many of these Brush Park mansions filled up with working-class renters, and the neighborhood started its downhill slide. When the jobs and money began trickling away in the '60s, the old beauties crumbled, and by the turn of the millennium, they were marked for demolition. A few preservationist associations struggled to save what was left of the mansions, but soon the city went bankrupt, the price of scrap metal skyrocketed, and scrappers ascended by night into the octagonal turrets and Mansard roofs, tearing copper and aluminum out of the grande dames. When the dust settled from the bankruptcy and the city began the long task of rebuilding, only a few houses remained on each square block, the rest a peaceful expanse of urban prairie, long grasses browning in the summer heat, the insects going about their business, the towers of downtown looming in the middle distance. The neighborhood's air of rural respite was fading now that Dan Gilbert's new block of condominiums had shot up at the southern end of Brush Park—three hundred and thirty-seven of them. But there were still a few old mansions left north of Edmund Street.

On the stoop of one of these mansions sat Jamal Dent, the proud owner of the John P. Fiske House, an 1876 "French Renaissance Revival." Scaffolding was up all around the narrow two-story house and the inside was a mess of sheet rock and drop cloths. He'd already spent more on renovations than he'd paid for the place, mostly on some I-deserve-it accouterments, like wireless integrated HVAC, smart lighting and security, and a new 4K OLED High Dynamic Range TV, which had such high definition you could put your face up to the screen and still not see pixels. There wasn't a ton of content that could really take advantage of this technology—aside from sports and porn. In a moment of weakness a few nights ago, he'd tested that out—the latest in hi-def wankspiration was as enthralling in the moment as it was horrifying the moment after. It made him realize that the more beautiful the house got, the more depressing it was to him that he couldn't seem to populate it, as if all it took were money and fancy crap to lure his family back.

Nina and Eve were with him now, playing with the hose in the gated front lawn, dousing the toasted grass with water—but he only had another ten minutes with them before Sandra picked them up. This was the second weekend of watering, and some of the grass was flirting with the color green. He'd been monitoring it with a nifty gadget named *Grow* that alerted his phone when the topsoil was dry. It was working.

What would John P. Fiske, famed importer of fine bone China and miscellaneous crockery, think if he could see the new owner, a black UAV pilot for a tech company based in a city that wasn't even part of the United States until a decade after the house was built? Of course, Jamal cared much less about that than about the smiles on his parents' faces when he'd first invited them over—his mother used to mention how sad Brush Park was when he was growing up. But even that small filial pleasure felt hollow so long as he couldn't get Sandra back.

Jamal divided his life into a series of projects. His career was a project. The house was a project. The damaged Skeeter he'd been repairing for the last week was another; it sat on the concrete walkway, almost complete, ready for some diagnostic flying as soon as the girls were done with the front lawn. Nina and Eve—they were the most important project. He needed them to be happy, and he needed Sandra to see how happy the three of them were together when she arrived, any minute now.

Jamal watched Nina spraying her little sister with the hose. The girls were growing up well, as he knew they would, although they spent too much time with babysitters.

$$((\!(\quad \begin{array}{c} \text{POP} \\ \text{POP-POP} \end{array} \quad)\!))$$

Gunshots. At least a few blocks away, but maybe less. Nina and Eve hadn't even blinked; they were now looking at Jamal, startled only by his own little jump. He'd grown up with this sound, oddly enough, but it'd been years.

"Do you know what that was, girls?"

They looked at each other. "Guns," Nina said.

"Yeah," Jamal said.

"Do we have to lie down?"

"No, baby."

$$((\!(\quad bzzzzz \quad)\!))$$

He checked his phone: it was *Grow*, indicating that the topsoil moisture was right as rain. Jamal shut off the water. The spray slowed to a trickle, and the hose drooped. Four-year-old Eve shook herself off like a wet dog. From the nearby stadium, the roar of plastered Tigers fans filled the air.

"You ready, girls?" Jamal said.

"Is it going to fly?" Eve asked.

"I don't know. I hope so! What do you think, do you think it's going to fly?"

Eve shook her head.

"No?! You don't think it's going to fly?"

"Yes, it's going to fly, dummy," Nina said.

"Don't call your sister a dummy," Jamal said.

"What's its name?" Eve asked.

"What's whose name? The UAV?"

Eve nodded, looking at the Skeeter, the yellow swooping arrow on its frame glowing in the heat, a faint rainbow from the hose's spray fading in the July sun.

"It doesn't have a name yet. What should we call it?"

Eve stuck a finger in her mouth and smiled, and Jamal smiled, too. It was in these moments that he felt like he couldn't understand the world in which he grew up. In his neighborhood, Jamal had been the weird one for having a dad in the house. Somehow, he'd become the absentee father he never had.

"Lucy!" said Nina.

"Lucy, huh? A UAV named Lucy. Okay. Let's see if Lucy will fly, how about that?"

Jamal bent over the Skeeter—Lucy—and gave each propeller a last twirl to make sure there was freedom of movement. He flicked the power switch on and checked the diagnostics on his tablet. Ready to go. The girls stood back as the props began whirring, the short grass in the walkway cracks fluttering in the miniature rotor wash. That old mans' buckshot had done a number on three of the rotors and the camera, but he'd replaced those components, and the rest of the damage was merely aesthetic. The rotor noise rose in pitch and volume, and Lucy ascended. Eve, unsure whether to smile or cry, ran to Jamal and grabbed his leg, then looked back at the Skeeter. Jamal brought Lucy up to ten feet and hovered her, checking for wobble. The new software was uploaded. Everything looked good.

"Look at this, girls," he said, showing them the live feed from the Skeeter's camera—a bird's eye view of the three of them. Nina's head shot up and down, playing with the realization that she could never see her own face on the screen, since she could only see the tablet when she was looking down. On the screen, a squad car rolled slowly down the block. Jamal looked up from the tablet and met eyes with the cop. His window was down. He smiled and gave a little wave, like everyone was where they were supposed to be, doing what they were supposed to be doing. Jamal waved back and watched the car roll away towards Woodward. Had it come in response to those gunshots? It was possible. Where he grew up, gunshots popped off all day long with nary a cop in sight.

"Should Lucy go on a little fly around?" he said to the girls. The Skeeter popped up to roof level, and Jamal sent her in a slow circle, then ascended to a hundred feet and began a tour of Brush Park. Once the noise had abated, Eve tried to grab at the tablet to see the footage of her daddy's new neighborhood. Here he was, finally—his professional skills had turned him into the master of one of the coolest toys ever. When Sandra had been pregnant, he'd wished for boys for precisely this moment, thinking then that UAVs were boy stuff, and girls wouldn't get it, but Eve was beside herself with excitement, and Nina, clearly, was dying to fly it.

"I want to try."

"Not yet. I'll get you one someday, but not yet, this is for Daddy's work."

Cue little-kid melt-down. Just as Sandra was arriving, of course. The Ford Focus wagon pulled up next to the house, and Sandra stood at the sidewalk as Lucy alighted on the freshly watered lawn. Jamal walked down to the gate. Sandra was wearing new glasses— square, dark red—they were cute.

"You want some iced tea? You should come in and check out the house," he said.

"Some other time," Sandra said.

Jamal saw her glance at the crumbling mansion two doors down—the back of that house had collapsed, like it had been hit by a Hydra rocket from an Apache helicopter. There was a lone three story brick wall still standing—clouds passed behind its window to nowhere. It was annoying they hadn't demoed that building yet.

"I don't let them play in there," Jamal said.

"I know," Sandra said. "C'mon girls. Mommy's gotta start on dinner."

Jamal could smell her from five feet away—not a perfume he recognized. Something new.

"Is Nate coming over?" Nina asked.

Sandra caught Jamal's eye, then looked back to the girls. "Not tonight," she said. "C'mon. Car time. Let's go."

Nina and Eve moped down to the car.

"Who's Nate?" Jamal asked.

Sandra sighed. "Jamal…"

"You're right. Never mind."

"Just. See you next weekend," she said.

Jamal waved to his girls as Sandra drove off. He picked up a sippy cup Eve had left in the yard, feeling that eerie, but not unwelcome quiet that always came when the girls left. He looked at his phone and thought about calling Ellis. Ellis always had a plan. Admittedly, those plans had never worked in high school, not for Jamal. But he wasn't in high school anymore. He tried out the name again in his head. *Nate. Nate.* How strange…he could fry a piece of his heart just by thinking a word.

6

The Amazon industrial campus at the old City Airport was surrounded by death on three sides: the Gethsemane cemetery to the south, the Mt. Olivet cemetery to the north, and to the east, the 48205, which everyone called the 4820die, where gunshots cracked on the hour like church bells. At that end of the campus, the new Amazon fulfillment center—a big gray block, lined with loading docks—rose out of the earth like a big…gray block. Barbed wire fences lined the perimeter, like the border between San Diego and Tijuana: the grass inside, green and tended; outside, clumps of brown weeds clawing at the chain link. Amazon UAVs buzzed in and out the aerial bay like worker bees.

The fulfillment center was 1.2 million square feet and looked even bigger from the inside. The fluorescent light from the airy rafters was softened and refracted in its journey to the concrete floor, where thousands of orange Kiva robots, three hundred pound Roombas the size of suitcases, moved in near silence along invisible grids, sliding under and lifting up eight foot high shelving units stuffed with action figures, vitamins, power drills, sex toys, the Kivas then ferrying their shelves through the warehouse in an intricate dance, sensing each other, never colliding, filing their shelves in dense arrays or bringing them to humans in neon yellow vests, humans like Ellis Wallace.

His ten-hour shift began at 6:30 a.m. After passing through the metal detectors, he was required to leave his cell phone and watch and even his gum inside a small locker before entering the warehouse floor. Then the medical associate would herd all three hundred and fifty Stowers, Pickers, and Packers into a circle for some light calisthenics—arm stretches, hammy stretches, deep knee bends. Ellis did this crap all the time, but watching this crew doing it—shouting A-M-A / Z-O-N—was remarkable. There was Elizonda, who, in her bandana and bangles, looked like one of the TLC girls on a second career as a fourth grade teacher. There was a big ass white guy with tatted arms who had to belong to one of those black leather motorcycle gangs up in Auburn Hills. No cute girls, but that was no shocker. On Ellis' first day, the guy next to him said, "What are you in for, bro?" He was a short Hispanic dude with Enrique Iglesias hair. It was a joke, but the strange thing was, everyone here had an answer to that question, just like in prison—*I used to sell real estate, GM laid me off, my restaurant burned down.*

"Just kidding, homes," the guy said. "Nestor Ortiz-Vega. Good to meet you."

It was his third day, and already, he had an infraction point for clocking in one minute past the seven-minute grace period. The job was simple: Kiva robots carrying four-sided shelves would queue up at his picking station, and the monitor in front of him would tell him which product to pick from which cubbie. Presently, the screen indicated PWRBANG MALE ENHANCEMENT SUPPLEMENTS in cubbie 2F↑. Ellis picked it, scanned it, put it in a yellow bin, then waited as the next Kiva robot slid its shelf into place. The rest of this order was…a BARBIE CAREERS OPHTHALMOLOGIST DOLL in bin 4C↑. Okaayy…His scanner began beeping and counting down: 12, 11, 10. He found the doll and scanned it, shutting the damn thing up. Before the Kivas, Pickers would walk the endless aisles of product, up to fifteen miles a day. Now that the shelves came to the Picker, the expected pick rate had increased from one-hundred and fifty per hour to three-hundred per hour. One pick every twelve seconds. Ellis wasn't quite hitting that benchmark.

"Sup sup?"

It was Amir from the next picking station over, an Iraqi dude with diamond stud earrings.

"What up doe," Ellis said. He picked two cans of *Off!*, then two citronella candles. Someone was going to the U.P. He tossed them in a bin and shoved it down the conveyor.

"You went to Denby, right?" Amir said.

"Nah, Pershing."

"Right, right. Rough, huh?"

"Eh, wasn't so bad."

An IT hobbit cruised past them on a bicycle, heading for some distant corner of the mile-wide facility.

"Word," Amir said. "I went to Fordson. In Dearborn."

"I mean, no shit, right?"

"Whaaa, cause I'm Arab? Sheiiiit, nigga. But that's the thing around here, yo. It's like all types of people. I bet every single hood in the three-one-three up in this piece."

Amir was trying to talk his way into being black, really laying down the slang. Even using 'nigga.' Ellis found it amusing.

"Wallace! Al-Awadi! Watch the jib-jab." It was Michael, one of the Problem-Solvers who roamed the fulfillment center with a laptop on wheels, fixing errors, prodding slackers. "You're at seventy-four percent, Wallace. You gotta make rate today, pal. I don't want to see you get another infraction point."

"Yeah, my bad," Ellis said.

"Just…you know, don't talk so much."

Ellis nodded, and Michael walked off, pushing his laptop cart like a baby stroller. Amir flipped a timid middle finger at Michael's back, looking to Ellis for a reaction.

Ellis picked a roll of duct tape, a *Satterly Bone Saw 13"*, and some Hefty bags, falling back into the rhythm, his thoughts drifting—his mother working the bar, the fight at The Sting, and Jamal and his new house and car and divorce and bills, all those working American problems, Jamal the schlubby sitcom dad with a sad, but uneventful life. But the repeated thought-worm burrowing through Ellis' brain was about where he was going to end up if this didn't work out. The fear of being a wage slave, going nowhere, his body deteriorating, was somehow worse than unemployment. His pick rate had

slowed—Concentrate: 1G↑: DEVIL'S PRONG G-SPOT THRUSTER. 4J↑:
CATNATION KITTY HARNESS—not a sex toy, Ellis was surprised to
find, but a leash for a cat. Product was moving; Detroiters were
buying shit from Amazon after all, credit cards maxed or not. He
tossed the items in a yellow plastic bin and shoved it down the rattling rollers, where it entered the circulatory system—fourteen miles
of conveyor belts—until it arrived at a Packer, who would shove it
in a box—the size auto-selected by computer—then send it down
to the SLAM line, where it would be scanned, labeled, and weighed
before being shunted down a metal roller to a delivery truck, or, if
the customer had ordered Prime Air, to the UAV take-off queue,
where an A-4 Skeeter would clamp onto the box and fly out through
an open bay.

Lunch break was thirty minutes, but it took five minutes to
traverse the fulfillment center, walking past neon yellow railings
and dormant forklifts, being tracked by GPS, then another five to go
back through security, leaving Ellis with just ten minutes to shovel
lunch into his face before starting the return trip.

The break room was stocked with several vending machines
offering frozen burger-like objects and twenty microwaves that
became a source of fierce competition for the two-hundred plus who
didn't pack their own lunches. On the wall above the microwaves,
the Amazon Fulfillment Center motto: "Work Hard. Have Fun.
Make History."

The floor manager called out from the front of the room: "This
morning, Anders was picking at one-hundred and twenty percent,
Boudinot at one-thirty-eight, and Al-Awadi at one forty-four!" He
began clapping, and a brief round of applause followed. A few people
clapped Amir on the back. Ellis looked at him from across the room
and gave him *the nod*, the one you give each other when surrounded
by white people. Amir nodded back a bit too enthusiastically.

"Shit bro, Picker's alright," said Nestor, "but Problem-Solver is
where it's at."

"Yeah? You got the answers?" Ellis said.

"I've been solving problems all my life," he said. Which for the
last few years had meant working overtime at his uncle's tire shop,

struggling to make the place profitable, and occasionally beating the shit out of his younger brother Julio when he caught him with meth. "This is only for a minute, you know?" Nestor said. "You put in your application to the drone factory?"

"Was I supposed to?"

Nestor waved him over to the bulletin board with several recruiting posters and a stack of applications.

"Looks like you need some certificate to apply," Ellis said. "It's a year at Wayne State."

"Yeah man, read the poster. You take classes for free, after work, and then you get the certificate, and then you get the factory job, making drones, bro, and you make like twice as much as here. And you get company stock. Weren't you listening during orientation?"

No, Ellis had not, in fact, been listening. He'd been playing out the basic set of behaviors that had remained constant for, damn, almost twenty years now: sit in the middle-back, zone out, think about sports (football back then, Krav Maga now) and girls (ideally, one that he was about to lay, otherwise someone in an earlier stage of seduction). Sports and chicks. He'd had a good run at it, but now here he was, a few years into his third decade of life. Still fit, but he could feel it wearing on the edges. Impacts hurt just a little more. A few weeks off, and the soreness was more debilitating. Hangovers just a little bit worse, like his body had some kind of repeat offender law that started throwing the book at him over minor offenses. And now here he was, working hourly at a warehouse. No shame in that, except for the shame of being poor and staying poor. It didn't used to bother him—he was king of the poor kids. Now he was a poor *man*, less than a decade away from being a poor *middle-aged* man, just like his father in the later days. Pops went from fairly solid factory work at the Chrysler plant in Hamtramck to uneven work at a non-union plant down in Sandusky, which was around the time Ellis stopped seeing him. He was now several years older than his pops was when he'd been born. He always told himself he'd never end up like Dad, and he'd thought it was enough just being happy and loving life, until now, since Tammy the college girl stopped coming around, and he found himself in handcuffs getting bailed out by his old high school sidekick. This job was the last rung on the ladder before he became one of those old *layabout niggas*—as his mom had put it to his dad—getting soft in the ass, always holding a cheap beer, walking slowly through the snow in an old jacket to find a good place to get a buzz on and watch the Lions get shitkicked again. Ellis wasn't going out like that. He took an application.

Maybe it was a black thing, or a class thing, or maybe it was a Detroit thing—the men Piper had known growing up would holler from cars, they'd look her up and down and say things like, *Yo girl wasup wasup let me get atchu.* That didn't happen at U of M. In fact, the whole experience was a slow-motion disaster. At Crockett High, she'd been the queen bee and the smart kid, but at U of M, she was neither. She struggled to catch up to the white kids who hadn't gone to inner city schools with metal detectors. And that was most everybody. Ann Arbor was overwhelmingly white. This was a first for Piper; although she knew she was a racial "minority" as far as US demographics went, she'd always been more or less surrounded by other black people. She made friends easily with the white students in her classes, but she couldn't escape the feeling that she represented some kind of exotic cool to them—they'd defer to her opinions about music and fashion, all while writing off her thoughts on more academic questions. Piper joined the Black Student Union, hoping she'd feel more at home, but the black kids at U of M tended to be suburbanites with nice little Volkswagen hybrids, and they were a bit cold to Piper, until they found out she was from Eastside Detroit; then they wanted to be best friends. It was as if Piper somehow anchored all their talk of white supremacy in real oppression. Instead of exotic cool, she was proof of the violence and poverty and racism that plagued all of black America. She saw how she could leverage that perception into social capital, but she hated the way they seemed to equate blackness with oppression; the oppression she felt most keenly in their company was the insistence on her own victimhood, when most of them had probably never heard a gunshot. At least she didn't have to deal with that with her white friends. By her sophomore year, she began to think that fitting into that world of business and money was more trouble than it was worth. She might have stuck it out another two years if weren't for one of the biggest disappointments of college life: white boys were either timid, awkward, or aloof. They didn't know how to mack. Or worse, they just didn't like her.

When Piper returned to the D, she ran into Curtis Washington—they'd known each other in high school. He had a nice ride, he was dealing, and he spit a lot of game. He was a gangsta clown, but he was funny, he was cool. He was the perfect palate cleanser after two years in Ann Arbor.

They dated for a few months, and he'd been there for her during Nia's decline, which meant a lot, but the drug thing got old, and it didn't seem like he was ready to give it up. She'd moved on about a year ago. Now he was texting her again. It reminded her that, though it could be laughable, annoying, and even threatening at times, a part of her loved that aggressive pursuit. She wanted it. She just didn't want it from Curtis. She wanted it from Aaron Thistle.

She hadn't seen him in two weeks. With Gramps laid up still, she was spending a lot of time at home, helping him out and going over their case with the lawyer. When the trial came around, they would put Luther on the stand and present him in the most sympathetic light possible—a regular church-goer, working man, a grandfather who'd raised two young women, one of them a community activist who, sadly, had died last year. Piper didn't like having to trade on Nia's death to gain sympathy, but she knew the lawyer was right about that. It was a lot to think about, and she'd told Aaron to give her space.

He had, mostly. But he still texted her once or twice. Earlier this afternoon, he'd invited her over. A few new artists had arrived at the Art Farm, and they were having a cookout. She had been playing host to the lawyer, Pastor Edwards, and the young city councilman he'd brought by to meet her grandfather. She'd fixed them iced tea while the lawyer explained that since Luther had admitted to shooting the drone, their only hope was jury nullification.

"It's rare," the lawyer said. "We're basically hoping that the jury will simply refuse to convict even while acknowledging that the illegal act was committed." The councilmember gave Piper a creepy smile when she handed him his glass of tea. His big white teeth gleamed under his pencil mustache. He wore a purple bow-tie. She popped into the kitchen to reply to some RNKR comments while they discussed how to raise awareness about his case in the local community. She was trying to keep a foot in both those worlds at once, and it was exhausting. She could smell Aaron's cookout from the next block over. She refilled everyone's glasses, then ducked out and walked over to the Art Farm.

She saw Aaron at the grill, tonging some eggplant and chatting with the girl who made shadow art. She wasn't wearing a bra. "Hey!" he said over his shoulder when she caught his eye. "There's beers in the fridge." He turned back to the girl. It made her jealous and annoyed at once. That *ignore the girl you like* passive-aggressive bullshit. Or maybe he just didn't want to be rude and interrupt the conversation he was already having? She tilted her head back in annoyance and found an otherwise tranquil sky crisscrossed by Amazon drones. Ugh.

Inside the house, she was met by a wiry guy with greasy hair. "Try the caprese," he said, after introducing himself as Nicolas.

"The what?"

"Tomatoes from the garden. And fresh buffalo motz—so good. Detroit Cheese Company."

"They milking buffalos now?" she said.

"Well, yeah, for like hundreds of years. In Italy. Water buffalo." Piper popped a tomato-basil-motz stack into her mouth, and Nicolas whipped out a small microphone and held it up to her neck.

"Wha da fuu!" Piper said.

"He always forgets to tell the person," said Hans, the filmmaker who'd been covered in shards of glass at the Amazon press conference. "He is to make music from, how do you say, schluken…"

"Sorry, yeah," Nicolas said. "I'm recreating Motown songs using only the sounds of people chewing and swallowing."

Piper finished swallowing. "Why?"

Nicolas furrowed his brow.

"Like, why would you do that? What's the point?"

"It is art!" said Hans.

"Yeah, art," repeated Nicolas.

"Oh, art," she said.

"You gotta see this guy!"

Piper turned and saw the braless bitch walking into the house, Aaron in tow. "Most interesting thing in hip-hop right now," she said. The girl ducked into a bedroom, and Aaron approached Piper.

"Hey, pretty lady," he said. "How's your gramps doing?" He rubbed her shoulder.

Goddamn if he wasn't sweet, though. "Better," Piper said. "Almost off the crutches."

The girl came back with a laptop and set it on the coffee table Aaron had built himself using wood from abandoned houses. She cued up a YouTube video. They all gathered round.

"Goldman Stackz," the girl said. "Local Detroit guy."

"Stackz?" Piper said. "He's just more gangsta bullshit."

"His early stuff, yeah, but have you seen his latest?"

Piper had not. She'd written off Goldman Stackz a few years ago as just another entry in that part of the Detroit hip-hop scene she liked least—strip club rap: pussy, money, weed. Guys like Big Herk, Icewear Vezzo, Young Amazing. At the other end of Detroit hip-hop was Eminem, Big Sean—the commercial pop-rap stripped of its Detroit flavor. The Detroit hip-hop Piper liked was somewhere in the middle. Indie rap with an edge to it. Black Milk, Guilty Simpson, and Danny Brown, Detroit's ODB. Her favorite emcees were women like Detroit Che and Mahogany Jones. They were probably destined for obscurity. Socially conscious rap just didn't get airplay.

The music video faded in to the sound of heavy 808s and sub-bass with an atmospheric tinkle layered on top—the ghost of a Motown melody abstracted into trap music.

Goldman Stackz, slender and effeminate, standing on a rooftop in front of a water tower, skinny jeans, Italian loafers, biker jacket, long straightened black hair coming out the side of his fitted Tigers hat. A few subtle face tattoos. Cartier wire-frame glasses.

Shout out Brewster Douglas
Sugar House Gang
Gilbert eat a dick

He was calling out Quicken CEO Dan Gilbert? Piper was intrigued. As Goldman Stackz began rapping, she noted that he wore no gold, had no shiny watch or chain. Instead, he wore a Burberry scarf—in summer.

> A lonely city bus passing a You Buy We Fry fish joint. Slo-mo pan: overgrown houses, hard black men on porches, hard teens on corners. Goldman raps:
>
> > *Eastside, in the summertime DE-cide*
> > *If you going out like a fuckboi, that's when the heat rise*
> > *Niggas want beef with the cheese fries*
> > *Take you a biscuit UP in the coney*
>
> Bangers ice-grilling the camera, smoking Newports outside a Coney Island joint.

Piper laughed. Goldman's lyrics were so playful and pun-filled. The double entendres on "beef" and "biscuit." But the subject matter was serious shit. She'd seen guns pop off late night outside the Hollywood Coney Island on Gratiot. Especially in the summer.

> Goldman's hands wavering like the weed smoke wafting through the air:
>
> > *D on the domepiece, hook rolling by like they lonely*
> > *Blow me, ain't never catch me with a custo*
> > *Only touch money, hands on my nuts though [cough]*

And his flow! He wasn't slavish to the beat, like 2 Chainz, and he wasn't in defiance of it, like Danny Brown, but somewhere in the middle, tripping in and around the beat, mixing up his cadence to exploit the structural and rhythmic patterns of the music, so that when his rhymes did fall on the downbeat, they hit with an extra pop. It seemed improvisational and calculated at once, like a jazz musician. One rhyme scheme would seem to end ("coney" / "dome-piece" / "lonely" / "blow me"), making way for a new end rhyme, "custo," but before that couplet could complete with "nuts though", the last rhyme scheme would pop back in with "money." And the way he said those words—he was highly articulate, but on certain words he'd intentionally slur, giving them an extra chime beyond the rhyme, ("coaaaney," "loaaanly" and "moaaaney").

> Goldman and his homie reclining in the back seat of a con-vertible box Chevy Caprice on huge rims. Cuddling almost, the two of them. Goldman holding a nickel-plated nine, the Chevy cruising past the new Otto Slice mural. Cut to packed front yard: posse-shot for the chorus—Goldman, shirtless, sliding his Burberry scarf off his neck, eye-fucking the camera as he sings:
>
> *We...don't need you*
> *Ain't nothing...you could save*
> *Ain't nothing...you could do*

The chorus was pure Detroit self-sufficiency, a middle-finger to all the wannabe saviors, to Dan Gilbert and Jeff Bezos, treating the city like a blank slate.

> The scarf slips from his neck.
>
> *We...got our own*
> *Suuuugar, my loves*
> *And we glazing each other*
>
> Goldman flings the scarf at the camera. Pan across posse: hard-looking niggas with chains, watches, guns in waistbands.

Glazing each other?!

Goldman Stackz was doing something in hip-hop that had never been done before. There were gay, bi-sexual, even trans rappers, but like most female rappers, they got sidelined from the mainstream, tossed into "indie rap." And it was kind of obvious why: they didn't rap about guns, drugs, money, and bitches. They didn't have that gangsta swag that seemed necessary to really blow up with the Drake and Rick Ross fans. There were a few artists, like Azalea Banks, who'd blended progressive attitude with gangsta swag, but not like this. This was too weird. Goldman Stackz had a scarf *and* a gun and cuddled up with his homies (which he called his "babies") while rapping like he never left the corner. He didn't seem gay, but he didn't seem straight exactly either. His whole being was a loud dismissal of that very question. And yet, he was Detroit as fuck! Shooting the video in front of a coney, and did anyone outside Detroit call the police *the hook*? His lyrics were clever, his flow fluid, his charisma undeniable. And there were the seeds of some anti-corporate ideology which wasn't fully developed. Imagine what he could do if he had a more articulated message, and if he could push the humor up a notch. The video already had a million views.

Piper felt Aaron's hand squeeze her ass. She leaned back into him.

As the song faded out over a final posse shot, Piper's eyes widened. Was that—? She reached forward and paused the video. It was…It was Curtis Washington standing in Goldman's posse, smirking.

7

The Packard Automotive Plant was one of the worlds' premier twentieth-century ruins. It was a massive complex of five- and six-story factory buildings, all in advanced stages of gutted decay. Jamal parked across the street, where the houses were boarded up or begging to be, and he and Annika stepped out. The sun was dipping red over the horizon, giving the broken and overgrown factory floors a tincture of orange. Chain-link surrounded the entire thing. *That* was new. Jamal spotted the inevitable cut in the fence. You couldn't keep urban explorers out of ruins like this.

"How long has it been abandoned?" Annika asked.

"Decades," Jamal said. "But it's actually cleaner than I remember. This whole place used to be a wreck. Now there's some event company in that red brick section near the freeway. And I think there's a new brewery or something at the far end."

Jamal had already taken Nik to some of the less embarrassing sights, but she'd kept up the pestering about ruins until he finally agreed. Jamal couldn't help but get swept along when an attractive woman paid attention to him. Though it wasn't like Nik was his dream girl or anything. Plus, he'd been socialized through the military to never pursue superiors, and had been socialized by life to show a complete lack of interest in whomever he was interested in.

And of course, his main romantic mission in life remained Sandra. But for all that, he couldn't help but feel, when he was with her, the glowing pleasure of being liked. It was probably just her charm; they'd made her the PR honcho for a reason. Annika planted her foot on a block of broken concrete and lifted her hand to her brow like Cortez spying the Pacific. God help him, he wanted to sweep her into his arms and kiss her.

$$((\ bzzzzz\ ))$$

Annika pulled her phone from her pencil case. An e-mail from her mother with an all-caps subject heading: "HAVE YOU SEEN THESE NEWS REPORTS?" Apparently, there had been a few incidents of gang rape up on Six Mile.

"So it's really coming back, then," she said absently.

"Slowly. There's like three million square feet of rubble still. It's gonna take like fifteen years to fix this place up."

$$((\ bzzzzz\ ))$$

Another e-mail, also her mother, also about the rape gang. This one with a link to a 7 Action News clip. Rape gangs, really? That was a thing happening in Detroit? Annika indulged a recurring fantasy about giving Amazonian Performance Reviews to her parents. *What's Principle Number Eight, Mom? Need me to remind you? Bias for Action. We value calculated risk taking. And one of those risks involves me moving to Detroit, okay? In Seattle, I was a mid-grade manager, and here, I'm the public face on one of the most exciting corporate roll-outs of the decade. This is why I went to college and graduate school, this is why, I thought, you pushed me to succeed. I'm leaning in, Mom. So chill the fuck out and let me do my thing.*

"C'mon," Jamal said.

Annika stashed her phone and finally looked up. "Is it dangerous in there?"

"Not anymore. I mean, just a few years ago, they were finding bodies in here still. And once a tiger got loose inside."

"*Jamal!*"

"Sorry," he said. "They got security patrolling the place now. My buddy and I used to explore vacant buildings all the time when we were kids." Which wasn't exactly true. They'd crept into vacants only a few times—not only was it dangerous, but there was something sacrilegious about creeping through the ruins of people's lives.

"And nothing bad ever happened?"

"Well…"

There was one time when he was twelve. He'd been reading a *Black Panther* comic when Ellis started pinging his window with bits of gravel. He'd found a new vacant down on McNichols with fresh looking junk. They rode their bikes down to check it out.

The back door had been forced open. It smelled like old people and detergent and rotting food and BO. Quotidian bits of life still filled the shelves: a family sized canister of Tang drink mix, half solidified with moisture; a roll of paper towels denuded of all its layers save the last one that was stuck on the cardboard at the factory. Fridge magnets held up some free calendars and coupons, a list of emergency numbers, and a child's picture, done on construction paper with stick figures and a crucifix in the middle, the shaky handwriting mostly illegible in the darkened room.

Ellis picked up a broken Lasonic ghetto blaster from the '80s. He hoisted it on his shoulder like LL Cool J would have done about the year they were born.

Jamal made an army-guy head motion for Ellis to follow him down the hall. This time, he was taking point. He wasn't going to let Ellis think he was pussing out again. The funk reached his nose about ten feet from the living room—boozy sweat, dookie.

The bum was lying on the couch in the living room with his shirt off and pants around his thighs, exposing old black underwear. He wasn't old, but his face had the tightened, dry look of exposure, with sores around his lips. At his feet, a plastic handle of Windsor Canadian and a black Hefty bag filled with bummy stuff. His eyes stared glassily at where a television had probably been a few weeks ago. They blinked and then rolled towards Jamal.

"Fuck you want," he slurred, his voice rising from some other world. He clutched at his junk. Jamal took a step back.

"Bishes, I fuck you up. I fuck you in the ass, bish. Punk bish motherfucker." His eyes moved from Jamal to Ellis. Jamal noticed now the sliver of sunlight through the curtains catching the slow, cosmic dance of the dust.

"Fuck you, nigga!" Ellis yelled, and he heaved the boombox at the bum, who spit out an 'oof' as the corner struck his belly.

They bolted out the back door, hopped on their bikes, not looking back, the doors and windows of the other vacants staring at them in wounded accusation as they sped by, the neighborhood silent, but for their own panting breath and the squeaks of their bike chains, not a car in sight.

"Nothing bad," Jamal said to Annika. "Got spooked a few times, that's it." They ducked under the chain-link and into the old factory.

Jamal led her up a concrete staircase to the long, open second floor, which was filled with busted concrete and trash, torn up wooden flooring, black steel drums, the kind bums make fires in, old car axles, pools of standing water, grass. There were large gouges in both the floor and the ceiling. And it just went on and on, over half a mile. And there were five floors of this.

"You know, it wasn't even like this until about ten years ago," Jamal said. "Packard went belly up back in the fifties, but this building was still occupied just a few years before I left for college."

"What happened?"

"They say it was the Beijing Olympics. China needed all this metal, and the price of scrap shot up. At the worst point in the recession. So all the hood rats started stripping everything, even smashing concrete for the rebar."

Annika poked a cluster of mushrooms with her shoe. "But that didn't happen in other cities," she said. "Was it the auto bankruptcies?"

"I mean, that was part of it."

The boom in automotive jobs came at a time when southern reconstruction had come to a creaking halt. Then the end of the Depression came, and with the war economy, the industrial north was yelling for workers while southern blacks were still getting lynched on the regular. Cue the Great Migration. But working class whites fought block by block to keep them trapped in the worst jobs and housing stock. After the '67 riots, the whites really started running to the burbs. When Jamal was growing up, the only whites he even saw in any given week were either teachers or cops, or else people on TV. He'd grown up in a shrinking, crumbling city on welfare, where less than half of the adults he knew had jobs. No one thing was responsible for Detroit's collapse. It was the deindustrialization that blighted the whole rust belt, it was the auto plants cutting jobs and relocating, it was the deep-rooted structure of racism, and it was the rise of automation, which he was now bringing back to his hometown. It made him feel sad.

"Do you think this a turning point?" Annika asked.

"I don't know," he said. "We're bringing some jobs over. But a lot of folks out here, they can't get most of the jobs we're offering. They can't even buy most of the stuff we're selling. I mean, there's no way to get around here without a car, there's like no grocery stores. Some of the kids I came up with couldn't even read. In high school."

"So how'd you do it?"

How indeed? Jamal thought back to one particular spring day in maybe fourth grade when he had told his parents that fully half of that school day had been spent in a spontaneous riot when a rumor started going around that one of his classmates had crabs. He didn't remember exactly why they thought that Kara had some kind of parasite infestation, but the whole class quickly erupted in the chant of "KARA GOT CRABS," a rallying cry that got restarted every time a new adult came into the room and every time Kara got up or sat down or tried to say anything. Ellis had been involved somehow. That summer, his parents nearly broke the bank sending him to a tutoring center up in Royal Oak. At first, he fumed about it, but he began to enjoy it once he realized that, rather than being a scrum of social status and crowd control, the other kids, nearly all of them white, were actually paying attention to the lesson. He went back the next two summers and by junior high, Jamal had realized that if he was going to learn anything in school, he'd have to do it by himself. He spent a lot of time at the Detroit Central Library in high school, which was just as well. He didn't have the personality or the juice to be someone like Ellis. For a few months in ninth grade, he was getting scoped out by some of the bangers, like they were seeing if he wanted to sling for them or at least provide some muscle, since he was a bigger kid. So they'd got friendly, started inviting him to shoot dice and all that, and it was almost like there was this coolness dangling in front of him. But he had a sneaking suspicion that their overtures were false, that he'd just end up being the fall guy or the outcast or the kid on the bottom of the pile in that world, too.

"I just wasn't cut out for the hood life and—"

((*bzzzzz bzzzzz*))

Sandra.

"Hey Nik, I gotta take this. Going up to the roof for better reception…come on, you should see the roof anyway." He answered the phone as he trudged up three more flights, Annika a few yards behind him.

Sandra cut to the chase. "*Look, sorry about the other day. We should be open with each other, right?*"

"Of course, yeah," Jamal said. He knew where this was going, and he really didn't want to hear it.

"*So, I've been seeing this guy, Nate. Just for a couple weeks. I just don't want to hide anything from you.*"

Jamal stared down at the old tarpaper roof where water had collected into small standing lakes, reflecting the fire of the sun setting over Western Michigan. "Thanks," he said.

"*And you should feel free to tell me if you, if anything's going on, you know, in that department…*"

"Of course," Jamal said. "Openness. That's best."

There were hundreds of trees growing from the roof, some of them nearly twenty feet tall. There was something reassuring about that, how robust nature was, that if humans ever left or died out, the earth would reclaim itself.

"*So, I have a favor to ask,*" Sandra said. "*I know I'm supposed to have the kids this weekend, but I thought, maybe you'd want an extra weekend…*"

Annika had been right behind Jamal, but she'd stopped on the third floor landing at the sight of some graffiti that piqued her professional interest. There, on a crumbling wall in relatively fresh spray paint: "GO HOME AMAZON. DETROIT GOT ENOUGH JUNGLE ALREADY."

((*bzzzzz*))

Priority message. Jasper. Ugh. She could never escape work. It was always around her, in the air, like pollen. She'd forgotten to take a hit of Claritin before leaving the office. She sniffed as her sinuses sent an advance party down her nostril, and as she did, she noticed a pungent, human smell.

"Hey." The voice was right behind her. She turned and found a man with a week's worth of beard staring at her. He was dressed in raggy sweatpants.

"Hey. Hey, can I ask you a question?" His face twitched, and he blinked rapidly.

Annika froze.

"Can I use your phone? I need to make a call. It's uh"—he grunted out a long, guttural, orgasmic cough—"it's important."

Where was Jamal? Upstairs? She tried to shout, but her voice wouldn't come. She took a step back, and the man stepped forward. *Run, run now.* She bolted left to the stairwell, her steps echoing through the hollow concrete box, sheets of water rising up as her sneakers pounded through a puddle. He was so close behind her she could hear his ragged breath. Her mind flashed back to Nigeria, seven years ago, where two men had followed her off the minibus, slowly gaining on her until she broke into a run, her legs moving faster than she ever thought possible, until she reached the door of her NGO building and shut herself inside.

"Are you going somewhere?" Jamal asked.

"*Well…Nate wants to take me to Chicago for the weekend. He's busy next week, so. But Nina and Eve really want to see you. I understand if you've got work or…*"

"Of course, I'd love to watch the kids." …while you go off on some sexcapade with Nate to Chicago. Why? Why did these two things have to be opposed? Did he really have to watch Sandra get carried away in some asshole's muscled arms just to get closer to his little girls?

Annika swung herself up the staircase, bits of rubble clattering off—up, up, two flights, only then realizing how very, very stupid it was to be running towards the roof! Her voice finally came—"JA-MAAAAL!!"—a calculated risk, siphoning the breath she needed to propel herself forward. The man was still right behind her as she vaulted a missing stair, hoping the concrete wouldn't crumble, pumping her legs and pushing herself up into the sunlight, calling Jamal's name.

Jamal saw her running toward him, and then saw the figure of the man darken the doorway. "*Jamal, hello?*" Sandra said. He dropped his phone and reached for his belt as Annika ran towards him.

Almost there—*run*. What was Jamal doing? That stupid clip-on belt thing so tacky god damnit Jamal *do something!*

As Annika ran behind him, Jamal snapped open his multi tool and whipped out the first blade his thumbnail could latch onto, which wasn't a blade at all, but a three-inch metal file—too late. He brandished the file, staring down the bum who'd stopped about fifteen feet away. He was sure as fuck back in Detroit. The bum was giving him the death stare—would he really come at them? He never should have left Nik alone. What had he been thinking?

"Security!" The voice echoed up out of the stairwell. Oh, what a sweet, sweet sound it was.

The bum peeled off across the roof, then scrambled through a hole to the floor below as the security guard emerged into the light.

"You can't be up here," he said. "This is trespassing."

Annika hugged Jamal in relief. Guilt had never felt so good. Out past the crumbling and revegetating roof, past the rusted, empty water towers, the broad blue wings of an Amazon Stork caught the last rays of the orange-red sun.

It was 4:59 when Ellis picked his last product of the day (a wall calendar called "Ghosts: Legendary Combat Aircraft of WWII") and tossed it into a yellow bin to be conveyed down to Packing. He'd made rate, just barely. Three-hundred and two picks per hour. He had exactly seven minutes to walk the length of the factory floor and clock out—a minute late and he'd get another infraction point. The Kiva robots went on ferrying their shelves in their inscrutable pattern as he hustled back toward the metal detectors.

The workingman's ritual. Just like his dad's at Chrysler. They both clocked out at five and got fourteen bucks an hour, except Dad had started at eight-thirty instead of six-thirty, and he got paid in 1975 dollars—he could probably fill his tank twice over on an hour's work. And his dad had probably clocked out by putting some cardboard strip into a slot, then yanking on a handle with a satisfying *chunk*. Ellis had to click through dropdown menus.

He grabbed a budget dinner at Royal Kabob in Hamtramck with Nestor and Amir. Nestor rattled on about his big-ass family. Ellis had his mom and sister, that was it, and didn't much feel like talking about them. Amir said he had a brother, back in Mosul. What he didn't say was that his brother had barely spoken in two years, after surviving an ISIS assault by playing dead, lying in a blood-soaked ditch for nearly forty-eight hours, next to the shot-up bodies of his friends.

They scarfed their food, then drove down to Wayne State where the Amazon UAV Factory Technician Training Program was held from six to nine, three nights a week.

They took notes with paper and pencil. No laptops—Amazon considered them distracting. It was a whole lot different from high school, where Ellis had spent most of every day making eyes with chicks, and generally goofing off in a tone of voice loud enough for the teacher to hear, but not loud enough to make her actually do anything.

The professor introduced the basic engineering principles they'd need to learn over the next few months, focusing on the tensile and load-bearing properties of common aircraft materials, especially those used to make the Amazon A-4. Ellis struggled to focus. The class was boring as fuck. Though he did find it interesting to be working toward a job where this much knowledge was even necessary.

About half-way through, they were all given tablets for a multiple-choice test. Out of habit, Ellis leaned towards Amir, hoping to catch a glimpse of his answers. He couldn't. He panicked for a brief moment, then steeled himself. Amir was just some guy like him, past thirty and working in a warehouse. Ellis could do this.

It was easier than he'd thought. Their tests were instantly graded, and the results sent to the professor's tablet. They weren't told how well they'd done, merely which topics the class needed to focus on. They spent the last ten minutes going over these low-comprehension areas. Ellis relaxed at this point. He was actually getting this stuff. Thrust moves the vehicle forward, drag holds it back, lift keeps it airborne. Maybe school had never been hard, but he'd just been lazy?

After class, Nestor said, "You wanna grab a drink, bro?"

"Maybe next time," Ellis said. He didn't explain why: Mom's car was in the shop, and she needed a ride home from work. Which meant burning through his gas tank. He was under a quarter-tank already.

He hopped on the Lodge, the first freeway ever built, and winged it up to Smiles Cocktail Lounge on Eight Mile: a sports bar in a strip mall, next to a barber shop, shitty Chinese, and a Metro PCS. His mom had been working there for years, since, well, since Ellis' dad moved out for good.

Ellis parked and checked his phone: a text from his ex.

> Quit texting me nigga. I told u we done.

He stared at it, confused, then looked up at the text chain—five or six texts he didn't remember sending. "Thinking bout you boo," the last one said. Then he remembered. It was *BroApp*—you gave the app your girlfriend's number, and it periodically sent her sweet nothings. He'd forgot to disable it. Whoops.

Inside, the usual crowd, mostly middle-class black Detroiters. It wasn't what you'd call classy, but it wasn't a shithole either. "Hi, baby!" his mom said. "Almost done."

Ellis sat at the bar and watched her take a finished plate of tenders away with the tip.

"So," she said, once they were in the car. "How's the new job?"

"It's good. Kinda tiring."

"Uh huh. And the school?"

"It's more like a training program, Ma."

"Looks like school to me. Ain't those textbooks?" She gestured to the 'Exploring Engineering' softcover in the back seat.

"I'm just saying, I'm not getting a degree or nothing."

"You're getting a certificate that gets you a good job, is what you're doing. That's a career. I don't have to remin—"

"No, Ma, I mean, you don't."

"—to remind you how important it is at this time in—"

"*Mom.*"

"*At this time in your life* to be thinking about a career. Being upwardly mobile. You know, that's what you need. It's either that, or get yourself arrested again."

"You *know* that wasn't my fault, though."

He drove in silence toward Grixdale. When he stopped at a light, he realized she was crying.

"Ma, what's wrong? What happened?"

Silence. She fished a tissue from her purse. The light turned green.

"I'm just so worried. I'm worried. You getting arrested at your age, a man just don't come back from that. Ain't nobody gon hire you. And then ain't no decent woman gon want a family with you, so you just keep messing with these *tramps*."

Ellis exhaled through his nose and scratched his shaved head. He loved his mom, but sometimes he hated himself when he spent too much time around her—like he was regressing into a child. "They ain't tramps, Ma."

"They tramps. They *tramps*, Ellis. And pretty soon, they be all used up with six kids. And meanwhile, all the *ladies* standing around clutching they purses because they too smart to get mixed up with the likes of you."

"*Ma.*"

"Even a boy handsome as you, and I know the ladies like you. That's why you need to *make* something of yourself." She started sobbing again.

Ellis watched her tissue fill up with moist and snotty makeup. "Alonzo came over, didn't he," he said. "You know I ain't like him."

She smiled and shook her head. That boy could read her so easily. But he was wrong. He was just like Alonzo, and that's what worried her. They were both fighters, and they could both be tender, but with Alonzo, it never lasted. She prayed Ellis had escaped that curse. "I know school ain't your thing, honey. That boy Jamal did something with his life. He's got a *career*, baby. He's going places."

Ellis thought he was done with this—the Jamal love and Jamal comparisons used to come nonstop when he was back in school, reaching their suffocating peak as Jamal went off to college, leaving the rest of them behind. It had been easier to take at the time, because even his mother could see how no boy would want to be *like* Jamal Dent, exactly. Jamal, in fact, had wanted to be like Ellis, back then, and even Jamal's mom said he could learn a few things from Ellis about being a normal person. The crushing thing now was that his mom was right. He wasn't ruling the school anymore.

"You know his wife left his ass and took the kids," Ellis said.

"Well, I don't know about all that, but if she don't change her tune, he'll be beating em off with a stick before long. But you have gifts Jamal doesn't *have*, baby. Everything so *easy* for you, except for doing well at school and staying out of trouble. And that's why I'm worried."

They drove in silence again until he pulled up at her house. It was a tired looking house, keeping up appearances, its porch slanting, barely.

"I just think this is your last chance, baby. I believe in you *so much*, but I just don't think you believe in yourself. Your daddy never believed in hisself neither."

Ellis said goodbye and drove off knowing she was right—he didn't believe in himself, at least not when it came to shit like school. How the hell was he supposed get there? On the way home, he stopped off for a handle of Black Velvet, but didn't climb back into the driver's seat. After a ten-hour shift, plus night school, he was bushed. He lay down in back, rested his head on his textbooks, and took a swig.

8

If a corporation jacks up your gramps in the middle of the ghetto, does anyone care? Depends how many people hear about it. The video of her grandfather's arrest had turned a few heads, but not enough. Piper needed a megaphone, and his name was Goldman Stackz. Which meant paying a visit to her ex-boyfriend, Curtis Washington, who apparently knew Stackz well enough to be padding the posse in his latest music video.

The last time she'd seen him, over a year ago, was at her cousin Darnell's birthday party. She'd asked him to pick up some pop and snacks. He'd arrived with a bottle of vodka and a lit blunt in his mouth. Which would have been fine at a different party, except this was at 6 p.m., Darnell was only sixteen, and the party was at her aunt's house. She'd shoved Curtis back out to his car, furious. He'd looked at her all confused, tried to crack a joke. She'd just said, "Bye. Don't ever call me." It was the last knot in a string of disappointments.

Of course, he did call, and call, and she never answered. The calls became texts she didn't return, and they eventually dried up. Until last week. When he sent her fucking flowers. Way out of character. Maybe he'd grown up a bit? Whatever. She needed a line to Stackz.

As Curtis pulled up in front of Piper's house in his Chrysler 300, he thought of the last time he'd been there, about a week before she'd dumped him. She'd given him an ultimatum—no more dealing, or else no more Piper. She laid it on him in the middle of a striptease in her room. Carrot and stick. She was slick like that.

He'd agreed. The problem was, the very next day, his connect hit him up for an out of town thing. A chance to make three grand in a single weekend. The Insane Clown Posse was having their annual festival down in Illinois. Ten thousand people. He couldn't pass that up. He told Piper he was going to see his Aunt in Cleveland.

The drive to Cave-in-Rock park was eight hours, and he'd arrived stoned and aching. He set to work immediately, going around to the tents and tailgate circles. The Juggalos, that's what these white kids called themselves. Green hair and lip piercings, raggy clothes, tattoos of evil clowns with meat cleavers. Even their bodies were weird, bony or doughy, girls with pale rolls hanging out under tank tops over jeans with no belts. Their whole thing was Not Giving a Fuck, which had to be some kind of defense mechanism for these weirdo losers, but it also made him look back at his own hood, his own crew, which had its own distinctive Not Giving a Fuck attitude—loud ass bass, tilted lids, smoking weed all day. Made him think maybe that was all anybody did—try real hard to look like you didn't give a shit what people thought.

He sold his product and got out of there fast as he could. When he got back, he offered to take her out to dinner. Said his Aunt gave him a little dough. They went to a fancy fucking steakhouse in Gross Pointe. He ordered a bottle of Moët. She called him out, and he copped to it. Drug money. Right then, he could see that it was over. Maybe not that night, but soon. The worst part was: she didn't even look mad, just disappointed.

He'd tried to win her over by popping bottles. But that wasn't her love language. He wasn't going to fuck up like that again.

Piper hopped in his car, and they cruised south toward the river. She asked where they were going, and he said it was a surprise. She was skeptical.

"Share this blunt with me, madam?" he said.

It was this kind of bad decision that led to other bad decisions. But if Curtis was nothing else, he was charming. He certainly wasn't healthy for her. She'd figured that out long ago. But junk food could be so good sometimes, especially after smoking up. Piper took a hit.

They did the catch up routine while listening to Way Back Wednesdays on WJLB, cranking it up for J Dilla's "Fuck the Police." They drove southwest on Fort, beneath the Ambassador Bridge, then Curtis turned toward the river, and they pulled up at Summit and West Jefferson, facing the old Boblo Island Dock building.

The massive ten-story warehouse, once a cold storage facility, had been vacant nearly two decades. A shipment of meat had been rotting in the basement for years, making the place rancid enough to keep out all but the most determined crack-head scrappers.

A small crowd had assembled across the street—photographers, even a news crew. And there were men in hard hats walking away from the building behind a protective concrete barrier. Piper covered her mouth: They were finally going to blow this bitch!

"I thought, you know, you'd wanna be here for this shit."

She reached for his hand.

Back in high school, her close friend Jordan wound up dead in the Boblo Dock building. Gunshot to the chest. They never found who did it. Cops thought she might have been in there on a drug buy. Piper shut herself in her room for two weeks, playing Jordan's mixtapes on loop, until her sister finally convinced her to get her shit together. They had a memorial. Piper wrote a letter to Jordan's mother. But the building remained. Many times in the years after, she'd been invited to go exploring in there. She couldn't. She couldn't even look it at. But now, she couldn't look away. She squeezed Curtis's hand. He squeezed back and gave her a soft look.

BWOOM! It was loud but muffled BWOOM! deep within the building BWOOM! in regular intervals BWOOM! what was that running BWOOM! out of the building? BWOOM! a small dog? BWOOM! Hundreds of them BWOOM! My god BWOOM! Rats BWOOM! Huge rats BWOOM! Swarms of them BWOOM!

The explosions stopped. The building held itself up for an interminable moment, as if gravity were waiting for the old warehouse to realize what was expected of it. The near side collapsed, pulling in the left, then the right, and a massive plume of concrete dust billowed out in all directions, cheers rising from the crowd, the building folding in on itself, the rooftop water tower the last to disappear into the brown-gray cloud of progress.

Piper took a deep breath. So did Curtis. He turned and looked at her. He was speaking her language now, barely. She smiled, tears welling up in her eyes. Good tears. She kissed him.

She pulled back abruptly. Curtis said nothing. He just stared at her, waiting, confident. Why do this? Because she felt happy seeing that building fall? Because she wanted to have some fun? Aaron's face flashed into her mind; she let it linger for a second, then pushed it out. She didn't owe him anything.

"That all you got?" she said.

Curtis turned his Tiger fitted backwards, grabbed her hair, and pulled her into him. They made out while the dust settled, the smell of it seeping into the car. He undid the button on her jeans, and she pulled back again. They looked outside. The cloud of dust was everywhere. No one could see shit.

They tumbled into the backseat, sliding their pants down to their ankles. Piper lay back, her head jammed against the door handle.

"Ugh. Can you, the seat?"

He slid the passenger seat forward, then entered her from behind. She didn't have to tell him—he grabbed her braids and pulled just hard enough. Car sex was always awkward. Better to go hard and fast.

The familiarity of his body, his rhythm, his scent, it all hit her at once, and she fell into it like walking into a movie she'd seen a hundred times, right at the climactic moment, every line memorized. But there was something different this time. Perspective?

Curtis pulled out, turned, and nutted on the door. His head swiveled back and forth like a startled bird, looking for something to wipe it up with. His car was his baby.

"Use your sock, dork," Piper said, as she pulled up her pants. He yanked off his boot, then his sock, and wiped up the jizz while Piper laughed, the demo dust still swirling around. She hadn't come, which was fine. For a brief moment, she had been a body more than a mind, and however dirty or low the act, she felt blessed to be a carnal creature, she felt the spirituality of bass. As they caught their breath, she wondered: could their movie have an alternate ending? She honestly didn't know, and that felt good. But exploring that possibility wasn't why she'd gone for a ride with Curtis.

As they climbed into the front seat, the radio brought it up for her: Goldman Stackz was in heavy rotation on WJLB.

"I saw you in that new video," Piper said.

"Ah yeah, we tight."

"Yeah? I gotta ask him something."

"I mean…we ain't that close—you know in those videos, niggas be asking they cousins of cousins to fill out the mob."

"So you can't, then."

"You just fuck me so I'd help you out?"

"No!"

"Yeah…"

"If you can't, whatever. Just asking."

The soft, swaggery voice of Goldman Stackz filled the space between them.

"Naw, I got you. I'll hit him up," Curtis said.

"You know we ain't back together."

"Shit, you think I'm stupid? You too good to be with me. I know that."

"That's not—"

"The old me."

"Oh yeah? There a new you?"

He flashed his old grin and started the car.

Annika opened the door and took in the small group: mostly women, stretching and wrapping their hands with rolls of black cloth. Her scare at the Packard Plant had rattled open her mind-cabinets, and the idea of assault had snuck inside. It was getting in her way. A quick Google search had led her to self-defense training at Motor City Krav Maga. She fired off a status update to Jasper, then set an "out of office" alert. From 5:50 to 7:20, potential phone dingers would be told: *Annika Dahl is unavailable.*

The gym was one big room with mirrored walls and a big padded floor lined with heavy bags. Annika lingered near the front counter until someone noticed her—a tall, beautifully built black man in a muscle shirt, with tats down both arms.

"Hey there, first time in?"

"I signed up online. Am I supposed to check in or something?"

"You just did. What's your name?"

"Annika Dahl."

"Annika?"

"Or just Nik."

He smiled. "Ellis," he said.

Shaking his hand, she felt like he could lift her into the air if he wanted.

"We're about to get started. Toss your stuff in one of those cubbies."

The class gathered in a line at the front of the room. "Any injuries, speak now," Ellis said. He made eye-contact with Nik. "No? Okay." He bowed. "Kida!"

The line of students echoed him.

He led them in a warm up—pushups, sprawls, bicycle crunches, a minute-long plank that had most of these newbs shaking.

He went over the fight stance: square hips, not bladed like a boxer. Then, basic left-right punches. There are no jabs in Krav Maga. Every punch should be a knockout. He partnered them up, one holding a pad to her chest as the other threw machine-gun punches on his cue. There were a few aggro grunts and yells. But it wasn't quite loud enough.

"This ain't a sport," he said. "You don't get points in a match with pads and referees and everyone goes home happy. I need you to be angry! Get mad! No half-stepping, you feel me? If you gotta strike someone out of self-defense, you go all the way. Say you get jumped. You don't know if the attacker's gonna knock you down, take your shit, and leave…or whether he's gonna do something much worse. That especially applies to the females here. You gotta hit like it's your life on the line. This ain't no pad," he said, holding up a pad. "It's some asshole's face. You gotta punch his head right off, got me? Let's do some hammerfists. Everyone good on hammerfists?"

Annika raised her hand.

"I'll come help you," Ellis said. "Jenny, why don't you partner with Craig and Sarah."

The class went at it. Ellis held up a pad for Annika.

"Okay, just like swinging a hammer. Hit with the meat of your fist."

Annika slammed her right fist into the pad against his chest, head-height for her.

"You gotta bring that hand back to protect your face. Lemme see a right-left."

She hit again—one, two.

"Harder! Break his face. Don't stop!"

Annika inhaled, gritted her teeth, and pounded away, work thoughts finally leaving her brain.

"Harder! It's him or you! Break him!"

She tried, flailing her arms as hard as she could, vaguely aware that she probably looked like some little girl slap-fighting, a feeling that only made her hit harder, until the sweat was pouring down.

"*That's* what I'm talking about. Hold on though, lemme fix your stance. Okay?"

Annika didn't answer. The blood had drained out of her head and she was hyperventilating.

"Nik, I'm gonna fix your stance, that cool?"

She came to and nodded, and he placed his hands on her hips. "So look, keep your hips square, left foot about half a step forward. Your striking power comes from your legs and torso. Every punch starts with your feet—you should feel your leg tensing, then your abs—all that power gets directed up into your shoulder, and whips out through your arm to your fist."

As he positioned her and showed her the proper hip swivel, Ellis noted her steely concentration. Chick was all business in a way that contrasted nicely with her, well, blondness. And small size. Sweaty girls didn't gross him out, not considering how much of his life he'd spent sweating. He came back around and held up the pad, and when she put her dukes up, her blue eyes met his. "Go," he said. Sweat-mist exploded as her fists impacted the pad, her ponytail whipping. Not a whole lot of power, as yet, but serious focus.

As soon as class ended, Annika beelined for her cubby. Five messages, one from Jasper. She stood next to the fan, prioritizing her priorities, making sure she wasn't ignoring anything just because it might be stressful or unpleasant. She looked back across the gym to Ellis. The girl with the neon sports bra was chatting him up. The guy basically looked like an underwear model who lifted more weights than the other underwear models. It had been a while since she'd dated a black guy. She'd gone through a phase in high school and early college when that was a bit of a thing for her. About when she'd begun to slim down from her chunky teenage self, until she was no longer fat, exactly, but not slender, either. The stereotype of black guys liking curvy girls had been repellent to her for being perhaps racist and for underlining the fact that she was one of these "curvy" girls, but it was hard not to be thrilled at the new attention, given that she'd grown into her teenage years more or less unnoticed by boys and hating herself for it. She'd gone to a truly integrated high school—one of those rarest of birds—about half white, thirty-five percent black, the rest, other. It began when Russell, who sat next to her in English, had asked her to homecoming. From there, she began hanging out with his crew and integrating into the world of the black kids of Garfield High, and by summer, she'd snagged herself a guy that she could just about, with a straight face in friendly company, call, her *boyfriend*. This experience led her to link up with some of the black kids at Stanford, but after the first month of freshman year, it got awkward as the froshes shook out into the gravitational pull of like-meets-like.

She changed into her street shoes as Ellis approached. "Nice job today, Nik," he said. "What brings you to Krav?"

"I just moved here," she said. "Too hot to run."

"Yeah, we got brutal summers. Lemme guess: Seattle. Amazon."

"That obvious, huh?"

She lifted her tank top up to wipe her sopping face, exposing a stomach with just enough to hold onto. Ellis would normally let his gaze linger there—chicks took the compliment—but Amazon Nik made him feel like he was overstepping some boundary, putting the mack down on a student, even if it was, for him, an extremely mild mack. He popped his head back up to her eyes just as she brought the shirt back down.

She noticed, but didn't let on.

"So, you a pilot or something?"

"Security guard," she said. "They pay for my Krav Maga."

Ellis laughed.

"What? You don't think women can be security guards?"

"Ahh, my bad."

"I'm kidding, I'm totally not a security guard."

He smiled sheepishly and ran a hand over his head in that classic teen idol style, revealing the kind of upper body musculature that gyms use to sell memberships.

Ellis almost started to say he worked at Amazon, too, but thought better of it; this girl definitely wasn't picking product at the warehouse. Come to think of it, she wasn't exactly a girl, neither, but a woman. She had that look of responsibility, authority even.

"Well, hope you got something out of it. And uh, here's my card," he said. "If you ever want to schedule a one-on-one training session." He loved whipping out this card to give to chicks, although giving it to Nik, he almost felt that pang again, that she would find this business card shit less…impressive than some other girls.

"One-on-one, huh?" She smirked.

"And hey, if you need someone to show you around the city…"

As she left the gym, she was hit with the aerosol swamp of July, and she puffed out her cheeks to exhale. She looked down at the card: *Ellis Wallace. Motor City Krav Maga.* Why not? It was time to reinvent herself, to become a citizen of Detroit, not someone trapped at a cocktail party of like-minded strivers on the way to money, power, and bitterness, but a new pioneer. She suddenly got what the deal was, with all these kids moving here, to this hollowed-out ruin of the American Century. They were snowflakes, trying to matter as much as their helicopter parents said they did, by coming somewhere both iconic and new. The very space lent itself to the freedom of reinvention. So why not become someone new, just as she'd done in high school and later college, when her sexual and social awakening (and it was hard to separate the two) had led her to become the high-achieving competent woman she now was, bedecked in yoga gear on off-times and skirt suits in the office, duking it out with all of the other girls, now women, in her own demographic.

She was like them, superficially. But she often felt that her present self was hollow or thinly rendered, and that her old self, the one in her childhood bedroom, overweight and bookwormy, with Lauren Hill pumping through her headphones, was still so real as to burn through the fictions of her present, working life.

9

Be brilliant, is that too much to ask? Bezos wanted customers in Brightmoor, in Kettering, and so far Annika had failed to deliver. Sales were still pathetic in the poor neighborhoods outside downtown. The black neighborhoods. She needed Jamal's advice.

The hangar bay was obsessively clean (you could eat off of the floor), and it felt a bit military with its high-handed disregard for any decorative finishing. The clicking of Annika's heels reverberated through the concrete and steel box.

She spotted Jamal at his workstation a hundred yards off; the long walk was hard on her lower thighs, thanks to that Krav Maga class. What was the instructor's name? Ellis? She pushed the thought away. As she approached, Jamal pulled a pair of First Person View video goggles over his head and grabbed a control pad. The Skeeter at his feet lifted into the air, its buzz magnified to a roar by the hangar's acoustics.

"What's up, Nik?" Jamal shouted.

He must have been watching her through the Skeeter's camera.

"Top priority from Jeff," Annika said. "We need to boost sales in the outlying areas."

"The hood, you mean." Jamal hit a button, one of the rotors stopped, and the Skeeter wobbled, then compensated. Bud's new stabilizing algorithm was working.

"We've gotta dive deep on this. Five Whys time," Annika said, referring to the famous Toyota corporate paradigm. "In the outlying areas—"

"The hood!" Jamal said again.

"*In the hood*…potential customers are shooting at our UAVs, thieving packages, and complaining about Prime Air on social media. Why?"

"Because they fear and dislike UAVs," Jamal said.

Annika thought back to her tour though the Quicken Loans campus with Bruce Schwartz, Quicken's own "Detroit Ambassador." Their offices were so hip—they had an indoor basketball court, an AstroTurf putting green—the kind of thing Amazon would never spring for. Bruce had shown her Quicken's security center, an underground vault filled with CCTV feeds from over five hundred cameras in and around Gilbert's eighty-plus downtown properties. "Folks have been fleeing the crime in this city for a long time," he'd said. "People *want* sushi joints and boutiques and all that good stuff. But they won't become customers until you make them feel safe. Then the barriers fall."

Bruce hadn't said it, but he'd been talking about white people. Did black Detroiters really want sushi joints? "Okay, why do people fear UAVs?" Annika said.

Jamal toggled off another rotor. The Skeeter wobbled, but again stabilized, now flying on only six rotors. His goggled head stared off into the distance. "Uhh…because they only imagine the bad stuff: surveillance, noise pollution, you know."

"So, why do they only imagine the negatives?"

"Who knows? Because they haven't seen the positives? This isn't really my area of expertise. Why are you asking—"

"There we go. That's our core problem: we can't show them the positives if they don't order anything, and they won't order because—"

"Hold on," Jamal said. "Let me bring Lucy down."

"Lucy?"

"Yeah, I was fixing her up at home. My daughters named her that."

"LANDING IN PROGRESS! PLEASE STAY CLEAR!"

Annika looked up. It was Jamal's nasally voice coming from the Skeeter. "What was that?"

"Pretty cool, right?" Jamal said, removing the goggles. Thin red lines marked his forehead. "Figured an audio warning would help improve landing safety."

"Could you make it say other things? In real time?"

"I guess, maybe…"

"Jamal! What if we made Lucy like, a diplomat to the outlying— to the hood?"

"Like a friendly talking robot."

"Exactly. But we'd need to make it—*her*—more friendly."

"Less octocoptery."

"A different paintjob?"

"You want to paint her black?"

"That's not what I meant. We could give her a face add-on or something."

"Googly eyes?" Jamal said.

"Yeah! You could fly her out to the hood and talk to people. We could make bumper stickers: I♥LUCY."

"But isn't that creepy? I mean, if we make Lucy a character, do we really want her to sound like me?"

"We could hire a voice actor."

"Like Flo in the Progressive commercials."

Annika thought of her father, who had taken up clowning in his retirement. Glip Glop the Clown, he called himself. Performed at children's birthday parties. "I'm thinking more like the Geico gecko," she said. "Non-human but with a personality. And it has to be interactive."

"So we need some kind of robot voice," Jamal said. "Text to speech."

"Great, but…what about the loud, insectile buzzing?"

"I wish people would get used to the buzz."

"No one gets used to the buzz. It's like a squadron of robot wasps come to slaughter your family."

"Oh my god, what is it with you people?"

"*You people?*"

"Luddites!"

"Just deal with reality, okay? Could we play music to mask the rotor noise?"

Jamal arched his eyebrows. Annika liked him like this—he was in his element with ideas.

"Yeah, we could do music. What're you thinking?"

"I'm way too Seattle to know. You're the Detroiter."

"Way too white, you mean."

"Sure."

"And I'm not? I'm a UAV pilot, not some Pocahontas to black Detroit."

This hang-up of Jamal's was why Annika had been hesitant to approach him in the first place. She just had to clear the air. "You really think Bezos promoted you just because you're black? Nobody doubts your talent. I don't. But your background is value-added here. So, use it."

Jamal huffed and pulled up Amazon Music. Who was that guy Ellis liked? Goldman Sachs? Oh *Stackz*, of course. He played the first track that came up. "*Scrooge McNigga* it is," he said. The beat dropped from Lucy's speaker:

Got these bunnies beggin' for my honey pot
Stack bread, spit raps like a gun assault
Whack emcees ducking lead doing somersaults
Won't stop till I'm swimming in a money vault

"Huh. People will go for that?"

"In the hood they will. You put some politically correct Macklemore crap in Lucy's mouth, everyone's gonna peg her as Seattle."

"I like Macklemore."

"Of course you do."

Stackz was now rapping about dipping his testicles in a vat of molten gold. How could a world-beating Seattle tech corporation send a mascot out into the streets, spouting this ghetto-ass shit? On the other hand, if Detroiters, *black* Detroiters, a.k.a. *real* Detroiters liked it, who would the S-Team be to question it? White cultural imperialists, that's who. Well, white and Asian, and south Asian…

"Okay, but, with the rotor noise and music, will you be able to hear people?"

"Sure. It's got acoustic echo cancellation. It ignores any sounds it's making itself, filters them out. Same reason Alexa can hear your commands when it's blasting music. But are you sure this is a good idea in the first place?"

Annika wasn't sure. She ran through the Amazon principles. *Think big. Leaders are right, a lot.* Bezos wanted Brightmoor. *Be bold.* She could swing and whiff, but she knew by now that not swinging, letting the pitch go by, was itself a choice. *Bias for action.*

"Could you have Lucy ready by Sunday?" Annika said. "We could do a little test run."

Jamal was supposed to have the kids on Sunday. Of course, if he didn't…then Sandra couldn't go on her trip to Chicago with *Nate.* Motherfucker was probably, let's face it, a bit like Jamal; Sandra wouldn't date him otherwise. The type of guy who hadn't exactly laid the village when he was young, but now that he had a real job was pulling all the single moms, given what the ladies around here had to work with. Basically, a down-market Jamal, pimping all over Westside Detroit with his middle-management ass. Well, fuck that guy. Jamal was the real deal: a veteran pilot, an engineer, a father. But what kind of father would bail on his little girls to keep their mother away from some douchebag?

"I don't know," Jamal said. "Shouldn't you run this by the S-Team first?"

Annika tapped her foot and listened to it echo through the hangar, wondering what it felt like to be brilliant, to not have to fake her way through it day after day.

It was awkward enough walking into The Sting—Piper had a distaste for strip clubs—but it was even stranger with gangly stand-up comic Danny Mikos at her side. They were here to see Goldman Stackz. Curtis said he came to The Sting on Friday nights to sit in one of the rear booths and write rhymes.

She'd found Mikos via RNKR and had invited herself over to

his Ferndale pad to pitch him on her plan. Her grandfather was awaiting trial, and the only hope was that a jury would simply refuse to convict an old black man, regardless of how clearly he'd violated the letter of the law. At first, it had seemed there was little to do but wait in the grip of anxiety for another month and half. But she'd soon realized that there was something she could do: steer public opinion against Amazon. And since Pastor Edwards and the church were taking care of the legal bills, she had a bankroll from the GoFundMe page.

She'd been playing the social media game long enough to know the markers of virality. The content that spread the furthest fastest hit four key qualities: it was provocative, artistic, it spoke to the cultural moment, and it was funny. Goldman had the first three in spades. As for the humor, that's where Danny Mikos came in.

When she'd arrived at his pad, he and his stoner friends had been hitting the volcano vape, which inflated a pillow-sized plastic bag with weed vapor. She'd joined them, manspreading on his couch while she asked about visual comedy, comedy in screenwriting, in music videos. Danny and his pals were Ferndale kids, not part of her usual set. A big part of why'd she'd gone there was simply to see if she could turn her digital following into real-world influence—could she get Danny and his white friends to trust her, follow her lead? At one point, Danny had tried sliding an arm around her—she shut that down quick. He'd taken it in stride. "I mean, c'mon," he'd said. "This hot chick wants to come over and 'talk about comedy,' if you know what I mean." Turned out, Danny was a huge Stackz fan. Before Piper could even explain the plan, he'd invited himself along to meet Goldman. Fair enough.

The bouncer checked their IDs. "What's the cover?" Danny said. "Self-respect?"

It was eleven, early in strip club land. TVs were on behind the bar. Most of the booths were empty and there weren't yet enough human smells to overpower the odor of last night's spilled beer. Nonetheless, the DJ was spinning the latest Young Thug, and there was a girl on stage half-heartedly working the pole, stretch marks on her thighs. Piper felt some weight drop inside of her. She wanted to offer her a smile, to say, *I see you*. But the woman was hardly there.

"She looks so bored," Danny said. "She should've brought a Sudoku book."

Piper scanned the booths, rising up in tiers from the central stage. There he was, Burberry scarf and all, sitting alone with a bottle of rosé, scribbling in a notebook. They approached, but before they could even say hello, a couple big boys stepped up.

"Y'all need something?" said the one with gold fronts.

"Oh thanks," Danny said. "I'll have a gin and tonic. Bombay. Piper?"

"He's an idiot. Can't help hisself," Piper said, her diction subconsciously melding to the hoodness of her surroundings. "But y'all need to move now, cause I'm bout to sit down." Piper waited, heart hammering her ribcage, staring up at the large men. She stepped forward, they parted, and she sat down next to Goldman. Danny slid through after her.

"What up doe," Goldman said in a silky baritone. He looked them both over equally, biting his bottom lip.

"This is Danny," she said. "I'm Piper. We gon make you famous."

"Oh?" He seemed amused.

"You Detroit famous. And you this close to breaking out." Goldman licked his finger and rubbed the rim of his wine glass, making it hum.

"What you need is a more articulate message."

"You boring me," he said. "Why don't you go bye bye now. Ricky, love…" He glanced towards one of the big boys who stood up.

"Wait." Piper pulled up the video of her gramps' arrest which had now been shared over half a million times on RNKR.

"That shit was fucked, no Vaseline," he said.

"For real. But you know what? People hyped on this shit."

"And what's that got to do with me?"

"That's my gramps," Piper said.

"So *he* gon make me famous?"

"We're pointing at the moon and you're looking at the finger," Danny said.

Goldman stared hard at Danny, who was fucking this all up, insulting the guy they were trying to recruit. Piper almost kicked him under the table.

Then Goldman, still grilling Danny, finally said, "You pretty."

"You should see the portrait hidden in my attic," Danny said.

"This Dorian Gray muthafucka," Goldman said, laughing.

Piper exhaled. Goldman wasn't about to have his boys toss them out. But that didn't mean he was willing to help them.

"How you feel about Amazon?" Piper said.

Goldman flicked open a pocket mirror and ran a finger across a delicate eyebrow. "I look like I give a fuck about Amazon?"

10

Barry Sanders, hoping for an ear scratch, trundled up to his master's knee and looked up—bad news: the big goggles were on and the pad was out. No scratches anytime soon.

Jamal was high above the city in his custom-modified Skeeter, Lucy—nay, not *in* Lucy, but *as* Lucy. The freedom of movement! No cockpit, no flight suit, no pretzeling around to toggle this or that switch. With the right optics and frame rate in a state-of-the-art pair of FPV goggles, his mind could take flight, leaving his body forgotten. The only thing missing was the g-force, the ground pulling at your guts as you lifted off. There was no replacing that. At least, not yet.

It had been a typical muggy summer, but today was substantially cooler, in the high seventies, and Detroiters were firing up grills and cracking beer cans. Annika stood behind Jamal, watching the feed as Lucy banked south in search of a good cookout.

The brunch crowd of A New Hope Missionary Baptist had gone whole hog for today's barbecue, the theme being, "Break Bread." In the grassy lot adjacent to the church: lawn chairs, tables, plastic silverware, and several smoking oil-barrel grills. The crowd was mostly well-dressed old women, a few men, and a couple teens with fitted caps and scowls, who'd clearly been dragged there by well-intentioned aunts.

"I don't see a whole ton of bread here, Pastor. Unless by *break bread* you mean cutting some ribs, but I think that might be a different part of the Bible."

Pastor Edwards let out a slow, low laugh. "Well, that's one of the blessings we can thank Him for, that we discovered some barbeque in these days."

"Oh, they had barbeque back in those days, Pastor," chimed in Ms. Jules, who, having laid her girth into a lawn chair, was nursing a plastic cup of lemonade.

"They had feasts with lamb."

"No pig, though."

"They didn't have no pig."

"Well, they didn't eat no pig, because it's not Kosher in the Jewish faith. See, they got a few rules in the diet that we don't."

Aspiring stick-up kid, Demetreus Reynolds, was sitting on a cooler as his older brother JT arrived from the You Buy We Fry. He set down a bag of fish, oil soaking through the paper, and wandered over to the cooler. "Move yo ass," he said.

Demetreus didn't react for a good two seconds, the idea being to maximize the time between the command and the execution, in order to minimize the reality that he was taking orders. JT saw through this petty bullshit, but didn't question it. He'd done it too, after all.

Darnell Parker, seventeen-year-old nerd, sat sipping a Faygo a dozen yards away, looking toward Demetreus. They'd known each other in junior high, but hadn't much spoken since Darnell got into Cass Tech. Darnell lusted after his swagger—meager as it was—as much as Demetreus feared that life was going to turn out much better for Darnell. Demetreus's moms had been on his ass lately for coming home blunted. He wanted to be blazing up right now. Fucking church bullshit. Where the hell were Sean and Clevester? He walked over to Darnell.

"Yo, lemme see your phone," he said.

"Umm, why?"

"I'm outta minutes. Give it to me."

Darnell handed it over.

Demetreus rang up Clevester, seeing if they were going to get their asses over here with the girls that Sean was supposed to be wrangling.

"I said five minutes!" Marc Jefferson barked, slapping a greedy hand with sauce-covered tongs. He had a belly like the Kool-Aid Man and was the undisputed grill-master of the congregation. Next to him, the Wilson clan was firing up their own grill. The thing about that family, it was well known, was that Daddy was Detroit Police.

Just as Demetreus hung up and handed back Darnell's phone, a buzzing music swelled from the clouds—Pastor Edwards wiped his chin and looked to the heavens. What in the Lord's name? The buzzing came closer, layered over with a hard-edged gangsta beat. The pastor's fleshy forehead contracted around his eyebrows, and he held his fork aloft at the drone as if to speak, but his mouth was still full of brisket. Demetreus snuck a splash of Aristocrat vodka into his Faygo.

Sean walked up with Clevester, no bitches in tow. "Look at that shit," he drawled, his voice filled with the alcoholic slur of aggression that seemed to be his default. "If I had a shotty, I'd show it what the fuck is up." He hitched his sagging pants.

"Yo, that bitch got a bomb or some shit," Clevester said.

As the drone descended into the cookout, they saw that it had a pair of large plastic googly eyes glued to its body, and instead of the usual blue delivery box, it held something else, something...

"Oh Lawd, Pastor. That little thing has got itself a watermelon."

A watermelon? Impossible. But true—it was one of those little, single-serving watermelons that one could now find at the Meijer's on Eight Mile—some sort of yuppie thing, or vaguely Japanese— what did anyone want with a *miniature* watermelon at a cookout? But Pastor Edwards had tried one himself recently, and he had to admit, they were juicy and good, not as mealy as the jumbo kind. Ms. Jules and Ms. Viv looked at each other with histrionic faces of baffled delight.

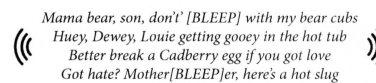

Mama bear, son, don't' [BLEEP] with my bear cubs
Huey, Dewey, Louie getting gooey in the hot tub
Better break a Cadberry egg if you got love
Got hate? Mother[BLEEP]er, here's a hot slug

"Well, *hi* there, little thing," said Viv. "You must be lost."

The hip-hop beat decrescendoed, and the drone, shockingly, spoke:

"WHAT UP DOE!" she, or it, said, in the voice of Alexa. "HOW YOU FOLKS DOIN'?"

The mouths at the cookout went slack, revealing all variety of masticated meat. For a long moment, no sound but the buzzing rotors of the drone. Then, several answers at once:

"How *you* doing?"

"Lord have mercy."

"The *fuck?*"

"Wai—*hold* on."

"I'M LUCY. I'M NEW HERE IN TOWN."

"Now *hold on*," Ms. Jules said. "You're one of those Amazon drones, right?"

"WELL, THE BETTER WORD FOR ME IS UAV."

"*UAV?*"

"UNMANNED AERIAL VEHICLE. BUT YOU CAN JUST CALL ME LU—"

"*Whoa, whoa, whoa.*"

"You do know this is Luther Prince's church?"

"He ain't here right now, but he gon find out!"

"You think you can just fly up in here playing some rap music and holding a *watermelon?* I mean, what in the name of…"

"We appreciate the offer, but—"

"Bitch about to get blasted."

"Now *hold on* there, young man."

"This is exactly what we brought you up in here to come correct about, with that mouth."

"Shhheeeeeiii—"

The pastor intervened. "Now calm down, everyone." He peered back at Lucy. "I understand you're trying to be friendly. However, I think some of these good folks take offense at the whole show you're putting on, with the rap music and the watermelon. Now, I know what the stereotypes are—"

"BUT I'M BLACK," the drone warbled. The crowd paused.

"You're saying you're an African American…drone?" Pastor Edwards said.

Jamal started to Panic. Annika stashed her phone and rushed across to the other side of the Bird's Nest. "Jamal…you brought a watermelon?!"

"That's what *I'd* bring to a cookout!"

"I'M FROM DETROIT. I WENT TO PERSHING."

Darnell's eyes lit up as it dawned on him what was happening.

"Ain't no *drones* grow up here motherfucka," Sean said.

Lucy hesitated, her watermelon payload swaying in the breeze as the rotors made micro-adjustments.

Inside the Bird's Nest, Jamal felt Barry's comforting doggy bulk against his shin as he stared down at the crowd through the FPV goggles. The more things change, the more they stay the same; pretty much every character from his childhood was down there: the moms, the pastor, the real religious folk, the people on welfare and those trying to get off, the men with their first jobs and unaffordable car payments, the hot girls, the fat girls, the ubiquitous aggro-thug bullies and poseurs and their male hangers-on and the women who loved them. And there, in the middle, that lonely figure in the ghetto: the kid who takes an interest in things outside the cage. For Jamal, it had been planes—the romance of the birds themselves, sleek and fast, angels of death punishing the guilty and protecting the innocent. He saw himself in the face of this teen, who in fact he'd seen before, at the Wayne State talk. And again, at the new Amazon Maker Space, where he'd given a lecture on UAV technology last week; this kid had been sitting in the front row. Darnell Something. There was no real option but to own up.

"JAMAL DENT, CHIEF PILOT, AT YOUR SERVICE."

A momentary silence. Viv fanned herself. "And why y'all here, again? This is just too strange…"

"JUST FLYING BY TO SAY HI. YO DARNELL: CATCH." The mini melon tumbled from the air toward the kid's hands. "SEE Y'ALL ROUND!" the drone said, and it ascended skyward.

The melon slipped through Darnell's fingers and broke open at his feet.

"You friends with that drone, Darnell?"

Piper's plans might have stalled at the starting line if she hadn't brought Danny Mikos along with her to the Sting, for he and Goldman Stackz had hit it off—they were both High Priests of the Word, which is to say Biggie's profound *Uh*, Flava Flav's tantric *Yeah Boy!*, Lil John's bewildered *What!*, those guttural trans-semantic noises between verses, the very same Word given breath by Homer Simpson's universal *Doh!*, Chris Rock's fuck-a-segue *SO!*, and Mitch Hedberg's opiate-laced *Alriiiight*. Growing up scrawny, they'd both found power through language, and was there any form of power more beautiful? The more they hung out, the more Goldman made passes at the comic; Danny liked the attention, and found himself contemplating what an encounter between them would be like. The only penetration he'd routinely enjoyed, he told Piper, was a Q-tip in his ear canal, but how did you know until you tried…

Piper kept them focused. For the last few days, the three of them had been working on a new song at Goldman's studio, an old Brightmoor house that had, believe it or not, been painted in trade-mark Burberry plaid. The place was ever-filled with weed smoke and bass. Danny and Piper had been storyboarding the music video with Hans, the filmmaker staying at Aaron's Art Farm. The video needed impactful visuals, and Piper knew immediately what they needed for a backdrop: a custom Otto Slice piece ripping Amazon. She'd contacted Otto, and he'd agreed to meet—the question was whether she could get him and Goldman to work together. Otto was already known outside Detroit, and he brought an anti-corporate cred, the kind of thing that would appeal to the people who'd voted for Bernie

Sanders. But if she really wanted to burn Amazon, she needed to succeed where Bernie had stumbled. Goldman would allow her to tie the anti-corporate message to the idea of racial justice.

There was also what Hans called the "iconic still," a moment that would stick in the viewer's mind. The idea for the still hadn't hit her until she'd run into her cousin Darnell after church last Sunday. Darnell Parker was seventeen, a junior at Cass Tech, one of the few good schools in the city. He was her third-cousin, the grandson of Luther's cousin Earl, who was long dead. Darnell was something of a whiz-kid, which made him stand out in a city that was still at the very bottom of the American scholastic heap. DPS had been under emergency management since 2011, with little improvement. More than half of the city's students were in charter schools, but they performed only marginally better.

Darnell had gone off about the robotics team at his high school. They'd used the VEXpro platform to build a robot designed to shake hands, give hi-fives, and even perform a five step dap with a left/ right slap followed by an up, down, and head-on fist bump. But they'd lost in the semi-finals of the FIRST robotics championship to a team from Davis, California who'd built an egg-cracking robot. Piper asked him if he knew about drones, and his face beamed with nerd-rapture: he and his team were building an octocopter for next year's competition. Later that day, he showed her his custom built UAV out in the park near the Armory where other drone hobby- ists—mostly balding late-forties white dudes—gathered to fly on Sundays. Darnell's drone was big, as big as the small Amazon ones. And with a little cosmetic modification, it could look pretty similar. Piper had yet to tell him the extent of the plan. He wouldn't be happy.

It was just after 9 p.m. when she, Darnell, and Hans arrived at the old Guardian Bank building on Fenkell. Otto and Goldman were on their way. The big concrete art-deco box was straight out of Gotham City, and it looked strange amidst the empty lots, bricked up liquor stores, and collapsing homes. The bank went under back in the '30s, and the building had since housed a post office and then a police station, until finally it had become a tombstone for the old working class neighborhood Brightmoor once was.

There was a mural on the side of the building already, but it was peeling and weathered and screaming for an Otto Slice piece. "Your drone got a camera, right?" Piper asked Darnell.

"A GoPro, yeah," he said. "It records in 1440p and—"

"Whatchu think, Hans? Swoop in from the east and you see the big mural here—whatever Otto throws up—and then Goldman and his posse standing on the roof, scarf blowing in the wind and shit."

"Yes, and we must want to film this crash from many angles—and so we can create that it looks like many times."

"Crash?" Darnell said.

"You know Chaz Miller did that mural."

Piper turned toward the voice to find Otto Slice walking up in the dusk, lighting a cigarette.

"Shit's peeling though." She swatted away a mosquito. "Plus it's already got some shitty tags over it."

"True. But that's a big wall," Otto said. "You want me to toss up a whole piece tonight?"

"Thought you was a pro, though," Piper said. "My bad."

Otto laughed and scratched his white beard. "Can't believe that bullshit still works on me. Okay, tonight it is, but I'm gonna need a few extra hands shaking cans and doing fill work…"

The air vibrated with bass as a white Escalade pulled into the lot. The back doors opened, and Danny Mikos stumbled out through a cloud of smoke.

Goldman Stackz strutted around from the other side of the vehicle, toting a pump shotgun.

"You've got to be fucking kidding me," Otto said.

"Who invited Uncle Sam?" Goldman said to Piper. Two of his posse joined him from the Escalade.

"Yo, chill," Piper said. "That's Otto. He gon be bombing this wall for the video."

"This nigga *Otto Slice?*"

"Put that gun away," Otto said. "Are you fucking stupid?"

Goldman clicked his tongue. "Shit, nigga. Calm the fuck down." He handed the shotgun to one of his boys who tossed it in the Escalade. "Gon need that shit tomorrow when we shoot the video."

"Piper…uh, hey, Piper…" Darnell was tugging on her sleeve. "You're not gonna, I mean—this took months to build and—"

Piper pulled him aside while Otto and Goldman kept at it. He was scrawny, had a seventeen-year-old's patchy beard, but he was taller than she was. "Look, D," she said. "We're not actually gonna shoot it. But—"

"But it's not even mine. It's the team's. And it cost over a thousand dollars."

"Don't worry," Piper said.

"But...what's so bad about drones? They're cool."

Piper sighed and glanced over her shoulder at Goldman and Danny and Otto, who looked pissed. "I know they're cool," she said. "And we couldn't do this without you helping us with the aerial shots. But look, just cause you think the technology is dope don't mean you have to support the multi-billion dollar corporation moving into our city, the company that has your uncle waiting on felony charges. That ain't cool, is it?"

"No, but..."

"This is bigger than you or me, D. You want another white-run outsider interest coming into our city and acting like it's a blank canvas they can do whatever the fuck they want with? This is gonna reach people. Don't you want to be a part of that?"

"Well, I guess that—"

"And don't you want to meet Goldman? I told him you were in. You still in, right?"

Piper felt bad playing on Darnell's nerd outcast status. She knew a part of him lusted after the aura of cool surrounding people like Goldman. But the video was nothing without the drone.

"Okay, okay," he said. "I'm in."

Piper turned back to the other three.

"I'm out," Otto said.

"What? No!"

"You didn't tell me this was gonna be gold and guns bull-shit. Thought you wanted to send a message. This misogynistic gangster—"

"Do you even know Goldman's music?!" Piper said.

"Gangsta is gangsta," Otto said. "Even if you dress it up in a fancy scarf."

Goldman stepped forward with his hands pressed together,

prayer-like. "Otto, may I call you Otto? A western ain't no western without no cowboy, feel me? Everybody knows the gangster shit's for show. It's a performance, an archetype, but it's a time-honored role."

Danny Mikos stared at Goldman like he was falling in love.

"The figure of the hustler embodies the braggadocio and reckless attitude which is the only path to self-respect for those caught in the trap. You get what I'm saying, nigga?"

"There's other ways to self-respect," Otto said.

"But no one gon give a shit about the message if it ain't G'd up."

"You see, that's the problem right there, and you just reinforce it."

"I'm just tryna connect, baby. I ain't gon shout in a language nobody speak."

"You oughta try respecting your audience."

"Nigga, I *do* respect my audience, by giving them what they want, a straight banger."

"Y'all done dick measuring?" Piper said.

Danny Mikos raised his hand. "I didn't get to go yet."

11

Centuries ago, before white settlers arrived, the Saginaw Trail cut through the forests of the Michigan Peninsula from Lake Huron to the Detroit River. The final stretches of the trail now lay beneath the pavement of Woodward Avenue, and at its terminus, where a gravelly boat launch once ferried people and pelts into the Great Lakes, stood that nineteen-eighties monument to delusion: the monstrous skyscraper complex known as the Renaissance Center, headquarters of General Motors. The "renaissance" referred to, of course, the rebirth of Detroit, something that decidedly did not occur in the wake of its unveiling. The makers of *Robocop*, which premiered six year later, were far more prescient about the coming decades.

On the seventy-second floor, Annika strolled the 360-degree perimeter of the Coach Insignia lounge, draining a dirty martini, and waiting for her date, Krav Maga instructor Ellis Wallace. He'd responded to her text with more emojis than words—which had given her serious pause—but her Amazonian habit of bias for action won the day.

The view of Detroit was spectacular, the rays of its arterials spreading out from downtown. Up here, you couldn't see the blight. The only hint that the city was still struggling was the emptiness of the streets. The Coach Insignia, too, was somewhat empty—whole banquet rooms closed off and silent. It felt like a fancy restaurant in Lagos or Accra, where even the most impressive accommodations had spotty plumbing and wi-fi. The décor was a few decades old, the carpet worn and thin. There were dust-bunnies on the rafters below and small stains in the gray fabric of the walls, as if someone had wallpapered the place with the steam-cleaned upholstery of some college student's old Ford Taurus. Apparently, the restaurant used to rotate. Annika circled the lounge until she arrived back near the hostess. She felt the urge to check her phone, even though it was set to vibrate for any incoming e-mails, texts, appointment reminders, Google alerts, and sundry social media tags and @ mentions. She tried her best to shut such thoughts into her mind-cabinet for work. The one she could never quite lock. *Relax. You're supposed to be having fun.* She laughed as she noticed a pair of huge novelty suede chairs. She climbed into one and let her feet dangle off the ground.

Ellis Wallace ascended rapidly in the glass elevator, a childish grin exploding on his face as he watched the Detroit River fall beneath him and Ontario spread out to the south. Up, up, up, it just kept going up. Ellis had never been on an airplane, and it occurred to him that he was now higher off the ground than he'd ever been. The doors opened onto the seventy-second floor lounge, and he immediately felt out of place.

Annika spotted him loping in towards the bar like a guy whose friends had put him up to something, looking over his shoulder, and brushing his nose with his thumb. That ass. But could he hold a conversation? Here's to hoping Ellis Wallace didn't blow his shot at not being annoying.

She hopped off the chair and walked towards him. "Hey, Sensei," she said.

"Ahh, now don't start with that."

She let him give her a squeeze. "So this where you take all the ladies?"

He laughed. "I have actually…never been here."

"What?! This is like the first building you see in pictures."

"Yeah, it's the postcard building. But you ever been to the Space Needle?"

She polished off her martini. "I've been all sorts of places," she said, raising an eyebrow and smiling. "Let's get you a drink."

As they waited, Ellis noticed her eyebrows were dark while her hair was blond. Was it possible that she…dyed her eyebrows? Blue eyes. Or did she dye her hair? He was on autopilot, making small talk and looking over at the bartender who finally approached. He had a moment of panic when he realized that he had no idea what a place like this would charge for a drink. "Whiskey, rocks," he said.

"Any particular kind?"

"Whatever you got, uh, *Jack?*"

Annika sensed it: Ellis was out of his element here, although of course, he was the one who'd picked the place.

"So, Annika. Nik. How's it been so far? You adjusting?"

"Yeah, but I haven't seen the city much. Spend most of my time at the office."

"They ride you hard, huh? Bad as they say?"

The short answer was, yes. There wasn't much time for a personal life at Amazon. Bezos didn't believe in work/life balance. But it was no secret. That was the cost of working with the geniuses inventing the future. "I'm here, aren't I?" Annika said. "But we totally don't have to talk about work." She wasn't quite ready to find out if this guy even had a job outside of Krav Maga. She was annoyed at herself for suspecting that he might not, just because of the way he talked and carried himself, like he was on some corner in hood. But what if she was right?

"You been hitting the heavy bag?" he asked, jerking into a quick shadowbox—left, right, left. He composed himself and straightened his collar when he saw an older couple staring at him.

"I can barely lift my arms!"

Ellis laughed. "That's how you know it's working." They strolled around the lounge, taking in the view. Out the massive windows to the north, the weathered buildings of downtown were encased in scaffolding. Above them, Amazon drones ferried packages through the sky, hundreds of them.

"So this is where the auto-execs eat dinner, huh?" Ellis said. He pictured a table of six dudes in fine suits who all more or less looked like Gene Hackman, but with subtle variations: a pair of glasses, a mustache.

"Until they went bankrupt!" she said.

This was the trophy dining room for an empire that was dying even when they cut the ribbon; GM had failed for a number of reasons: commitments to unions, unsustainable pensions, and old-school chauvinism—none of them had believed Americans would buy Japanese. They were killed by their own tired complacence, by a corporate culture of *good enough*. Amazon was the opposite, constantly self-challenging, constantly evolving, never satisfied, and that was why they'd never be begging for a life ring from Uncle Sam. "Evolve or die out, right?" Annika added with a laugh. Ellis was strangely solemn.

"Lot of people lost their jobs and houses and shit," he said.

"Yeah…" Annika said. They strolled on in silence for a moment. She felt stupid for that laugh, for not realizing—*it was so obvious*—that to Ellis, the auto bankruptcies were a staggering blow in the long destruction of his city.

He was looking out towards the Book Tower wistfully. "You wanna get out of here?" Annika asked.

Ellis raised his eyebrows—he'd been asked this before, but he hadn't sensed this date was going as well as all *that*. "Uh, sure, what are you thinking?" he said, before downing his whiskey.

"What are *you* thinking?" Annika forced a laugh. "I'm thinking we skip on the dinner res here and hit up some place you actually like!"

They cruised up Gratiot in Ellis' charger. Downtown gave way to the wide, flat expanse of the eastside, with crumbling concrete buildings interrupted by gas stations, liquor stores, and churches. But Annika also spotted a few greenhouses and tilled fields—what other city had this much farmland right in its midst, among beauty parlors and fast food restaurants?

"Hey what's the deal with that You Buy We Fry stuff?" Annika said. "I've been seeing that everywhere."

Ellis leaned back in the driver seat, wrist draped over the wheel. "The fish joint? What, you wanna go *there*?"

"Just wondering why it's called that."

"Don't got that out west? It's so you can use your Bridge Card. Can't buy cooked food with EBT, but you can buy the fish on the card, then pay a couple bucks to get it fried up."

"Oh," Annika said, a little sadly.

Ellis had never thought of the You Buy We Fry as *sad*, but maybe she did. He didn't want to be apologizing for Detroit, but he also couldn't act like everything was roses, could he? "I know where to take you," he said.

Ellis pulled off Gratiot and parked on a side street. Annika surveyed the block. Every fourth or fifth house looked abandoned, but there were cars in most driveways. A teenage kid carved a languid zig-zag up the street on a tiny bike. What was the deal with tiny bikes? Ellis walked around the side of the car and opened the door for her, presenting the crook of his arm, and they walked up to Capers Steakhouse, a squat, white concrete number with a red awning. It had a sign advertising…

"Steak by the ounce? Now we're talking."

On a bulletin board just inside, Annika spotted a notice that read, "WE NOW CHECK FOR COUNTERFEIT MONEY." Ellis guided her through the tables. Every single person in the restaurant was black, and Annika would have felt very out of place if not for his big hand on her hip. Huge hand, really. It made her feel dainty.

The whole place felt surreal. Here she was in a steakhouse that served filet mignon…for $1.65 per ounce. And the table had no tablecloth. The forks were wrapped in paper napkins. Ketchup and steak sauce in squeeze bottles on every table. The walls were tiled three feet up with fake marble. Large flat screen TVs hung over the bar. When their drinks arrived, she knocked her martini glass against his massive 32-ounce mug of Bud Light. His smile was almost debilitating. For someone who had apparently grown up on the wrong side of the tracks, Ellis had big rows of straight, white teeth. He was like the boys in high school that were so unattainable she tried to not even daydream about them taking her out to steakhouses. Contained in all of us are the people we used to be, but Ellis seemed like he was that person more than most. He'd ordered hot wings to start, and he gnawed on them with casual aggression.

"I got something on my face?" he said, wiping his mouth.

"No…"

"Oh, you just keep staring at me," he said with a grin.

"I'm looking for reasons not to like you."

"Find any?"

"Not yet." Which was true. He was so unpretentious, direct, confident, he was funny, he was handsome and tall. And most of all, he held her gaze. She thought of Spencer. During their last few months, they'd both spent more and more time on their phones during dinner, responding to work stuff. Putting out fires, he sometimes called it, although she'd thought most of his fires stemmed from an inability to prioritize and focus properly.

The waiter brought her six-ounce filet and Ellis' plump twenty-ounce Delmonico ribeye. He set a baked potato the size of a tennis shoe in the middle of the table. It was overstuffed with bacon and cheese. Annika gawked.

Her filet was tender, buttery, and nourishing—better than she'd expected. "Why didn't you just invite me here to begin with?" Annika said.

He gestured with a chunk of ribeye on his fork. "Honestly? I thought you'd be into classier shit than the girls I usually see."

"Hah. And who are these girls?"

"You know. Girls who can dance."

"What, you think I can't dance!"

"Naw, I mean, I'm sure you can."

Oh shit, had he meant strippers? If so, it was both off-putting and kind of hot. She made a mental note that if they hooked up, he was sure as hell using protection. *If they hooked up*…she was thinking that already! Something about the way he sat, arms forward, was it his confidence, rubbing off on her?

"So tell me more about Nik Dahl. What's new in your life?"

"Everything."

"Ok, well, what about family? You got parents? What's their deal?"

"They're retired. Actually, this is funny, they just moved to this polyamorous compound in Northern California. It's like, a gated community for senior swingers."

Ellis laughed, and clapped several times.

"My little brother's freaking out about it, even though he's the backpacker hippy."

"See, that's what I like about you—you're in a position to judge, but you don't."

"Oh, I don't judge?" she said with raised eyebrows.

Two drinks each, two steaks, baked potato, and hot wings for less than fifty bucks. Ellis waved off her attempt to pay. She touched him softly on the shoulder as she excused herself to the ladies' room.

Ellis knew what that meant. This chick was *down*. As long as he didn't do anything stupid from this point on. When the bill came, he was about to write in the usual couple bucks for the tip, but he stopped himself and decided to actually calculate what a good tip would be. He left a generous fifteen percent.

Every square inch of the bathroom was covered with marble tile. But the sink was stainless steel, the mirror was stainless steel! Was it really too dangerous to have glass in here? In a steakhouse? It was too funny. This whole situation with this Krav Maga muscleman, it was all just too much. She caught herself smiling in the steel mirror. On every date she'd ever been on, at some point in the night, she would ask herself: am I or am I not going to fuck him? Better to decide that up front before hormones or alcohol got the best of her, then lock it away in a mind-cabinet and have fun. She tried to imagine him undoing her bra—a good revealing self-test—but her imagination didn't stop at the bra. Oh my god. She hadn't been with anyone but Spencer in over three years. And she'd known Ellis for less than three hours. Yet here she was, giddy with the realization: she was so going to fuck him.

When they got back into the car, she let him lean over and kiss her, and she kissed back, until it was a full-blown make-out session, her mind's bare foot wedged firmly against the cabinet labeled *work*. She bit his lip, his hands moved over her ass and between her thighs, and she decided she'd let him get her off right here as a nice end to the night, especially considering that as fun as he was, he probably wasn't going to be, let's face it, boyfriend material. But as she leaned back into the sounds of the neo-gospel radio station, she began to feel a burning sensation where his fingers had been, up until now, doing a pretty pro job…

"Wait, stop."

He did.

"Did you…"

"What's up?"

"Did you wash your hands?"

"Huh?"

"Oh, shit." She started to laugh. "The hot wings."

"Oh…my god. Really?"

She squirmed. "Yeah, really."

"Ohhh, damn girl, my bad, my bad. What—should I go get… some of those wet wipes or something?"

"No, no, it's fine." And it was; the look on his face was almost worth it. Plus, he was being sweet about it. And now her phone was buzzing again, and she considered for a moment whether she should just ignore it. The work drawer was fighting against her heel, and she figured she'd indulge it, make sure it was nothing pressing. An email:

> Sender: jeff@amazon.com
> Subject: ?

The single dreaded question mark. You didn't want to get that question mark.

On the scale of Amazon's internal emergencies, a Sev-5 was a non-critical tech problem the engineers could fix, a Sev-1 required an immediate response. Then there was the Sev-B, for Bezos. The dreaded single question mark: drop everything you are doing and attack this problem. Fix it, explain how it happened, explain why it won't happen again. You have two hours. The clock is ticking.

She adjusted her underwear and smoothed her skirt out, then opened the e-mail, which was nothing more than a link to a YouTube video. A music video?

"What's up? Everything okay?" Ellis asked.

"Uh, sorry, an e-mail from Jeff. Shit."

"Jeff?"

"Sorry. I have to watch this."

A soft piano fades in. In slow-mo: police pushing an old black man into a squad car. Fade to black. The bass drops with a patter of snaps and claps.

GOLDMAN STACKZ
#NOFLYZONE

Flying low over west side blight—Brightmoor liquor stores, vacant lots—to the art-deco brick of the Guardian Bank building, its western wall freshly muraled: A frog flicking its tongue around a bald disembodied rotor-powered head—Jeff Bezos as an octocopter. Panning up to the roof, the man himself, Goldman Stackz: slender, tattooed, wireframe glasses, Burberry scarf whipping in the wind, crew standing hard behind him, muthafucking pump shotgun in his muthafucking hands.

We keeps it gritty in the D, this a no fly zone
No delivery is free, this a no fly zone

Goldman aims into the sky. A drone hovers overhead—the swooping yellow arrow, could it be?

Look up in the sky, it's a bird, it's drone
[chk-shik, BOOM BOOM] this a no fly zone

Barrel smoke and nothing but bass. The drone hits ground—hits ground—hits ground. Cue horns. Goldman's crew shuffles a choreographed dance.

That dance! It was so...pop...so Michael Jackson, so lighthearted after that hard-faced shotgun blast. Annika's head hurt. There was even a hipster white kid in the crew who was dancing some cross between the sprinkler and charaded shotgun blasts. She couldn't help but smile. As the rapper started in on the verse, the footage cut to images of Detroit poverty, forlorn black people standing in front of collapsed houses, looking up as Amazon drones whizzed by overhead. The video moved so fluidly through emotional registers, from humor to sadness, but it returned, inevitably, to the righteous anger of the opening shot.

> *Fuck that, grab a Mossberg or a deuce-deuce*
> *Bust caps, let loose if you hear a rotor spinning*
> *Drones over Motor City, never asked the voters if they*
> *Wanted that, this is why you vote with the automatic*

There was no coherent argument, but Annika could already tell that didn't matter. The song was channeling anti-corporate resentment, it was trading on racialized images of economic inequality, it was presenting the criminal destruction of Amazon property as not only necessary, but fun! The fact that she wanted to laugh only made it more infuriating.

> *Listen up, Amazon fuckbots:*
> *You deliver in the D, we delivering the buckshot!*
>
> And the chorus returns as drone after drone after drone gets blasted by the pump shotty, from this angle, from that, slow slow motion as rotors bend and break on impact, frames buckling against the concrete.

Ellis stopped laughing when he saw Annika's stricken face. "What's wrong?" he said.

"This! This is wrong!"

"It's funny."

"I know! That just makes it worse!"

Girls trip over the weirdest shit. How was he supposed to play this now?

"And who the hell is *Goldman Stackz!?*"

Bryce Berg
@VanillaBryce

Follow

I say we all start blasting @amazon. Critical Mass.
They can't arrest everyone. #NOFLYZONE

3:41 PM - Jul 29

💬 5   🔁 18   ♡ 43

Liz Markleson
@Liz_Marky

Follow

Got Prime day after I got pregnant. What a life-saver.
@amazon will you deliver my baby by drone?

11:15 AM - Jul 30

💬 11   🔁 12   ♡ 34

Darth Flavor
@DarthFlavor

Follow

WTF, where's my pizza? It's been like an hour.
@amazon, can you get into the pizza biz? We need u.

2:22 AM - Aug 01

💬 1   🔁 3   ♡ 28

Reggie Gables
@Renniggade

Follow

Takes true evil like @amazon to turn pussy-money-
weed rap political. #NOFLYZONE

2:22 AM - Aug 01

💬 8   🔁 11   ♡ 24

Danny Mikos
@Mikosystem

Follow

Bezos unveils new @Amazon Surprise. Deliveries based on browser history. 80% are lube & cheez-its.

5:18 PM - Aug 05

💬 14 ♻ 39 ♡ 65

Louis Oglethorpe
@OgleSmash

Follow

Finally, a gun-toting anti- @amazon thug all right-thinking Americans can get behind. #GROWUP

7:29 PM - Aug 05

💬 2 ♻ 9 ♡ 5

Keisha Jones
@ChiefKeish

Follow

If @amazon sold time machines, baby Bezos would be toast. #NOFLYZONE

8:17 PM - Aug 05

💬 21 ♻ 22 ♡ 67

Mike Butts
@captainbuttstuff

Follow

@amazon stock: sell, sell, sell! @winchester stock: buy, buy buy! #NOFLYZONE

3:28 PM - Aug 08

💬 3 ♻ 15 ♡ 44

Patty Kowalski
@PKowala

Follow

@amazon just offerin wut people want. #noflyzone bad advice. U just get arrested by racist cops.

11:13 AM - Aug 09

💬   🔁 9   ♡ 6

Alan Shoop
@Shoopsedaisy

Follow

I stand in solidarity with the victims of @amazon drone strikes. #noflyzone

9:51 PM - Aug 09

💬 6   🔁 22   ♡ 43

Troit as Fuck
@TroitasFuck

Follow

#FF #NOFLYZONE resistance: @GoldmanStackz @NeptuneFrost @OttoSliceCream @Mikosystem

12:44 PM - Aug 10

💬 3   🔁 125   ♡ 81

III

12

#NOFLYZONE might never have caught on if not for a woman named Kira Dodson who'd given an interview to 7 Action News the day after the Goldman Stackz song was released. Dodson's neighbor had been arrested for firing a shotgun at an Amazon drone. There was something almost musical and performative about her speech patterns. "Getting my kids up for school, DRONE, working in the kitchen, DRONE, tryna take a nap, DRONE. Inside, DRONE, outside, DRONE. I'm tryna sleep at night, DRONE. Loud as anything. What the hell they think gon happen? BOOOSH. This a no fly zone." The clip of Dodson went viral, and it drove traffic to the music video, catapulting Goldman beyond the world of Detroit hip-hop.

It was annoying to Piper that they were getting traffic from this video, from the fact that white people loved, meaning laughed at, the flamboyant cadences of hood-speak. But she wasn't about to question a lucky break. Within a week, #NOFLYZONE had over a million views—Goldman's last video had taken six months to reach that count—and it was only climbing higher. *Slate, Salon,* and *BuzzFeed* wrote thinkpieces about Goldman and the Amazon drone program in Detroit. And as Piper had released the video through her RNKR account, Neptune Frost's following had skyrocketed to over half a million. She and Curtis drove to Chicago for Lollapalooza to see Goldman perform to a massive crowd. He pulled her up on stage during #NOFLYZONE as thousands sang along with the chorus. A drone camera filming the festival from above captured a sea of middle fingers.

Curtis was after her more and more—it had been a mistake to fuck him again. She shooed him off. She didn't have time. She was talking to the fashion designers at CrookedCrown, a local label, about a line of #NOFLYZONE apparel—they told her some corporate woman had been asking about her. She was planning out the next music video with Danny and Goldman—who told her some Amazon bitch had called. She was brainstorming a massive bombing campaign with Otto Slice—who had heard through the graf community that some executive lady was looking for Neptune Frost. It was a little frightening. But that meant she'd touched a nerve. It was hard to breathe in the whirlwind of social media activism she'd fallen into. Aaron Thistle and his slow world of urban farming was her oxygen. She'd wound up in his bed again after returning from Lollapalooza. It was better than the first two times—she didn't have to ask to be choked, and he'd done it carefully, but firmly, cutting off her blood supply without crushing her windpipe. The next morning, he'd made her breakfast, then asked if she'd help harvest some greens to take down to Eastern Market. Piper had never been the type to play in the mud, but she found herself strangely enjoying it. Getting her hands dirty, kneeling between rows of kale, smelling the earth!—it connected her to the world of physical things that slipped away so easily when she spent hours a day swimming through the cloud of postings and comments and upranks, curating and expanding the narrative surrounding Goldman, keeping #NOFLYZONE afloat atop everyone's feeds.

This was a nightmare for Annika Dahl. Bezos was furious, and she knew it was her ass if she didn't develop a good counter-offensive. Lucy wasn't enough. She drafted and discarded a dozen ideas (~~Amazon gift cards? Wrangling Kid Rock into a free concert?~~) before hitting on the idea she'd present to the S-Team.

There were over 1,500 urban farms in Detroit, and their biggest customers were the emerging crop of upscale farm-to-table restaurants. The rest of the fresh produce went to Eastern Market on Saturdays. She'd been there once; it was full of the same money-eyed white crowd who ate at the nice restaurants. With so many urban farms in the city, and with so few grocery stores, why weren't the low-income families in Brightmoor and Kettering eating local greens instead of fried chicken and fried fish and fried cigarettes? Detroit still had the highest obesity and diabetes rates in the country. She surmised it was a cultural thing: poor black Detroiters had established eating habits and didn't feel welcome at the bougie Eastern Market, just as the Corktown kids didn't feel welcome at Brightmoor block parties. And a budget issue: organic produce was expensive. But why was it expensive? Part of the reason was that the urban farmers had to guess how much produce to pick and haul down to market each week, letting much of it go to waste. The farmers' costs would be considerably lower if they could pick only what was already sold and not have to leave their gardens. Introducing: *Amazon Prime Air...Salad Bowl? Salad Toss*—ooh, no!—*Garden Copter?* No, simpler: *Amazon Prime Air Farmers Market.*

This was the brilliant idea Bezos had been asking for, something that would garner Amazon good press and provide quality produce to the food deserts of the city. She spent the entire weekend working on her six-page narrative—Bezos had banned PowerPoint long ago, calling it the Most Holy Sacrament of the Church of Dumb. All new initiatives were to be introduced at meetings with a six-pager, which everyone in the room would read in silence before discussion began. Like the leadership principles, this practice was designed to encourage everyone at Amazon to think like Bezos, amplifying his genius and spreading it to every corner of the company.

As expected, there was pushback from the S-Team. Her plan called for *free* UAV delivery, from farm to house, *without* an Amazon Prime membership. That was half the point of the entire UAV program: to entice more customers to become dues-paying Prime members. And it violated the frugality principle.

"Jeff," Annika had said—it still felt strange to address him by name—"We're never going to get people in Brightmoor to spring for Prime anyway."

"You know why I don't hire defeatists?" Bezos had said, his fore-head wrinkling as his eyes widened. "Because they get defeated!"

"It'll be a loss in short-term profit, but if we think of it as a long-term investment…" That was right out of the Amazon playbook, one of their bedrock principles.

Bezos paced the conference room in silence for nearly a minute. Then he stopped abruptly, turned to her, and said, "I want it up and running in two weeks."

That was ambitious, but doable, since it could be built off the platform they were already developing for Amazon Third Party sellers. The programmers back in Seattle set to work round the clock to get the website ready and to develop a seller-side tablet app for the participant farmers who would fulfill orders. The quant-heads modeled process and demand scenarios with an eye to maximizing free cash flow. Annika, meanwhile, corralled whoever she could into helping her approach urban farmers throughout Detroit. She, Jamal, and a few interns had been going out daily, pitching these sunburnt, green-thumbed, overalled entrepreneurs on the idea of partnering with Amazon. Prime Air Farmers Market had become a Jeff project—something Bezos had taken a personal interest in, sending Annika emails with detailed and brilliant recommendations, often late at night. But the negative press from the Stackz video had continued to multiply, more anti-Amazon graffiti was popping up in the city, and six more UAV shooters had been arrested and charged—none of them elderly men, thank god, but as FAA regulator Thad Burrows had said, fault was irrelevant. Amazon had now accrued seven minor incidents. Three more would trigger a review of their flight clearance. So while trying to get Prime Air Farmers Market off the ground, she was also frantically researching this Goldman Stackz character. From what she could tell, he hadn't had much of a developed agenda before #NOFLYZONE. The coverage surrounding the video led her to Otto Slice, noted Detroit graffiti artist, and that led her to one of RNKR's rising stars, a certain Neptune Frost. But Frost was surprisingly elusive. Annika hadn't been able to turn up any info on who he actually was—she could only assume he lived in Detroit.

All this was swirling in Annika's mind as she arrived at Eastern

Market on Saturday, August 11th. There were a few more farmers to approach, and the clock was ticking. She strolled past hundreds of booths, selling everything from locally ground chia-seed sausage to elderflower infused honey, then approached the Detroit Art Farm booth, where a strapping blond guy and a thin black girl were shoveling greens into compostable bags for eager yuppies.

By now, Annika had learned that before pitching Prime Air Farmers Market, it was best to ask about the farm: its size, how many people they had harvesting, what they grew. Those details were irrelevant—their ability to fulfill orders in a timely fashion would self-sort the reliable from the unreliable, and the seller-buyer-connection algorithms would take care of the rest—but opening with those questions made the farmers more likely to sign on.

"Nice looking arugula," she said.

"Wasabi arugula," Aaron said. "Has a great kick."

Piper looked the woman up and down—some kind of partially unbuttoned office drone—yoga pants and a loose t-shirt, but hair pulled back in a bun, blue-tooth headset fused into her ear canal.

"I gotta bounce," Piper said to Aaron. "Photoshoot."

Aaron bagged up some kale for a dude with a curly mustache, then leaned over and kissed her on the forehead. "Thanks for helping this morning, babe."

She slapped his ass and left.

Annika watched the girl strut off in her vintage Reebok pumps. She was about to ask the dude about his monthly yield and seasonal crop rotation, when she noticed the button on his shirt:

"Not a fan of Amazon, huh?"

"Amazon's one element of the real problem," he said. "Globalization, corporatocracy."

Well, this was a long shot, and she really wasn't in the mood. But they needed urban farms on board if this plan was going to work. And they were still under the crucial threshold. "I can't speak to the intricacies of global economics," she said—though in fact, she could, having majored in behavioral economics at Stanford before running a micro-finance NGO in Nigeria, but she didn't want to alienate Farmer Marx here. "Amazon's doing some interesting things, though, like the new Prime Air Farmers Market."

Aaron shook his head. "You work for Amazon." He leaned over to the left and snatched a five-dollar bill from an outstretched hand, replacing it with a bag of radish greens. All around them, money was changing hands to the sounds of market chatter and clatter, to the smell of earth and sugar and sweat.

"Let me at least ask you this: what's your goal here? What are you trying to do?"

"Lots of things," Aaron said. "I'm trying to grow sustainable food in an earth- and human-friendly way. I'm trying to work hard and enjoy life. I'm trying to provide fresh food for people who don't have access to it. Amazon's goal is to make money. Our interests don't align."

Annika had to consciously resist shaking her head. The *poor, benighted soul*. She used to be a little pie-in-the-sky herself, which is why she wound up at the Stanford Center for International Development, where the kids who actually took their own application essays seriously prepared to Save the World. That was where anti-corporate sentiment crashed up against the latest and greatest data about what actually works. Handouts don't work for anything beyond immediate emergencies. Cutesy Peace Corps projects where kids from Bellevue are sent to Chad to teach crop rotation…don't work. Feel-good tech projects where solar powered internet learning centers are dropped in malarial deltas worked for about thirty days before all the computers were busted or malwared to hell. All of that stuff made for glossy donor pamphlets and sounded wonderful to fresh faced undergrads who carried around backpacks strapped with Nalgene water bottles. But none of it worked, not according to the Gates foundation types and their outcome studies.

What worked was, basically, capitalism. Figure out a way for companies to invest in poor populations, figure out a way to keep local governments from shaking them down too much, and you start getting development. Once there's a foothold, get some infrastructure in there. Maybe seed some subsistence farmers with start-up cash and watch them get a fruit stand going. Figure out which farmers are the best investments through social vetting. Check the outcomes from data-driven development groups to see which vetting systems work best in different types of environments. Get bitten by so many mosquitoes that the malaria breaks through the wall of Stanford Student Clinic-prescribed Doxycycline, and spend 48 hours in feverish Mefloquine fantasias, lying in bed under a ceiling crawling with insects so big and heavy that they occasionally lose their grip on the ceiling and thump thorax-first on your chest. Feel a deep satisfaction that the miniature credit union you set up in Nigeria with Gates Foundation seed-money is still going strong, eight years later.

If helping people was a moral prerogative, then it was a moral prerogative to do what worked, and not do what didn't work.

"Seriously," Annika said, "How many of your customers even live in Detroit, or are they coming in from Ferndale and Royal Oak?"

The next customer materialized in a few seconds, her canvas tote sporting the logo of a famous Manhattan bookstore, its interior smudged with topsoil from a recent root vegetable purchase. Aaron rang her up for a handful of shallots.

"Think about all of the locals who aren't coming to these markets," Annika said. "They buy their groceries at convenience stores. Or get dinner at a You Buy We Fry. You ever been to a You Buy We Fry? Didn't think so. People outside of downtown don't have a lot of healthy options. Now, that's not my fault, and it's not your fault. But I'm trying to remedy that situation. You're just selling kale to white people. But if we worked together..."

"It's a marketing gimmick."

"Even if you believe that, so what? If Amazon decided to advertise by setting up free drug treatment centers, would you be against that?"

"I'm against a system in which basic social services are provided by corporations looking to advertise."

"Fair enough," Annika said, holding out a pamphlet and wiggling it, ever so slightly. "But you shouldn't be against poor people getting free deliveries of fresh produce."

Aaron snorted, but took the pamphlet. As the woman left, he shoved it in his back pocket. Piper would kill him if he even brought it up, but the Amazon lady was at least trying. Was that a good thing, corporations paying lip service to the problems of social inequality? Better than mercilessly ignoring it, but perhaps more insidious, for they'd never do it if it didn't benefit their bottom line. Whether they were a force for good in the world was a secondary question, at best. Was he any better? Was he a force for good, or was he just selling kale to white people?

Annika wandered down to the next urban farm booth. This woman didn't have a #NOFLYZONE button, thank god, but that didn't necessarily mean she'd be more sympathetic. Were those buttons everywhere in Detroit, or did that blond kid have some particular connection to the elusive Neptune Frost? She shoved the question into a mind-cabinet and readied her spiel: first, compliment the microgreens.

13

The smell of glazed BBQ ribs masked (mostly) the manure from the tilled lot next door as the menagerie of hipster weirdos swilled Griffin Claw IPA and sang-bucha, which is as delicious or disgusting as it sounds, depending whether or not you like your wine adulterated with fermented effervescent tea made from gelatinous mounds of bacteria and yeast. Aaron Thistle was throwing a BBQ fundraiser to support the Detroit Art Farm, which meant pretty much everyone there was white, excepting Piper Prince and the newest Daffy (ie. D.A.F. resident), a Korean dude who made miniature dioramas of ruin porn that had to be viewed with a magnifying glass. The demographics would change shortly when Goldman Stackz and crew arrived. Piper had invited him, both because he had a few fans at the Art Farm, but also because getting these white hipsters on board with #NOFLYZONE was crucial to the success of the campaign. If Amazon's downtown customers dried up, it would be a crushing blow. It wasn't just about her grandfather's trial anymore. The rush of burning a big corporation like Amazon was the best drug she'd ever had—precisely because it gave her purpose, the feeling that her actions might actually effect some positive change in the world. And with half a million followers of her own, and Goldman trending on every notable social media platform, the next hit was sure to be even more intense.

"Ah, you must be the charming negress Aaron spoke of. He's quite enamored of you, you know."

"The fuck?" Piper said. "What did you call me?"

"You modern women talk like dock boys—I love it! I must say, I've been admiring your, how would one put it—exotic?—coiffure."

The white girl in front of her was in her mid-twenties and dressed like a flapper, complete with flat armless dress and bell-shaped cloche hat. "Your hair, my dear."

"No, I know what *coiffure* means," Piper said. "Why are you talking like—nevermind." Piper was learning to expect this kind of shit at the Art Farm, but still—fucking white people—call something art and they feel like they can start tossing around words like *negress*.

"I really shouldn't speak of it," the girl said, leaning closer, "you'll think me mad."

"Probably, yeah," Piper said, leaning against a porch pillar and scrolling through RNKR, hoping the crazy chick would take the hint.

"Well," said the flapper, producing a cigarette affixed to a long, slender holder. "It was a man, as usual, but not just any man. The most brilliant scientist of the century, Nikola Tesla. He was a poet, too, you know. I had been visiting him at Wardenclyffe Tower in Long Island, where he was working on some new inventions. I was doing my own experiments, you see, on which type of feminine charms might work on such a visionary, coming into his workshop at all hours, making any and all excuses, wearing *all sorts* of outfits, but always he responded with shortness and irritation, until one day he invited me to place my hand upon a metallic sphere. How could I resist? I felt a terrific shock! The next thing I knew I was here! Among you dear, strange people. Future people, to me."

Piper looked up from her phone. "I'm sure it was an accident," she said, and wandered off to find Aaron in the kitchen, cutting pieces off a big placenta-looking kombucha culture. The whole place smelled like hippy armpit and marijuana, but especially the kitchen.

"I see you met Leslie," Aaron said. "Performance artist. She's acting that role for an entire month without falling out of character."

"Shouldn't she be walking around all dazed, going, *This can't be real? I'm dreaming, I must be dreaming?*"

He dropped the rubbery thing into a giant glass jar and poured in a pitcher of tea. "I think it's the kind of thing that works if you suspend disbelief a little," he said.

Piper ran her hands up his shoulders. "This whole scene is like that, boo."

They wandered out to the porch just as some booming automotive subwoofers announced the arrival of Goldman Stackz. Everyone turned to see the rapper and his posse strutting in—which, with the acoustic stylings of Father John Misty on the Art Farm stereo and Goldman's ride still bumping base at the curb, looked like some impossible hybrid of a slow-mo club video and a Wes Anderson denouement. Piper noticed the DAFFY kids stiffen up, adjust the suspenders on their wooden shorts. They weren't used to this. Goldman grew up in the D though—you don't wander in alone to some strange party. Who knows what could happen? You roll deep. Goldman doffed his straw cowboy hat as he approached the porch and bowed like a Versailles courtier while his crew ambled up after him. And there amidst the posse, one Curtis "Chips" Washington. Piper instinctively sidled closer to Aaron, her subconscious attuned to the power and play of sexual jealousy.

Curtis nodded at her, but kept his distance as Goldman's crew cracked brews and assimilated into the crowd. It didn't take long for someone to commandeer the music—instrumental hip-hop washed over the BBQ, weed smoke rose in the air, and a rap cipher swirled into existence. Some of the drunker white kids joined in, including Hans. No one could understand his German flow, but they cheered him on anyway. When Goldman took the invisible mic, he rapped directly to Danny:

> *Got a dick for a brain, got a brain for a heart*
> *Got heart for a dick and I'm feeling so naughty*
> *Lawdy, damn look at that body*
> *Make me wanna write a poem to get it on me*

The flirtation had become a running gag between them.

Curtis approached Piper while Aaron was off getting another beer. "Don't tell me it wasn't good," he said.

It hadn't been, but Piper was feeling nice. "That the new you talking, or the old you?"

"Shit, girl. New me still got swag. I'm saying though."

"Hey," Aaron said, walking up. "I'm Aaron."

Curtis gave him a stoic nod. "Curtis."

"So how do you two know each other?" Aaron asked.

"Shit, nigga, how—" He caught himself. The new Curtis wouldn't go off like that. "We go way back. High school."

Aaron nodded, and they all took an awkward sip of their drinks.

"So, this your…farm?" Curtis said. "Shit's nice. Nice farm."

"You can be real with me," Aaron said. "I know you don't give a shit about the Art Farm."

Piper had been drawn to Aaron precisely because he cut through the bullshit like that, but here it seemed like trouble. Curtis took a step closer and stared up at Aaron, who was nearly a full head taller.

"You right," he said. "I don't give a shit bout some white boy planting seeds cause it ain't gon do shit. Ain't gon fix nothing. But I guess you cool being useless."

Their chests were so close now, people nearby had stopped talking to gawk.

"That's sad," Aaron said. "That's real fucking sad. Giving up on your own city. No wonder it looks like this."

"Hey," Piper said.

"You know who fucking gave up on this city? White people, bitch."

"Babies, babies," Goldman said, sliding his hands between them and spreading them apart. "It's all good. Y'all remember why we here or what?" He walked over to the big donation bucket, took out a massive stack of banded bills—at least a thousand bucks—and tossed it in. "Gotsta support each other, loves. Now who wants to hit this blunt with me?" He withdrew a finely rolled blunt from the front of his pants. Had it been in his underwear?

Piper took a hit, and by the time the blunt rotated back to her, she felt a strange discomfort, her hair follicles at attention. But it wasn't the weed. It was that distinctive sound, that high-pitched metallic growl. They were everywhere, and here she was, without Gramps' pump action. As the sound grew louder, the partygoers looked up: there were dozens of zipping dots in the sky and one of them was descending towards the party.

"My! Will wonders never cease!" The time-travel chick blushed, fluttering her eyelashes, and fanning herself with a paper plate. "I'm not sure I could ever get used to it."

"Nobody can," Piper said.

The drone hovered about twenty feet above, and they noticed it had large googly eyes glued on. "DELIVERY FOR DETROIT ART FARM!" it said in a robotic female voice.

Aaron frowned. "Did someone order something?" Crickets. Piper glared at him. "What? Don't look at me!"

There's something in the human brain that is exquisitely attuned to the gazes and postures of other humans, especially if those postures evince surprise or danger. Whatever that is, it fired in Aaron and Pipers' heads, which both swiveled simultaneously to the same thing everyone else was looking at: a blackened .45 pistol in the outstretched arm of one of Goldman's boys, aimed at the drone.

"Put that away!" Aaron barked.

"It *is* trespassing on private property," mumbled Curtis.

"Yeah, *my* private property," Aaron said.

"Now, hon, let's put the piece up and take a breath," said Goldman. "Ain't the time or place."

The drone seemed to hesitate, then settled gently on the grass, its music still pumping. It unclamped the box, then hovered back up. "PEACE, GODS!" it chirped, then flew off.

Aaron pulled a dirty multi-tool from his belt, cut open the box, and removed an Amazon Fire tablet.

"What the hell is that?" Piper demanded.

"Don't know," Aaron said.

"How you gonna lie to my face, though." Piper stalked off.

"Piper, wait!" Aaron called.

"Yo, Neptune," Goldman yelled. "We just getting started!"

Curtis Washington scurried after her.

Aaron turned on the tablet and a message popped up:

It's our pleasure to offer you this free Amazon Fire Tablet, which comes preloaded with software to connect you to local residents hungry for fresh produce. We hope you choose to participate in our new Prime Air Farmers Market program. The tablet is yours to keep regardless. To learn more, tap the green button.

Aaron looked back, but Piper was already gone. She would have chucked this tablet in the garbage. But what was the harm in learning more? He wasn't agreeing to anything, not yet. Aaron tapped the green button.

As the drone drifted away from the Art Farm, gaining elevation, no one there noticed it following Piper and Curtis toward Clarion Street, to a house it had visited once before.

14

Ellis Wallace hadn't seen Nik since that night at Capers, which he was already solidifying in his story-bank as 'the wing sauce incident.' Miracle of miracles, she'd agreed to meet him for a second date, here at his apartment in the Leland Hotel. He spent the hour before the date blasting Parliament Funkadelic and cleaning up. Sheets washed, check. Laundry done or stuffed in the closet, check. Wipe up obvious urine stains around toilet, check. The plan was to do a little urban exploring in the abandoned lower floors of the building—that would provide the illusion this wasn't just a booty call. He'd used this routine before, but he'd never been so concerned about the state of his apartment. Then again, he'd never brought home a high-level executive. He'd found out exactly who she was during his lunch break earlier that day. The break room TV had been showing a live press conference about the new Prime Air Farmers Market program, and there she was: Annika Dahl, Prime Air Ambassador, answering questions from reporters. The skin on his arms had prickled with anxiety while his dick went half-chub. Knowing how high up she was had him second-guessing his time-tested game plans. Would it be better to come clean, just tell her that he knew? Or would that ruin things? She hadn't volunteered that information, so maybe she didn't want him to know…

He straightened one mirror and paused at another—the sex mirror next to the bed. He could leave it there…it was a bold statement that usually set the tone right. He took it down. It was annoying, actually, to be judging his room by her standards, which he assumed were corporate and even bookish. Of course, if she was looking to hook up with some kind of bookworm, she wouldn't be dating him in the first place. He thought for a second about calling up Jamal. He'd appreciate being asked for girl advice for the first time in the history of his people, the nerds, but Jamal's advice would undoubtedly be wrong. And worse, Ellis would have to explain that he was banging someone Jamal knew. Bad idea.

((*bzzzzz*))

Incoming call: "Mom." He blinked and stared at it for a second, then put it on speaker.

"Sup, Ma?"

"*Hi hon. Just checking in. How you doing?*"

"Getting ready for a date," Ellis said.

"*A date, huh? An actual date?*"

"Yeah, what? I'm thirty-two, I go on actual dates."

"*With actual women?*"

Ellis tossed a takeout container in the garbage. "What, as opposed to…yes, actual women. You know what, this 'actual woman' happens to be an executive at Amazon."

"*Really?*"

"What? Yes, really."

"*Well, I'm not surprised.*"

"Yeah, you are."

"*She white?*"

"Just because she's an Amazon exec doesn't mean she's white."

"*I know that.*"

"Yeah, she's white."

"*That's fine baby. I don't judge, I only—*"

((*bzzzzz*))

Downstairs.

"Gotta go, Ma."

"Okay, baby, I love you. What's her name?"

"Nik."

"Nick? You not—"

"Gotta go. Love you." Ellis hung up, lit a stick of incense, and went downstairs.

Misha pocketed the phone and peeked in her purse to make sure she had everything, then got out of her car, and walked across the street to Alonzo's house. He opened up after one doorbell ring, wearing slacks and a sport jacket, no tie. "Hello, gorgeous," he said. He had a beard on these days, which looked good. Made him look his age. He poured her a glass of Moscato, and she sat on an upholstered cube that was evidently meant to be some kind of chair. It was nice. Everything in his house was nice. He had a piece of fish frying in a cast iron pan. She really hoped he'd be nice, too, this time around.

She had meant to tell Ellis that she was going to see him again. Not to ask permission, because Lord knows she didn't need her son's permission. Just to let him know. Maybe to ask for his blessing.

Ellis didn't get along with Alonzo, and it was mutual, she knew. It wasn't fair to have expected a twelve-year-old boy to take to a man who stomped in the house one day to give loving to his mother, especially if that man wasn't no model of patience or understanding. By the time Ellis was fourteen, Alonzo couldn't very well demand respect based on physical size alone, and Ellis was the sort of boy to test him. It had taken everything Misha had to keep the man and boy in her life from each other's throats. She would have kicked him out sooner if not for the money. It was always about money. It was still about the money.

"You like it with a little black on there, right?" asked Alonzo, pressing the fish against the pan with a spatula.

"Just keep me in wine, and you cook it how you like," Misha said.

Alonzo had never hit her, but he hadn't always been too kind with his words. Made her feel like she deserved to be right where she was and nowhere better. But it must have been hard on him too, dealing with someone else's kid disrespecting him all the time. When he'd called her last week, it had been hard to resist seeing him. Misha had been lonely, and tired, working too many nights at Smiles Cocktail Lounge, on her feet. But she didn't want to run back to Alonzo just because he could change her financial reality. She wanted the man who had danced her through the living room, holding her close, singing Smokey softly in her ear, *And inch by inch we get closer and closer / to every little part of each other / ooh baby.*

"You still working at that shithole?" Alonzo said.

"It ain't so bad," Misha said. "I got friends there."

"Woman, you sound like some fool locked up in a cell too long. Till you forget what's out there. *It ain't so bad.*" He laughed. "Always like that about you. Find a way to convince yourself to be happy."

He flipped the fish, and leaned in and kissed her on the neck. Misha could smell his breath. It was sickly sweet, like a rotting apple.

Annika followed Ellis through a brass revolving door, then up a carpeted staircase into the cavernous lobby of the old hotel. Framed by fluted pilasters and large vases, the room was lit by weak electric chandeliers hanging from the ceiling, where the paint curled off like dead skin. Between two cathedral windows, a fireplace decorated with two massive—could they be real?—elephant tusks.

"Wow," Annika said. "You live here?"

"Yeah, I don't how this shit's legal. I pay rent in cash at the bar." Ellis nodded toward the bar at the far end of the room, where a guy with a trim stache sat on a stool reading a newspaper, liquor on the shelves behind him, a TV on mute. Ellis guided her around the corner toward the elevator banks where an old Coke machine collected dust with a sign that read: "working."

The Leland Hotel dated to the twenties and once housed Detroit's wealthy visitors in eight hundred air-conditioned rooms. By the 1980s, it was a seedy flophouse. On its ground floor, the famed City Club had catered to the industrial goth crowd, a grimy demographic swath that cut across race and sexuality lines. By 2009, when the city went bankrupt, the Leland was a wreck, its lower floors filled with garbage and squatters. The top floors were in decent shape though, and in the last decade, the owner had been renting out rooms as apartments.

They stepped out of the rickety elevator on the twelfth floor, and Ellis led her down a hallway laid with worn red hotel carpeting.

"This here's my humble home," he said, opening the door to his studio apartment, which suddenly felt really fucking humble with a corporate executive walking in just behind him.

It reminded Annika of nothing so much as her own college studio. A counter and kitchenette, a smallish flat screen with a beanbag chair plopped in front of it. A few posters and mirrors. The bed was made, but clearly by a bachelor. Beneath the incense, she detected essence of...gym bag. She posted up at the counter, and Ellis said, "Thirsty?"

As he grabbed a couple beers, she peeked inside his fridge: some leftover takeout, protein shakes, a half-gallon of milk.

"Ready for some urban exploring?"

"Yeah! Should we call an Uber?"

He laughed and handed her a flashlight. "No need. Jungle's right below us." He nodded for her to follow him back into the hallway. She did, but slowly, as if expecting a surprise party on the other side of the door.

"My floor's pretty nice," Ellis said. "But there are whole floors of this building that are totally wrecked."

As soon as they entered the stairwell, Annika's understanding of the place changed. The walls got rougher, with chunks bitten out of the concrete and artless tags on every surface: *Minx 237. DRED. Scum.*

They popped out on the ninth floor and looked down the hall. Red carpet, like on Ellis' floor, but stained and torn at irregular intervals, a few hallway lamps burnt out.

"People live on this floor?"

Ellis walked up to the nearest door and jiggled the doorknob, then did the same with the next one. "Mostly occupied up here." She looked amazed already. This was going too well. His instinct had been right: fancy girl, play up the grit.

"What is that!?" Annika said, pointing to the end of the hallway.

"Oh, that's just the blood door. C'mon." He walked forward, and she followed him. The door was a horror of red and purple paint dripping down from horizontal strokes that looked like lacerations. Below the door, a marble threshold—a small reminder of what this place used to be. "I think some artist used to live here." The door was bolted shut, but the doorknob was missing. Annika shined her flashlight through the circular hole. "Can't see anything," she said.

Ellis put his hand on her hip, and she turned up and into him. They stared into each other's eyes. Annika said, "Well?"

Ellis kissed her, then pulled back before she could. "Let's go down a few floors."

The seventh floor was a murder scene waiting to happen. It wouldn't be the first time. About five years back, a gay man was found beaten to death in his apartment in the Leland. Ellis didn't need to tell her about that.

No carpet, just stained concrete floor, flickering bare bulbs on the walls. The doors were mostly closed, but some were hanging on bent hinges. Darkness crept in at the edges where the wallpaper was torn off. Little bits of carpet-padding and exposed floor staples jutted out from the old moldings. The ceiling was a mosaic of water damage.

"It's like the set of one of the Saw movies," Annika said. "I can't believe you live here."

"Crazy, right? All these rooms are abandoned." Ellis pushed open a creaking door, and they entered a room with five tattered mattresses leaning against the wall and the skeletal remains of an upright piano. He banged a random detuned key—it wasn't loud, but it gave her chills at how eerily quiet this entire floor was. She peeked into the bathroom, which was now a pile of shattered tile and porcelain—someone had sledgehammered a hole in the wall to get at the copper piping.

They ducked into the next room over, stepping on old beer cans and rotting clothes. Their lights danced over the dead place. A refrigerator stood in the center of the room like a bleached monolith. Annika reached for the handle.

"I wouldn't open that," Ellis said.

Annika spotted a rusted pan with some ancient burnt ramen noodles sitting on the unplugged stove.

"It's like Pompeii, like they just dropped what they were doing and left."

"Most of this shit's from squatters. Junkies."

"What's in there?" Annika shined her flashlight at a jagged man-sized hole in the wall. Wisps of dust curled in the beam.

They crawled through to the adjacent room. Pictures from nineties magazines were taped to the walls: Hugo Boss ads, LL Cool J, and Bo Jackson, in his old black and white football pads, holding a baseball bat—the two-sport wonder.

They crawled back through the hole to the other room, and when they rose, Ellis spun her around. She could barely see his smile in the darkness, their flashlights angled on the junk-strewn floor. Ellis leaned in and kissed her, softly, his hands grabbing her hips. He started nibbling her neck, and then, it came out, the thought he'd been holding back all this time: "I saw your press conference today," he said. He pulled back and stared in her wide pupils. "Prime Air Ambassador."

Annika offered an uncertain smile. "Oh, that's just…it's a new position."

"Don't act like you ain't a big deal, though," Ellis said, leaning back in to kiss her again. "So that was your idea? *Hood Fresh?*"

"What?" She bent back at the waist, his hands still holding her hips. "Did you just make that up?"

"Naw, that's what they calling it."

"Who?"

"On RNKR, Twitter, you know."

"Oh god. Is that bad or good?"

"Ah, I wouldn't worry bout it. I mean, first thing on people's minds probably ain't gon be organic kale or whatev, but it might catch on with the health-conscious crowd."

"You're health-conscious."

"Why you say that, cause of my rock-hard warrior body?" He bit her earlobe.

Annika's verbal centers were fritzing out. "Uhm…Duh."

"Wanna take it for a test drive?" He pushed her against the wall and kissed her. Her hands slipped under his shirt and felt the taut muscles of his lower back. She pushed against him with her mouth, taking her turn as the aggressor, and they stumbled through the room, bumping into shadowy junk. Then Annika felt the junkie squatter ramen pan pressing into her back. "Upstairs," she said. "Don't want to be attacked by zombies when I'm naked."

Their clothes hit the floor before they could make it to his bed. Ellis pulled a condom out of thin air, and they started fucking right in his little kitchenette, Annika bent over the counter. He turned her around and hoisted her up, her arms roped around his neck and his hands on her hips as she slammed into him. He carried her over to the bed and dropped her, then stood over her, holding a dramatic pre-pounce pose. He licked his lips. But before he could fall on top of her, she said, "Wait!"

Annika grabbed the mirror near the wall and propped it up at just the right angle.

Ellis broke into a grin, and climbed on top of her. They put on a show of sweaty acrobatics and deep massage to a rapt audience.

15

Piper Prince bombed east on 94, the hot summer air gusting through the Granada's open windows, the envelope in her glove box now lighter by a thousand bucks after paying a visit to Darnell at the Amazon Maker Space. She had hesitated ever so slightly before handing him the money—after all, it had come from her GoFundMe page. While spending the money on destroying drones in music videos wasn't exactly in accordance with the page's description ("Legal defense fund for Luther Prince, arrested and injured by DPD"), Gramps was now current on his legal fees, and further activism was more in line with her donor army than, say, opening up a savings account. Darnell had been excited to take it, and she'd been annoyed at the flicker of surprise she'd seen on the kid's face—she *had* told him she'd get him back for the drone. Also vaguely annoying was how Darnell nerded out over the Amazon drones—he wanted to fly one, bad. She'd walked into the maker space right at the end of a presentation given by some Amazon drone pilot, Jamal something, a guy in business casual who talked like he was from the hood and who Darnell was glomming onto like dude was Jay-Z here to give him a personal lesson in pimping. But Piper figured that Darnell would be down for the cause when the time came for Phase II of her grand plan.

Back home, she found Gramps doing his grandpa thing, sitting in front of the TV, the news on, way too loud. She watched over his shoulder as she put the oven on for a frozen pizza, the coverage moving from Tigers mid-season stats to more about that awful rape gang, to a new spot about the Amazon drones. She looked up from the pizza's ingredient list ("sodium ascorbate" and "flavoring") to see some chirpy blond Amazon lady talking about how they were going to save the hood through lettuce, now that drones were picking up produce straight from the little hippy farms and flying them up to momma's house so she could make salads for the rugrats.

"It's bullshit, though," she said.

Luther craned his head around. "What's the matter?"

"Don't you see what they're doing? They're just co-opting the hippy white people."

"What hippy white people?"

"The farmers. The ones on TV right now? The guy I'm dating?" Oops. Now they were going to have to talk about that. She wasn't *dating* him exactly...

"You're dating a white farmer? Where?"

"He lives a block away. On Armour."

"There's a white farmer a block away? Where does he live?"

"He lives a block away, Gramps. There are white people in the neighborhood now."

Luther was silent for a few moments, as if considering this information. "Well, I suppose you oughta bring him over and introduce him."

Piper laughed. "You just need to get out more! But you know what? I'll see if he's home. I'm setting the timer on this pizza, don't let it burn." And she was out the door, walking a block over to Aaron's place, trying to stitch together game plans both for her mission and her relationships, and wondering if they could work in concert.

Aaron Thistle had come to believe that his natural element was hard, physical labor. He'd taken to farming at Deep Springs College in California, where the curriculum had him roaming the west on horseback, tending to bum calves. He had always dreamed of being a modern-day cowboy, and one autumn morning at Deep

Springs, while cutting through a stump, the chain saw bucking in his hands, the vibrations rattling his bones as the sky stretched out wide before him, he'd achieved self-actualization. He wanted to mark that moment in some way, and he found himself staring down at the wool socks peeking out over his boots. Like most of the kids on his high school baseball team, Aaron had developed the kind of magical thinking that allowed clothing or Byzantine dugout rituals to make the decisive difference in physical contests, when the pitch came too fast for thinking, and the mind-bat-ball connection was harnessed or lost. A not unreasonable belief, in light of the placebo effect. In this vein, Aaron had kept the socks he wore that morning out in California, and had not washed them, and from time to time, when he was feeling like he had fallen off of the pyramid of self-actualization, or when his energy was ebbing, he would take the socks from the plastic storage box in his closet and put them on, and wear them around. Rarely did he then put shoes over them and go out of the house, but today had been one of those days, a day that, it seemed to him, would be decisive—the day he either "sold out" to the larger corporate culture, or the day in which he used new technology to turn his small pipe dream into a viable business, the day he would begin to effect real change in the world.

And so, in the ninety-degree sludge of a Detroit summer day, his feet were melting in the petri steam wrap of the dream socks as his business flattened into a blur around him.

A small landing pad had been demarcated in the backyard where an Amazon drone was waiting. Blue cardboard boxes rose in stacks next to the house. On the Fire tablet Amazon had given him, the Prime Air Farmers Market fulfillment program showed him live-data on produce requests. Amazon must have done a killer job getting the word out, because orders were rolling in fast. A turnip order flashed on the screen, and his finger darted towards it, but it grayed out before he could confirm—a competitor had pounced on it. Who else sold turnips…Greg over at Brother Nature? Aaron looked down at the tablet again, and saw an order for *Russian Red Cabbage or Similar*. He stabbed the screen, hit it again to confirm, and a two-minute timer popped up on the tablet.

"Clint! Order of red cabbage!" he yelled. Clint was the newest resident at the art farm. He made clothes out of wood and actually wore them around. A ball cap made of polished fir, cedar-board t-shirts, and clogs of course. You could sometimes see his junk through the slats in his boxy pine shorts. He was from—meaning not actually from—Brooklyn.

"On it," Clint said, and he hobbled like a wooden robot, painfully slow, through the garden rows. Aaron checked the tablet—an order for spinach and mustard greens. Tap-tap, confirm. "Hans!" Aaron yelled. Where the hell was Hans? "A minute, please!" came the reply from inside. "Leslie!" He called, before remembering—the time-travelling performance artist had begged out of her daily farm hours on account of a bad case of "the vapours." He was doing double duty, both delegating order fulfillment and harvesting at the same time. Clint clopped up with a handful of *green cabbage*.

"Clint, no—" He looked at the tablet. Fifty-one seconds left to fulfill the red cabbage order and a minute thirty on the spinach order. Aaron handed him the tablet and bolted to the other end of the farm plot, leaping rows of kale—if they kept going over the two-minute window, Amazon would prioritize orders to other farms. He plucked a head of red cabbage, sprinted down the aisle to the mustard greens, snatched a handful, turned back toward the helipad—*shit, the spinach*—he reversed course, ripped a grip of spinach leaves, gathered it all in the basket of his t-shirt, and leapt back over vegetable rows toward the delivery point, where Clint was standing right in his way in his stupid wooden suit, totally useless. Aaron juked left, then vaulted over a stack of blue Amazon boxes, going airborne at the exact moment that Clint turned, his wooden shoulder moving into Aaron's flight path, causing him to attempt a mid-air evasion—his foot caught on the stack of blue delivery boxes, shunting him earthward, his face landing inches from a pair of size five Air Jordan Velcros.

"What the fuck!" Piper said.

"Hold on," he said, popping up and dropping the cabbage into one box, the greens into another. He sealed the cabbage box and slid it underneath the waiting drone, which autosensed it and whirred to life. Another drone was already landing to take the mustard greens and spinach. He ran back to Clint to check the tablet. Made it, with four seconds to spare. He walked back to Piper, touching the rising welt on the side of his head.

"*Aaron!*"

"Little busy here. Can't really talk."

"Yeah, you can't jump either."

"Another spinach order," Clint said. "Confirm?"

"Yeah, confirm. Hans! Get out here!"

"So what, you just gonna ignore me?" Piper said.

"Order for tomatoes," Clint said. "Confirm?"

"Hold on!" Aaron said.

"How can you be fucking with Amazon?"

"I'm trying to sell produce."

"You were selling plenty before."

"Yeah, but I was only selling to hipster white kids. Now I'm getting food to people who actually need it. But it won't happen if I don't work my ass off, so—"

"So you and Amazon are saving Detroit?"

"I don't know! I'm just trying it out."

"I just can't even—after they threw my gramps in jail and broke his ankle?"

"He committed a *crime*, remember? And you told me he tripped! Amazon didn't just come over and break his ankle."

"Are you fucking serious right now?"

"What? Yeah, I'm serious—*Hans! Spinach, go!*—Look, I get the anti-drone thing, and I'm for it, in principle, but if free drone delivery, *free*, can get my produce onto people's tables, what is so damn bad and evil about that?" He wiped a lock of blond hair from his sweaty forehead.

Piper glared at him.

"See," he said, "you're so wrapped up in this little mission of yours, you can't even tell me what it's about."

"Loyalty," she said.

"Oh, loyalty, really? You're telling me you didn't fuck your ex-boyfriend in Chicago?"

"No, I didn't!" Which was true, she hadn't, *in Chicago*. But it's not like they'd promised each other anything.

"Yeah, sure."

"I really like you, you know that? But I ain't down with this."

"Did you even consider that it might—"

"Don't bother calling me till you quit Hood Fresh."

"I'm trying to give them the benefit of—"

"Bye," she said, turning before the word even left her lips.

"Piper…goddamnit." Aaron spit towards the dirt, but his saliva was thicker than he'd expected, and the loogie landed on his own boot.

Piper had half a mind to call up Curtis, but was mostly depressed at the idea. So, Aaron Thistle was definitely not on board. Maybe that was a good thing. She'd lived much of her life surrounded by followers, but she'd never actually dated any of those guys, the do-whatever-Piper-wants types. She couldn't maintain an attraction to someone who didn't resist her.

When she got home, she found more than half the pizza uneaten and cooling on the counter. She wrapped several slices in foil and walked to the house next door, the not-quite-collapsing-but-not-not-collapsing house in which old Crazy Richie lived alongside this or that addict of the month. The addict of the month was the one who opened the door on this occasion, a young emaciated guy with jeans sagging so far down that thick tufts of pubic hair curled up over his waistband. Piper reined in a grimace. Richie was home, and this skin-and-bone guy hollered up for him. Richie came shambling down the stairs and lit up when he saw Piper bearing gifts.

He'd lived next door long as she could remember, and she used to call him Uncle Richie. She realized he wasn't a real uncle at about the same time she learned that his house was an Adult Foster Care Home. She didn't know much about Richie, except that he had some kind of mental disability, and that her gramps knew him from way back and cared about him. She'd been bringing him food on and off for years.

Richie thanked her and invited her to come in and watch TV, which, as always, she declined. As she left, she heard the sound of a drone descending across the street. It was Dolores' fat ass. Piper yelled over to her: "Why you buying shit from them?"

"Why you care?"

"You know they threw my gramps in jail, right? You know they suing him?"

"Girl, that ain't got nothing to do with me. I'm just trying to live my life."

"Whatever," Piper muttered. She dragged her body inside. Luther had gone to bed already. The house was oppressively quiet.

16

Though sexual conquest was not the greatest achievement Ellis could imagine, it was the one that most demanded braggadocio. Crowing to his homies about last night's lay, in glorious detail, had gotten him into minor trouble before, the sort of trouble that made it difficult get back with that same girl, or with one of her friends. But those difficulties were easily overcome with his persistent charm. This time though, the potential fallout was much worse: if anyone found out Nik was screwing a guy who worked in the fulfillment center, her job could be in jeopardy. And though this didn't directly affect him, he actually liked Annika. He'd never been with anyone like her. The thought of her suffering from his actions was painful. But it wasn't painful enough to stop him from telling Nestor and Amir that he'd bagged the Amazon Prime Air Ambassador! He had to tell someone how she'd gone right for the sex mirror!

And good thing it had been Nestor and Amir. Otherwise he might have spilled the beans to Jamal, which would have been a disaster, both because Jamal was terrible at keeping secrets, and because as Chief Pilot, he'd probably met Nik at some point or another. And if Nik found out from Jamal that he worked at the fulfillment center, at the very least, she'd stop fucking him. So when Ellis arrived at Jamal's Brush Park house on Sunday afternoon, six-pack in hand, he made a mental note to lock that particular sexual encounter in the vault, which would be hard given that he liked impressing pretty much everyone, and the only thing he had going that would impress Jamal was his skill with the ladies.

Jamal had invited him over to help out refinishing the old hard-wood floors. He'd already sanded them, but they needed to be sealed and stained. Ellis had a test coming up on Monday for the UAV Factory Technician Training Program, and he should have been studying, which was precisely why he had jumped at Jamal's request to help out with the remodel. At least he could feel productive while procrastinating.

Jamal would have been spending time with his girls this weekend, but Nina had begged her mother to let her go with her friend Brit to YMCA day camp in Farmington. And Sandra wanted to take Eve up to Flint to visit her grandmother. Which was good. They needed to make friends and connect with their grandparents. Jamal worried that that's what he was like to them: someone important, but not at the top of the list. That would always be Mom. But once this remodel was done, the house would be a lot more kid-friendly, and hopefully, Sandra wouldn't be so apprehensive about their spending time here. Maybe she'd even join them…

Ellis cracked beers for the two of them, they threw some fans in the open doors to ventilate, then started applying coats of sealant and wood-stain. He noted that Jamal was sweating way too hard for work that wasn't all that physically demanding.

"So how's that Hood Fresh thing going?" he asked.

"They really calling it that?" Jamal said. "It's going better than you'd think, though. Believe it or not, there's people in the hood buying fresh veggies. And we're getting good press. Which is crucial after that Stackz video. You see it?"

"Hell yeah!"

Jamal frowned and took a swig from his beer.

"C'mon, it was funny." Ellis slopped sealant over the wood slats.

"Maybe so, but ill-informed. Doesn't matter. We know who's behind it now. Gonna shut that shit down."

Barry trotted by with Eve's Doc McStuffins doll in his mouth.

Jamal shooed him outside, away from a patch of freshly stained wood.

A few hours later, the floor stained and waiting to dry, they posted up on the porch, finishing the last of the six-pack, staring out at the sterile townhouses covering the once vacant prairie of Brush Park. Jamal sighed.

"Alright, spill it," Ellis said.

"Oh, just Sandra."

"Nigga, you don't need that bitch."

"Dude. Don't say that. She's the mother of my kids."

"Yeah, sorry. You're right. You're the bitch."

"Oh, fuck off," Jamal said with a smile. He socked Ellis in the arm.

"For real though. You want her back, don't just whine about it. Do something."

"Like what?"

"Go get laid, nigga. Then she'll come to you."

"Oh, *get laid*, why didn't I think of that?"

"All about right place right time. That's half the reason I still teach at the Krav gym. Met this fine ass white girl. Classy executive type, you know? Which means she likes it rough. Anyway, you don't need the gritty details."

"Thanks."

"But ain't there somebody you got your eye on? Just somebody to have some fun with? Really, you gotta do that shit just to get your mind right before trying to get Sandra back, feel me?"

"My boss Nik is kinda hot."

Ellis swallowed his own throat.

"I don't really get the vibe that she'd be into it though."

"Yeah, boss, bad news. Don't mess with that." *Jesus Christ. Nik was his boss?* "Let's go out. See what we see," Ellis said.

So they drove down to HopCat, a hipster spot in Midtown. On the way there, Ellis gave him the basic playbook: if you find yourself talking to a woman, smile, laugh, make fun of her, just a bit, but it was mostly about body language and physical touch. Keep your chest open, lean forward, find a way to touch her hands. Then touch her shoulder. Her back. Then just kiss her, and if you can't seal the deal at that point my friend, you're hopeless.

After a beer and a half, the moment presented itself. The woman Jamal had been eyeing was finally alone after saying goodbye to her girlfriend. She leaned against a table, finishing her drink, scrolling through her phone.

"Go over there, Romeo," Ellis said. He nudged Jamal, who downed his beer and went for it. Ellis remained at the bar nursing a vodka-water. It was quiet on Sunday night, which was better for Jamal—the only flirtation skills he'd ever developed were verbal.

The girl had straightened hair, a nose ring, and padding in all the right places. Jamal asked her name. It was Willow. "So your parents must've been trees, right?" he said.

She laughed and sipped her rum and coke. From wher Ellis was sitting, it seemed like Jamal was actually getting this.

Jamal glanced at Ellis, and Ellis nodded at him. *Make fun of her, just a bit.* He could do this. "Nice bangles," he said, pointing at her earrings. "They really...distract from your face."

"What?"

"Sorry," Jamal said. "Bad joke."

"You a Taurus, ain't you," she said. "I'm a Gemini. We gonna clash."

Ellis had only looked away for moment, but already, the girl did not look pleased. Question was: how to rescue Jamal without drawing the girl after him?

"I don't think I'm Taurus," Jamal said.

"You don't know?"

"No, I don't really...know about...all that."

"Refill," she said, handing him her empty glass. She went off to the bathroom. Jamal walked up to the bar. "I tried making fun of her," he whispered to Ellis.

"Okay, that was bad advice for you. Just...be nice."

"She started talking astrology. I don't know if I can get down with someone who—"

"You're not putting a ring on it. Just be funny. When she comes back, say something like, well...what's she drinking?"

"Rum and coke."

"Alright, tell her the bartender screwed up her drink. Made her a coke and rum."

"That's not funny."

"Nigga, just say it."

When she returned, Jamal said exactly what Ellis prescribed. She laughed and touched his arm. Conversation moved to jobs—she was a shift manager at the Double Tree hotel downtown. Jamal told her he was a pilot, but instead of mentioning Amazon right off the bat, he told her about his time in the Air Force. She seemed impressed, but clueless. She had no idea what a predator drone was. Jamal whipped out his phone to show her.

Back at the bar, Ellis took note of a lonely looking white girl who was staring at her drink. Not as cute as Nik, but cute enough. He looked back toward Jamal—he and the girl were leaning over his phone, and he had his hand on her shoulder—about time!

"Why all the pretty ones gotta be alcoholics," Ellis said, taking the stool next to white girl.

"You think everyone drinking alone's an alcoholic?" she said.

"I was talking about me," Ellis said, flashing his weaponized pearly whites. "But you right. Alcoholics can drink together." He ordered two shots of whiskey. Turned out, girl was on her way to some salsa night in Ferndale and was just drinking up a little dance courage beforehand. Ellis didn't know how to salsa, but he could dance, which meant he could fake it. He noticed a tattoo on her arm of an EKG heartbeat line, and they started comparing tats. This was too easy. But when he looked back to Jamal, the girl was leaving! Jamal glanced at him, dejected. Ellis put the salsa girl on hold and walked over to him.

"That's fucking impressive, nigga. How did you fuck that up?"

"Amazon came up and she went off about *Hood Fresh*."

"Ah shit."

"Yeah, she's a big Goldman Stackz fan."

"Well, *The More You Know*. Maybe don't mention that next time. You can get an Uber home, right? I'm going salsa dancing."

"You know how to salsa?"

"Shit no. But we ain't gon be there long." Ellis gave him an insufferable, exaggerated wink.

17

Piper slouched on the couch, idly scrolling through RNKR, watching the Sunday night news with Gramps, who sat in his easy chair half asleep. As if things weren't bad enough, some idiot had tried to assassinate Trump, throwing a climber's chalk bag at him that supposedly had anthrax spores in it. Except it didn't. It was just chalk. But that's what the news initially reported. Some burn-out Occupy kid who ranted about the 1% as they dragged him away. It was all anyone was talking about on social media, and it was killing the momentum for #NOFLYZONE. Piper tuned back into the TV when they moved to local coverage. The anchorwoman went live to a correspondent:

"A twenty-one-year-old woman and her boyfriend were walking back from the liquor store a few blocks east of here when they were confronted at gunpoint by six men who led them behind an abandoned house and forced them to disrobe. All six men proceeded to rape the woman while the man was held to the ground and forced to watch. The perpetrators are described as in their late teens, early twenties, between 5'7" and 5'10", of medium complexion, and wearing dark clothes. We spoke with the cousin of one of the victims earlier today."

Cut to a tall black man with dreads: "We been up all night. All night. It's just. This ain't right. Something gotta be done. They gotta catch these [beeeeeeep]."

"Investigators are pursuing leads in the case, but ask anyone with information to call Crime Stoppers at 1-800-SPEAK-UP. All callers remain anonymous. Our thoughts and prayers go out to the victims and their families. Live at E. McNichols and Goddard Street, Jenna Samson, 7 Action News."

Back to the anchorwoman: "Now, we turn to some more lighthearted news. Hot on the success of Amazon Prime Air Farmers Market, the company has announced a new joint venture with Domino's Pizza, called Amazon Sky Pies, which will deliver pizzas by air in the Detroit metro area. And, for a limited time, each delivery drone will also carry a second large peperoni pizza, free for the first lucky customer in the flight path to hit the "FEED ME!" button on the Sky Pies app. When we return: Twitter users say the Force is strong with a Detroit toddler who was caught on a baby monitor humming the Star Wars theme music."

Watching the news was the exact wrong thing for Piper's mood. It just made her more depressed. Why couldn't she just live in a normal city, without rape gangs and drones everywhere? The high from the #NOFLYZONE video had begun to fade even before Aaron joined Hood Fucking Fresh. The most annoying thing was that it seemed like it was actually helping people, bringing fresh food to people in the hood, across race and class lines. That's what made it insidious, because even if it helped in the short term, it made people dependent on a huge corporation like Amazon, a corporation planning to automate away more and more jobs the bigger it grew.

They weren't after any kind of social justice; they were just using the trappings of justice to make bank. It was sick. It was sad. How could she compete against something like that? Amazon's whole business model was to make things as cheap and convenient as possible. Of course no one was protesting.

"Hey, Gramps, how did it happen back in '67?"

Luther startled awake. "Huh?"

"The riots. How did that get organized? You were there, right?"

He cleared his throat. "Oh, it wasn't all like that. Just a lot of random violence. The feeling was there—been bubbling up for a long time. Just took the right thing to kick it off. Nobody can make a thing like that happen. Can't see why you'd want to neither."

"But it changed things—they got fair housing laws or something passed, right? You didn't break nothing? C'mon, not even a window?"

"Ain't I told you about the riots?"

"No, maybe you told Nia?"

"Alright child. Why don't you fetch your grandpa a glass of the good stuff."

Young Luther Prince was working down at Linsky's Grocery in Hamtramck. He had the morning shift, stocking produce, so although the riots had started late the night before, he hadn't heard nothing about them until some old lady come in first thing talking to Abe Linsky about the blacks done rioting over on the west side, burning buildings and what not. He was checking the bananas right then, removing ones with too many brown spots, and hearing that old lady, first thing through his mind was, *Oh lord, they must of killed somebody.* They'd shot the president a few years back, and maybe now they'd shot Dr. King, and that's why people were rioting. Of course they hadn't, but they'd get to that just about a year later. Turned out it was just some cops trying to arrest some brothers drinking at a blind pig over on 12th, that's what set them off. Same thing, just about, had happened over in Los Angeles. It must have been something in the air at the time. The Panthers were just getting started, and the Nation of Islam. Folks starting to think and dress different. He never got in with that crowd. Was working too much and mostly around white folks like Abe Linsky, who for the most part treated him decent so he didn't have much of a bone to pick with them, though he certainly knew brothers who did. The only reason he ever got close to the riots was for the same fool reason young men get caught up in all kinds of trouble. What else? He was chasing a girl.

No, not Piper's grandmother. This was a very different girl. Susaye McGown. She was deep into liberation and Black Power, wearing Kente cloth and head wraps and all that. Now he'd known Susaye since grade school, and since grade school, she'd been the one true love of his life, which she didn't know, he told himself, though of course she did. By '67, Luther was beginning to think he'd never have a chance with her if he didn't get a little revolutionary himself. The hitch was, he'd just about been hired at the Rouge Plant through some union contacts from his uncle. So he had a lot to lose at the time, and getting involved in a riot very well might get him arrested, which would mean losing that Ford job before it even started.

But knowing that Susaye would surely be down there, he punched out at Linsky's and hopped on a bus to the west side, where a big pile of smoke was rising over 12th Street. The driver started getting antsy as they got closer, until he finally stopped the bus about a half mile away and said he was ending the route and calling the dispatch, so everyone get off.

Now there were young black people everywhere, and cars jammed up in the streets, everyone yelling and honking, excited to see what the fuss was all about. Oh, the youth was fed up alright—black folk been getting the short end of the stick since before there was sticks, and often not even the short end, but just the bruise it left when the white man swung it, but it wasn't any worse in '67 than ten years before or ten years before that. There was plenty to say it was better, even. Maybe they just weren't afraid anymore. Malcolm was dead, but they had Martin and momentum, and if they weren't exactly winning, well, it didn't seem so impossible. Or maybe it was just fashionable. As Luther went further in, the chaos grew. The windows on Hardy's department store were smashed to pieces, people running out with clothes and radios and all kinds of things, even naked mannequins. But Luther was there for one thing and one thing only, which was Susaye McGown. He didn't know what he was gonna do once he found her. He wasn't thinking too far ahead. He walked around for hours looking for her, with all sorts of craziness breaking loose, people flipping cars over, setting cars and houses on fire—this was a black neighborhood mind you, so people were burning their own damn houses. Sweat as thick in the air as the smoke. The black business owners were running around painting "Soul Brother" on their windows and doors so their stores wouldn't get looted, but half the time it didn't help. The police mostly hung back, all in their white helmets with night sticks out. Either there weren't enough of them or else they were just content to watch the blacks burn their own neighborhood to the ground if that's what suited them. Luther was just putting one brown leather shoe in front of the other, scanning for Susaye, when a gunshot popped off nearby. The whole crowd seemed to flinch, and the cops at the end of the street drew their revolvers. No one seemed to know where the shot came from. Luther stopped at a car flipped on its side, leaning up against a phone pole, with a little gang of kids sitting on it, looking down the street. One of those kids was Richie McGown, Susaye's little brother. Richie was one of those kids with mental problems, wasn't right in the head, had trouble controlling himself, so it wasn't normal for Susaye or her mom to let Richie out wandering the streets, much less on a day like this. He was just sitting there on that car, sucking on a bottle of pop, like he didn't understand what a gunshot was.

That's right, the very same Richie that would one day be living right next door. Luther asked the kid what he was doing out here and where's your big sister, and Richie just pointed into the crowd. There she was, standing next to this tall fella dressed in leather who was yelling slogans and waving about pamphlets or something, and Susaye was looking up at him, snapping her fingers like he was some kind of beatnik black pope preaching the gospel. And Luther just watched her for a minute, wondering why he had to fall in love with a girl like her. For one thing, he was trying to get that Ford job and be a Ford man, and for another, he just wasn't one of these militant guys. Now, everyone wants to be a different version of themselves sometimes, especially young people. But that whole leather jacket and beret and fist in the air stuff, that wouldn't have been a different version of Luther, that was someone else entirely.

When Susaye saw him, her eyes lit up—that's how she kept him coming back for more, for so long—and she threw her arms around him and then begged him to watch over Richie.

It was right at that moment that this big wide boat of a car pulled up, big even for '67, this hulking shiny car, and this man got up on the roof. He was wearing a Tiger's jersey, and after a moment of confusion, Luther realized it was none other than Willie Horton, the Tigers' left fielder, still in uniform from the game that Luther had been listening to at Linsky's. He'd hit a home run earlier that day over in Tigers Stadium, which used to be in Corktown. Now if you think this story's not going anywhere, you just wait, cause it is.

Luther turned around and saw Susaye heading deeper into the mob, and he said to Richie, "Wait right here," and Richie didn't even nod cause he was staring up at Willie Horton, who was telling folks how they got to calm down and stop burning the city, how they can all live in peace and protect what's theirs, staring up at Willie Horton, so big and strong, the word DETROIT stitched across his chest looking like it would split right down the middle, the buttons barely holding it together.

So Luther pushed forward into the mob, going after Susaye, but little as she was, she was slipping between folks and getting farther and farther ahead, to the point where Luther called out, "Susaye, wait!" but she was hopping into the bed of a pickup truck with that leather jacket fella and peeling off. She saw Luther and blew him a kiss, which was just cruel. So Luther fought his way back to Richie, but he wasn't staring up at Willie Horton no more, he was a dozen yards off and he was chucking a bottle straight at the heads of some police. The bottle missed, but it smashed into their patrol car. It all happened in slow motion as that policeman shook his head and twirled his baton, then jumped at young Richie, his partner right behind, and soon enough, they were beating the poor kid on the ground, stomping him, saying, *You stupid niggers just asking for it,* and what was Luther supposed to do, run up and pull them off and get beat himself? And Richie wasn't even his brother, not his responsibility, but something had to be done, and he was already yelling, *Stop! He's just a kid!* and they weren't paying him no mind, and that's when Luther found his hand reaching down for a baseball bat someone'd dropped on the street. Now, you might be thinking he was about to do something real stupid, but you'd be wrong. It was only a little stupid. He went right up to that patrol car and started banging on the hood, loud as he could, denting the metal and yelling, *Hey pigs! Hey pigs!*

As you can probably guess, that did the trick. The police left Richie in a pile and ran at Luther full speed. Luther dropped the bat and took off, knocking a few people out of the way and jumping over piles of garbage and shattered glass. He ran and ran, turning corners till he lost those fat white cops and caught his breath, circling back around through an alleyway. He poked his head back onto the street, and there was Richie struggling to get up. Luther grabbed him and ushered him out of the fray, then walked him home.

Susaye's mother took one look at Richie's swollen face and started cursing her oldest daughter while hugging her son, and asking Luther where she gone to, which he couldn't say.

The riots got worse over the next few days. With looters running amok, burning thousands of buildings down, well, the folks in charge were worried that the whole city might go up in flames. So President Johnson addressed the people of Detroit, told them to settle down, then sent in the National Guard. The 82nd Airborne, too, fresh from Vietnam, and they were white and black, fully integrated, not nearly as brutal as the Michigan Militia, which had beat one of his neighbors to a bloody mess. Luther stayed inside with his family, feeling his belly ache—not enough food in the house to feed them all and they weren't about to leave the house. Sometime in there, Susaye got arrested for breaking curfew. By Tuesday, the looting had died down, but the real militants were taking it a step further, hiding in dark windows and shooting at police. So of course, the helicopters flew in low over Linwood to shine lights in the windows and the tanks blasted their machine guns up at the snipers. *Horrific* doesn't even really do it justice, does it? Forty-three dead, most of them black. Not to mention those three in the Algiers Motel murdered by police, without much reason anyone could drum up.

A little while later, Susaye wound up with a baby from one of those Panther fellows and ended up on welfare. She lost track of Richie, and so did Luther, who'd moved on to be a Ford man, finding himself a proper wife and nice house. It wasn't until decades later that Luther saw Richie outside a coney, his clothes ragged, picking up a cigarette butt from the gutter. He bought Richie lunch that day, and the next. He did a little research, and that led him to Detroit Central City to see about getting Richie a place to live. There was already a foreclosed home next to his own that they'd acquired for Supportive Housing. They agreed to place Richie there, and Luther promised to check in and look after him. When you love someone, it never really goes away, even if that someone disappears into the fog of drugs, or money, or simply moves to another state. Luther never saw Susaye again, but he remembered the ghost of that love every time he brought Richie a plate of food, his smile all that remained of hers.

18

Jamal zoomed in on the brick wall, trying to get a better look at the graffiti.

I♥LUCY

There was even a crude, but cute UAV painted above the words. After all the negative press, at least someone was responding positively. Nik had to see this. The mural was on the side of an overgrown tire shop on Van Dyke, across the street from shuttered Kettering High. Jamal brought Lucy in low over the empty lot to get a better shot of the mural, lit up by the soft summer sun of early evening.

The rotors seized. Lucy dropped twenty feet to the ground. *Thunk.* Something white in front of the camera. A net? Fuck fuck fuck!

Two people in black ski-masks bent down in front of the UAV. One of them stretched out a length of duct tape, and Lucy went blind. Shit. *Think.* The Incident Response teams were up and running, but this wasn't just a crash, it was an abduction! Time to scramble. Jamal clipped his phone on his belt, grabbed his control tablet, ran for the door, then stopped, ran back to the console and set Lucy's audio to record to internal memory. Evidence. He ran downstairs and out to the parking lot, his knee aching with every step. He'd left Barry at home today so he could ride his crotch-rocket to work, a neon green Kawasaki Ninja. He shoved his helmet on, almost breaking his glasses, then peeled out, heading southwest on Gratiot.

Curtis Washington sped north on Van Dyke, the drone rattling in his trunk, which was ajar but held down with a bungie cord, as they crossed the Ford Freeway. Piper sat in the passenger seat, Darnell in the back, all three of them with adrenal grins and getaway eyes. Darnell's custom-built PVC pipe net-gun lay at his feet along with the black ski masks. Piper squeezed Curtis' thigh as he gassed it north. A part of her felt like she was using Curtis—she'd needed a getaway driver, and he'd agreed without hesitation. "Aint no thang." To help her commit a straight-up crime. She didn't want to lead him on, because this didn't mean they were getting back together. But there was something so sweet, so perfectly Curtis about his eagerness, how it bled through his hustler's nonchalance.

"You sure you can disable the GPS?" Piper said.

"I think so," Darnell said.

"D! You said you could!"

"I mean, I can, probably. It just might take a minute."

Curtis screeched to a stop in front of her house. They hopped out and lifted the sheet-wrapped drone out of the trunk. "Wait," Piper said. "Not here, they know my house. We can hide it in the house next door. I know the guy."

Richie was shirtless and crazy-eyed, as usual, one eye off to the left, taking in the void, the other lasering in on her face.

"In the basement," she said. "Just for a bit."

He nodded rapidly in silence, which didn't mean yes, but meant he was thinking real hard.

"I'm cooking up some spaghetti tonight. I'll bring it by," she said. "I know you love spaghetti."

The dam burst, and his phlegmy voice came out in a torrent: "Okay yeah yeah spaghetti mmm yeah the basement that's fine the basement real quick little bit that's fine game on later you gon watch hot out today okay yeah."

Piper gave him a big smile and nodded at Curtis and Darnell to carry the drone around back to the rear door. Poor Richie. He was really so sweet. She wondered what he'd been like before he started losing it. She excused herself and dashed around back.

Curtis stood at the doorway to the basement. "Alright, whachu need, girl?"

"You should go!" she said. "If they come, I don't want you getting in trouble."

"You sure?"

Piper stared at him for a moment. She hadn't thought Curtis would actually change. But he seemed…genuine in a way he never had before. She pulled him in for a quick kiss, then pushed him away with a smile.

"Aight. Holla at me," he said.

Piper poked her head inside and saw Darnell going at it with a screwdriver. "Hurry!" she said.

Jamal turned onto Clarion street just as the GPS cut out. Everything kept leading back here, to Clarion, the scene of the initial shooting. There was that kid with the patchy beard. Darnell. Walking down the street, a little too quickly. Jamal stopped in front of the Prince residence and pulled off his helmet. There she was, lounging in a chair on the porch, her legs sprawled wide.

Jamal walked up to the sidewalk, but went no further. "I know you have it," he said.

"Have what?" Piper said.

Jamal held his breath, then let it out slowly. "This isn't going to work out for you," he said. "Just give it back, and I won't call the police."

Piper could feel sweat collecting at her hairline, but she remained motionless. "Do what you gotta do."

Jamal stared her down, rage boiling up inside him, at her, at himself for being too weak, at the whole situation. She didn't even blink. He walked back to his bike and dialed Annika.

"Lucy's been abducted," he said.

"*What? Hold on.*" Jamal heard the sound of a bag zipping up. "*What do you mean abducted?*"

"It's that fucking girl, again. Neptune Frost. They used some kind of net-gun. I tracked it, but the GPS cut out a block away from Clarion street. I know she's got it. She's just sitting there on the porch like a big middle finger!"

"Ugh. Annoying. I'll call the police," Annika said. *"But don't leave, okay, you gotta stay there and watch the house until the cops get there."*

"I won't even blink," he said. Jamal posted up against his motor-cycle and stared down Piper Prince. He said nothing, he waited, he didn't blink.

Piper fought the urge to get up in his face and yell at him. She licked her finger and wiped a smudge off her Nikes. She didn't stare at this Amazon loser so much as she looked through him, wearing a face of utter boredom, which did exactly what she wanted it to do: she could see his jaw clenching even from thirty yards away. But he didn't budge. And the cops probably were coming, but it didn't matter. They wouldn't find shit.

Jamal's phone rang. He unclipped it from his belt. Sandra!? He turned forty-five degrees, keeping Piper in his peripheral vision, and answered softly. "Hey there. Was just thinking about you."

"Yeah, I bet you were," she said.

"What's up?"

"You free? I was thinking, it's been a while since, because Eve is starting kindergarten soon and, well, she got a bad progress report from her pre-school day camp. We should talk. I got a sitter. Meet me at Slows?"

Holy dinner date! Really? No wonder she had trouble getting it out. Eve was going to start kindergarten in the fall, and a bad prog-ress report, how did you get a bad progress report in pre-school? They did need to chat about that, but it couldn't be all that pressing, could it? She wanted to see him! Just rein in the enthusiasm. "Yeah, that would be good, I mean we should talk about that stuff. But, I... there's this work thing. Maybe I can get it covered. I'll text you in a few minutes, K?"

He glanced back to Piper as he dialed Ellis. She hadn't moved, but she had her phone out now and was thumbing the screen rapidly.

"What up doe?" Ellis said.

"Dude, need your help."

"Ah man, I was just about grab some grub, yo."

"One of our UAVs got captured," Jamal said.

"Oh right, I mean, what?"

"For real. I tracked it to this house. Cops are on their way, but someone has to stay here and watch to make sure they don't move her somewhere else."

"Why can't you do it?"

"Sandra! She wants to have dinner. I have to go. It's my shot, dude."

Ellis sighed.

"Nigga, I fucking bailed you out of jail."

"Yeah, no, you right, you right. I got you, homes. Text me the address."

"Ah shit. I gotta help my stupid friend," Ellis said to Annika. They were standing in front of Slows BBQ, still sweaty from their Krav session.

"What happened?"

"Some shit with his ex-wife. Don't worry about it."

Annika pulled him close by the sides of his shirt. "You're gonna make me eat alone?" She clicked her teeth together. Ellis threw his head back in mock frustration. "Call me," she said, and she ducked inside.

Ellis sat in his car, parked across the street from the house Jamal had fingered. The girl sitting on the porch had gone inside when some skinny hipster had walked up. Ellis was curious, but he was also starving. He'd burned a lot of fuel during Krav. How long was this shit going to take? He looked down the block, trying to will a squad car to appear around the corner so he could get the hell out of here and go find Nik. A drone whizzed by overhead, carrying what? Books, socks, bok choy, or…a pizza. He'd seen the announcement about Amazon Sky Pies. He installed the app. It gave him the option to order a pizza through Dominos, or to scan for passing deliveries for a chance to get a free large peperoni. He hit scan, and a map screen appeared with a dotted circle surrounding his location and with small green dots zipping this way and that. The "FEED ME!" button at the bottom of the screen was red. It blinked green as one of the dots entered his circle, but flashed back to red just as he hit the button. Shit. Not fast enough. The green dot continued on its flight path, outside the dotted circle.

Danny Mikos sat on the floor in Piper's room, nodding to the beat from her stereo, smoking a joint.

"So that car with tinted windows out front," Piper said. "It showed up just when that pilot asshole left on his bike. Amazon is staking out my fucking house, yo!"

"Well, you did steal their drone!" Danny Mikos offered her a hit.

"Can't be doing this in here," she said. "My gramps hates it." She took a hit, then blew the smoke out the open window and passed the joint back.

Danny's phone buzzed, and he said, "Goldman's texting me new lyrics. *Dollar signs in they eye sockets. White hands in our black pockets, we blast rockets to slash profits, they all muppets and hobbits.*"

"There's something there," Piper said.

"God, he's good, isn't he?" Danny said.

"I should go back out to the porch," Piper said. "Hook probably roll up any minute now."

"Hey, Piper. Do you think..."

"What?"

"I don't know."

"Spit it out."

"Do you think he likes me? Or is he just like that?"

"Who? Goldman? Sure he likes you."

"No, I mean—"

"Oh...I kind of assumed he was just like that. What, you like him? Like you want to..."

"I don't know. I've never...done anything like that before."

"But you're curious?"

He nodded.

It was a slight shock that Danny was seriously considering that, but even more surprising was his candor. He felt comfortable enough with her to be that vulnerable. Not even her sister had opened up to her like that. It felt like a gift. Piper wanted to offer back real advice, but she had no idea if Goldman was even gay. There was no doubt he was an omnidirectional flirt, but she'd always thought of him as sexually alien, like Andre 3000, impossible to categorize.

"Shit, I'm curious, too," she said. "You know what? I say, do it. What's the worst that could happen?"

Danny thought for a moment, then said, "I'd need a whole new wardobe."

Across the street, Ellis fixed on the green dots traversing his map screen. One of them entered his circle, and the "FEED ME!" turned green again. He hit it, and a box popped up:

> **Answer three questions to get your free pizza!**
> **Hurry, the clock is ticking!**
>
> 1. Have you ever purchased carrots at a farmers
> market? Yes ( ) No ( )

Ellis answered the first two questions in a flash. The third gave him pause.

> **Answer three questions to get your free pizza!**
> **Hurry, the clock is ticking!**
>
> 3. Would you buy intimate products online?
> Yes ( ) No ( )

But whatever, sure. His phone vibrated as an image of a pizza popped on the screen.

> **Congratulations! Your large peperoni will arrive**
> **momentarily!**

Sweeeeet. Ellis got out of his car as an Amazon drone descended to the sidewalk. A moment later, he brought an oozing slice of pizza to his mouth, the box sitting on the hood of his car, as Officers Cross and Shepard pulled up in front of the Prince residence.

"Well, look who it is," said Officer Cross, walking up to the porch. "Better bust out that camera phone."

"Fuck off," Piper said.

"That sound like Contempt of Cop to you?" Cross tapped his thumb on the top of his holstered baton.

Piper knew it was stupid to be mouthing off while black, but she couldn't help it. Cross was an asshole.

"Miss, we've got a report that a stolen Amazon drone may be inside this residence," Shepard said. "May we take a look inside?"

"You ain't gon find shit," Piper said. "Go ahead. Look."

Sandra Dent sat at a table waiting for her ex-husband, trying to recall details from their first date, nearly a decade ago. They'd gone out for coffee somewhere, but she couldn't remember the place. There were grains of rice in the saltshaker. Jamal had been awkward, but adorable. At the end of the date, he'd said, *I would like to kiss you now. Is that okay?*

Slows BBQ was suffused with the smells of slow-cooked meat and thick, sweet sauce. Sandra found her eyes drifting to a white woman with a Bluetooth headset who was alone at the bar, mawing on some brisket.

Jamal saw Annika first. What the hell was she doing here? He scanned for Sandra, and found her near the back. They made eye contact, but walking to her table would mean walking right past Nik. Was he supposed to walk fast and avoid her? Too late. Annika turned in his direction. Her jaw froze, mid-chew. He leaned in close to her. Sandra was watching.

"What are *you* doing here?" Jamal said through his teeth.

She swallowed. "What are you doing here?"

"I'll tell you later." He nodded at her as if they'd just exchanged pleasantries, then walked on and sat down across from Sandra.

"Who's that?"

"Just a friend," he said, unsure why he was lying.

The waiter came by, and they put in their orders. Soon as he left, Jamal said, "So, what's up with this progress report?"

"She won't do the hand gestures to this dumb little song, *Gray Squirrel Swish Your Bushy Tail.*"

"Why not?"

"Lord knows. And apparently, she refuses to sit in her assigned seat, which is next to this boy Michael who bit her last month."

"Oh right, the sugar cube something, what was it?"

"She smeared his sugar cube sculpture with pink glitter." Sandra sighed. "Anyway, one of her day-camp counselors teaches at the kindergarten, and I'm worried they'll label her 'rule averse,' or whatever they call it."

"Well, what should we do?" he said with a smile. Eve would be fine, he knew, but he wouldn't miss this discussion for the world. The girls had this insane ability to reconnect he and Sandra when they couldn't find their way back to each other on their own.

Annika caught Jamal's eye. He was probably wondering what she was doing here just as much as she was wondering about him. She'd carved out tonight to hang out with Ellis, and even though he wasn't here, she wasn't about to uncarve that time. She'd drawn a line in the sand. She needed just a few hours without thinking about work. A few hours to recharge before the relentless e-mails from Jeff, the meetings with the S-Team, the kowtowing to Thad Burrows and the FAA. But with Jamal here, what the hell was happening with that captured UAV!? She tried to beam that thought to him with her eyes. Jamal beamed back: *Leave me alone, please.*

"She thinks she's smarter than everyone. I blame you!" Sandra said playfully.

"Well, she is. But I'm not the one who made her so smart. I can talk to her this weekend about being patient with the dumbs."

"The dumbs?" She laughed.

"You know, most of society."

Sandra had been thinking a lot about Nevada, and how miserable she'd felt there while Jamal was piloting drones. But seeing him this last month, hearing the kids talk about their time with Daddy, she'd begun to realize that it wasn't him, it wasn't that their spark had fizzled there, it was the Air Force, it was the cultural desolation of Nevada. They were home now.

"You know, Eve will be fine. How are *you* doing?" she asked, reaching forward and grabbing his hand, which was gripped around his water glass. Just a few hours before, Sandra's friend Crystal had told her some disturbing, but not unexpected news. She'd matched on Tinder with a guy who looked a lot like the guy Sandra had been seeing, Nate. Crystal showed her the profile. It was Nate all right, posed with a stack of books like some pretentious author photo. She'd figured he was dating other people, but seeing him on Tinder hammered home a truth she'd been hiding from herself: she didn't want a guy like Nate. He was a distraction. And whatever his charms, they couldn't stack up to this sweet, shlumpy man. There was something sexy about being a good father, and Jamal didn't even know he had it.

"I'm doing alright," Jamal said. "Keeping busy at work. Been on a date or two." Which was a huge exaggeration from *Tried to chat up a girl at the bar*. But he had to seem desirable. And nonchalant about it. That's how Ellis did it.

Sandra pulled back. "Really?"

"What, you think I can't get a date?"

"No, I'm just surprised."

God damnit Ellis! Jamal's heart clattered up a gear. "You're still so beautiful," he said.

"Still? You waiting for it to fade?"

"Damn, c'mon. I mean—"

"I'm just giving you a hard time," she said, but the joy from just a few moments ago had drained out of her voice.

"We should take the girls here sometime," Jamal said. "They've never been, have they?"

Their food arrived. Ribs, mac-n-cheese, collards. "Can I get you anything else?" the server asked, hooking his thumbs through his suspender straps, like some hip, white Steve Urkel.

"No thanks," Sandra said. "We're fine, just like this."

 **Bobby Kirkpatrick**
August 23 · 🌐

Fucking Amazon. Unbelievable. They srsly need to be stopped. I'm cancelling my prime account tomorrow.

The first hit's free: how Hood Fresh exploits poor communities of color

Amazon's new Prime Air Farmers' Market yokes urban farms and urban poor, taking capitalism to insane new low.

SLNM.US | BY ROBERT BOSTICH

12 Likes 19 Comments 1 Share

👍 Like   💬 Comment   ➡ Share

Annie Kim **and** 11 others **like this.**

1 share

 Janet Stolz I do NOT agree...I get why people think Amazon drones are creepo but isn't it kind of a good thing that they're delivering organic food to people who need it? Detroit has had a problem with food desserts for a long time, causing malnutrition, etc. I agree that Amazon is problematic but what is the alternative for people living in food desserts?
August 23 at 12:21pm · Like · Reply · 👍 1

 M Montauk Great, now Amazon is taking away our desserts!
August 23 at 12:22pm · Like · Reply · 👍 2

 Richard Sims Bobby Kirkpatrick you said the same thing last time when that thing about the working conditions came out and you still didn't cancel your Amazon your addicted lol
August 23 at 12:24pm · Like · Reply

Terrence Shots Oh no, is it going to turn Detroit into some fucked up ghetto? TOO LATE
August 23 at 12:28pm · Like · Reply · 1

 Ellen Blick Whatever, I guess any black neighborhood is a "ghetto" to you!?
August 23 at 12:33pm · Like · Reply · 3

 Joachim Grubs Amazon is a monopoly. Teddy R would have busted it. Trump will just take it's money.
August 23 at 12:39pm · Like · Reply

 Woody B Oh Joachim...It's not Amazon that's the problem, it's a gov't that provides no incentive for corporations to keep jobs here and does little to actually stimulate the economy.
August 23 at 12:41pm · Like · Reply

 Neil Abalone "It is no crime to be ignorant of economics, which is, after all a specialized discipline and one that most people consider to be a 'dismal science.' But it is totally irresponsible to have a loud and voiciferous opinion on economic subjects while remaining in this state of ignorance." -- Murray N. Rothbard
August 23 at 12:47pm · Like · Reply · 1

 Patty Svalbard Neil, have you even read Karl Marx "Capital Vol 1"??
August 23 at 12:51pm · Like · Reply · 5

 Sara-beth Kirkpatrick Bobby remember the sweater your grandfather and I sent you on your birthday well that came from Amazon. We miss you.
August 23 at 12:58pm · Like · Reply

 Samira Dalbey I've worked for Amazon for three years and I have to say that it's hard, yes, but they're doing good things. I'm not an economist, so I can't say how this affects capitalism, but I know that the people there have their hearts in the right place.
August 23 at 1:03pm · Like · Reply · 1

 Dade Plum Where's that, Samira, the freezer? #NOFLYZONE
August 23 at 1:12pm · Like · Reply · 5

 Kyle Q I will continue to use Amazon Prime until the day they destroy the earth and plug my mind into the matrix and my body into some weird goo cage. And probably after that.
August 23 at 1:20pm · Like · Reply · 3

 Annie Kim I agree that's messed up. They're offering free food to poor people, and then when they get hooked on it they'll ramp up the price and those people will have no where to go.
August 23 at 1:25pm · Like · Reply · 2

 Jason Rubenking TRUMP
August 23 at 1:37pm · Like · Reply

Halifax C All hail our corporate masters!
August 23 at 1:39pm · Like · Reply · 1

 Ayelet Orenstein Can we go a day without some corporation exploiting poor POCs? Oh wait, this is America...
August 23 at 1:49pm · Like · Reply · 8

 Cal P. Molar Ayelet Orenstein so getting free delivery is getting exploited now? I wish Amazon would exploit me, I have to pay for same day Prime. I guess that's just my white privilege.
August 23 at 1:51pm · Like · Reply · 1

 Jes Zimmerman bitch bitch bitch
August 23 at 1:56pm · Like · Reply

Write a comment...

19

"Just get it back, I don't care how." Annika stood outside the Fulfillment Center, waiting for Thad Burrows, who had just now parked and was walking towards her. "And keep it quiet. According to Legal, we have no obligation to tell the FAA about captured UAVs."

"Okay, but if it wasn't in her house, then—"

"Gotta go, Jamal. Solve this, K? Thanks. END CALL."

Annika waved to Thad Burrows as she calculated the fastest way to run through this Fulfillment Center tour without it feeling rushed. Start with the Kiva robots and the Robo-Stow hydraulic arm, showcase the UAV shipping lane, then meet and greet a few Pickers, and send him on his way. She had a lot on her plate; Prime Air Farmers Market was steadily gaining customers in the very demographics Bezos wanted, refocusing public perception of Amazon away from that #NOFLYZONE nonsense, but the *Hood Fresh* name had taken hold, and combating that required a concerted effort. The capture of Lucy was a further headache. The value of the UAV was negligible; the worry was what this Piper Prince character might do with it. If she indeed had it, which Jamal was convinced of. The cops had searched her residence and turned up nothing. If only Annika could sit down with her and talk some sense into the girl. She shoved those thoughts into a mind-cabinet, then found the Ellis Wallace cabinet ajar. She indulged a quick peek inside—the feel of his hands gripping her thighs—then shut it as Thad Burrows bounded up like he was chewing gum with his ass.

Ellis was zoned into the job, working alongside the Kiva robots, picking product from the shelves they ferried him, feeling more like a meat robot himself than a fully realized human. Then he saw her. The sour alertness of adrenaline flooded his chest. She hadn't seen him yet. He could duck out now for the bathroom, but then his pick rate would plummet. He glanced at the Plush Moses Sock Puppet™ in his hands and threw it in a bin. Why hadn't he just told her already? The sensible thing was to keep his head down and just hope she didn't notice him. But that's not what a badass player (who made fourteen bucks an hour—but forget that) would do. So he stood tall, and when she rounded the corner with some jittery old dude, Ellis looked her straight in the eyes and gave her a little *sup girl* head nod, slow, saucy, mouth slightly ajar.

Annika's heart stopped, or it felt that way as her voice dried up mid-sentence. Ellis worked in the Fulfillment Center? Was this some kind of joke? Why hadn't he told her? Because she never would have slept with him, obviously. And the way he was looking at her now, like, like—
"These Kiva bots really are something," Burrows was saying. And what was she supposed to do? Be mad at him now and then be the petty person for being mad about a thing like this, for caring about that fact that—
"Orange, that's a good color for a robot. Very visible. What's the injury incidence rate for workers interacting with the Kivas? Ms. Dahl?"
Annika mentally restarted her heart, gave Ellis a single glance that communicated nothing but existential exasperation, and steered Thad Burrows away.

Ellis went back to picking. That had gone about as well as he'd hoped. At least she hadn't yelled at him or kicked him in the balls or gotten him fired. He ruminated on the sad possibility that he might never again get to fuck Annika Dahl, which was sad not just because she was hot, but because she was smart and passionate, and being around her gave Ellis visions of some better version of himself, a self not working in a warehouse and behind on his car payment. At least he'd owned the reality of where he was. What else could you do?

Jamal unlocked his deadbolt and punched in his seven-digit alarm code—it was an annoyingly stressful system, requiring him to enter it perfectly within ten seconds of opening the door, or else the whole place would light up like a night raid on Dresden. He almost didn't make it in time. His brain was thoroughly wiped by another fourteen-hour day—he'd been doing route development for Prime Air Farmers Market with the added responsibility of formulating a plan to recover Lucy.

He tossed his keys on the table and let Barry into the backyard, then went upstairs to work on a little project of his own, a little Batman detective job. He woke the desktop in his room and logged on remotely to the UAV footage database. The UAV cameras were strictly for navigation, but the footage was kept to augment Amazon's predictive marketing algorithms. They weren't technically surveilling the public as no human eyes were watching the video. The one exception was Jamal, who had clearance to check the footage against the navigation logs as they continually tweaked the UAV's sense-and-avoid software. But that's not what Jamal was doing now. He was searching for any UAV footage near E. McNichols and Goddard Street at 11 pm last Saturday. He'd been following the news story about that horrific rape gang, and it seemed like the DPD wasn't having much luck tracking them down. They'd even asked Amazon to look through their UAV footage, but the higher-ups had said, no. Maybe they'd change their tune if he happened to "stumble" on something useful.

There was nothing at that intersection at that time, unfortunately. Jamal scanned footage from adjacent blocks from 10:45 – 11:15. Nothing, nothing, a whole lot of nothing, until—there: a group of figures walking on McNichols at 10:49. Could it be them? Two of them wore hoodies, the others wore ball caps. Seen from above, there was no view of their faces. But that didn't mean there were no useful clues. What would Batman do? Jamal zoomed in on the hats, looking for a logo. It was small, blurry. He took a screenshot, opened up Photoshop, and sharpened the image, refined the edges. The logo came into focus: the Tigers' 𝔇. He sighed. That didn't narrow it down much.

Eddie Noble was on a bender. It wasn't his fault—it was a periodic immune response to living in close-quarters with his beautiful, black-hearted ex-wife, Detroit. She was moving on without him, into the future, and she made sure to let him know on a daily basis. He'd just left Downtown Louie's after drinking them out of Maker's, and had lit his last cigarette. He'd been on the Amazon beat for months, covering its slow, creeping success. He needed a scandal. The drone shoot-down was something, the #NOFLYZONE video had made a stir, but the real story was about surveillance: the Amazopticon. He'd nearly given up on this angle, but that was the thing about this city—if you kept your eyes open, it would eventually deliver you exactly what you were looking for.

A few blocks away from Downtown Louie's, at Motor City Krav Maga, Annika beat the ever-loving hell out of stick-limbed Christy Park, who barely managed to keep the pad up, tripping backwards with each blow, stumbling into other students. Ellis had never seen Nik look so fierce. God, it was hot. Christy twisted her ankle and had to sit out, so Ellis took her pad and stood in front of Nik, then called for the class to do a thirty second burst of hammerfists—he wanted to see how hard she could hit.

Nik wailed on him, slamming her fists into the pad on his chest, her technique getting sloppy as her rage increased, like she was trying to beat a heart-attack victim back to life. *Live, damnit! Live!*

Ellis sidled up to her after class, and she ignored him.

"Invite me over," he said.

"Why?"

"Because you only hit somebody that hard if you really like them."

Annika didn't say yes, but she didn't say no, so Ellis followed her out of the gym into the evening humidity, the only sounds coming from their footsteps and the satisfied buzz of drones overhead, taking care of business.

Eddie Noble recognized her from a block away: Ms. Dahl, the Amazon Prime Air Ambassador, walking towards him with some beefcake. Interesting. He flicked his cigarette and leaned against his car, waiting for her to close the distance.

Annika jumped at the sound of her name. The man was leaning against some '70s gas guzzler, shades (at night), goatee, unbuttoned vest. "Can I help you?" she said.

"Eddie Noble, Detroit Free Press."

"I know."

"Mind if I ask a few questions?"

Ellis looked at her quizzically. She exhaled. "It's late, Eddie. Make it quick."

He clicked on a small recorder and held it up near her face. "Members of the Detroit PD believe that video footage from Amazon drones could help solve crimes and keep Detroiters safe. Do you agree?"

"Do I..." Careful, now. It was an easy question with an easy answer. Too bad the public wasn't...sophisticated enough to hear it without freaking out. "UAV technology...has the potential to improve many facets of public life, but the question of whether to use this technology for anything other than commerce is something that only the people and government of Detroit can answer."

"So, you agree that the cameras on Amazon drones *could* be used for law enforcement."

"That's definitely a question that Amazon is not focused on right now."

"Okay, but, considering that the DPD has already requested

drone footage for a criminal investigation, isn't that a question Amazon *has* to consider?"

"To what investigation are you referring?"

"For one, there's the drone shooting that happened on the northeast side involving Mr. Luther Pr—"

"Yes, I'm familiar, but I can't comment on an ongoing criminal investigation. That's something you should ask the police department."

"There have also been federal requests. From the Department of Justice."

She almost made the mistake of asking how he'd heard about that. He'd tell her his sources were confidential and then get her on tape acting clueless and defensive. "I'll have to get back to you on that," she said.

Noble flashed a smile. "Thank you, Ms. Dahl. And I'm sorry," he held out his hand to Ellis. "Eddie Noble."

"Hey. Ellis Wall—"

"We gotta run, Eddie," Annika said, breaking away and pulling Ellis after her.

Ellis looked back at the reporter. So that's how it was. He was good enough for the bedroom, but not the sidewalk. They walked back north in silence.

She breathed a sigh of relief when they finally reached the Broderick Tower. The elevator rose to the 30th floor, and when they stepped into Annika's apartment, the lights and A/C clicked on automatically.

"Sweet pad," Ellis said. The aesthetic was Crate & Barrel: clean, modern, and with an artsy edge sanded down by the pressure of corporate mass-appeal. The view was a class divider; only people of a certain strata lived this high up.

"I'm hopping in the shower," Annika said, looking over her shoulder. Was that an invitation? Ellis disrobed and joined her. The shower was so nice (two shower heads, marble tile), it actually distracted him from her naked body. She didn't seem in the mood to talk, so he didn't, but he did take the soap out of her hand and wash her. A kiss on the neck was all it took.

The sex was fast and rough and wet.

Afterwards, they stood under the hot water, rinsing off the sweat. Annika let it run over her neck for a long time, turning up the heat, breathing in the steam. The shower was the only place in the entire state where she was free from sinus discomfort, which made it so much easier to think, and to decide. After a while, she said, "We can't do this anymore."

Ellis stared at her back, the water splashing off her head and spraying his chest. Yes. He wanted to just say, *Yes, Yes we can, we should, we deserve this!* It was a strange feeling, difficult to wrap his mind around—not that he deserved her, or that she deserved him, but that they both deserved to see where this would lead. "I should have told you," Ellis said.

"You don't have to be embarrassed. I don't care where you work, I care that—"

"I ain't embarrassed. I just thought, you know, you might get in trouble…"

She turned around to face him. "Sorry," she said, placing a hand on his chest. She let it drop. "I just have a lot going on and…"

"Yeah, I get it."

"I'm sorry."

Ellis said nothing. Annika shut the water off. Already, cold air was rushing in to displace the steam.

20

Darnell and two of his nerd friends, Tre and Kyle, had been at it all night, picking at Lucy's guts under the light of a naked bulb in Crazy Richie's basement. Darnell had Lucy hooked up to his laptop, which was wallpapered with stickers—a Lions logo, the Star Wars Rebel insignia, *Detroit vs. Everybody*. He was attempting to edit the flight control code so Lucy would accept input from his third-party radio controller. A task like this narrowed the world—it was just him and the code. There was no better place to be, for here he didn't have to think about his pop's diabetes, or Katie Pulaski, the fine-as-4K-HD white girl at Cass Tech who didn't know he existed, or about Magi-Tech downtown, which wouldn't hire him as a computer repair tech even though his friend Kyle already worked there, Kyle who had learned basically everything he knew about computers from Darnell, Kyle who was—coincidence?—white. But Piper had given him the best kind of problem by asking him to hack this UAV, the kind that forced him to learn something new to solve it, a problem that voided even the annoyance of having to fuel his body.

Piper had been checking in periodically, resupplying Darnell with two-liters of Faygo and barbecue potato chips—anything to keep him working. They were running out of time. They'd already filmed Goldman and crew for the new music video, but they needed a sequence of shots with Lucy, and Piper's videographer, Hans, was heading back to Germany tomorrow.

Piper popped in just before noon on Sunday to find Darnell finally screwing the case back onto the drone. Tre and Kyle were asleep on a ratty couch. Darnell smiled, and pushed the throttle on his controller—Lucy's rotors spun up, and she lifted off and hovered two feet above the basement floor, blowing dust and potato chip crumbs to the corners of the room. He spoke into a headset mic around his neck, and Lucy's robotic voice came out: "GOOD TO GO!"

While Darnell and his nerds loaded Lucy into the trunk of the Granada, Piper ran down a block to the Detroit Art Farm to get Hans. She knew she'd see Aaron there, and she wasn't sure what she'd think or say when she did. An Amazon drone, ferrying DAF produce, took off from behind the house as she approached. She called inside for Hans. As he gathered his camera gear, she walked around back and found Aaron tapping a tablet and barking orders at his haggard artists—even the time-travelling racist—to harvest more carrots, to water the tomatoes. He was more in control than the last time she'd seen him. A single word tripped out her lips: "Still?"

Aaron looked up from his tablet and said, "Hey! How've you been?"

Piper crossed her arms and said nothing.

Another drone landed behind Aaron and lifted off with a box of greens. "Piper," he said. "Yes, still. Look how empty the field is! We're selling faster than we can grow. We were breaking even before. Now we're actually making money! It's crazy."

"Yeah, because you don't pay for labor," Piper said.

"That's not—the residents are paid in room and board, you know that."

"Which one's chard again?" one of the residents called.

"Hold on," Aaron said over his shoulder. He touched Piper's elbow. "I know it's crazy," he said, "but people out here on the eastside, they're buying fresh greens. This is a good for the community."

"Community?" She shrugged his hand off. "How you gon build a community if everybody at home just getting shit dropped off by drone. You gotta interact with people face to face. How do you not—"

"Yeah? That what you're doing on your phone all day? Building a community on RNKR? Face to face?"

"That's different."

"No, it's not. But whatever, you're just mincing words. I've seen the delivery map of where our produce is going."

"But how does it make you feel, working for fucking Amazon?"

"I'm not working *for* them. I'm—"

"How does it make you *feel*?"

It didn't make him feel good. He knew that. But he wasn't doing this to feel good. What mattered was whether or not he was helping the community, right?

"Ready!" Hans called. He was standing behind her, loaded up with camera bags.

"I don't—" Aaron began.

"I'm out," Piper said.

Piper, Hans, Darnell, Tre, and Kyle piled into the Granada, the teens in back, their feet surrounded by an odd assortment of items Piper had picked up early that day—delivery options.

All around the city, fans were pushing the soup-thick air back into the afternoon heat. They drove for miles, looking for promising opportunities, Darnell taking Lucy up to spy down from above when safe. Eventually, they found a low-rise apartment complex on a quiet street, an open window, a dude in a chair, but was he…? They parked around the block, took Lucy out, and crept back to a bush across the street from the guy's building.

"I can't quite tell," Darnell said.

"No, he totally is, dude," Kyle said.

Piper picked through the delivery options, found the perfect object, then loaded up the blue box—they'd cut a hole in the side and rigged it with a spring plate that would launch the object out when Darnell hit a button on the controller. Piper glanced down the street—clear—up in the sky—no other drones. She nodded to Hans, who hit record on his Canon EOS 5D.

Darnell brought Lucy up to a hundred feet, moved her across the street, then brought her down slowly toward the guy's window.

Hans crept closer with the camera—the guy was sitting in a

La-Z-Boy, his arm pumping up and down, staring at the TV which was tuned to…Sportscenter? As Lucy dipped into the guy's view—the rotor buzz blowing his curtains inward—he jumped out of his chair, boner bouncing behind his fat hands.

Tre started choking on his Milky Way, and Kyle was rolling on the ground, but Piper flicked Darnell on the forehead. "Launch it already! And say some shit!"

The guy was jumping up and down, trying to get his pants on and get out of the room at the same time, when the tube of Astroglide lube shot out of the spring-loaded delivery box and hit him in the belly as Lucy's feminine robot voice boomed out: "TRY SOME LUBE FOR THE DICK CHAFING!" which caused Tre to spit a soggy chunk of candy bar onto Kyle's back. Darnell lifted off and ran down the street, Lucy overhead, and they rendezvoused back at the car, laughing their asses off.

"Shit," Piper said. "You can fly alright, but on a comedy tip—I got the one-liners." And she did, for the fat mom pushing a double stroller down the sidewalk—"DAMN BITCH, PREGNANT *AGAIN*?" Lucy said, launching a box of condoms. For the clutch of black kids tossing a football around in the park—"SMOKE UP, MONKEYS!" Lucy said, scattering five packs of Newports at their feet. For the thugs sipping beers on their stoop—"EAT UP, NIGGERS!" Lucy said, chucking drumsticks and wings onto the cracked cement walkway in front of the house. They chased Lucy down the street, one of them throwing a baseball bat into the air, and Darnell had to bring Lucy down blind two blocks over; they scooped her up and peeled out.

The day was getting long in the tooth, and Lucy's battery was running low. They prepped for one final bit of harassment, but just as Darnell was taking off, Piper yelled, "No! Down." She pointed up as two Amazon drones cruised by overhead. As they waited it out behind a couple garbage cans, a red Ford Focus wagon drove by on Florence street, heading east away from U of D Mercy, and—holy shit! It had one of those Amazon I♥LUCY bumper stickers! Perfect!

They followed at a distance until the car pulled into a driveway on Linwood Ave, a few blocks south of McNichols. The woman got out with two kids and went inside as lightning bugs made slow loops through the sweating heat of early evening.

Hans got in position with the camera, and Piper rummaged through the stash for just the right delivery.

Sandra Dent sat down with a glass of Riesling and an open copy of Robinson & Kovite's *Deliver Us*, which she was reading for her book club and not hating nearly as much as she'd expected. She looked at the author photo again. Two white guys from Seattle. Huh? Nina and Eve were ensconced in a Doc McStuffins rerun. A familiar buzz washed through the open window, that sound people hated, but which she'd grown fond of—the sound of Jamal. She set the book down and smiled. Lord, Jamal, bringing that drone around just to come after her. And she'd begun to admit to herself, she was open to—maybe even wanted—Jamal back in her life. He'd been annoying the other night at dinner—him, dating, please!—but she could tell he was just trying to impress her, however wrongheaded he'd gone about it. She'd been avoiding the very idea of Jamal. She didn't want him to be the convenient answer to her fear of becoming the single mother on the prowl. She didn't want a reminder of the career opportunities she'd sacrificed to deal with the slog of motherhood—there were still unpacked boxes from Nevada stacked in the closet—while he pursued his dreams. But he was practically begging to share that slog with her. It had taken her a while to see it, to remember, like picking up a half-finished novel she'd set down ages ago, that the two of them—the four of them—were a story that had been waiting here in Detroit, a story worth finishing. It wouldn't be perfect, it wasn't exactly what she wanted, but it was good enough, it was real.

So when she opened the door and was hit by Lucy's breeze, she was half hoping that she'd see Jamal at the end of her driveway, looking like Levar Burton from Star Trek. But it was only Lucy, hovering back and forth somewhat erratically.

"LOOKING A LITTLE THICK THERE," chirped the drone. Sandra wrinkled her nose.

"Excuse me?"

"TALKING BOUT THAT FAT ASS, BITCH! THIS ONE'S ON THE HOUSE. DEUCES!"

And the blue box ejected something into the driveway.

"Jamal?? What the—Is that you?" But Lucy was already rising. Sandra walked toward the driveway to find a bottle of Lipo-Zapp supplements and a single can of Slim-Fast. She hurled the bottle of pills toward the ascending drone, not getting anywhere near it. She shook her head in disbelief, her tear ducts pumping to life, as the bottle landed in the middle of the street, and diet pills scattered over the sunbaked pavement.

It was an excuse and Annika knew it. She did need a status update from Ulrich Richter, the head of the fulfillment center, on the daily package volume and the number of full-time hires—essential PR info—but she could have acquired that over e-mail. And yet here she was, touring the fulfillment center with Rick-Rick, who, as expected, had launched into a long, pointless story, this time about his blind corgi chewing up an old pair of shoes he was going to throw out anyway, not because they were too worn to walk in, but rather because of unpleasant emotional associations surrounding their purchase in Yokohama the day before attending the 2002 World Cup final, where his beloved Germany suffered a crushing defeat in the 90th minute when—Annika shoved all that in a mind-cabinet as she saw Ellis at his pick station. She interrupted Rick-Rick, speaking loud enough so Ellis could hear.

"Fascinating," Annika said. "I've got to run to the ladies' room. I'll meet you back at your office in ten." She made eyes at Ellis, then strode off.

Ellis' hands slowed. Was she really here for that? Maybe she just wanted to talk. Whichever it was, he had to find out. Ellis kicked into high gear and started picking faster—books and wart cream and armpit hair...extensions?—if he could bump his rate up now, he could afford a quick bathroom break and hopefully avoid an infraction point.

Ellis hustled to the men's room, bent down and looked under the stall doors. Heels. He'd guessed right. He tapped softly on the door, it opened, and she pulled him in and stuck her tongue in his mouth.

Ellis pulled back. "You think you can just come by whenever and I'll break you off?"

"You know it," she said, leaning in and kissing him again.

Ellis slid a hand down the back of her skirt as she went at his neck. After a moment, he pulled back again. "But only if no one knows about it."

"Ellis, c'mon."

He'd never had a problem with being kept a secret from strict parents or jealous boyfriends. This was different. He wasn't a threat here, just a loser.

She pressed herself against him, and something shifted in his horn-dog brain: an unfamiliar circuit had been activated.

"You know what? Nah. I ain't your little side piece."

No one had ever said *that* to her before. Annika was at once aware of many things: the ID card dangling around Ellis' neck, the ambient noise of the warehouse, the fact that he knew, just as well as she had, how far beneath, or at least, outside her range of "dateable" he was.

"I'm…I'm sorry. I wasn't thinking."

"I ain't mad. I know I'm the least of your problems right now. But—"

"No, you deserve better."

"I said I ain't mad. Just, if you're gonna be with me, you gotta respect me." He chuckled. He'd sure as shit never said *that* to anyone before.

"I like you, I do," she said.

"So…"

This would be so much easier if he were dumb and hot, or even a bit of jerk. But he wasn't. He was nice, and he was smarter than he gave himself credit for. "I should go," Annika said. "Can you check… see if the coast is clear?"

Ellis did, and Annika gave him a sad, embarrassed smile as she ducked out. He listened to the sound of her heels click away and dissolve into the hum of the Fulfillment Center, then he washed his face, doing a mental post-game analysis: based on today's performance, what were his future prospects—of sex, of love? How strange. He had no fucking clue. Outside the bathroom, he checked the wall clock. Great. He'd just earned himself a nice fat infraction point.

21

"I don't want to be late for class," Ellis said, when Jamal asked him for yet another favor. He needed this UAV factory certification more than anything else in his life right now. Time was, he would have taken any excuse to skip. But Jamal had begged and promised to pull strings if there was an issue. And it was hard to say no to being called in as muscle.

Ellis parked his Charger down the block from the house.

"Okay, what's the plan?" Jamal said.

"Nigga, you the one wanted to squad up. You ain't got no plan?"

"I don't know. We go talk to her and you just…look big."

"Man, your dog is drooling all over my car."

"Sorry," Jamal said, reaching back and wiping the seat with Barry's towel.

"Ah forget it. Let's do this."

They walked up to the Prince residence, Jamal's head in bird-alertness mode, Ellis doing his gorilla-walk. They knocked on the door and as they stood there waiting, the impending failure of this plan knocked around inside Jamal's skull like an angry bee trapped in a hot car. Was she suddenly going to crack just because Ellis was standing next to him, grinding his fist into his palm? But what the hell else was he going to do? He had to solve this, fast. There had been sightings over the weekend, so said a few angry Twitter users. A drone with googly eyes harassing people. Could this girl really have figured out how to fly the damn thing? Footsteps from inside. Game face.

The door creaked open, and there was the old man. "You again," he said. "And who's this dumbbell?"

"Sorry to bother you, sir," Jamal said, trying to keep acid from creeping into his voice. "We think your granddaughter may have taken something that doesn't belong to her."

"They turned my house upside down, didn't find nothing. So why don't y'all move along and stop bothering this family. Hmm?"

"We know she took it," Ellis said, leaning towards the old man, neck veins bulging.

"We just want it back," Jamal said. "That's it."

Luther wiped his cokebottle glasses on his shirt. Piper had been pressing him hard not to take the plea deal, to fight his felony charge in court, and now here she was committing crimes of her own, if these Amazon thugs were to be believed. He'd noticed her going over to visit Richie quite a bit more than usual the last few days. He sighed. It felt wrong, like selling her out, but Piper was walking toward a cliff edge and he couldn't bear to see her fall.

"You don't know squat," Luther said. "Especially bout my grand-daughter. She got nothing to do with this. But you might find what you're looking for next door."

The Lincoln Street Art Park was a grassy lot surrounded by graffiti murals and filled with sculptures made from found junk, including a truck-sized brontosaurus. Inside a repurposed shipping container on the property, Otto Slice taught summer art classes to high school kids. A few boys were leaving as Piper walked up, and they put on surly faces.

She'd texted Otto earlier with her idea for a hashtag to use in the next Goldman Stackz video, requesting another custom piece, and he hadn't been thrilled. She was going to have to work her charm in person. And if she could get him on board, she might be able to tap into his network—he knew graffiti artists all over the country—and spread this idea, through paint and paste, beyond Detroit: the more places the hashtag popped up physically, the more coverage it would get on social media; with the right boost to kick it off, the two forms of promotion would feed into each other.

She found Otto inside, flipping through his sketch book, listening to some techno. The interior walls of the container were covered in newspaper clippings from decades back—important events from Detroit's past. "Otto. What up doe?"

He gave her a sad smile, his blue eyes deep and gauzy. Earlier that morning he'd visited his mother. She didn't have long. Her mind was somewhere just out of reach, but she'd occasionally grab hold of it long enough to utter something decipherable like, "I like the black doctor, he's friendly. Smart, too." Her best old-person attempt at progressivism. Her heart was in the right place, but words like that built up a wall around your heart every time you said them. It made him sad, not for her, but for the country, for in those moments he saw America like that—demented half the time, its heart aimed in the right direction, but walled off by its own bad habits of language. "Rough times," Otto said. "Mom's in hospice."

"Damn. I'm sorry."

"Eh, she's ninety-seven. Been a long time coming. And one good thing about hospice: packed with all flavors of Detroiters. Not just vanilla. Death, the great equalizer, right?"

Otto was trying to lighten the mood, but it only made Piper feel crass coming here for her own stupid project.

"We gotta get you some new music, O."

"Yeah, you probably never heard of Derrick May. One of the founders of Detroit Techno."

"AKA: Stuff White People Like," she said with a laugh.

"You'd think that, but you'd be wrong. Back in the late '80s, it was the black intelligentsia and the gay community filling these techno clubs. But, I know you didn't come here to talk music," he said. "You're here to convince me."

"It's a good idea, yo. People gon be pissed."

"I know that's what you're going for. But I don't like it. It's too incendiary. Too divisive. Think about Black Lives Matter. That idea's framed in positive terms."

"Yeah, but it still about getting people angry that cops keep shooting black people. I mean, fuck, just last week was Philip Klyde."

Otto shook his head and turned off the music. "There's a lot of broken shit in society," he said. "But how or why shit broke, that doesn't matter so much. What matters is how we respond, right? Do we embrace blame, or do push past 'rightness' and 'wrongness' into 'loveness'?"

"Loveness?" Piper laughed.

Otto nodded.

"But it doesn't have to be just one, though. Can't have Martin without Malcolm, right? Togetherness, love, that ain't me. That was my sister."

"Yeah, she was something."

"But that's not my skill, it ain't where my heart is. Let someone else do the love shit. Me, I'm a take a stick, shove it in a beehive, and shake it around. See what happens. You don't think the world needs that?"

"Sure, *sometimes*, but—"

"C'mon, Otto. Please?"

Otto laughed. "Shake the beehive, huh? What're you thinking?"

#NOFLYZONE had racked up close to three million views, but it had been a slow build. She needed something that would hit nation-wide, overnight. Their whole project was still anchored in Detroit. But Amazon was destroying small businesses and automating jobs away across the US. And soon enough, they might have drones over the entire continent. So how did you get other cities to join in, if not through social media? "You know any graf writers in Chicago?" Piper asked.

"Yeah, I know POSE pretty well."

"What about New York?"

"Oh, there's a ton in New York. I've known Lady Pink for thirty years."

"OK, this is gonna work, I think. LA? New Orleans? Ooh, what about Seattle?"

"Well, There's Revok in LA—though he's pissed at me. Then let's see, TARD in New Orleans—does the snaggle toothed faces. Though the Gray Ghost is down there, Fred Radtke, you know him? This ass who paints over all the graffiti in New Orleans with gray splotches. And Seattle, Seattle…I don't think I—oh wait, TRED and PeanutLincoln are out there. Those guys are nuts."

"Otto, you gotta do this for me. You gotta."

"What exactly are we talking here?"

"You design the main mural for the hashtag. Like a…a template. Then we get like twenty writers in twenty cities to throw up a piece overnight, the same night, all with the same hashtag. The next morning, we put out the video on RNKR, Twitter, YouTube, and that shit will EXPLODE!"

"A crowd-sourced ad campaign. Hah!"

"Yeah, and if you know these dudes well enough, get em to hustle other kids in their cities to do it, too. Get like five bombs up in each city!"

"But it's not just about knowing these guys," Otto said. "You're talking about cats who don't follow rules, almost by definition. Hard crowd to organize."

Piper paced the width of the storage container. There was a way to frame this that would sell it. Why did it matter to graffiti writers, specifically? "You see that Free Press story, though?" Piper asked. "DPD been asking Amazon for drone footage."

"I did."

"They trying to stop that rape gang and shit, right? But if Amazon says yes, you think it's gon stop there? That's eyes in the sky, everywhere, all the time. You know what that is? That's the death of graffiti. They'll do it, Otto, you just gotta ask the right way."

Otto scrunched up his mouth, his eyes wandering over the newspaper clippings on the walls, coming to rest on an old image of Hazen Pingree, Detroit's famed four-term mayor from the 1890s, who'd fought against corporate corruption. Otto sighed, then said, "Damnit."

"What?"

"I knew you'd do something big, I just didn't think I'd be helping you." He laughed. "Alright. Let's whack the beehive, huh?"

"Hello? Anybody home?" Jamal called through the screen door. From the little he could see inside, the house was a wreck—a stairwell with no railing, a tipped over chair, random garbage on the floor, the smell of rank sweat. Ellis stood behind him, arms crossed. Jamal knocked gingerly on the edge of the screen door. "Hello?"

Ellis pushed in front of him, pulled open the door and peeked inside. Should they just walk in? Ellis and Jamal, back sneaking through smelly vacants, just like old times? "Police!" Ellis yelled. "Come on out!"

Jamal hit him in the arm. Ellis shrugged. Eyeballs! Jamal jumped back. The guy had come out of nowhere: bald with a ring of bristly gray-black hair, face like dried leather, the skin over his breastbone stretched like a shrunken t-shirt. "*Y'all ain't no police now ain't no police come up in here and fuck with me the fuck y'all want?*"

"Sorry to disturb you," Jamal said. "We're looking for a missing UAV."

The guy's eyes bulged even further out.

"A drone," Ellis said over Jamal's shoulder.

"We were told that this...uh, drone, might be in your house. Do you know anything...about that?"

The guy grunted, walked back into his house and let the screen door shut behind him.

"You think he's gonna come back?" Jamal said.

A loud clatter from deeper inside. Ellis nodded reassuringly.

The old man didn't just come back, he came marching back with a giant butcher knife and a hammer. Jamal tripped backward into Ellis, and they both stumbled down the steps, almost eating it.

"*YOU WANNA DIE YOU WANNA DIE NOW!?*" the man yelled, swinging the hammer in the air. Across the street, a lady with curlers in her hair leaned out her window with a phone to her ear. Crazy Richie at it again.

Officer Cross parked near the Mt. Olivet Cemetery a block south of Seven Mile while Shepard filled out the paperwork for their last stop: this kid Mikey who they picked up about once a week. Known mental. He was actually twenty-eight. Mikey had gone into a rage inside the Marathon gas station a few blocks away. He ran when they saw him, lugging his blubbery self down the road in big bounding steps. Cross chased him down. As usual, once the cuffs were on, Mikey giggled like the whole thing was some kind of game. Which it was, in a way. Each time they asked his mother if she'd petition him for involuntary mental health treatment, and she declined, saying she'd look after him. And so it went. Cross typically kept his head down and plowed forward—nab the bad guys, don't ask questions. But hanging out with Shepard the last few weeks, he'd found himself wondering what it was all for—if they were actually serving the community they patrolled.

"Hey, Shepard," he said. "You think that—"

"I know I am," she said, without looking up.

"Christ, can you let me finish my—"

"It's what you bring to it. Why you think they give us a certain measure of discretion?"

"Okay, but do you think—"

"You got a good heart, mostly. But yeah, you could do better."

The computer console lit up: PRIORITY 2—MNTL, ARMD. Cross took the call, flipped on the lights, and gunned it down Outer Drive. For some reason, calls seemed to come in clusters. You might have a Robbery day or a Domestic Violence day. Today just happened to be a Mental day.

Cross rolled up to the house and parked. There was the mental, pacing on the porch, shirtless and screaming. And armed...dispatch wasn't kidding. Guy was clutching a big, mean looking kitchen knife in one hand, the kind you carve a turkey with, and a hammer in the other.

Shepard walked up to the two guys standing on the sidewalk, a paunchy nerd type and a guy who did too many deadlifts.

"You know this man?" Shepard asked.

"Not exactly," Jamal said, "but—"

"He stole our drone," Ellis said.

"We have reason to believe," Jamal said.

"We'll handle this," Shepard said. "Stay back."

"I CUT YOU UP YOU WANNA DIE C'MON I SLICE YOU UP!"
Cross radioed for backup.

Piper slowed when she saw the squad cars. She parked two doors
down and marched up to find that Amazon douche and his muscly
sidekick standing on the sidewalk watching as four cops stood in
Richie's lawn trying to talk him down. Oh god. Poor Richie. Off his
meds? He was holding a knife. Did they know the drone was in his
basement? Piper shot Darnell a quick text:

> get your ass over here!

She flicked Jamal on the back of the shoulder. "Hey, asshole,
what did you do?"

Jamal startled. "What?"

"How you gon harass my neighbor, though? Seriously? Richie's
fragile."

"You…!" Jamal said. "You stole our damn UAV. Don't even try
to act like this is my fault!"

Ellis stood behind him, arms crossed, chin lifted. Another
squad car rolled up, parked in the street, and two more officers
spilled out.

"I didn't steal shit," Piper said.

Cross and Shepard inched toward the porch, where the mental
was bouncing on his feet in a boxer's fight stance. *"C'MON FIGHT
ME I'M READY TO FIGHT I'M READY TO DIE!"* His left eye was
straining to pop free like a dog fighting its chain. And as if things
weren't complicated enough, another mental waltzed out onto the
porch. This one younger, drooling, eyelids drooping, the ribs on
his bare chest individually countable, his filthy jeans sagging low
enough to expose a thatch of pubes and—could it be?—the base of
the shaft of his dick. Just another day in the 9th. A fourth squad car
pulled up.

"Sir, we just want to talk. If you can put down the hammer and
knife," Cross said to the berserker.

The drooler shambled down the steps to Shepard, got on his
knees, and put his hands behind his head.

"You don't have to do that," Shepard said. "Why don't you just go stand out by the sidewalk, okay?"

The drooler stood up slowly, walked toward the sidewalk, then got back down on his knees and put his hands behind his head again. Dolores from across the street came over and patted him on the shoulder. "It's okay," she said. "You ain't in trouble, boy."

"I'M READY I'M READY TO GO TO DIE I CUT YOU UP!"

"Any y'all got a riot shield?" Shepard called back. A few of the cops popped their trunks and shook their heads.

"Staties got tasers," Cross said. "I'll call."

Shepard nodded and began inching up to the porch, getting dangerously close to the mental's flailing reach, way inside the Department's 21-foot rule.

"I get that you're mad," Jamal said. "But look—"

"You can eat a dick," Piper said. "And you—" turning toward Ellis, "eat a bigger dick."

Ellis loomed over her, his chest inflating with pent up air—fight fuel.

"What you gon do? Punch me, right here, front of the hook? Get the fuck outa here."

"Yeah, Ell, just, let me talk to her."

"Whatever," Ellis said, and he strolled back towards his car.

"That's right! That's right!" Piper yelled after him.

Jamal rolled his eyes. "Look," he said again. "This doesn't have to be a thing. We just want the UAV back. Your grandpa told us to—"

"Oh, you harassing my gramps now, too!?"

"Nah, you know what's happening? *That's* what's happening," he said, pointing at the porch. "Yeah, I called the cops, because you stole Amazon property. Property we *will* get back. Now you can do the right thing, get that UAV, calm down the neighbor, pull the plug on this whole situation."

"I told you I didn't steal shit."

"That guy's gonna get his ass kicked because of you, you watch."

As Shepherd approached, the mental ducked inside and locked the door, then immediately poked his head and his knife out through an adjacent window. Cross advanced up behind her. Shepard was a known Mental Whisperer, and Cross gave her space while she laid it on thick.

"Come on out, now, no one needs to get hurt, we just wanna talk to you."

"*I SLICE YOU UP!*"

"No one's gonna take your knife away, but why don't we just set it down for a second and we can talk? There somebody that look after you, sir? A relative? Someone we can call on the phone?"

The guy just moved his head back and forth, like a starved pit bull eyeing a stranger with a pork chop. Every cop had her own idea about good policing. Cross thought the faster he could run, the more he could whip out the cuffs. Well, he was young. He thought Shepard had some magic touch, but it was only patience. That's the job, showing up at a bad time, seeing people at their worst. It was a lot like gardening—you had to water, and fertilize, and sometimes you had to get down on your knees and pluck the aphids off your lettuce, one by one, and if you had the patience for that, hopefully you wouldn't have to throw out a whole head. It wasn't a battle you could ever win. Only one you could manage.

A crowd was gathering across the street. It wasn't the first time the cops had been here. But this was an eight-cop affair, with four cruisers parked haphazardly on the street, forming a kind of cop-car maze.

And then—you can't make this up—a ghetto-ass ice cream truck, rattling its tinny song, rolled up the street: a rusting steel cage on tiny wheels advertising cartoon-themed popsicles with peeling stickers. Officer Tannin left the yard and waved for the truck to turn around and go somewhere else while Shepard kept calm in front of the mental, who was yelling, "*COME ON NOW YOU WANNA DIE PIG HEAD ON A STICK PIG C'MON!*" The ice cream truck, undeterred, began maneuvering through the gauntlet of cop cars. Only in Detroit. Tannin marched up and started yelling at the driver.

"This ain't just theft," Jamal said. "It's espionage."

"Oh, fuck off!" Piper said.

"You think I'm joking? That UAV is proprietary technology."

Piper spied Darnell creeping up from behind Jamal. She whipped out her phone. "You know what, I'm a film this shit," Piper said, but she didn't activate her camera, she texted Darnell:

> Sneak through the backyard. Get it ready to fly. Meet me in the car.

Darnell paused, whipped out his phone, then reversed course and ducked behind Piper's house.

"Yeah, just wait till the feds come knocking," Jamal said.

Piper ignored him and started filming.

The ice cream truck was rolling up onto the curb to maneuver around the cop cars, *The Entertainer* still blaring from its speakers. The mental was riveted, poking his head out the open window, the butcher knife still in hand.

"Oh, you want some ice cream?" Shepard said. "If you put the knife down, you can have some ice cream."

The truck was finally past the cop-car logjam and about to drive off. Cross shouted to Tannin. "Wait! Stop it. Get some ice cream!"

Another squad car arrived and the LT stepped out, put his hands on his hips, and surveyed the chaos with a smile, his protruding belly a statement of its own.

Tannin ran up to Cross with a bomb pop. He unwrapped it and held it toward the mental. Shepard and Cross were both within feet of the open window now. The mental jabbed his knife out. Cross gripped his nightstick. Some dog was barking like mad from a parked car.

"Put down the knife and you can have it," Shepard said.

The mental was staring hard at the popsicle, dripping onto the porch, tasting it with his eyes. He looked down at the sill like he was going to put a leg through the window. Cross moved the popsicle back, trying to get him onto the porch. This mental was more twitchy than the average. His eyes kept moving from the bomb pop to the service weapon still holstered on Shepard's hip. She saw it, too, and placed her hand over the grip.

Just as the tableau on the porch froze, Piper and Jamal heard that unmistakable hum and looked up to see Lucy rising over the house. Piper's head shot back and forth between the drone, the porch, and Darnell, who was leaning out of the window of the parked Granada. Jamal looked at Lucy, then at the cops on the lawn. The cops on the lawn looked at Lucy, then, since Lucy wasn't the one with the knife, looked back at the porch. Jamal looked back at Piper. Piper saw Darnell's friend Kyle walking down the sidewalk. She bolted. "Film this shit!" she blurted as she raced past him to the Granada. She hopped in, kicked into gear, and drove south on Clarion, Lucy following a hundred feet up, Darnell leaning out the window with a radio controller.

Jamal stared in disbelief. Holy shit! Darnell had hacked into the flight control code. Unbelievable. Jamal jumped into Ellis's Charger, Barry barking and leaping in the back seat. Ellis did a jerky three-point turn as Jamal strapped on his goggles and readied his own controller. No way was he getting this close and letting Lucy slip away. Those punks had another thing coming: Jamal Fucking Dent.

Ellis peeled down Clarion after the Granada, whipping around the corner at Georgia, fishtailing onto the unkempt grass near a vacant lot before veering back onto the road, accelerating up to forty, then fifty. Neptune Frost was speeding west toward Hamtramck, but Jamal couldn't see her car—his eyes were now Lucy's eyes, but Darnell had control of her. He'd figured out the control frequency and his remote was strong enough to keep Jamal's from taking over the signal.

"Get closer!"

"I'm just about ramming the bitch, dude."

"Not the car, get closer to the *drone*." Jamal tightened the head strap of his FPV goggles and leaned out the window, thrusting the controller out in the wind to try to hook the signal. "It's in front of us, right?"

They flew past burned out houses and small brick Baptist churches, blowing through stop signs on the suburban street. Ellis ducked down to get a better look. "Hold on—yeah." There it was, out in front of the Granada. Ellis floored it and swerved left to pass, then realized that Jamal was leaning way too far out the window. He pulled left, nearly throwing Jamal out of the car, then shot his hand out to grab his friend's shirt, swerving back to the right.

Piper was ducked down herself, trying to keep a bead on Lucy, when Jamal's big goggled face thunked into her driver side mirror. She took a hand off the wheel and wonked him on the head. The Charger bolted past, and Piper was hit with a rope of drool from the bulldog hanging out the back window, its tongue whipping in the wind like a pink, disgusting flag.

"Jesus, fuck, nigga!" Jamal yelled.

"Sorry, sorry." They crossed Van Dyke, narrowly missing a pickup, swerving a quick left then right to stay on Georgia, passing a shuttered high school. The Granada was right behind them as they cruised past a trucking facility, veering around a pile of wet asphalt. Plastic bags wavered on the barbed wire fence.

Jamal jammed the goggles back over his eyes. This was personal now. This was some Panjwai shit. He wasn't going to flinch, and he wasn't going to leave Lucy behind. He had a strong stomach for air sickness and was basically fearless when it came to moving at high speeds, so as long as Ellis refrained from shearing his head off on a light pole, he'd keep his eyes matched up with Lucy's and his hands on the remote, angling it for a better purchase, his thumbs indented on the small metal spikes of the control sticks. He kept the rudder stick on a roll to the right, waiting for Ellis to get close enough. Georgia came to a T at Vincent, and they whipped left, nearly slamming into a concrete retaining wall, swerved right again, and as they charged toward Conant Ave, a four-lane arterial, Lucy finally pitched right.

"I got her, I got her!"

"Should I stop?"

"Turn right, turn right!"

"Oh, no," Darnell said. "I'm losing it!"

"What do you mean losing it? Losing it how?"

"He's got a controller too, and they're closer now! You gotta pass him. Get closer."

"I'm hella close already, you wanna crash?"

"Not closer to the car, closer to the *drone*."

They sped under an overpass coming into Hamtramck, signs in

Arabic, the Bustan Café, Al-Ameera Foods, Hookah and Tobacco, Islamic gifts.

Ellis looked up, saw a drone cutting sharp left, then swerved the Charger down a side street.

"Whoa, whoa, where you going?!" Jamal yelled.

"Following the drone!"

"No—that's a different drone, that's a delivery!"

Ellis slammed on the brakes and backed into the main road, braking again when another car cruised past, laying on the horn. The Granada was ahead of them again. Jamal tried banking Lucy hard left to bring her back around, but it was already too late—his goggled view screen pitched back to the right. Darnell was in control again. The Charger's engine roared as Ellis pulled a quick three point turn and zoomed after them. They were pushing fifty, and Hamtramck definitely had more cops per square mile than the eastside. The traffic was getting thicker. The Bangladeshi shops gave way to Polish community centers. Fortunately, they were now heading in a useful direction.

"Okay, there's a spot nearby I can bring Lucy down. Just need to get her there," Jamal said. They'd caught up with the Granada, which had slowed to the speed of traffic. A young white woman jogged down the street in yoga pants and neon running shoes.

"What spot?" Ellis asked.

"We call em bivouacs. They're little safe houses for UAVs. In case of weather or a hardware malfunction, we can fly the drones near the bivouac, and they automatically shut off comms and land inside."

"So, it's like a tractor beam?"

"No, but, yeah."

"What?"

"Just, get them to turn at Caniff. At the light."

The Charger was still behind them. Piper couldn't shake them, and thinking she might have to give it up, she pulled out her phone, preparing to record. If they were going to confiscate the drone, she could at least get footage of these corporate assholes being corporate assholes. Then as she sped into the intersection at Caniff, the

Charger cut her off—that fat nerd oreo and his dog both hanging out the window, forcing Piper to swing right.

"Perfect, keep her headed east," Jamal said. "Just a few more blocks. When I say, you gotta punch it and get me right under Lucy. Only need a second."

"There's fucking traffic here!"

"I don't know, get up on the sidewalk!"

"And pancake some old Polish lady with a walker!?"

"If you have to!"

"You gon bail me out again!?"

"Three, two, okay now, go!"

Ellis found a hole in the oncoming traffic and gunned it. Jamal raised the controller over his head, a receiver leaping for a catch in the end zone.

Jamal punched the emergency land button like some old arcade game where the main skill was to jam the fire button as fast as possible. For several long moments, Lucy was unresponsive, staying straight and then beginning to bank left as the kid tried to get her back over the Granada. He dimly heard a chorus of horns over Neptune's curses. And then: the view straightened out as Lucy accelerated in a diagonal toward the bivouac site, a small building with "Amazon Prime Air—D3" stenciled on the roof. Jamal watched the roof get bigger and bigger until a trap door opened, and Lucy dropped inside. She was home. Jamal threw the controller at his feet, lifted his goggles, leaned as far out the window as he could, and gave Neptune Frost a well-deserved double bird.

By the time Piper pulled back onto Clarion, her pulse had slowed, but it immediately jumped again when she saw the scene. There were six cop cars now, plus an ambulance. Darnell looked at her nervously. "Should we turn around?" he said.

"If they're gonna arrest us, they'll do it now, or they'll do it later. I don't got nowhere else to stay anyway."

Piper parked a few houses down. The cooling engine popped and creaked, and she opened and shut the door with a muffled metallic *thunk*. Just as she stepped into her driveway, she noticed Kyle walking across the lawn toward her, his eyes fixed on the grass. A fog lifted from her brain as she looked from the boys to the ambulance still over at Richie's house.

"Oh, shit."

Kyle started relaying what had happened. Piper could barely listen. Something about how Richie dropped the knife, but then the cops dropped the popsicle, and Richie jumped at the female cop, and then...Kyle was holding up his phone. He had a video. Piper looked over to the porch. There a was white lump at the foot of the steps. A sheet covering something. Oh god. She couldn't even. "I got it," Kyle said. "I got it." Piper took his phone and hit play. For some reason, it was easier to watch through this five-inch screen than to look at the scene still playing out a dozen yards away.

> The knife clatters to the porch. Police crowding the view. An officer drops the popsicle. Richie lunges at the female cop. Screams. A gun shot! The camera shakes. Richie is on the ground. The white cop is holding his pistol. Cops racing in. Heavy breathing, a wordless whimper from behind the camera.

Piper closed her eyes. Was this what she'd gambled on? Had she put money on this square right here? An innocent man, shot, dead. A man her grandfather had known and helped all these years, since that riot so long ago. Because she'd got him involved. Shot by the cops, not her. Oh god. Richie. She felt her stomach rising. But not at the image of his body, at the fact of his death, but at a small but growing thought in the back of her mind, a thought that sickened her the more she acknowledged it: here was a black body, and here was a video of it. Was it wrong to use this, would she be trading Richie's life for fucking publicity? But keeping it quiet wouldn't bring him back, it wouldn't fix anything. She looked to her own porch and saw Gramps standing there, his glasses in one hand, the other hand pressed against his eyelids. She handed Kyle his phone back. "Send me that video," she said softly. And she went to her grandfather.

22

It was Monday night, and Smiles Cocktail Lounge was mostly empty—just a few regulars and the quiet hum of the TV, tuned to some reality show called *Rags to Riches*, where bums are plucked off the street, dressed up as billionaire CEOs, and tossed into corporate boardrooms and exclusive restaurants. Misha Wallace was wiping off the bar and shaking her head at poor Philadelphia Joe, who'd just puked in his duck confit, when she heard the door open. There was her boy, and…

"My god, is that little Jamal Dent?!" she said.

Jamal gave her a shaky hug, adrenaline still coursing through his veins. "Good to see you, Mrs. Wallace."

"Was about to ask how you been, but I can tell you need a drink. What're you two having?" She reached up and rubbed Ellis' shoulder.

"Tanqueray tonic?" Ellis said.

His mom winked, and they sat down in a plush red booth lit by the soft yellow light of a paper globe lamp from *Ikea*.

"Seriously though," Jamal said. "I'm sick of being the whipping boy for everyone's personal moral crusade. Same shit as in the Air Force. People going off about drones hitting terrorists, as if somehow it'd be different if there's a dude in the cockpit. Man, dead is dead, whether it's a drone or a fucking plane. Ditto with the delivery stuff. It doesn't get more innocuous than that, right?"

"Wait, than what?" Ellis asked.

"Than a little drone cruising by with a package. I mean, these are delivery bots, dude. They're like the little gopher carts in the death star. You'd think people would think they're cute."

"Gopher carts?" Ellis said.

Jamal sighed. On the TV, Philadelphia Joe, shaking with the DTs, voted his proxy shares at a Nabisco board meeting.

Ellis' mom came by with their drinks, and a water bowl for Barry, who lay under the table.

Jamal took a long, slow drink, draining half the glass, the lime bobbing underneath his nose like some surreal mustache.

"Listen, man," Ellis said. "I need some advice."

"Shoot."

He searched Jamal's face for any sign of how awkward this was going to be. Jamal was the only person Ellis knew who might actually have some wisdom about how to get Annika back. "So…I been seeing this chick," Ellis said.

"What a surprise," Jamal said.

"Yeah, right, but you know this one."

"Nigga, if you even say what I think you're gonna say."

Ellis laughed nervously. "Who do you think I'm gonna say?"

Jamal's eyeballs waxed insane.

"*Sandra?* Nigga, please. I'm not a straight up asshole. You tripping. I'm talking about Nik. At Amazon."

"Annika *Dahl*, my fucking *boss*?"

"She's your boss?"

"Well, it's not that straightforward, but she's one step away from the S-Team. Jesus man, you're just…you know what? I ain't even mad."

Ellis glanced at the TV, where a horrified masseuse at Clinique Tribeca kneaded the cyst-riddled back of old Philly Joe. "Really? You ain't mad?"

"I mean. It's a little annoying."

"Annoying?"

"Dude, this chick is pulling six figures. And she still goes for the high school jock?"

Ellis flicked his glass with his index finger; it made a loud *ping*. "You're saying she's bottom feeding."

"Look, I get it when chicks are young and nobody's doing much, and so they go for the fly dudes. But isn't there some point where they..."

"Where they what?"

"Where they prioritize guys with *jobs*? Shit."

"I have a job."

Jamal rolled his eyes.

"Fuck you, nigga, I *have* a job."

"Okay, alright, alright."

"You're saying she's bottom feeding."

"I'm not saying that. All I'm saying is, it would be nice if...if all the hard work I've done translated into...you know?"

"What, booty? Thought you wanted Sandra back."

"I do, but, still. You *know* what I mean."

Ellis caught his mom's eye and nodded for two more. "Yeah, I know."

"I live in a castle."

That got them laughing.

"Yeah, nigga, you do live in a castle."

"A fucking *castle*."

"But, hey, I wanted to ask you. She's calling it off."

"What happened?"

"She found out I worked at the warehouse and freaked."

"You didn't tell her?" Jamal rubbed Barry's noggin under the table.

"How could I? Girl like her would never go for a scrub like me."

"I don't know. Just move on? It's not like you got a shortage of—"

"But I really like her. She's way smarter than me. And she gets after it."

"Well maybe you shouldn't have kept things from her, then. It's like you're embarrassed. That's not exactly...baller, right?"

"Yeah, you right," Ellis said with a sigh.

Mom came back with another two G&Ts. She sat in the booth next to Ellis. "You boys been passing that sad face back and forth. What's the matter?"

"Girls," Jamal said.

On the TV, Philly Joe rummaged through a trashcan at the 18th tee, pulling out a bottle of MGD with a few swigs of beer left. "It's our lucky day!" he said, handing it to his mortified caddy.

Outside, three hooded figures scoped out the front of Smiles Cocktail Lounge.

"You can get your brother's car, right?" Sean said.

"Yeah, I told you, nigga," said Clevester. "On Thursday. That's his day off."

"Alright, so you park behind the Metro PCS, right? After we get the cash, we run out the back through the kitchen."

"Alright, but ain't we skipping over like, the most important shit?" Clevester said. "Like, how do we get the cash?"

"Nigga, is you stupid? You asking why niggas do shit when they got a gun in they face?" Sean held his index finger up to Clevester's temple.

Clevester swatted it away. "Yeah, yeah."

"Then we bomb east on Eight Mile," D said.

"Nah, nigga. We gotta do what they least expect, like Chips said."

"He ain't say that."

"Whatever, I'm saying it. We head west, out to Farmington or some shit."

"You trying to pick up some white bitches?" Demetreus said, laughing.

"You think the hook come looking for niggas in Farmington? My point exactly. We just lay low for a minute, then roll back east when the heat die down."

The door to Smiles Cocktail lounge swung open, and a bulldog trotted out.

"Keep walking," Sean whispered.

Jamal dialed Nik as they walked out to the car. Ellis cocked his head ever so slightly. The night was humid, traffic on Eight Mile was light, and though the sky was filled with more drones than ever, they were far enough up that it was quiet below—just a couple kids walking off toward the Chinese restaurant.

"Yeah, we got Lucy…Smooth? No, but it's fine…Just a friend. Actually," Jamal glanced at Ellis. "I'm with Ellis…Yeah, since grade school…He wants to see you." Ellis was shaking his head violently and mouthing the word *no*. Jamal smiled. "Yeah, he said he can't stop thinking about you…Anyway, I set the audio to record to internal memory when they stole her…yeah, good chance I think…okay, b—" He turned to Ellis. "She always hangs up before I can even say bye."

"I hate you," Ellis said as they got in the car.

"Yeah, you'll thank me," Jamal said.

Demetreus sat in the back of the No. 29, heading south on Linwood, leaning his head against the window, watching the churches and liquor stores and gas stations pass, imagining that they'd already done the job, that it went down clean, and word filtered out at Denby that they pulled off some real shit, details unknown, and then he could hang up his jersey and declare his gunpoint robbery days done, pour one out to those they'd lost, and then he'd decide, his adulthood glowingly achieved, to retire from the street life and either try getting a job at an auto body or maybe even the new Amazon place. He pulled the yellow cord a few blocks from Collingwood and sauntered out. Durfee Elementary was a few blocks away. He'd promised his Aunt Camille that he'd meet his cousin Darby—she was only five—and walk her home.

Nina Dent sat on a bench near the main entrance of Durfee Elementary wearing a purple backpack nearly as big as she was, staring down at her tablet. Other kids and their parents filtered out of the school into the afternoon heat. Nina looked up toward the parking lot as a car pulled in. Not Mom.

Demetreus walked up through a squad of little kids to the front of the school, where a teacher sat on a plastic chair under a banner that read, "Detroit Growing Summer Program."

"Yo, first grade class out yet?" he asked.

"Soon, honey. Five minutes."

Demetreus sat down on a bench next to a little girl, maybe a year younger than Darby, playing on a tablet. The girl looked up.

"Hey, what's up," he said.

"Do you play Hungry Hippos?" the girl asked.

"Hungry Hippos?"

"It's a game."

"Oh yeah? How do you play?"

Nina loaded up the game and showed him how to tap the screen to have his hippo gobble up the food floating in the pool. "You're the blue hippo," she said. "I'm the green one. The green one is my favorite. Ready?" They poised their fingers on opposite sides of the tablet, then, when the timer started, began tapping madly, their hippos chomping away. A merciful breeze floated over the school parking lot, causing an old Faygo can to roll over the asphalt with a gritty metallic scrape. Nina's pigtails shook as her head twisted and bobbed with the exertions of her fingers, as if really tapping hard on the screen would cause her voracious hippo to leap with greater zeal.

Sandra left the car idling in the parking lot, Eve buckled into her booster seat. There was some man, some teenager leaning over Nina on the bench. "Nina," she called. Her daughter looked up, then back down at the tablet. "Okay," she said, but she kept tapping the screen. The teen boy glanced at her, too, and took his hand away. "I win!" Nina shouted. "Sorry," the boy said as Sandra approached. "We just playing Hungry Hippos." He offered a bashful smile.

"C'mon, Nina," Sandra said, and Nina leapt off the bench and took her mother's hand, but she turned back to Demetreus and waved at him. "Bye!" she said. "You can be the green hippo next time!"

Demetreus waved back at her. The girl's mom smiled at him just as his cousin Darby walked up and tugged on his long white t-shirt.

Just after midnight, at the corner of Outer Drive and Gratiot, only a few blocks from the Amazon Industrial campus, on the side of a two-story brick building that once housed a beauty salon advertising "100% human hair," Otto Slice shook a can of Montana Gold spray paint—low pressure, quick drying, superb line quality. He was used to working in the dark. He sprayed two precise vertical lines of white paint—the edges of a column. He'd drafted a handful of design templates to send out to his contacts—nothing too concrete, they were all talented (and ego-driven) enough to give it their own spin. Forty years on the scene, he'd done a lot of favors and hadn't called in a single one. He was blowing his load with this stunt, but he always had a soft spot for firebrands like Neptune Frost. And she'd been right, the threat of aerial surveillance to graffiti as an art form had been enough to get a dozen prominent graf writers on board. Otto painted another column on the opposite end of the wall, then the triangular pediment above: the outlines of a stately marble bank began taking shape.

In Chicago, POSE swept back his blond, paint-flecked hair, took in the hashtag he'd just emblazoned on the brick wall, then switched nozzles on a can of Ironlak, and began outlining a series of disembodied black hands underneath the words, grasping for bills being blown away by a downward wind. Otto was gonna flip when he saw this shit.

Just east of Boston University, where the B line dips underground heading towards Kenmore Square, Mad Money Mise crouched in the shadows, waiting for the T to pass, looking over a folded printout of the sketch he'd received that morning from Otto Slice. As the T rattled into the tunnel, he hopped back across the tracks to the concrete wall—he was too old for this guerilla shit. Most of them were, Otto included. And any piece here would get covered up in a few days, but not before trainloads of people saw it. He spun his white ball cap backwards, then clutched four cans against his Celtics jersey with his left hand, and began filling in the hashtag—he'd done it in smooth wildstyle, not over-arrowed. More of a Copenhagen vibe. The goal was often to encrypt the piece so only those who spoke the visual language knew what it said, but not this time. Otto had been clear: it had to be legible.

Lady Pink and Otto Slice had been an item for a hot minute back in the '90s. But she could never leave New York, and Detroit had called him home. She'd been surprised to hear from him, with this kind of request no less. Her train-bombing days were long past. She had shit in the Whitney and the Met for fuck's sake. She didn't need to be painting a U-Haul truck parked under an overpass in Queens. But she kept up with the younguns, and she'd been following Neptune Frost for a while. Lady Pink painted the side of the truck with a close-cropped shot of a feminine torso, belly exposed, the skin a dark, purply black, hands turning empty pockets inside out. It took ten cans of Molotow. Now for the hashtag to finish it off.

Nether's mural of Trayvon Martin had lasted quite a while on this particular Baltimore vacant. But just recently, in the wake of the Little Rock riots, some racist asshole had defaced it. Otto had caught him at the perfect time. It wouldn't take long to paste over his own work. He tied a bandana around his face and started rolling wheatpaste on the wall. Within minutes, the new piece was up—a black dollar bill caught on a fishhook.

Agua had been released from the Pennsylvania State Pen just a week ago, and had been itching to paint. And if he owed anybody anything, it was Otto Slice, who'd sent him books on the reg while he was locked up. Philly had never been a mural town—it was all about wicked hand styles. Agua got a few cans of cheap-ass Krylon and starting throwing up quick tags, thirty seconds here, thirty seconds there—by tomorrow morning, this hashtag would be inescapable.

TARD didn't paint much in New Orleans anymore—don't spray where you sleep—and when he did, it was commissioned work, which meant the Gray Ghost—Fred Radtke, the anti-graffiti crusader—couldn't paint over his shit. But Otto was right—Amazon drones were coming to New Orleans soon enough. He'd gone for a twist on one of Otto's designs—throwing up his own trademark, big-toothed, jawless figure, in white, standing at a cash register while an infinite line of black silhouettes, money in hand, stretched back to a vanishing point.

Revok had decided to keep it simple. On a high retaining wall of the LA River, he threw up ten-foot tall letters with cans of black and white Plutonium. Just the hashtag. He and Otto had beef, but this was too good a chance to stir up some shit.

Otto Slice smiled at the pic from POSE, then went back to his own piece. The marble bank front was nearly done—it was detail work from here on out. In the center of the pediment, an abstracted drone logo. And the on the architrave, the following words, painted as if chiseled into stone: COLORED MONEY WELCOME. All it needed after that was the hashtag at the bottom. Otto lit a cigarette when he finished, then checked his messages again—texts from across the country, and from Fel and Malt here in the D, who'd finished their own pieces just minutes before. It was really coming together. If TRED could pull off the Seattle job, they'd be golden. It was a big ask, but the BTM and 3A crews did not give a fuck.

Seattle was tough on graffiti—shit typically got buffed the next day, forcing most writers to paint on authorized walls or in hard to reach spots. But tonight wasn't about throwing up something that would last. It was about making a statement. TRED had rallied twenty dudes with cans and markers and wheatpaste and they were going to hit the new biodomes at Amazon HQ—three conjoined hundred-foot tall glass domes at 7th and Lenora that were just begging to be defaced. If they didn't want to end up in jail, they'd have to be in an out in less than ten minutes. Plenty of time to toss up a few dozen wheatpastes from Otto and to spray that hashtag a hundred times over on the glass panes of the enemy's sanctuary. TRED gave the signal—an actual flare gun—why the fuck not?—and the hood-ied figures raced in from all directions, cans in hand, ball-bearings rattling with their impending triumph.

In the bedroom of his Lake Washington mansion, Jeff Bezos dreamt of first contact with an alien race, moving lucidly through the treaty negotiations—even his dreams were under his control, thanks to his LED lucid-dream-inducing sleep mask—securing whole new worlds to explore, billions of new customers eager to join Amazon Prime Universe.

23

Blackness, blackness with white creeping in, blackness taking shape with a slow zooming out: a face in black, inside an oval, the face of Goldman Stackz, zooming out, his face, black, in the center of a black $100 bill, the bill over a white background dissolving into whiteness. The bass drum kicks as

GOLDMAN STACKZ

stamps onto the screen. The bass drum kicks:

#BLACKMONEYWHITEPOCKETS

Drum roll into a '70s funk shuffle, woodblock popping through the mix, a funk rhythm guitar strumming in joyfully. Pan over a crowded auditorium to a stage where a massive screen shows an Amazon drone buzzing over Detroit. Applause as Goldman Stackz walks on stage in blue jeans, a corporate button-up, collar undone, head shaved, and his face—his face painted a pale peachy white! Pounding piano chords as Goldman raps:

They ain't got much, but they got a lil' bit
And that lil' bit oughta be inside of our pockets
Black gold to fire my rockets (uh)

Eddie Noble sat at the bar top in the Sweetwater Tavern, sipping a glass of *Jameson* and gnawing some hotwings, thinking over the interview he'd just conducted with Thad Burrows of the FAA—Prime Air was closer to getting shut down than anyone realized—when the bartender pulled up a YouTube video on the wall-mounted TV. And there was Goldman Stackz, in *whiteface*, with a lapel mic. He was dressed as Jeff Bezos! Noble dropped his half-eaten wing and whipped out his notepad without even licking his fingers.

> *Every corporation need kindling*
> *Can't sell em books cuz niggas illiterate.*
>
> Goldman throws a Kindle to the ground. On the screen behind, the drone swooping low over a park, black kids tossing around a football.

A young, busty Whitehouse staffer approached President Trump in his sitting room. She held a tablet with the video cued up. "Mr. President? You asked to be notified about any possibilities of…racial unrest."

> *Let's see, what the black man need?*
> *Well, he's a animal, probably need something to eat.*
> *[But he got sharp teeth, best leave him alone!]*
> *That's it! Deliver his kibble by drone!*
>
> On the screen behind Goldman: the drone drops five packs of Newports at the kids' feet, then chirps: *Smoke up, monkeys!*

Trump glanced at the video. "Ehhhhhh, these people," he said. "They don't want to be part of America. Maybe they want to go to some shithole country in Africa. They don't have drone delivery there. They don't have much commerce at all. They've got flies on their eyeballs is what they have."

A phased-out guitar solos in, swelling the mix to anthemic heights as the crowd stomps and sings:

[BLACK MONEY!]
Everything under the sky, you buy from us!
[WHITE POCKETS!]
There can only be one true god in the marketplace!

Goldman points his thumbs chestward, while on screen behind him, the drone drops diet pills for a black mother, her face wrought with rageful sadness, her kids watching from the window.

Sandra Dent threw her phone across the room and buried her leaking eyes in her sleeve.

"What's wrong, Mommy?" Eve said.

Look what you did to your city [your city]
You burned it down, it couldn't turn around
So we're coming to deliver you out of your shitty
Existence—open that ass for our business!

The drone descends to a stoop and tosses fried chicken at the hard-looking dudes on the porch. It chirps: *Eat up, niggers!*

In their retreat mansion in Steamboat Springs, Trey Parker and Matt Stone sat hunched over a laptop, a glass of red wine seeping into the carpet. They didn't care.

"It's like double-reverse minstrelsy."

"What's his name? Goldman Stackz?"

"Shit, we gotta bump up the drone episode."

"How many times you think they'll let us get away with the n-word?"

> *Look at all these fourteen dollar, blue*
> *Collar, factory jobs that we're offering*
> *Betta get em quick'r than we figga how to automate em*
> *All away to raise our profit, while meanwhile every*
> *Customer is sucking on the titty of the god*
> *Of convenience, that's why they call me a genius!*

Riding the 48 towards the U-District with his skateboard tucked between his knees, sixteen-year-old Seattlite Johnny Dott stared at his phone, trying to shut off his growing grin, both for the general rule of always looking cool in case any girls were watching, and for fear that, as a white kid, he wasn't allowed to find this video funny. Was it supposed to be funny?

> *BEZOS! Multiply bread like Jesús!*
> *Ain't here to save yous, here to pave ways*
> *For the gentry, for a cent'ry, every drone is a sentry*
> *here to make the black man send me...*
>
> The whole crowd now at the top of their lungs, arms up in ecstasy:
>
> *[BLACK MONEY!]*
>
> Goldman dancing as the screen behind him displays graffiti murals of the hashtag in New York, Chicago, Atlanta.
>
> *[WHITE POCKETS!]*
>
> In Boston, New Orleans, Los Angeles, Seattle: the glass domes of Amazon's very own HQ covered in the hashtag.

Ta-Nehisi Coates sat in the kitchen of his Paris apartment, bent over a wobbling Eiffel-Maki Sushi Tower—the specialty of the local

Japanese restaurant—the video playing on his tablet. He stopped chewing and began live-tweeting the experience.

Ta-Nehisi Coates
@tanehisicoates

(Follow)

Stackz in whiteface as Bezos. Cognitive dissonance astounding. #BLACKMONEYWHITEPOCKETS

1:55 AM - Aug 30

💬 61   🔁 415   ♡ 1014

Ta-Nehisi Coates
@tanehisicoates

(Follow)

Song triumphant, anthemic, yet title an aggressive indictment. #BLACKMONEYWHITEPOCKETS

1:56 AM - Aug 30

💬 34   🔁 275   ♡ 883

Ta-Nehisi Coates
@tanehisicoates

(Follow)

Whatever this is, it's mind-blowing. Need time to process. #BLACKMONEYWHITEPOCKETS

1:59 AM - Aug 30

💬 17   🔁 86   ♡ 401

The music cuts as Goldman speaks to someone through his Bluetooth headset. "They stole a drone? Well call the darn cops. I don't care what they have to do, just get it back!"

The footage cuts to a shaky cell-phone video:

> Police crowd around a shirtless black man, one of them holding out a popsicle. A knife clatters to the porch. The popsicle drops. The man lunges at a female cop. Screams. A gun shot! The camera shakes. The shirtless man is on the ground. A white cop holds his pistol. Others rush in. Heavy breathing.
>
> Fade to black. Heavy breathing on loop. White letters fading in:
>
> R.I.P. Richie McGown

Annika Dahl bounced nervously on the balls of her feet, staring at the monitor on her standing desk, a pile of tissues on the floor, her hair all crazy. She was breathing through her wide-open mouth. In the last twenty-four hours, her face had exploded in a fury of allergies. This was bad. Extremely bad.

((*bzzzzz*))

Call from a 206 number. Oh, shit, shit.

She gave a nose-clearing honk, tossed the tissue onto the small mountain spilling out her Ikea KNODD wastebasket, then answered.

"Nik, it's Jeff. Tell me you've seen it."

"I just watched it."

"Good. Now explain to me what we're paying you for."

"To manage all aspects of public relations and marketing specific to the Amazon Prime Air project in Detroit, and to plan and implement local and national messaging in order to positively influence public opinion on UAV delivery, which—"

"Now please explain how you allowed this to happen. Because I've never seen this level of negative pushback to any major corporate project, ever. It took Monsanto a decade to provoke this kind of vitriol. *A decade. Monsanto!* Exxon had to cover a Delaware-sized chunk of pristine Alaskan coast with ten thousand tons of crude to make people this mad. As far as I know, we're not dumping oil on baby seals out there. We're just delivering products people want! Including free, repeat, *free aerial delivery of organic…*"

$$((\ bzzzzz\ ))$$

She pulled the phone away from her face. It was Ellis calling. Ellis? He was probably calling about the video, too. Or he wanted to patch things up. And actually, talking to Ellis sounded a whole lot more pleasant than what she was doing now, but she couldn't exactly cut Bezos off mid-rant, and he was still going off at a rapid clip in her ear, and she *hadn't been listening.* She dismissed the call.

"…just makes me wonder what year it is. Is there so much deep-seated race-hatred over there that any major corporate venture results in the CEO being turned into a white-supremacist cartoon? Where's the music videos mocking Dan Gilbert and Mike Illitch! What in god's name is it that we're supposedly doing over there that makes me a *racist*? And that clip at the end, please tell me that has nothing to do with us!"

Annika reached for the tissue box; her face had started to fill up again. She gave a long honk and dropped the tissue on top of Snot Rag Mountain.

"I don't think so," Annika said.

"You don't think? You don't think? Hold on… *What? …Now, yes…*I have to go," Bezos said. "Fix this!"

He hung up and Annika crumpled to the floor. She wanted to cry, to have the right constitution for weeping, but she didn't. She wasn't a weeper. She just felt like trash. She wanted to talk to someone, anyone, Ellis, but she couldn't, not now. "Alexa," she said. "Tell me a joke."

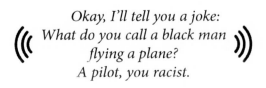

Okay, I'll tell you a joke:
What do you call a black man
flying a plane?
A pilot, you racist.

Had it really said that? Or was she hallucinating? She imagined the dialogue continuing in her head:

That's not funny, Alexa.

I think that's your privelege talking, Annika.

((*bzzzzz*))

It was Jamal. She let it go to voicemail, then listened to the message as soon as he hung up. He'd recovered audio from the stolen UAV. Proof. They could hand it over to the cops and get Piper Prince arrested. That should have buoyed her spirits, but it didn't. Would that even help her? Would it makes Bezos happy? Maybe she'd be better off sitting down and chatting with the girl instead. Maybe it was too late to save her own career no matter what she did. That poor man had been shot by the police, and somehow, it felt like it was her fault.

► ▶❙ ◀× 0:00 / 3:15   CC ⚙ 🔊 ⛶

Goldman Stackz - #BLACKMONEYWHITEPOCKETS

Neptune Frost
✓ Subscribed 24,978

312,156

╋ Add to   ➦ Share   ••• More   👍 28,057 👎 3,559

Published on Aug 29, 2018
Music video by Goldman Stackz performing #BLACKMONEYWHITEPOCKETS. (C) 2018 Sugar House Music

#BLACKMONEYWHITEPOCKETS on iTunes: http://itunes.apple.com/us/album/black$whitepockets/id5782748238
#BLACKMONEYWHITEPOCKETS on Amazon: http://amzn.com/B00715FFGU
RNKR @GoldmanStackz @NeptuneFrost

SHOW MORE

ALL COMMENTS (1,487)

  Add a public comment...

Newest first ▾

 Marcusg2000 2 minutes ago
One of illest ways to off yourself would be to cruise around blasting this song and then when you get to 2:52 crash into a telephone pole at full speed and let the song carry you away.
Reply · 👍 👎

 ROBIN 4 minutes ago
Holy shit, cops shot that black dude. Was that for real?
Reply · 1 👍 👎

 Jay D 7 minutes ago
Count money all day
Reply · 10 👍 👎

 Swagnutz 11 minutes ago
D town baby erbody know we be straight BLASTIN bitchaz drones ERYDAY shit bang so hard. Eastside shit you dont feel this shit youa h8er straight up #NOFLYZONE
Reply · 18 👍 👎

 Matheus Peter 14 minutes ago
This music is so racist, how can black people like it?
Reply · 9 👍 👎

    Darius Garner 18 minutes ago
   +Matheus Peter Are you stupid? The whole point is to comment on how racist the white power holders are.
   Reply · 👍 👎

    BattleChicken 19 minutes ago
   +Darius Garner Seriously? Not everything is about race.
   Reply · 21 👍 👎

   View all 4 replies ▾

 Choco Chapman 15 minutes ago
What good is it to gain the whole world, yet forfeit your soul? YOU SEE WHAT HAPPEN WHEN GOD JUDGES
Reply · 6 👍 👎

 AstroProductions88 22 minutes ago
What good is it to look up videos just to comment that shit?
Reply · 👍 👎

Ray Ray 24 minutes ago
STACKZ IS SO TALENTED BUT THIS SOME RACIST BS, DIDN'T THINK HE WAS WORKING FOR WHITEY
Reply · 3 👍 👎

KatetheWizard 29 minutes ago
"When music hit you can't hit it back." – Marlon James – A Brief History of Seven Killings
Reply · 23 👍 👎

YaBoyNico 31 minutes ago
Oh fuck, that shit at the end is real. Makes me sick, cops still killing unarmed black people.
Reply · 11 👍 👎

Bethany Royal 33 minutes ago
2024 GOD WILL RISE. Goldman for PRESIDENT
Reply · 4 👍 👎

SomeDudeontheTube 35 minutes ago
hah Bezos can rap! Amazon fuckboi.
Reply · 49 👍 👎

Moneywolf 41 minutes ago
Y'all don't even get how many levels this shit is on. Parody, obviously, and Amazon isn't stealing money from
black people, but in the context of the larger system, concentrations of wealth and power perpetuate themselves,
and they are disproportionately held by white americans. But you can't just say that or nobody will listen, so the
genius is to put it in cartoony whiteface. But that final clip shows this isn't a stupid joke. R.I.P Richie McGown.
Reply · 27 👍 👎

Matty Smart 44 minutes ago
He talked over a beat. "Rap."
Reply · 6 👍 👎

Lucifer Oswald 10 minutes ago
Hating ass nigga they everywhere
Reply · 1 👍 👎

DeonM 13 minutes ago
white people are sheep rap was nigga shit now every niggas doin it even british asshole its colors bitch
Reply · 1 👍 👎

SpeedJuice 53 minutes ago
enlightened Black people know the system Haha we made Egypt fool he saying that SOCIETY IS DESIGNED
to put the black $ into white pockets but we should be fighting the gov Not Physically but with our minds
Stackz is a genius
Reply · 28 👍 👎

Show more

IV

24

Behind the Metro PCS off Eight Mile and Chapel, Sean, Demetreus, and Clevester sat in Clevester's brother's rust-bucket 2001 Chevy Malibu, black with a white hood, a bumper from the junk yard, a shitty tint job bubbling from sun exposure, and stock speakers pumping some Icewear Vezzo. It was just after 8 p.m.—the perfect time, Chips had told them, when the hook had their highest call volume, and response times were slowest.

"Ay yo, turn that shit down," Sean said, tying a black bandana over his nose. "Y'all ready to do this?"

Clevester had his on already, and was spinning the cylinder on an old revolver. "Nigga, I *been* ready," Clevester said.

Demetreus looked out of the window. He couldn't see the entrance to Smiles Cocktail Lounge from back here, but he could see people walking in and out of the Metro PCS. He'd never actually committed a crime before, aside from a few handoffs for Sean. His biggest worry was explaining to his mom if he got caught. Which meant: don't get caught.

"D, what the fuck, nigga, you up?" Sean demanded. He looked into the back seat and ice-grilled Demetreus.

"Shit. Let's get paid," D said.

"Told you he was soft," Sean said to Clevester.

"Yo, kiss my ass, nigga. Let's roll this joint," D said.

"Yeah, that's what I'm talking bout!"

They hopped out the car, left it running, and crept up the side of the building, guns in hand. "Hold up," Sean said.

Two women clicked across the parking lot in heels, the last rays of twilight sun reflecting off their earrings. They opened the door to Smiles, and just as it closed behind them, Sean said, "Let's hit it!" The trio sprinted across the lot, Sean holding his pump action shotgun out in front of him. Demetreus brought up the rear, and before he knew it, they were inside. For a split second, it seemed like they could do this quietly, or even not at all, but then Sean racked the Mossburg and yelled, "NOBODY FUCKING MOVE!" Sean and Clevester ran up to the bar. It was D's job to cover the booths lining the wall. He pulled out the .22, and a cone of silence formed as he held out the weapon, pointing at no one in particular.

"D, GET THOSE MOTHERFUCKERS' WALLETS!" Sean yelled.

Misha Wallace found the barrel of the shotgun six inches from her face. She'd been through this drill before—she'd worked in Detroit bars for decades—but every time, her breath caught in her lungs, and her ears and neck went hot with sweat. The kid's eyes were boiling, darting around the bar, and he seemed to be hopping from one foot to the other. Maybe he was on something.

"OPEN THE FUCKING REGISTER!" he yelled. He racked the shotgun again, popping an unspent shell out of the chamber. Well, now they knew it was loaded.

Edgar was at the end of the bar with his hands up, the other kid leaning over the counter and holding his pistol sideways, nearly touching Edgar's head with the barrel.

"Okay, okay!" Misha said.

The shotgun kid turned to see his friend in the back standing motionless near the booths. "D, WHAT THE FUCK?" he yelled. The kid didn't respond—he just stood there motionless with his .22. "I got it," said the kid aiming at Edgar. He ran to the back, and Edgar started lowering his hands—they kept a bat behind the counter. *Edgar, don't.* The shotgun kid swiveled, took two steps towards

Edgar, then fired! The glass behind the bar shattered, and screams erupted, then silenced as the shotgun kid panned the room with his barrel. Misha was shaking. The smell of burnt powder stabbed up her nostrils. She looked down and saw Edgar writhing on the floor, clutching his ear. She didn't see any blood.

"Open the fucking register," he said again, the barrel back in her face.

She did, and one of the others came up and swiped out all the cash, a few hundred bucks. He flipped through it. "That's it?" he said.

"Where's the rest?" The shotgun kid said.

"That's, that's all there is," Misha said.

He racked the gun again, wasting another shell.

"Son," Misha said. "You boys got to get out of here."

"BITCH, THE FUCK DID YOU SAY?"

"You gotta get out of here before the cops—"

He swung the butt of the shotgun in a short, nasty arc and caught her square in the face with a dense, wet sound—Misha's head popped back, and she remained standing for a second, seemingly resting at the back of the bar, and then blood gushed from her nostrils onto her necklace of wooden beads, staining her lavender blouse. She pitched over like a felled maternal tree and hit the floor, hard, her temple shielded from the linoleum by a sticky rubber matt with a Bacardi logo on it.

"GRAB THE LIQUOR!" Sean yelled. They ran behind the bar and swiped whatever they could reach, plastic handles of Monarch, Seagram's Seven, then the three of them bolted out the back. Clevester hopped behind the wheel as D and Sean dumped the liquor in the backseat. "DRIVE!" Sean yelled, and Clevester peeled out onto Eight Mile, nearly hitting a motorcycle. They pulled a u-turn and sped west toward Farmington as Sean counted the money. Just over four-hundred bucks. D wondered how badly that woman was hurt, his heart pounding in his ears, blocking out the sounds of traffic and the constant overhead hum of Amazon drones whizzing through the evening sky, delivering small goods to customers with a speed and accuracy unmatched in the history of human commerce.

#BLACKMONEYWHITEPOCKETS was everywhere. It was trending on RNKR, on Twitter, on Facebook, even on Google+, which was apparently still a thing. Wide-eyed blond women on chirpy morning talk shows were saying it quietly as they covered their mouths—were they even allowed to say it? Kids on playgrounds were taunting each other with it, not even knowing what it meant. The music video had racked up 1.2 million views in less than twenty-four hours, helped along by the nationwide graffiti campaign. Instagram had exploded with photos of #BLACKMONEYWHITEPOCKETS murals in Chicago, New York, Atlanta. *The New York Times* had covered the plastering of Amazon's biodomes with the hashtag. Amazon had it cleaned up within a few hours, but the images were already in the cloud, immortal. But it was Richie's death that had really grabbed the nation's attention. Black Lives Matter was demanding that the DPD release the name of the officer involved in the shooting and conduct an investigation into police misconduct. DPD claimed the officer had fired in defense of his partner, but the video clearly showed the knife clattering to the ground before the shot was fired. Then again, the man had lunged at the female officer, but did that threat justify the use of deadly force? The DPD claimed he was reaching for her weapon—the video was unclear on that count. The whole situation was unclear, which made it the perfect fodder for disagreement. Piper had thought long and hard about tacking the footage onto the #BLACKMONEYWHITEPOCKETS video. A part of her felt irredeemably base for using his death to promote her agenda, even though doing so brought far more attention to the injustice of his death than it otherwise would have received... an injustice carried out by the police, but one that would never have happened if she hadn't stolen and stashed that Amazon drone at his house. It was a bargain with the devil. It had exacted a high price and delivered more than she'd asked for.

Amazon's stock had plummeted fifteen percent, but they'd yet to make any public statement. Goldman had been invited to perform on the *Late Show* with Colbert and to host *SNL*. Piper's own follower count was closing in on a million. There were essays and articles and twitter rants by David Brooks, Ta-Nehisi Coates, and Roxane Gay. Even a few sound bites from President Trump ("White this, black that—money's got one color: green!"). There was even a new meme making the rounds: a picture of Goldman in whiteface wearing his wide Bezos-grin with captions like: *Free money, why thank you!* or *Admission to Yale, but I didn't even apply!* or *He went that way, Officer!* or *Those negroes, they think everything's about race!*

There seemed to be two camps: those who thought the music video was stupid, incoherent, and insensitive, doing more harm than good by dividing people, and those who thought its very incoherence was what made it brilliant, that it showed how tangled up our notions of race and privilege are, how much of the seemingly rational debate is fueled by irrational emotion. The beehive had been righteously shaken. Piper was high on success, too high, and she'd gotten there by climbing up the ladder of Richie's body. The guilt gnawed at her from below while the pressure of responsibility crushed her from above—she had everyone's attention and they were waiting to see what she'd do next. On top of all that, there was the fear that Amazon might find a way to tie her to the theft of that drone. Meaning she might have landed herself in the very pot of hot water she'd been struggling to pull her gramps from.

Luther was more broken down than broken up over Richie. He wasn't the type to cry; he just sat in his chair and looked out the window. Piper had tried to talk with him earlier in the day, but he hadn't said much. She'd made him a sandwich for lunch, but he'd only taken a few bites. He'd said *no thanks* to dinner, but she'd gone ahead and boiled up some spaghetti anyway. He saw her eating alone and finally pulled himself out of that chair to join her.

"Are you mad at me?" she asked.

"About what, child?"

"Posting the video. Of…"

"I'm not mad. I just." Luther twirled some buttered spaghetti on his fork. "This whole mess," he said.

Piper squeezed his hand, feeling useless. How was she supposed to comfort him? He'd been looking after Richie for decades. He no longer had anyone to care for, to check in on.

"That city councilman's been talking to Amazon," he said. "Trying to work something out."

"You really think—"

"I'm tired, Itty."

Piper cleared the table when they were finished—Gramps had barely touched his noodles—and found her phone blinking with a new notification: an e-mail from Annika Dahl, the Prime Air Ambassador. She wanted to meet, to have a discussion. Gramps was back in his easy chair, staring out the window, watching the sun set. He usually went to bed around this time. Piper poured him a glass of water and set it next to him. Annika Dahl. She wanted to meet…

Orchard grass, chicory, yellow sweet clover. With your eyes closed, you might think you were in a woodland meadow filled with wildflowers. Aaron Thistle inhaled deeply as he rolled through the hood in his Toyota pickup, windows down. The sun was setting over the boarded up houses overtaken with mugwort, crabgrass, and was that spotted knapweed? A pit bull stared at his slow-rolling truck from behind a chain-link fence—didn't even bark. He rounded the corner past a vacant lot, the old concrete foundation of someone's house buried beneath a thriving patch of Queen Anne's Lace. He'd been out here for the last hour, cruising the quiet, half-abandoned streets of east-side Detroit, thinking, smelling, nodding at the people sitting on their porches as he passed. Black people. Poor black people. Amazon drones whizzed through the sky overhead. Every now and again, one would descend a few blocks away, then rise back up to return to its hive. He wanted to see one land.

He'd spent the day harvesting vegetables for the Amazon drones to whisk away, and when he'd clocked out of the system as evening came on, he'd surveyed his ragged patch of farmland—he'd sold so much produce it looked barren, picked clean. Melancholy had overtaken him then. He'd seen the data on where his greens were being delivered. Prime Air Farmers Market was doing something good, providing real food to people otherwise stuck with things that came fried or in a bag with preservatives. But loading produce into drone delivery boxes, it just didn't feel...*authentic*. Like he was somehow betraying the vision of his dream socks. He'd lost the simple connection of handing someone a head of broccoli, a bunch of radishes, of two human faces meeting, sharing a smile, even if they were white hipster faces. He needed to remember what that was like. If he was going to continue partnering with Amazon, he needed to see a human on the other end, the person who would eat the food he'd grown. It didn't even have to be his food. He just wanted to see with his own eyes that actual people were opening these Amazon boxes and smelling the produce grown in their own neighborhoods by weirdos like him.

He slowed to a stop as he saw a drone land on someone's front lawn. A tall black woman, poofy hair held back in a bandana, walked down her porch and picked up the Amazon box as the drone lifted off. She opened it right there and pulled out a bunch of greens— mustard greens maybe. It was hard to tell from this distance. She caught his eye, then turned and walked back into her house. And that was it. No catharsis, no great feeling of connection. Aaron put the truck back in gear, but stopped. Why not? He parked and walked up to her door and knocked.

The door opened a crack, and the woman peered out at him.

"Hi, sorry to bother you."

"Uh-huh."

"I'm a farmer, with Amazon, not with, but...I live over on Armour Street."

"You live in *this* neighborhood?"

"Because you just got a delivery order, I thought—"

"What, you want it back?"

"No, no. That's not even from my farm," Aaron said.

The woman looked confused. Aaron heard someone calling from the back of the house. "Sorry," he said.

"Okay, honey," she said, and the door closed.

Aaron climbed back in his truck and sat there for a moment. What the hell was he doing, out here bothering some lady? As if she'd have any desire to talk to him at all. But that was the whole problem, wasn't it? The transactions of daily life were the stitches that held together the fabric of a community. And as soon as you start delivering everything, you lose that. You insert a layer of abstraction. But still, people find a way to connect. Back in Eureka, California, growing up, his own parents knew the name of the postman who delivered to their house. Gregg. They tipped him on Christmas. But you turn the delivery man into a drone, that's a further layer of abstraction. There's nothing left to stitch into. Everyone retreats into their bubbles. That was no way to live.

By the time Aaron got home, the decision had solidified. He pulled out his phone and texted Piper:

> I'm quitting hood fresh.

She found him on his porch, his feet kicked up on the railing, a journal open in his lap, a pen in the corner of his mouth. It was dark out, and the lights from inside his house framed his silhouette.

"Finally saw the light?" she asked.

Aaron nibbled the end of his pen, then finished writing a line of what was beginning to turn into a poem about soil. He looked up at Piper and held her gaze, doing his best to project "meaningful thought." He hadn't *seen the light* exactly. He didn't suddenly hate Amazon. By participating in Hood Fresh, he'd been helping the community he was gentrifying—he was convinced of that—but he'd chosen, selfishly, his own feelings of authenticity. He needed the warm glow, even if it meant he was less effective at helping the community. He felt guilty about that, but he didn't quite know how to explain that to Piper.

"Started feeling drone-like myself," he said.

"That's how they want it, right?" Piper said

Aaron just shrugged.

"She wants to meet," Piper said. "That Amazon lady."

"Yeah?"

"I'm a record it."

"And?"

"I don't know, lead her into saying something racist?"

"See, that's your problem," Aaron said. "You think she's actually racist? You're not exposing anything if you have to trick her into saying something."

"I don't want to *trick* her. I just want to her say what she really thinks. That'll be enough."

"What are you trying to accomplish? This last thing, the #BLACKMONEYWHITEPOCKETS thing. It doesn't even make sense. It's just getting people angry."

"People need to be angry. My neighbor Richie is dead!"

"I saw. It's awful. I'm mean, fuck, right? But…you know anger is what they call a *secondary emotion* in emotion-therapy. It's always predicated on some deeper primary feeling—fear, despair, disgust. That's what—"

"Really? You gon delegitimize black anger?" So typically male, so typically white. It was the kind of attitude you could only have if your whole life felt safe, if you could go after whatever you wanted without the world shutting you down. Just because you couldn't articulate something completely didn't invalidate the emotion behind it. How hard was that to understand?

"That's not what I'm saying," Aaron said. He stood up and cupped her shoulders. "You're gonna meet this woman, right? All I'm saying is, you gotta respect her viewpoint. You can't just dismiss it, or parody it. That shit might get YouTube views, but if you're not engaging with the actual ideology, then you don't do it any real damage. A few days or weeks pass, and everything's back how it was." He let his hands drop to his sides.

"You're saying I should listen to her."

"I mean, yeah."

"You think Amazon'll listen to me, to anyone who's not a fucking shareholder?"

"What are you willing to risk?" Aaron asked.

It wasn't about her gramps anymore, it wasn't about drones, it wasn't even about Richie. It was about the link between corporate power and black disenfranchisement, it was about the whole system, the context that enabled something like Richie's death to happen, to be an expected result. "I'll figure that out when I get there," Piper said. She turned and walked down the steps.

"Let me know how it goes!" Aaron called.

She gave him a sad smile, then walked home without looking back.

Aaron watched her until she disappeared around the corner. The front door opened, and he turned to see Jacque, one of the new residents. He was holding his wooden "smell box," a polished mahogany cube with a nose-shaped hole cut in one side. Jacque pointed at Aaron's pit-stained t-shirt. "You offered…" he said.

"Yeah, of course," Aaron said, "but I want it back." He stripped his shirt off and handed it Jacque, who danced back inside with glee. Aaron looked down at the stark line of his farmer's tan—his dark forearms stuck to his pasty white torso, like a mismatched Lego man.

25

Ellis thought he was keeping it together on his trip to fourth floor recovery, but his rage radiated via such unmistakable signals that two hospital security guards had already been paged and were milling around the door by the time he made it to the desk of the ward.

"That's my mom in there," he said, and they kept a respectable distance as he approached her bed. She was asleep, her head in a cast with a cut-out for her left eye and a drainage tube threaded through the plaster, the rest of her barely covered in an undignified paper gown. Mom probably had insurance, although he hadn't asked about it in several years. He curled his hands around the bed's crib-like barrier and closed his eyes. The gentle sounds of hospital equipment beeping down the hall, people pattering by, rolling gurneys. He tried to visualize something calming, but kept coming back to fists and blood. There was a crust of eye-gunk in the corner of Mom's good eye. He reached over to clean it away, but the eye opened.

"Ell?"

"Yeah, I'm here, momma."

"How I look?" She sounded somewhat druggy.

"Beautiful," Ellis said. "Like always."

She made a wheezy stutter that must have been an attempt at laughter. "Well, I'm not feeling too hot," she said.

"You need anything?" he asked, looking around for a nurse. "Did they…they break something? What's going on under there? With your head?"

"Jus' a little," she slurred. "It's a hairline fracture, they said."

"You got an eye crunchy," he said.

"Oh?" She brought a slow arm out from under the hospital blanket and tried to pluck out the crunchy with her press-ons.

"Ma," he whispered, "Who was it? Did you see their faces?"

She exhaled, and gestured for him to get it.

(((*bzzzzz*)))

It was Nik calling. He silenced his phone, then reached over and wiped the crunchy from her eye as she flinched.

"Ell, come here. Look at me."

He leaned over. She couldn't move her head.

"You're not gon do anything."

"They broke your face," he said.

"Listen to me, son. Are you listening? You're not gon get hurt or locked up. I went too damn far for you."

"Did you see their faces?"

"No."

"Did anyone?"

"Ellis. You're going to promise me you're not going to do anything. Hold my hand and promise me."

Annika sat on the edge of her bed scrolling through her contact list. Why hadn't Ellis picked up? She knew what she needed and she felt stupid for needing it. She just wanted someone to tell her she was brilliant, that she'd take this girl down, easy. Not because she didn't believe that already—she did—but because those words were a sign that she was loved, that she was lovable, and that was something she sometimes doubted. She'd underestimated Piper Prince—not her determination or intelligence or resourcefulness, but her level of rancor, her antipathy. Annika still found it hard to believe that the girl hated Amazon enough to produce something like #BLACKMONEYWHITEPOCKETS.

The girl had agreed to meet tomorrow night, and Annika had been gathering her thoughts on index cards, but had found herself unable to organize them into a coherent narrative. It was this stupid emotional insecurity—it screwed with her productivity. She stopped scrolling, her thumb hovering over Spencer's name. They still hadn't spoken since the break up in Seattle, now, what, almost three months ago. And there was that ringing sound—her thumb had gone ahead and made the decision for her.

"Nik? Hey, what's up?"

Hearing his voice chilled and warmed her at once. The very timbre of it conjured his appearance, his small but protuberant ears, tall forehead, sarcastic eyes.

"You there?"

"Hey, Spence. How's it going?"

"Oh, man, the summer's been crazy. I think I'm gonna plant some palm trees in my little planter thingy and grow coconuts."

"Cool. Taking advantage of that climate change."

"Something wrong? You sound…"

"I'm fine."

"I saw that black money video. Big man can't be too happy about that."

Annika sighed. "I don't really want to talk about work."

"Okay. So, how you been? You got friends out there?"

"Not really. I mean, there's one guy."

"A guy?"

"Sorry, I shouldn't—"

"No, it's fine, you can tell me. I mean, I've been Tindering."

"Oh. How's that?"

"Been on a few dates. Everyone's so young, though."

He said it as if it were a bad thing, but there was an undertone of smugness.

"How young?"

"You don't want to know."

"Yeah."

"So, who's this guy?"

"A local, Detroiter, but not a techie or anything."

"You're dating a townie?" He laughed. "What's he do?"

"You are so shallow." Annika was aware she was starting to flirt, despite herself. "I met him at Krav Maga, actually. He's a trainer."

"He's a—oh wow, like, that's what he does for a living? Did he go to college? Am I an asshole for asking that? I'm not judging."

"You're totally judging."

"Am not! I get it, I get it. This is your...I don't know—*Eat, Pray, Love* phase."

"Okay, you're definitely being an asshole now."

"Sorry. Didn't mean it like that."

"Yeah." He didn't, but he did. Part of his insufferable charm.

"I miss you," he said.

"Don't."

"I do though."

"Spence..."

"You never think about me?"

"Of course I do."

"But as soon as I pop up, you shove me away into one of your mind-cabinets."

Spencer was the one who'd given her that term, comparing her to Napoleon, who could open and shut doors in his mind at will, planning battles one moment, then writing letters to his wife, then drafting large sections of the Napoleonic law code, all from an Army tent at Marengo. Spencer was a short, small guy, and his obsession with Napoleon had been a source of amusement to Annika and her friends, although she only brought it up to him once.

"I've got a whole other life out here," she said. "I have to prioritize." She knew now that though she'd been in love with him, she'd never been madly in love with him. That was the problem. Everything had been comfortable without building to anything. He could have changed that, of course, if he'd taken the hint and proposed. Wasn't she worth it?

"You ever think about coming back?"

"Why didn't you do it? Why didn't you just buy a fucking ring?"

"Whoa, uh. That's..."

"You know I would've said *yes*." She could almost hear him thinking.

"I don't know...I guess I felt like you deserved better."

"Really?"

"Yeah, you're so…"

"What?"

"So…you."

"What does that even mean?"

"I don't know."

"I gotta get back to work," Annika said. "Let's talk again sometime."

As Annika hung up, she could feel the accumulated melancholy of their conversation harden into drive, purpose. Maybe that was what Spencer had meant, that she was too driven for someone like him. Or was that a flaw? Maybe he'd meant that he deserved someone better, someone who wouldn't armor up and fly into mission-mode whenever the two of them probed around the soft spots. Annika shoved those thoughts into a mind-cabinet. Right now, she had an opponent to crush. But first, she needed to irrigate. She filled up the plastic Neti Pot and clenched her teeth while the solution flooded up one nostril and out the other. Pain just meant it was working.

"Sandra, please! Just open up and talk to me!"

She stood inside crying, her back against the door. Jamal knocked again, and she felt his fist thudding through her chest.

"You know that wasn't me!" Jamal said, his voice loud, but muffled. "I would never do that! Sandra, *talk* to me."

She wiped at her eyes and said nothing.

"It was that girl—they captured Lucy and used her to harass people for that stupid music video!"

"Well maybe you shouldn't have let that happen!" Sandra said.

"Well, it happened, and I'm sorry. I can't change that. But we're going after that girl. She's gonna pay."

"That fixes everything, doesn't it?"

"Sandra…"

"Go away."

Jamal could feel his eyes welling up. It was all coming back: the helpless pain of their failure, year after year, to make it work. He had thought he could make this one woman happy, and he'd told her so, and she'd believed him once. But the more miserable she'd grown under his roof, the more ashamed and despairing he'd become. And angry. Angry at her for showing him what a failure of a man he was, angry at himself for being that failure, angry at life for blessing him with seemingly special talents, and then sprinkling this accursed dust on him that made others around him, but especially women, recoil, as if he had some unsightly deformity of the soul. So maybe he couldn't ever make this woman happy. Lord knew she had her issues with happiness anyway.

"Jamal?" Her voice barely penetrated the door.

"Yeah?"

"Leave."

He stood there for a moment, then placed his palms over his eyes and wiped them dry with one stroke. The sky overhead was a thickening mesh of UAV traffic. All those Amazon A-4s and A-9s, thousands in the sky at any given moment. They were winning. It didn't make him feel any better. He shuffled back to his car.

As she heard him drive off, Sandra slumped down to the floor and buried her face between her knees. Jamal hadn't done anything wrong. She knew that. And he was trying his best, he really was. But in the days since that drone had dropped diet pills at her feet, anger had calcified her heart and right now, in this moment, she had no idea how to soften it, how to love this man who loved her before, and who loved her now, and would keep on loving her. Thin, fat, young, old, when she was smiling at him, when she ordered him away, he would be loving her. How could he be so consistent? It was infuriating.

"Give it back!" Eve said.

Sandra looked up and saw Nina holding a juice box over Eve's head. The TV was blaring some cartoon. Toys and books littered the floor. Next to her, a dead fly on its back. She couldn't remember the last time she'd had a chance to vacuum.

26

A few months back, Curtis had rounded up the crew to cele-
brate—their nigga Joey was back home after fifteen months in the
state pen. They climbed to the roof of the abandoned Kettering
High School to smoke joints and drink some Hennessey—the basic
bottle was only forty bucks—three hours work at Hot Wheel City.
You could see all the way to downtown from the roof. They used to
go up there all the time back in the day. Getting up was easy, and
getting down wasn't no problem either, you just went to the west
side of the roof, stood on the birdshit covered tar panels, tucked
your arms in, and jumped the ten or twelve feet down into a clump
of sturdy, green bushes with pink flowers.

At least, that's how they used to do it. This last time, Curtis had
stood at the edge, looking down, wondering if there might be a gas
meter or pipe or something in the bushes. He hadn't remembered
there being one, but he'd never checked. And even if it was just a
bush, there might be some branches sticking straight up, some sharp,
hard wooden spine, waiting to stab him…There was a moment
of silence as the small band stood at the edge. A little hesitation.
Then everyone jumped. Just a few scratches, but no one hurt. They
probably wouldn't be back there again, Curtis had thought. No one
had to say anything. It was like their brains had developed some

kind of alarm or insurance system that forced them to imagine bad outcomes to risk. Made them Give a Fuck. He didn't like it.

It was that part of his now adult, filled-out brain that helped him put the drugs up on the shelf and get a straight job, after starting to imagine a jail cell every time the hook rolled by or a deal felt weird. It was also this Give a Fuck part of his brain that started ringing real loud when this swoll-ass nigga came stomping into Hot Wheel City asking for Chips. Dude was big. Cop? Curtis almost said, *who?* at the mention of his name. But nah, he wasn't no punk. He nodded and said, "Sup?"

"I heard you might know about a thing that went down the other day on Eight Mile. Smiles cocktail lounge. Black Malibu, white hood."

The kid's face twitched, then went blank. Pleasant, polite, blank. That twitch was all Ellis needed. This kid knew. One of the Smiles regulars had seen the getaway car peeling out. There couldn't be more than a few Frankenstein Chevy Malibus in Detroit. Ellis had asked around, and one of his old roughneck pals had pointed him toward Denby High School—didn't know who owned that car, but did know a dude named Chips who'd done a few stickups, who probably still knew people. Word gets around. It's a small town, really. "I ain't a cop," Ellis said. "And I ain't trying to cause problems. Ellis Wallace." He held out his hand.

Curtis paused for a moment, and shook it. Blank face. "I know I got a history round here, but I don't bang no more."

"Yeah, I know. But look. One of the ladies behind the bar got laid out. Kid busted up her face with the back of a shotgun."

"Shhh, damn. Sorry to hear that. You know her?"

"That's my mama. She in the hospital now."

"You know stickups. Shit goes wrong sometimes."

"Yeah. But she was telling these niggas to head out before the hook rolled through. They already had the cash. But one just decided to go a little wild, impress the squad or some shit."

Curtis had heard something about that. Made him regret ever talking to those idiots.

"I ain't looking to go to the cops," Ellis said. "I go find this nigga, no weapons, whoop his ass a bit, that's that."

Curtis wasn't about to get his ass kicked for Sean, but then he couldn't just roll over like it was nothing. "I might have heard something about that. Lemme think for a second," he said.

"Yeah, you think on that. Take your time." The guy walked a few paces away, like he was looking at some matte black *Borghini* rims, but he never turned his back on Curtis. Fucking hothead Sean and his little jit wannabes, popping some nigga's moms in the face so they could brag about some stickup. And Sean would brag about it. Only a matter of time. Funny thing was, Curtis wanted Sean's ass kicked, too. But he was in a tight spot. He didn't have the juice anymore to roll on those kids and expect them not to come back at him. If he did it just because he was scared of this Ellis nigga, that would look even worse. He needed some reason that was street-legitimate.

"Not that I'm trying to go this route," Ellis said softly, wandering back over to the counter, "but I know the dude who flies the Amazon drones. If I can't find these niggas, I'm gon call in a favor and get that footage. You know those things are always overhead. Then the cops just trace the car, see where it drove to."

Curtis tried to roll his eyes in the most polite way possible. "C'mon, nigga," he said, quietly.

"I ain't even fucking with you. Amazon head pilot, Jamal Dent. Look it up. He's in the news. We came up together from grade school. Tight from way back." Ellis was bluffing, of course—Jamal had straight up told him that he wasn't allowed to scan through drone footage, let alone hand it over to the police. But this kid didn't know that. "I can get this done," Ellis said. "No cops."

Curtis looked down at the laminated wheel poster on the counter. He smiled. That's legit then. Keeping cops out of it is legit. "I give this nigga up, you gotta let him know. It's you and him. One and done. I ain't a part of it," he whispered.

"One and done," Ellis repeated. "What's his name?"

Nia's room was an unvisited museum. In the weeks after her death, Piper and her grandfather had come to the unspoken conclusion to leave the room exactly as it was. Piper had gone inside once, to cry, about two months after Nia was gone—one final cathartic burst so she could move on with her life. But aside from that, neither she nor Gramps had disturbed a thing.

As Piper opened the door, the changing pressure kicked dust into the air—she watched it swirl in a column of evening light slanting in through the window. The room still smelled like Nia—patchouli. The double bed was made up, several pillows artfully arranged. A dashiki shirt hung over the back of a chair. Beads and kente cloth headwraps on hooks. Above the desk, a poster, in Papyrus of all fonts:

Piper scanned the bookshelf: *Black Feminist Thought*, *Critical Race Theory*, Flannery O'Connor, *The Poems of Robert Hayden*, Ralph Ellison, James Baldwin, *Angela's Ashes*, bell hooks, *The Autobiography of Malcolm X*, *A People's History of the United States*, *I am Malala*, *Bad Feminist*, and Tina Fey's book. Piper hadn't read any of them. There was a gap which must have been where Thomas Sugrue's *Origins of the Urban Crisis* had been shelved. Nia had lent it to Piper just before she wound up in the hospital. It was currently lost somewhere in Piper's room. She'd gotten about half-way through.

On top of the bookshelf was a cardboard file box. When Nia had realized she wasn't going to leave the hospital, she'd asked Gramps to bring her books and journals and he'd also brought her some small totems of comfort from her room. And whenever her friends in the activist community came to visit, they would leave her with something new. It had been so hard for Piper to see her deteriorate, and she didn't have anything to bring, so her visits had been brief, but she would always ask what she could do, and Nia would always say that she was doing it already. Piper had thought about volunteering for AIDS awareness, but she'd never gone through with it. When Nia passed, they had put everything she'd collected in her hospital room into this box. Piper had never looked inside. What did she expect to find? Courage? She was supposed to meet this Annika woman in a few hours.

Inside the box, she found stacks of pamphlets and flyers. The Detroit Food Policy Council. The Community Land Trust and Conservancy. Water rights, Black economic development, the March against Monsanto. They were causes that Piper supported, a hundred percent, in theory. Nia had always gone beyond theory. She'd made it a point to do measurable good in the world. Piper wanted to believe that #BLACKMONEYWHITEPOCKETS was more than controversy, that it was addressing the root problem, but what was the root problem? Racism? Or was racism a symptom of some deeper human dysfunction, an overriding need for comfort, complacency? For every box you unpacked, there was another one inside it. Maybe there was nothing at the core.

Below the pamphlets, Piper found one of Nia's spiral-bound notebooks. She flipped through it until she hit the last page of writing—about a third of the way through. The hand-writing was shaky, but recognizably her sister's.

> I wonder if the kids in college right now have ever heard "The Revolution Will Not Be Televised." And if so, do they even get the irony that today, it is televised, it's tweeted and shared and ranked. And they're helping it stay that way. Heron's whole point was that you had to get off your ass and do something. And reposting another NYT op-ed about white guilt and micro-aggressions and safe spaces—all without a single reasonable policy prescription, then shaming the people who disagree with you on Facebook—that's not doing something, it's the illusion, the delusion of doing something, which is terrifying, because one day you'll wake up and realize that instead of dressing your country's wounds, you've just

been instagraming them and talking about
how painful they look. The revolution will not
be televised because the real revolution is love,
Jesus taught us that, and love happens under our
noses, without the dramatic events which feed the
media—coverage of protests sells ads, sad but
true. I feel like I'm trying to convince myself
out of protest, which I don't want to do. Protest
is essential. But I feel conflicted. I guess it's that
some fights seem much sexier than others. The
fight against racism head on, through things
like BLM, it stirs shit up. But it's so hard to
fight ideas like that. You reduce the world to one
equation: white supremacy supported by violence against black bodies, and you erase indi-
vidual responsibility from asshole cops as much
as from heroic protestors—and there I go playing
into the category, as if cops couldn't be heroic
and protestors hateful. That categorical thinking
boxes every beautiful complicated human into
either oppressor or oppressed. It leaves you staring
into the abyss. It's poking our deep historical
wound, and then offering nihilism as a band-
aid. That's not disruption. It's anti-disruption.
The better way, I think, is to fight for the less
sexy causes—water rights, affordable housing,
decentralizing food and energy—because if you
make headway in those areas, you help the people
at the bottom, who are largely black anyway,
without having to stir up racial enmity. On my
most cynical days, I feel like it's some kind
of shell game: the people with real power aren't
racist, they're just plutocratic. Money over everything. If ending systemic racism would make
them money, they'd find a way to end it. And
what could be better for them than an endless
race debate that never gets anywhere, pitting

those without real money against each other so we don't come together and rebel against the rich. But even when I'm not being cynical, and I don't feel cynical today—even though my t-cell count is down to 36—I think we have to return to our humanity, what unites us, if we have any hope of reducing inequality in its many forms. We need a communal, collective response, not a battlefield of opposing dogmas. We need to be waging love. We need to forgive, even the worst offenses. I've been thinking a lot lately about the man who assaulted me, the man who put me here in this hospital bed. It's so hard for me to forgive him. But with God's help I'm trying. I can only believe that any man who would rape someone must be so wounded inside. So hurt. So in need of love. And it feels wrong, so wrong to say it, but so <u>deserving</u> of love. Love isn't earned. It's for everyone, even the worst of us, even him.

Piper's hands drooped to the floor. Nia had been raped? She'd never said anything. When she'd tested positive, all she'd said was that it could have been this boy at a club, a night she made some decisions she wasn't proud of. Maybe she'd been too embarrassed? Maybe she wanted to look invincible in front of Piper? All her energy, her activism, it had never been about herself. Piper found her own kneeling reflection in a mirror next to the bed. She looked so put together, so color coordinated, so Neptune Frost. She could feel her eyes welling up and she turned away from the mirror.

Inside the file box, under few more pamphlets, was a shoebox. She opened it: hundreds of photos Nia had brought with her to the hospital. Gramps with Grandma, before she passed, the two of them posed formally at a church barbecue. Seven-year-old Piper wearing huge sunglasses and doing an 80s rapper lean with crossed arms. Then Piper on Nia's back, both of them laughing, water behind them. Were they at Bell Isle? What were they laughing at?

Beneath the photos lay a jewelry box. Nia's cowry shell earrings. Grandma had given them to her. Nia had practically slept in them.

Luther hung up the phone and hoisted himself up with a grunt. He caned his way down the hall to Nia's room and found Piper kneeling on the floor, her back to him, a mess of photos at her knees. "How you feeling, child?" he asked.

Piper didn't turn.

"Lawyer just called," he said. "Said there might be another way out of all this if I talk with Amazon." He paused. Piper said nothing. "That councilman said…look, I know you can't stand the idea of—"

Piper turned to look at him. Tears were streaming down the poor child's face. She was gripping tight on a jewelry box. Luther waited, but she couldn't seem to get any words out. He sighed, thinking back to Pastor Edwards' sermon last Sunday. About faith and trust. Trusting in God, mostly, but also having faith in your loved ones, trusting your kin. But the poor girl just looked so pointless right now, like a broke-down car. Something must have happened, or she just flew too high and cracked her head against the sky. He didn't understand all that app nonsense, followers going viral and what not, but he knew she was good at it, that she had a talent like very few people for steering the spotlight, and he knew that when she was in the thick of it, her eyes lit up with purpose, and how could you deny somebody her purpose?

"Come here, child," Luther said. Piper stood, and Luther put his arms around her, and they held each other in the fading light of this room that belonged to Nia, which meant it belonged to no one.

27

Gordon Park wasn't a complete shithole. There were a few clean benches, a small playground, minimal graffiti, and yes, empty cigarette packs and unlucky lotto tickets dotting the overgrown grass, but that was expected. More surprising to Annika was the hacked and blackened picnic table—clearly doused in accelerant and torched, but still bolted to the ground—an unintentional piece of modern art. At least the park was surrounded by occupied houses. Well, mostly. Across the street, a charred three-story house stood quietly like it was waiting for the right moment to collapse. The sidewalk was spangled with glass shards—*Detroit diamonds*, Ellis called them. The rays of gentrification hadn't yet reached the corner of Rosa Parks and Clairmount. It was stuck in limbo, a place waiting to see what the rest of the city would do before deciding if it would wither or flourish. Why had the girl chosen this spot? The sun had dipped over the horizon—it was just after 8 p.m.—but it was still plenty light out. Amazon Skeeters whizzed by overhead. Annika checked her phone—she was exactly on time. She felt eyes on her and spotted a black guy in reflective jeans eye-fucking her as he walked down Clairmount. She tensed her forearms and visualized a hammerfist combo.

Piper peered at the woman from behind a Rizzo construction

dumpster across the street. She looked hard, her jaw set. But that probably just meant she was nervous. Let her wait, just a few more minutes. To calm her own nerves, Piper had dressed her flyest: she was sporting her ShiftWear hi-tops, which were made of flexible e-paper screens that would, with a tap on her smartphone, display whatever animation she chose—currently, a pulsing #BLACKMONEYWHITEPOCKETS. But it wasn't the hi-tech shoes or the rather creepy necklace made of human hand-bones that was fueling her confidence. It wasn't even that her phone, tucked in the left front pocket of her jeans, was already recording. Piper brought a hand to her ear and rubbed the cowry shell earring between her finger and thumb—it was so hard and soft at once, like Nia, it was fragile but polished armor, strong because of its beauty.

Ellis had been circling the blocks near Denby High for a good fifteen minutes, windows down, music off, his body in a state of tense calm. His eyes darted back and forth in search of a black Chevy Malibu with a white hood.

According to Chips, the punks he was looking for were three high schoolers: Sean, Clevester, and Demetreus. And he could find them somewhere near Denby. School was out for the summer, but the building still exerted that teenage gravitational pull. Ellis remembered the feeling. It was a sort of security, like having a parent at home, even if you didn't want to be home hardly ever. Denby High was so far east that it was almost in the burbs, the ones that used to be called Gratiot Township and East Detroit, but changed their names to Harper Woods and Eastpointe during the lean years to convey a sense of Anglican safety and propriety. The demarcation line was about a quarter mile from the school, and at that point, the crumbling gray asphalt and vacant body shops abruptly became smooth blacktop and lawns.

There was a chance of Ellis getting his ass kicked, of course, but he was a champion scrapper and these were dipshit teenagers. There was also a chance of getting arrested again, though that was vanishingly small—none of these punks would go anywhere near the cops. Then there was the chance that these kids were packing heat. Ellis decided not to think about that. Because he didn't have a choice. The street had as powerful a code of justice as anywhere else. Someone cold cocks your moms like that, next time they'll just kill her, and kill you, and people would think it's a bad thing, sure, but if you don't hit back, then you're asking for it, like you lack the basic instinct for self-preservation. At the very least, you dip your fingers in the holy font of vengeance, whether you mean it or not. Ellis meant it. Just an ass whooping for an ass whooping, and that would be that, and then they could all get a good nights' sleep and get on with their lives, and the cops would futz around with the investigation until it petered out, and it would be just another little speck of grime in the long map of the history of the city.

And lo, there it was: black Chevy Malibu, white hood, outside some party store at Whittier and Roxbury. Three kids leaning, brown-bagging, smoking, bumping some Goldman Stackz. Ellis rolled by slow and caught the eye of the kid sitting on the hood, the largest of the three. He parked across the street, next to the Touching Lives for Jesus Ministries. It was Friday, dusk, the strip club two doors down from the church would be jumping later, but it was empty now. So was the party store parking lot, except for these punks. Ellis walked up slowly, without breaking eye contact, doing his best to refrain from setting them off with any overtly threatening gestures, but his blood was up, and he couldn't resist a small hint of his intentions, a little neck crack, side to side, *pop-pop, pop-pop.*

Piper approached like she was too cool for the party. The exec smiled and extended her hand. Piper looked down at it, then back up to her face.

Annika dropped her hand, but held her smile in place. Such hostility. "Piper, right? I'm Annika. Thanks for meeting me."

"You know why I chose this spot?" Piper said.

"No," Annika said. "Should I?"

"Yeah. You should. The '67 riots started right here. Can't even tell, can you? There were tanks on this street. There were snipers shooting motherfuckers from second story windows."

It was dead quiet.

"Let's have a seat, huh?" Annika said. She walked towards a concrete table with an inlaid chessboard and sat in one of the concrete chairs.

Piper sighed, then slouched into the chair opposite. "So?"

"You're trying to speak for Detroit, for the neighborhood," Annika said. "I get that. That doesn't mean we need to be enemies."

"It does, though. You think what's good for Amazon is good for Detroit, but it's a lie."

"We've hired close to a thousand people at the Fulfillment Center."

"Please. This ain't the second coming of Henry Ford. A handful of folks from the hood will get a job for a few years, then they'll be replaced by robots. Amazon gets even richer. And rich people get their bullshit delivered in ten minutes by drones flying over all the burned down and boarded up houses in *my* neighborhood."

"When they first started making cars, they were luxury items," Annika said. "They didn't stay that way. You know why? Automation. Quality goes up and price goes down, and then people can afford more things they need, and companies like Amazon can afford to run programs like Prime Air Farmers Market—"

"Hood Fresh."

"—delivering, at no charge, fresh produce to people without access to decent grocery stores."

"So white people will feel comfortable moving in."

"What's the problem with that? Your grandpa's house might actually be worth something in a few years if Prime Air succeeds."

Piper grilled her for a second. A mosquito landed on the exec's ear; she didn't react. This woman was tough, and she was probably surrounded by men who constantly doubted her.

"Do you really believe that? I mean, I know it's your job to say that, but do you really, personally, think that way?"

Surprise flashed across Annika's face. "Yes, I really do. I think I've come to this understanding honestly, through a lot of coursework on development, a lot of reading, and a lot of experience. From what I've seen, business is the main thing that helps struggling communities."

Piper took a breath, and tried to recall what Aaron had said. Listen, engage with the ideology. What this woman was saying made sense, in a theoretical way. Piper could see how you could maybe believe it, if the real-world results weren't so starkly visible.

"Look at these collapsing houses," she said. "Playgrounds littered with junk. The deal you're offering sounds good, right? People like it, because it sounds good. But it's the same deal we've been taking for the last fifty years, and look what we got for it. Amazon's not here to fix the city. It's here to make money. That's it. Ain't no other goals. And it takes money to make money, right? And who's got the money? White people. That's what you don't get. On a macro tip, when you zoom the fuck out, everything Amazon does just magnifies imbalances that already exist."

Annika looked the girl over, her perfect hair, wooden bracelets, her expensive new-fangled digital sneakers, animated with that awful hashtag. "You know how hypocritical you are?" she said. "How much did those sneakers cost? Where'd the money go? You have an iPhone? You buy gas for your car? You support existing power structures every day."

"You wanna act like it's all or nothing, but it ain't like that. Yeah, I've bought a fucking latte at Starbucks before. But that ain't what matters. Consumerism, it's like…a drug. Nobody resists that shit completely. And expecting people to is stupid. What matters is that you don't become an addict. You know what consumerist addiction looks like? Amazon fucking Prime."

"The fuck you looking at?" said the kid sitting on the hood. He wore an all-black Tigers hat. Clearly the alpha, Sean.

"Thought maybe y'all could help me out with something," Ellis said. He stood ten feet away.

"Doubt it."

Ellis eyed the other two. The one with the gold-plated figaro chain stepped on a joint roach. The other kid—scrawny, wife-beater—screwed the cap on his brown-bagged forty and tossed it in the back seat of the Malibu.

"You acting like a cop, motherfucker," said Sean. He hopped off the car and pushed his chest out. "You a cop?"

"Nope," Ellis said. "Just wanna know about a thing."

"What kind of thing?"

"Thing up at Smiles Cocktail Lounge."

"Smiles?" The kid smirked. "Don't know nothing bout no Smiles." He turned back to his boys. "Y'all know bout Smiles?"

"Nah," said figaro chain.

"What about you, D?"

Wife beater shook his head. He must have been Demetreus. Meaning figaro chain was Clevester.

"What you want to know bout that shit, nigga? You looking for your purse?"

"Yeah, you got it?" Ellis said.

D and Clevester snickered nervously. Sean was oscillating between smirks and hard stares.

"No? Well maybe you can help me with this other thing. See, my moms works at Smiles, and some shithead broke her face in for kicks."

Sean stepped forward. He was tall, well built for a teenager, but only for a teenager. "Yeah I think we can help you out with that," Sean said. "Hey, yo, let's help this faggot out." He pulled his t-shirt up to show a pistol grip sticking out his waistband. The other kids hesitated, then walked up behind him, trying to look hard.

"You want some payback for your mamma?" Sean pointed the gun at Ellis' head and cocked it. Five feet of air crackled between them. "See, that's some schoolyard bullshit. This look like a school-yard, nigga?"

"Power begets power," Annika said. "I get that. And it sucks that there's so little power and capital in the hands of black Detroiters. But the solution to that is black entrepreneurship, not blaming things on non-existent racism."

"Non-existent!?"

"I'm not saying racism doesn't exist, just—"

"Yeah, you just gon blame black people for white supremacy. *Black entrepreneurship, that's the solution*, but how we gon support black businesses if everything we buy comes from Amazon. Isn't that the master plan?"

"When I said 'non-existent' I was referring to motives you and Goldman Stackz imputed to Amazon in your video."

"Oh, I get that you think #BLACKMONEYWHITEPOCKETS is stupid. Wake up. We all know it's stupid. Nobody thinks Bezos is scheming on how to fuck over black people. But he's a convenient symbol. Deal with it. He represents the systemic racism embedded in the fabric of society!"

"You're just rejecting capitalism. That's not going to get you very far."

"I'm rejecting hyper-consumerism. I don't have to hate capitalism to hate the idea of living under a cloud of Amazon drones dropping off dildos and Cheeze-Its to idiots who gon kill themselves if they can't shove something in one of their holes in the next thirty minutes. If a silly music video can steer us away from ending up in that place, even a little, it's worth it."

"Piper, all those people you harassed to make that video are going to come after you with lawsuits. They'll be asking for more than we asked from your grandfather. Is *that* worth it?"

"Yeah, it is."

"Is it worth jail time?"

Ellis stared not at the gun, but at Sean's eyes. The kid had Ellis pegged as one of these Good Men of the Community types, giving tough love to "at risk" teens, mentoring them off the street and back into school, the kind he could intimidate with a piece he barely knew how to hold. He was mistaken. Ellis was still five feet away from Sean, but only three feet from the barrel of the gun. This was no different than Krav Maga drills with bright orange rubberized glocks. The solution was simple, as it had to be when your heart was hammering, your vision narrowed to an ultra-bright tunnel, adrenaline hitting so hard it was almost pleasurable. The gun is controlled by a computer; destroy the computer.

Ellis' head darted left, out of the gun's line of fire, his left hand shot up and clapped over the barrel, forcing it right, bending Sean's wrist back as he lunged forward, pushing the barrel sideways into the kid's stomach, knocking him a step back. His right arm torqued forward sending his massive fist through the kid's face: Sean's head popped back, and he stumbled into the car as Ellis wrenched the gun from his grip.

Sean wiped blood from his mouth, sneering. No apology, no backing down. The other two were waiting to see what Ellis would do. It made for a strangely classical portrait: three Gs in front of a

Malibu, a grimy party store in place of the standard Roman ruins. Ellis popped the clip out and tossed the gun. All three of them watched it clatter on the cracked cement.

Sean charged. Ellis side-stepped, arced his arm down and locked him in a guillotine choke: he pulled up, wrenching Sean's neck, and the kid flailed. Ellis took a hard shot to his kidney from Clevester. Sean slipped free and jabbed at his stomach. Ellis winced, swung a #3 elbow back at Clevester, then heaved a knee towards Sean. Where was the third kid!?

"You stole an Amazon UAV, Piper. I'll save you the embarrassment of denying it. We know you disabled the GPS and covered the camera lens, but the UAV was recording audio to internal memory the entire time it was missing. We've got hours of tape implicating you, Goldman Stackz, Darnell Parker, Curtis Washington, and several others.

"So you wanna do me like you did my gramps? Take the whole family?"

"Have you talked to your grandpa lately?"

"What's that supposed to mean?"

"I think we're coming to an agreement. We drop the lawsuit and ask the county to drop the criminal prosecution. Luther comes and joins us for a press conference. We bury the hatchet."

"He ain't doing it."

"I wouldn't be so sure about that. We've been talking it through with your city councilman, and with the pastor at New Hope. I'm offering you the same deal. All I want is for you to do something else with your life than shit-talk Amazon. That's it. You do that, and we're good. If not, well, you can get some real street cred once you get out of prison about five years from now."

Piper's pulse was hammering behind her eyes. Was she going out like that? She had close to fifty grand in her war chest from the GoFundMe page. Could she just apologize, take it and run? Freedom or jail? Maybe it was best for Gramps to apologize, shake hands for the cameras. He'd be free, as he should be. But people were suffering, and the country was all too happy to not care. Someone had to make them care. Piper was still young. Getting locked up had not been the plan. But how could she live with herself if she just rolled over? Fifty grand in the account. She could post bail and fight it. Raise more money, get more lawyers, get more press, fight harder.

She pulled her phone from her pocket and set it down on the inlaid chessboard of the concrete table. "Hope you like the sound of your voice," Piper said. "I've been recording this whole conversation."

Ellis caught Clevester with a left hook to the body just as Sean kicked him in the back of the knee, sending him tumbling forward. Ellis popped up to see Demetreus emerging from the passenger side of the Malibu with a .22 in his shaky hands. Clevester was rolling on the ground, clutching his ribs.

"Blast that nigga!" Sean barked, blood pouring out his nose.

Demetreus cocked the gun.

"DROP IT OR I WILL BREAK YOU!" Ellis roared.

Ask any youth counselor in the inner city about who rejoins the living and who gets sucked into the vortex of the street. They'll tell you about fear, greed, insecurity, narcissism. How a kid about to go straight ends up shooting someone. How difficult it is to predict. How it often comes down to a single inflection point, a moment where two vastly different futures, equally likely, vie for a place in reality. Here it was. Demetreus stood frozen, looking down the barrel.

"Fucking do it!" Sean yelled.

His hands dropped an inch.

Another inch.

Ellis saw it in D's eyes. He wouldn't shoot. Sean lunged, and Ellis caught him in the hip with a round kick, sending him to the ground. He spun to find Clevester back up and swinging. Ellis took the blow on his right forearm, then clocked him with a left hammerfist, knocking him against the car where he couldn't escape. Ellis hit hard, again and again, keeping an eye on D, who was still holding the gun, Clevester's head bouncing against the car, his hands flailing as he tried to fend off the blows, Ellis barely registering that he was taking hits from behind until Sean connected with his temple. Ellis fell, but managed to kick out Sean's ankle. He jumped up while Sean tumbled down next to Clevester. The two of them were twisting on the ground. D was still staring at him from behind the car, and he brought the gun back up to level when he caught Ellis' murderous stare. Ellis brought a hand to the side of his head to feel the growing welt. "I just want to know," he said, through ragged breaths, "Who? Who did it?"

Demetreus glanced towards Sean, then back to Ellis. "Just leave," Demetreus said.

"This nigga, huh?" Ellis said. He could smell the fear in their sour sweat.

"Bitch—" Sean began, but Ellis' boot caught him in the head. Twice. Sean rolled over and stumbled up, then fell, blood running down his shirt, painting his white sneakers—he stumbled up again and ran two steps away, then fell again, his body refusing its commands. Clevester was up now and standing by Demetreus; they both stared at Sean's twitching body.

"Get that nigga to a hospital," Ellis said.

They didn't move.

Ellis stepped back to give them room. "The fuck you waiting for?"

They walked forward and pulled their friend into the back seat of the Malibu.

"I figured you'd record it," Annika said. "I stand by what I said."

"You still don't get it, though. I've got an Amazon executive on tape threatening to have a poor little black girl from Detroit sent to prison. How you think that's gon go over, huh?"

"I don't think you want to find out."

Piper gripped the side of the chessboard park table and leaned over, her eyes hot. "You don't think that's what I want? This ain't some PR stunt for me, this is my life. This is my home. You're asking me to just forget that my neighbor, Richie, is dead."

"No one's asking that. Your church, your councilman, your grandpa, they all want to grieve and move on with their lives. You know, for someone who claims to represent her neighborhood, you're looking kind of alone out here on this ledge."

"I keep saying, and you keep not hearing me. It's bigger than this neighborhood. Richie was unlucky enough to be a mentally

ill black man in a spot where guns pop off every four hours and
cops are just looking for an excuse to shoot. You've never been in
that position and you never will. And your kids never will. Every
Amazon success just reinforces this fucked up status quo, padding
the pockets of the white people who own Amazon stock, and doing
shit for people like Richie."

"You're right," Annika said. "I will never be in that position.
And Amazon can't fix inequality. But what Amazon can do is keep
innovating to bring down costs so that even people at the bottom
can afford to have food and medicine and books delivered to their
doorsteps—you had to be fantastically wealthy to get that kind of
service just a few years ago!"

Piper took a deep breath. *Wage love*, Nia had said. This woman
wasn't evil, she wasn't soulless. But she was assuming that Amazon's
vision of the future was what everyone else wanted, without even
thinking to ask them.

"You and your grandfather," Annika said, "you say a few words,
smile for the cameras, and that's it. It's done. Don't you want this to
be over?"

"Yeah," Piper said. "And all it takes is two more 'incidents,' right?
You think I don't read the news? That's what the FAA guy said. It
doesn't matter what you get my grandpa to say up there. If the neighborhoods decide to make a few *no fly zones*, you get shut down."

Annika stood up from the table. In some other time, in some
other reality, they'd fight it out right here, pounding each other's
faces like a pair of Krav pads, until someone tapped out. Then maybe
they'd shake hands, and that would be it. But that was Ellis' world.
Annika lived in a world that was perhaps more peaceful, but no less
cruel. Perhaps more cruel.

"I guess we'll find out, then," Annika said.

"Guess so," Piper spat, and she walked out of the park.

Annika's fists were clenched as she watched the girl leave, her
futuristic shoes still pulsing with the animated hashtag.

Ellis looked at the torn skin on his knuckles, the blood on his
shirt, finally catching his breath. The moment after a fight was like
the moment after sex, the body flooded with endorphins, high on

its own physical extremity. It was always in these moments that he felt like his truest self—a body only, a perfect body running on instinct. But it never lasted. You couldn't just lie back and enjoy the comedown. There was always the condom to take off and flush, or the gun to pick up and toss. He kicked the clip into the bushes behind the party store, then picked up the pistol, wiped it off with his shirt, and tossed it in the dumpster. There was a camera up on the corner of the building, but knowing this part of town, it was probably a dummy. As he walked back to his car, incipient bruises on his ribs and knees making themselves known, a sadness crept over him. He'd fucked that kid up, but at least no one had been shot. Even so, how did he go from here back to picking product at Amazon, grinding through night school, moms still banged up in the hospital? What did it say for his future if it was shit like this that made him feel alive?

28

Piper parked in front of Goldman's house, gave a quick knock on his door, and walked right in. She found the rapper sitting in his breakfast nook, wearing a silk boxer's robe, eating a bowl of Grape Nuts, and watching *Aqua Teen Hunger Force* on his laptop.

"Hey, baby," he said through a mouthful of cereal.

"I talked to that Amazon spokeslady last night. I got her on tape saying they're gon throw me in jail."

"They ain't tryna cut a deal?"

"Oh, they trying. They want me to apologize."

"But you ain't gonna."

"Serious?"

"Hey look, I'm down. I'm just saying, like, you young, right? You smart. Gotta think about your future."

"They throw me in jail, I just get stronger. King did."

"You ain't King, though, girl, no disrespect..."

"I ain't going back to posting pics of nigga's kicks all day."

"So whatchu wanna do?"

"Burn her. Put out the tape of her threatening me. And if they arrest me, fine. Then we do the thing we talked about."

He swallowed a spoonful. "You wanna make that no fly zone for real. Sure bout that?"

She nodded. "Your boys ready?"

"They ready. Got masks and everything. But you sure? You ready?"

"No." Piper said.

"Your gramps know bout this?"

"No."

"He ain't gon be happy."

"I know."

"So who you doing this for?"

For Richie? For Nia? Or was it just for her, for her own ego? It sounded so stupid to say she was doing it for everyone, for society, but that's what felt the most true. "Do I have to know?" she said. "It just feels right."

Goldman finished off his Grape Nuts, then drained the milk. He gave her a long look. "Whatever you decide, boo, I got you."

The doors of Detroit Receiving Hospital slid open, and Annika walked to intake with the name and room number. She'd finally texted Ellis and he'd told her where to find him. Some kid was choking and braying in a restraint gurney a few feet away, surrounded by cops and orderlies. Annika paid it no mind. Her thoughts were swirling around that disastrous bull session with Neptune Frost. And her e-mail was exploding with Google alerts, but not for "Prime Air" or "Hood Fresh," but for "Annika Dahl." Content was popping up on the web, mentioning her by name. She followed a link to a YouTube video: "Activist threatened with jail by Amazon Executive." The still frame thumbnail was her very own face. The elevator doors opened, and she stepped in with an elderly patient and a few nurses. *Threatened with jail.* That was a risk, saying that, but Annika had thought it was a good one. Now everything was up in the air. She clicked on the video, but her phone had no service inside the elevator. She closed her eyes for a moment, breathed in the sterile hospital air, and zipped the phone up in her pencil case. The old woman next to her had a small plastic tube taped to the papery skin of her wrist; it ran up through the arm of her dress and ended in a portacath just underneath her collarbone, a light bruise radiating out from the subdermal implant. The woman looked up and into Annika's eyes, and Annika looked away. *Threatened with jail by Amazon Executive.* The elevator doors opened, and Annika walked down the hall, her eyes back on her phone, willing it to catch the invisible 4G breeze as her heels clicked past the nursing station where two police detectives were inquiring about an eighteen-year-old male in critical condition. Annika found the room and poked her head in. There she was, sitting up on a reclining hospital bed and staring out a window at the sun falling pink over the lower peninsula. She turned her head to focus her good eye on Annika.

"Mrs. Wallace?" she asked.

"Yes?"

"Hi...I'm Nik Dahl. Ellis said..."

Misha smiled. "Oh, he should be back soon. Come in."

Annika sat on a chair near the bed.

"So you this special friend. He said you was pretty."

"I brought you something," Annika said, and she pulled a small box of chocolates from her purse.

Misha thanked her with a wince, then patted them, and said she'd get to them soon as she could chew.

"Ellis told me what happened. I'm so sorry."

"So it goes. Lord's still watching over me, though it does seem like he blinks now and then. And how you doing, honey? Detroit treating you right?"

"Mostly. Work has been...tough recently."

Misha took in the girl—frazzled hair, tired eyes. "Has it now?" she said.

"You don't think Amazon's evil do you?"

"Evil? No. The drones are creepy, don't get me wrong. But you get used to anything. I used to think cell phones were creepy, and now I'm on mine every day, checking this and that. Drones will be the same, I expect."

"Yeah, but right now, they're still getting shot at."

"All in good time. You know, people around here, they're used to getting banged up a bit. Look at me. People will carry on. You be all right. You hand me that water, honey?"

Misha took a shaky sip and handed it back. "You a bit of a departure for my boy, I gotta say."

"He's a bit of a departure for me."

"I bet. Ha. Ow." Misha settled her head back to the pillow. "I have to rest my eyes, dear. Ellis be back any minute now, I'm sure."

Annika leaned back in her chair, her phone beckoning to her. She tried to fight it. It won. She popped in a pair of earbuds, and clicked on the video:

Neptune Frost and Goldman Stackz sitting on a porch, speaking to the camera, inviting their guests to check the latest Amazon bullshit. Cut to: silent clips from #NOFLYZONE and #BLACKMONEYWHITEPOCKETS—that cell-phone footage of the police shooting, that man's death, and in audio over the footage, the unsettling sound of Annika's own voice: *"All I want is for you to do something else with your life than shit-talk Amazon. That's it. You do that, and we're good. If not, well, you can get some real street cred once you get out of prison about five years from now."* Neptune speaks to the camera: "Go ahead, lock me up. See what happens."

Annika stopped the video. Incoming e-mail from Jasper: "Call me." A quick swipe down the email chain and she saw the message from Bezos containing the dreaded single question mark and a link to the video. She jumped as a large hand plucked an earbud from her ear.

"Hey, girl, you okay?" Ellis was holding an ice pack to his head. "Oh my god, are you okay? What happened?"

"Nothing." His voice was softer, less spirited than usual.

Annika cocked an eyebrow.

He glanced at his sleeping mother, leaned down, and whispered: *"I found the kids who banged up my moms. Taught them a lesson."*

"You what? Oh my god, you beat them up?"

"Shhh. She'll kill me. You saw what they did to her. That's how we do."

"I get it, but you don't want to get arrested or anything," she whispered.

"I know, it was dumb, but those kids ain't telling nobody. It's done."

"Feel good?"

He looked at her, then took her hand, and lifted her out of her chair.

"You know it did," he said.

She put a hand to her face.

"Hey, you don't have the sniffles today. Maybe you're finally settled in here?"

Annika tried to smile, but it wouldn't stick.

"What is it?"

"I met with that girl. That's what I was calling about earlier."

"You Krav Maga that bitch?"

"I wish. That might have been a better idea. I threatened her with a little jail time for stealing Lucy."

"Ooh."

"And she recorded me saying it. Now it's all over the internet. I think I might lose my job."

"Oh, shit."

She nodded. "But we still got her dead to rights. We hand over the evidence from Lucy, and then cops will take her in."

"What then?"

"I don't know."

"Well," he said, glancing over at his mom, "it's good to see you. If you do lose your job, does that mean your schedule's gonna be freed up for some more…urban exploring?"

Her gaze hardened. Wrong time to bring up sex? But no, she smiled, a little sadly, and fell into his arms. He held her, swaying side to side, while Mom pretended to sleep.

Curtis had called her after he'd seen the video, and he'd told her, through joyous laughter, that it was the most baller thing in the world, daring Amazon to have her arrested. Piper had been telling herself for so long that she had important things to do, that she was so much better than someone like Curtis. But he got it, on a deep level, he understood why she was doing this. Enough to laugh. Enough that she could share her underlying insecurities about the whole thing. He'd asked to see her. It was her idea to go for a night-walk.

"You sure they not bluffing?" he asked.

"Don't matter. *I'm* not. But that's not what I'm worried about."

Lightning bugs pulsed in and out of existence. The air was moist and sweet.

"What, then?"

"I'm just worried I can't put it down. That I'm doing it all for some sick ego thing. You don't know what it's like. I've got over a million followers on RNKR now. A fucking million. How am I supposed to stop feeding that shit?"

Curtis draped his arm around her and just nodded. "I ain't worried about you," he said. "You more like your sister than you know. Just got your own style."

The first time wasn't an accident, exactly, but they didn't know they were gon rape the bitch until it was happening. The night before they'd been at a house party in Brightmoor when some nigga called Bo a faggot just for the way he was leaning—so they threw down, Bo and Adam, but they got stomped when the nigga's homies jumped in. The next day, they decided to find that nigga and teach his ass a lesson. Adam had a piece his cousin left him when he caught an assault charge. They railed some coke to get ready, then found the nigga leaving a Coney on Fenkell Ave, him and this bitch, about 11:30. Adam pulled the piece, and they ordered them out behind a vacant. Adam kicked the nigga to the ground and put the gun to his head. They was just gon scare the nigga, but his bitch started mouthing off. So Bo grabbed her and threw her down. And it just happened. Adam made the nigga watch, the whole time thinking about how Shar, his ex, had been fucking some nigga behind his back. He'd been having violent, vengeful dreams for months—she didn't even live in Detroit anymore. When Bo was done, they shared a look and didn't have to say nothing. Bo took the piece, and Adam took his turn.

They kept it between them for a minute, but it was hard not tell the homies. Cal and Damon thought it was the funniest shit. Cal wanted to know everything, every detail about how she squirmed, what she whimpered. He'd never tell his boys what happened when he was twelve—his older brother's friend, nigga back from two years in the pen—how he'd cried the whole time. But since then, he'd felt a sick impulse to make someone else feel that way. Damon was just a violent and stupid nigga, punch a fucking brick wall if you told him to. Once Eric and Frankie found out, the thing started taking shape. They were only sixteen and neither one had touched a pussy wasn't they momma's. Frankie was Adam's cousin, and he'd lick Adam's shadow just for a nod. So it became a mission. Eric and Frankie wanted to run with his crew, they had to prove they wasn't no bitch-niggas.

They did it just like before, only this time, they was rolling six-deep. They met up in a shitty park at Van Dyke and Sylvester, smoked a couple blunts, passing a fifth of vodka around, then Bo brought out the coke, and they got turnt. Didn't have to wait long—some nigga and his bitch walking down Van Dyke in the summer heat. Adam put his boot on the nigga's back and put the gun to his head, just like last time. Then he told Frankie to do it. The bitch was shaking, crying. But he just stood there, till Damon punched the bitch in the face and held her down.

The time after that was even easier. They'd all fallen into their roles. Adam liked holding the gun, making the nigga watch his bitch get fucked in every hole. After, they got blunted at Bo's house, but Cal starting saying shit, that it was fucked. He bounced, and when they saw him a few days later, nigga had bandages on his wrists. Fuck it, they didn't need him. Frankie was acting hard now, and Eric was wearing those dead-eyes. Thought they'd be done after that. Shit was on the news, risky. But there wasn't nothing to do except smoke, drink, roll around in Bo's shitty car. Not like niggas had jobs. But it was easy doing nothing in the lazy days at the end of summer. Then Adam got rolled by the hook on some bullshit—threw him against the hood and searched him, just for walking while black. Good thing he wasn't holding. But that shit got his blood up again.

So here they were, everyone but Cal, squaded up, high as fuck, looking for another fix. And there it was, walking right towards them. Short-ass nigga, skinny bitch. Damon, Eric and Frankie were waiting a block away. Adam nodded to Bo and cocked his piece.

Piper noticed them when they crossed Harper and walked south on May. Two dudes in hoodies. Probably just lived in one of these shitty houses. Curtis still had his arm around her and it was starting to feel heavy. A billboard on the corner of Harper showed the stern face of a black lady and bold text: "YOU KNOW WHO KILLED ME."

"I don't think I know how to be alone," Piper said.

"Shit, you ain't gotta worry bout that—you magnetic."

"No…That's what I'm saying, though." She slipped out from under his arm. "I never get a chance, and when I actually am alone, it's like I'll suffocate if I don't start posting and ranking shit."

"Girl, you need to relax," Curtis said, pulling out a joint. He slowed his walk, and bent his head down to light it. That's when Piper saw the other three, rounding the corner at Duncan, walking with that barely restrained animal purpose you didn't ever want to see— her eyes jerked backward so fast they whipped her head around after them—the other two were closing in—*RUN*—her bones vibrated to the word, every muscle sour and taut. She clutched at Curtis' arm and whipped him around, then walked straight into the two men behind them. Curtis dropped the joint as his perma-chuckled face flattened with fear. Maybe it was nothing, paranoia. That thought evaporated when she saw the guy's face. Her body carried her forward—it had its own plan, and she could tell what it was going to do: it was going to walk right up to this motherfucker, kick him in the balls, and run. But then she saw the gun barrel, and her autopilot failed. Curtis turned back only to get jumped by the other three. The guy with the gun approached slowly, and Piper walked backward in short halting steps, the distance between them closing.

"Turn around, bitch," he said.

She did.

"Walk."

She did. Past a sign that read, "NO OUTLET." *Breathe*, she told herself. The other three had Curtis's arms pinned behind his back.

One of them held a knife to his neck. They marched him forward. The overwhelming sound of silence, of night—then a car passing behind them on Harper, already gone.

Piper hit the ground, the back of her knees throbbing. Smell of burnt garbage. Curtis was ten feet off, his face pressed to the dirt, a foot on his back. They were out behind a charred pile of rubble. The siding on the vacant house next door looked like melted, blackened marshmallow. She could hear the low hum of the Ford Freeway a block to the south. Three of them were passing around a small plastic baggie now, doing key hits, snorting.

"Don't, don't hurt us," Curtis said. "Just take whatever, nigga." The guy pressed the gun to his temple and Curtis whimpered out a barely intelligible *please*. The other four surrounded Piper. *Move. Get up.* She reached deep into herself to pull out something, anything, like clawing a bullet out of her chest with her bare hand. "FUCK," she said. "YOU." And she could breathe again. "FUCK YOU FUCK YOU." The dam broke—"You little dickless bitches, fuck you, fuck all you ugly ass niggas, y'all ain't shit, fucking cowards."

Two of them grabbed her legs and pulled—her head hit the dirt and her world filled with a high-pitched whining...

"Grab her fucking arms."

Head throbbing, the whining growing louder and louder...

"You want this dick, bitch?"

Louder, a buzzing, a whirring, a droning...There above her, a light...

"The fuck?"

The Amazon drone descended to the yard adjacent the vacant house just as a shoeless, shirtless man stumbled out of the wreck holding a half-empty vodka bottle and a glowing smartphone. "That's my goddamn pizza!" He yelled at everyone and no one.

"Shit!"

"Hook!"

"Shit!"

"Ain't the hook!"

"Yo, B!"

"Fuck."

"Where the fuck you going!"

And there was the drone lifting off, and there was the nothing tugging at her legs. Piper sat up as the noise faded into the sky. She caught the last of the figures disappearing around the corner. Curtis had struggled to his feet. He held out his hand. Piper looked at it, confused.

"You okay?" he said.

She stood up on her own, stared right through him, then ran away.

Home, the front door shut and locked behind her, her bedroom door shut and locked behind her, her comforter, much too hot for any other night, pulled all the way over her head, she listened to her own breathing, just her breathing, hoping her body would calm down, that it would shut down from exhaustion. It didn't. She'd trained herself to process everything through that glowing rectangle. She brought her phone under the comforter and opened up RNKR. She linked the last *Free Press* article on the rape gang, geo-tagged the Harper and May intersection, then attached a two-second video, the first she'd ever posted of her own face: "Motherfuckers almost got me. Where the fuck you at DPD?"

29

Jamal let the alarm buzz a few times before hitting snooze. 0600 on a Sunday morning. He felt the mattress shift near his legs as Barry stretched out and lumbered up to his face, putting a paw down on his leg and another right on his crotch. Jamal tossed him off.

"Jesus, buddy."

He checked his phone. Some work emails about the conference. A Google alert for a new Neptune Frost RNKR posting. Too early for that shit, but he clicked on it anyway. No one has free will anymore; it's all up to the phones. It was a selfie video of Piper. That was new. Holy shit. The rape gang?

"Barry, get up."

Dog and human hit the floor with a pair of heavy thuds and moved over toward the desktop. Jamal logged on to the UAV footage server. Harper and May. Just last night. He toggled through a few flights with nothing much to see, then moved on to a Sky Pies delivery running west by southwest from the Hamtramck Domino's to just about the spot in question. There was the delivery, guy collecting his pizza. Nothing notable. But, ah, the Skeeter had another pie to deliver, a Buddy Pizza promotional thing. Delivery address looked like a collapsing vacant. He'd love to get the metrics on how many deliveries went to vacants.

And sure enough, there was a group of men. They were closing in on a couple: one male, one female. Not just any female. Piper Prince.

As the Skeeter descended for delivery, the gang took off—squirters, they called them during combat ops—and a moment later, so did Piper. Jamal ran the footage back. The assailants had come from Harper. And there was one of them walking into a building. Was that a…? He scrolled forward again until the Skeeter was right above the building. It was. *Prince Liquor.* There had to be security cameras all over that place. They'd keep that footage for at least a day, right?

His phone rang. Annika.

"Hey Jamal. Change of plans on the press conference today. We want you to take the lead."

"You want me in front of the cameras? You know I'm not great at—"

"You won't have to say much."

"Just stand up there and be black."

"That's what I always do…"

He waited for her to jump into some mile-a-minute Nik Dahl master class on PR theory, but there was silence on the other line. Barry put a paw on his leg, and Jamal stood up to go let him out.

"I'll do it," he said. "No worries. But hey, I think I've got something for you."

"What?"

"Well, you know that thing on the news with these rape guys?"

"Yeah…you see Piper's RNKR thing?"

"I did. And I looked through some of last night's Skeeter footage."

"That's against policy," Annika said.

"I know, but I found some clear images. I think the cops can ID these guys."

"Yeah, but it turns our Skeeters into police surveillance tools. People are gonna freak."

"No, they won't. They'll love us."

"I don't think you get people's attitudes towards your little flying children."

"Tech people are worried about surveillance. People in the 313 are more worried about getting attacked. This can be a one-off thing.

And come on, it's too good. Make nice with Grandpa and stick it to the guys that attacked the granddaughter. We could make the announcement today. Just give me the word, and I'll send it over to DPD."

"Yeah. I don't think I can make that call right now. I'm on the shitlist."

"Piper's not gonna take the deal, is she?"

"Doesn't look like it."

"And you being on the shitlist…that's why I've got the speaking role today?"

"Yeah."

"I think you've been doing a great job," he said.

Annika sighed.

"I mean it. You're in a difficult spot. No good answers."

"Thanks."

"You really think Grandpa will show up to the press conference if you have his granddaughter arrested?"

"We're gonna ask DPD if they can serve the warrant during or after the conference."

"That's cold."

"You have a better idea? It's gonna be open season on Skeeters if we let people just get away with this stuff and shoot music videos about it."

"I know."

"Or we could see if she shows up to the press conference and try to have cuffs slapped on right there, next to Grandpa. That sound good to you?"

"Jesus, Nik, sorry. I get it."

"I'm sick of being the wicked witch. Maybe I should go chain myself to a water meter. I'm doing the right thing here."

"Okay. Just ask Jasper, okay, about the footage?"

"I'll let you know what he says."

"This is a good thing. We can do a good thing."

"You've got an hour. Get dressed."

Piper awoke to a knock on her door. She was prone, her clothes still on, her face resting in a warm drool spot. She didn't open her eyes. Images from last night flashed into her mind.

The knock came again, and the door cracked open. Her gramps.

"Itty? I'm going along to this thing with the Amazon people."

She didn't respond.

"They're not asking much, just to say a few words. Piper? I understand you don't like it, and I respect that. But. Well, it's my decision. I want to put this behind me."

"Okay," she said. It was all she could manage.

"Why your shoes still on? You fall asleep like that?"

She didn't lift her head from the pillow, but she could feel his eyes on her, scanning for trouble. She looked up at him. "I'm good. You do your thing. I'll see you after." She heard him sigh, then gently shut her door.

She lay there for a few minutes, listening to the birds outside, willing herself to drift back to unconsciousness where she didn't have to think about last night, or what her gramps was about to do, a song and dance for Amazon.

A faint smell of baking tar and synthetic lubricant wafted off the tarmac of the Amazon airfield. Luther Prince stood on a low platform behind a podium. Above him hung a gleaming vinyl banner sporting the Amazon logo. He hadn't worn a suit for anything other than church and funerals since his retirement ceremony at Ford over a decade ago. The jacket was sticking to his back in the heat, and sweat was pooling between his toes and on his wrist under the gold retirement watch that he still wore. He was surprised with how much media had shown up. Piper must have really stirred up some trouble. Pastor Edwards and the councilman were here, too, along with some of the congregation. As the camera people did their last light checks and the microphones were tapped and thumbs-up given, Jamal Dent approached—the man who'd shown up on the doorstep the morning he'd shot down that drone.

"Mr. Prince? Jamal Dent."

"I remember you, Jamal."

"Sure. Thanks for coming today. I appreciate it."

Luther nodded.

"We'll start in just a moment," Jamal said. He excused himself and found Annika on the periphery.

"What did Jasper say? Can we give the footage to DPD?"

"He brought it to the S-Team," she said. "Still waiting to hear back."

"Okay, so I can't say anything about that?"

"I'll signal you if word comes in. You'll do fine. Now get up there."

Jamal lurched back on stage next to Luther.

"Thank you, everyone, for, uh, coming here today," Jamal said into the mic, reading off note cards. He rattled off a few pleasant things about Amazon's present and future cooperation with the city of Detroit.

Annika covered her mouth to hide her smile. Jamal was stilted, but actually rather endearing. The press sat there politely, eating it up. Jamal was so bad at this, he was good at it. Or at least, he was the right kind of bad at it. It made him seem guileless, homespun. It was a relief, honestly. The only thing worse than wondering if she'd get sacked was the thought that everything she'd been working on was about to fall off the shelf. But this was going well. And if DPD had done their job, they'd be rolling up to the Prince residence right about now. Annika felt bad about the timing, hiding that from Luther, but they couldn't risk him backing out at the last minute, and they would lose all credibility if they let Piper off the hook for stealing a UAV. And if the S-Team gave the go-ahead on handing the rape-gang footage to the DPD, Amazon would come out of this looking golden.

"And now, Mr. Luther Prince has a few words to say," Jamal said. He stepped aside and nodded toward Luther with a smile.

Luther took a moment scrutinizing Jamal's face—it was an honest smile. He approached the mic and cleared his throat. Lord, was he really going to do this? Even after poor Richie?

Piper startled awake at the sound of a loud knocking. It didn't stop. She struggled out of bed and opened the front door to find Officer Shepard with some other cop she hadn't seen before.

"Good morning, Ms. Prince."

"Where's your asshole partner?"

"We've got a warrant for your arrest."

She gave her watch a mock glance. "That's a fast response for the east side. This city must really be turning around."

"You knew this was coming. Don't make me the bad guy here."

Piper held her hands out in front of her. Shepard put the cuffs on loose around her bony wrists, the steel ratcheting in time with the old wind chimes her grandmother had hung from the porch decades ago.

Luther surveyed the crowd as they stared him down, waiting for him to speak. He knew damn well why they wanted him up here—to be a black face, a Detroit face telling everyone that Amazon wasn't so bad. He'd been angry, angry at life that it would allow a hard-working man like himself to be stuck in a dying neighborhood, getting his water shut off. That wasn't Amazon's fault. It was a million things. But he wasn't even angry anymore, just sad. "I'd just like to say...that I apologize for...shooting at that drone. That was a mistake." He made eye contact with Pastor Edwards, who nodded at him. Admitting you were wrong was supposed to be a good thing, a Christian act, humility, but this felt more like humiliation. "I was annoyed at the sound, but there were better ways to handle that. I'd also like to say that I'm glad that the charges against me are being dropped, and I can go back home to my granddaughter."

"Mr. Prince," said a reporter, "what do you think Amazon should be doing for the people of Detroit?"

Leaving them the hell alone? Letting them decide how to fix their own problems? "Well," Luther said, "I think Amazon should try listening to the people who live here. This city's had problems for a long time, and people have been thinking hard and working hard to fix those problems for a long time. Detroit ain't a blank slate. So don't treat it that way."

"What do you think about the new Goldman Stackz video?"

"I don't listen to rap much," Luther said. "I understand that it gives some respects to my old neighbor and friend, Richie McGown, and I appreciate that. He didn't have to die like he did.

And if it wasn't for this drone business, he wouldn't be dead right now. I put that on the city, I do. I put it on the healthcare system, which bankrupted me when my wife and granddaughter passed. Bankrupted, after thirty years of working for Ford. You've got folks here trying to make it like you're supposed to be able to make it in this country."

Sweat rivered down Jamal's neck. Oh god, the old man was starting to ramble. He looked to Annika. *Cut him off?*

Annika refreshed her inbox. Nothing from Jasper. She bit her lip and gave him a micro-shrug.

"Have you seen these neighborhoods? Have you walked down the streets past vacant afer vacant?" Luther caught a whiff of Jamal's fear. They weren't liking this. Good. Was this what Piper felt making her videos? It was hard to resist. "Drone delivery ain't a solution to the problems we got, and a bad solution's nothing but another problem!"

Annika refreshed her inbox again. There it was. Jasper. They had the go-ahead. She caught Jamal's eye and gave him a thumbs up.

"Thank you, Mr. Prince," Jamal said, stepping back in front of the podium. "Just one more thing before we end here. I found, I mean we, in a routine footage check, we stumbled across some evidence that may lead to the arrest of those men who've been going around assaulting young couples, and we'll be handing that footage over to the DPD."

When Luther got home, he found Piper's room empty. He called through the house, and not finding her anywhere, went out to sit on the porch. She was probably off doing her thing. Which was fine. He wanted her to do what made her happy. Still, would be nice to have her here now. The sun was out, not a cloud in the sky. Just those little black dots zipping back and forth. What passed for a beautiful day, these days.

Sandra was late with the kids—it was almost seven. Maybe she wasn't even coming. Jamal had made them dinner and was keeping it warm in the oven. He looked outside again—no cars—and checked his phone again—no calls. He thought about texting her, but—well, she didn't seem like she wanted to talk to him at all, maybe ever again, and bugging her about being late today, or not coming, that would just sour things further. It was frustrating. And the kids didn't deserve this tension. They deserved a family meal. They deserved a family. And he needed them now more than ever, just to breathe, to give his mind a break from the constant headache of work.

The press conference with the old man had gone over fine, and the girl had been arrested, but that probably wasn't the last they'd hear from her. Annika was still freaking out. There was an S-Team meeting on Monday where she would likely get a lashing from Bezos. They were coming up on the end of their two-month review with the FAA, and they were still just a hair under the incident limit, but with public perception so negative, they might not get nationwide approval anyway. For Jamal, that meant pulling long hours to make sure there were absolutely no further screw-ups or malfunctions. Even now, Bud was at work monitoring the UAV traffic, giving Jamal a chance to see his kids. He felt guilty not being at work and he felt stupid for feeling guilty about that. It was a lose either way. It seemed like every day at Amazon was a crisis situation. Jamal thrived under pressure, but his nerves were getting frayed. A part of him thought he should just leave.

A buddy from Seattle had just forwarded him an email about a job opening at Google. He could cut his losses, move to Mountain View and leave Amazon, and Detroit. He'd heard that work-life balance was better at Google, or at least a topic that wasn't taboo. But if he left Detroit, if he left Sandra and the girls, what life would he even have to balance? What life would he have without the smell of their hair as he tucked them in and kissed them goodnight, without their hip-hop dance recitals and goofy elementary school musicals. Leaving them seemed impossible, even if he barely saw them.

And leaving Amazon seemed impossible, too. Never before had he been surrounded by so many talented and driven people. Every day, he witnessed inspiring feats of creative problem solving, the pure aesthetics of ingenuity. As for what problems they were solving, well, streamlining commerce and delivery had never seemed like the most noble or exciting job, but lately he'd begun to see how much of a gift it was, to students who could spend more time studying, to the elderly who had trouble making it to the store, to the mothers and fathers who could spend less time shopping and more time with their kids. For every second Amazon shaved off the shopping experience, the customer had another second to focus on what really mattered to them, whatever that might be. I mean, Christ, he had the table set with plates and silverware that had been delivered by drone while he was at work.

Jamal snapped to at the sound of a car door. She was here.

Eve squirmed as Sandra unbuckled her from the car seat. She almost hadn't come, but the kids had wanted to see Daddy. They felt something for Jamal that she used to feel. Excitement. Longing. She wanted that. Could she just choose it? Her pastor had said last week that love is a choice, that if you choose to love God, you will feel him enter your heart, but if you wait for the feeling to come, you may wander lost and alone for years. Forever. But that was God. And this was poor, flawed, Jamal. Jamal who had chosen work over family in Nevada, in Seattle. Jamal who had been too busy to see their marriage dissolving. Was it different now? Was he? Could she just choose to love him again?

Before she could ring the bell, the door opened, and the kids jumped up and hugged their daddy.

"Hungry?" he said. "Food's on the table."

The girls ran inside. She looked over Jamal's shoulder and saw that he had the table set. For four.

"There's a chair for you," Jamal said.

"I don't know," Sandra said. "I probably…"

The kids climbed into their chairs and dug in, dipping their grilled cheeses in tomato soup. The smell of fried bread, tangy tomato—she saw the two of them, eight years ago, on their third date. Was that still all he knew how to make? Jamal was holding his hand out with a brave smile, a smile prepared to tip into the abyss. Sandra's eyes watered. She grabbed his hand and squeezed it. "I'd like that," she said.

And for the first time in four years, the Dent family ate dinner

together, Nina and Eve splashing soup, talking up a storm, while
Jamal and Sandra just stared at each other, their feet touching under
the table. Was this what it felt like to choose love? Sadness and anger
have a way of making you feel alone, even when surrounded by
people—there is no fellowship between the sad and rageful. It's quite
the opposite with love. Love is a door opening into a party of the
hopeful, an invitation. As they ate their grilled cheese sandwiches,
the Dents could feel the presence of countless other families in the
city of Detroit, sitting down to their own dinners, right this second,
sharing air and words and food, all of them engaging in a city-wide
communion, all of them dreaming of a brighter future.

30

Luther Prince sat in his living room with an intermittent smile on his face. He was feeling pretty good about life, better than he had in a while. It was like that time, a long while ago, when he'd scratched his cornea at the Rouge Plant after working with some glass shavings. He'd been blinded and in agony at the aid station until a nurse put some numbing drops in his eye, and when the pain left, he had started laughing right there on the table. That feeling when pain is added and then suddenly taken away. He was a bit concerned, though. Piper hadn't come home last night. Not that that was unheard of, but she ought to be around at a time like this.

There was knock on his door. Luther opened up and found a white kid—young man, really—standing on his porch in jeans and a t-shirt.

"Mr. Prince?"

"Mmm hmm?"

"Hi, I'm Aaron. I've got the farm over on Armour..."

"Aaron. I believe Piper mentioned you. She ain't here at the moment."

"I know, sir. She's...downtown. They arrested her yesterday. For stealing that drone. Do you...know about—"

"The drone. Oh, Jesus, Lord."

"I'm heading down there. You want to come?"

Piper was rubbing her handcuff-free wrists when the door opened with a clang. Goldman Stackz stood at intake in an all-white denim ensemble, signing a metal clipboard with a Stackz-y flourish. He winked at her.

"That's a day of my life I ain't never getting back," Piper said.

"They gon regret pissing you off, boo," he said, leading her past security.

"Hey," she said, grabbing his arm to stop him. She pulled him in for a hug. She needed to feel another body. That night in jail had been an irreducibly physical experience. Sitting in that cell, she'd become acutely aware that the overflowing praise and love directed at her virtual self, at Neptune Frost, could never satisfy her the way a simple hug could. And she had so few people in her life to touch in that way. And whose fault was that but her own? "Thanks for coming," she said.

Goldman squeezed her, then pulled back and gave her a nuggie. "Girl, I ain't the only fam you got."

He opened the door to blinding sunlight, and they stepped out onto the sidewalk, where a small throng awaited them. There was Goldman's crew, and Otto Slice with a cheeseball grin, and Danny Mikos wearing Goldman's scarf, and Curtis just about skipping up to meet her. And a bunch of weirdo white kids—the Daffys—and there was Aaron Thistle pulling up in his pickup, and climbing out the passenger door, her sweet old gramps, smiling his grandpa smile, eyes wet behind those huge glasses. What a strange loving crowd. She reached for her phone to snap a picture, but stopped. No, this didn't belong on RNKR. This wasn't for Neptune Frost. It belonged to Piper Prince.

"Burrows files his report tomorrow, and we're over the incident limit. They could make an exception, but we should expect to stay confined to Detroit through September." Bezos stalked the perimeter of the Seattle conference room like an angry sentry patrolling the battlements, the evenly spaced heads of the S-Team forming the castle's crenellations. Annika, jet-lagged from her red-eye from Detroit, sat with her hands folded in her lap, picking at her nails, trying to focus on the meeting in which she would likely get fired. It was coming, soon.

"These last ones were deliberate shoot downs. They put us over the limit on purpose," Jasper said.

"There's no exception in the new regs for that."

"That's absurd. We need to get Burrows to push this in Washington!"

"The FAA's still skittish. They'll take any excuse to stiff-arm the program."

"Come on, the people want this. We have polls. It's only a matter of time."

"Oh come on, Rajit, they'll drag their feet for years if they can."

"Gay marriage happened fast."

"Not fast enough!" Bezos thundered. "If we can't get into the major markets in a few months, our whole production schedule will be screwed. If it takes a year, we're looking at major competition from day one."

"So we press Burrows on this and get amended language for the next go around."

"Do we need more lawyers?"

"If we don't get those no-fault terms nixed, Google's going to start giving out free net guns at Lions games."

"We'll get some more legal talent to try to move the ball in DC," Bezos said. "Production wise, we continue to gear up. This technology is inevitable, remember that. Aside from outside interference, our record's been flawless. And the latest polls are encouraging. Think legal weed back in 2015. There's going to be a lot of grumbling, but there's just too much money to be made. The bureaucratic opposition will turn into leeching—taxes, concessions, etc. Leeching we can deal with. It's only temporary. As Prime Air takes off, we'll have increasing leverage to push back against any regulation that cuts into our margins or screws with the flywheel. So, regardless of immediate approval, we'll continue UAV production at full capacity as well as PR efforts in Detroit. Under new direction."

"I was gonna ask about that."

"Probably necessary."

"Sorry?" Annika said.

"You're sharp, Nik," said Bezos. "And you've been trying hard. And you have had to deal with some…unexpected resistance. But it's pretty obvious, after recent events, that we'll need to bring in someone else to fill the role of Prime Air Ambassador."

Oh god, was that it? Had she just been fired?

"Now about using the UAV footage for—"

"Jeff, sorry," Annika said. "What does that mean, for me?"

Bezos gesticulated wildly. "Are you even reading your e-mail these days? Christ. I'm moving you to Product Manager for Prime Air Farmers Market. Less personal drama. Now, the UAV Footage. Actually, first, Jasper, what's the news on Shu-Yen?"

"Well, apparently, the body rejected her head yesterday."

"Ah. Well, let's have two to three seconds of silence for Shu-Yen the chimp."

"No, no, she's alive! They're trying a new donor body. She went into surgery today."

A moment of horrified silence hung in the conference room.

"Wow, that's…let's continue. So we turned over some footage to the cops. A risky move, but maybe the good kind of risk. We'll see how it pans out. Let's talk about using it internally for customer demand metrics."

Jasper droned on about impulse-buy percentages as Annika tuned out. The image of the poor chimp Frankenstein filled her vision, and she struggled to lock it into one of her mind-cabinets. She hadn't been fired…that was good, wasn't it? But as soon as you start moving laterally, you're no longer a rising star, the sparkle fades. This was the death-knell for her career at Amazon. She would never make the S-Team.

"There's no legal question if there's no humans watching the footage."

"All done algorithmically!"

"But what can they actually identify?"

"What kind of car is in the driveway?"

"Is there a barbeque in the backyard?"

"Are the gutters clogged?"

"Then associated products are automatically suggested!"

"New car mats for your Honda!"

"Grill tongs!"

"It's a whole new level, really. If we could match addresses up with IPs through the service provider…"

"What about the creep factor here, once the ads start popping up?"

"Nobody cares," Bezos said. "Remember *The New York Times* exposé? Our stock went up a hundred and seventy-eight percent that year. We're trading privacy for convenience and safety. The people have chosen and will continue to choose Amazon, as long as we stay true to our guiding principles."

And what was the point of staying at Amazon if she'd just be shuffled from one middle-manager role to another, without ever making it to the top? Annika wasn't meant for the middle. The middle was a Chuck-E-Cheese for the unremarkable—a life-long diversion where no important decisions were made, where nothing that mattered ever originated. Or was that some sickness talking, the disease of over-achievement? Ellis seemed happy where he was. So did Spencer. So did so many people. Could she find a way to be happy in the middle? It seemed so impossible. The ladder started at the bottom of the ocean, and only the top rungs stuck out above the waves into the salt-sea air.

"…I didn't just buy this island for kicks," Bezos said. "At this moment, it's being sculpted into a world-class golf course. And this time next year, it will host the first ever Amazon Invitational, broadcast exclusively on Amazon Video."

"The networks will be livid!"

The booming Bezos laugh filled the room. "And golf is just the first step. Imagine the possibilities!"

"Poker!"

"Billiards!"

"Curling!"

And if she left Amazon, then what? Apply at Google, Facebook? Or she could strike out on her own, found a start-up—doing what? Something unequivocally good? Which was?

"Football?"

"That's a fight we're not ready for."

"*Foos*ball!"

The core of Annika's being felt raw, sandpapered by failure, by the sadness of not being good enough to rise to the top of Amazon. But that rawness also felt like exposure, like something had flung open all the windows of her body, all the cabinets in her mind, and the outside wind of possibility was racing in and swirling around her heart. She could do anything, she could go anywhere. Overseas? She could move back to Seattle? She could even stay in Detroit, with Ellis. She could get up right now and leave, without a word, just leave the room and walk until she felt like stopping. What do you call that feeling? Freedom?

"Jasper, I want you to hand select the team for Amazon Sports League. Now, many of you know that Blue Origin has a crucial rocket launch tomorrow. What many of you *don't* know is how this ties in with our operations here. Well, I'd like to let you in on

Up here, anything is possible—a woman stands on the green copper roof of the Book Tower, where falcons nest and spiders the size of children's fists spin webs for high-flying insects, while down below, thousands roll slow on bicycles through the city's streets—and there, Michigan Central Station, where Remingtons clacked ribbon against paper, and thousands in fedoras jostled under vaulted ceilings before the Goths and Vandals gutted it, left it windowless as lattice—somehow, now filled again with glass—and there, the lost city of the Packard Plant, once sprouting trees from its collapsing roof, home to growling packs of wild dogs, now a thriving business park—up here, the smells of cookouts and coneys and car exhaust and welding smoke mingle in the current, connecting the girl on a mission to the muscled man in the hospital window, the would-be thugs without their leader to the alcoholic newsie and the histrionic pastor, the philosophizing farmer to the nerdiest kid in East Detroit, and a father to the mother of his children, packing boxes for a move across town to a spruced up Victorian mansion—up here, the hovercars zoom past while the mag-trains rocket below, carrying human and android alike through the veins of Neo Detroit, rainforest lush atop every building—or is it the sulfurous air, thick and hot above the ruins of Lost Detroit, where roving gangs on jerry-built bikes run down and capture those foolish enough to stray from the protection of a tribe—the black, the white—raping, killing, leaving the carcasses for the outsize rats and glowing crows—up here, both of these futures co-exist—the rising, the falling—waiting for the people below to choose.

Deliver Us: a novel Hardcover – Feb 22

by Christopher Robinson ▾(Author), Gavin Kovite ▾(Author)

Top Customer Reviews

 **Astounding Achievement**

By Nancy Dwight on Feb 22

Verified Purchase

It has been a while since I've found a book that I hoped would never end.
When reading the synopsis, I couldn't have imagined I'd feel so close to an
Amazon executive, a former military drone operator, a Krav Maga trainer,
and a hip social media guru. But the idiosyncracies of each character
made them come alive and pulled me into the pages. I was amazed at
how it felt like I was really in Detroit, the sounds, the smells, the weird
minutiae of social behaviors. What impressed me most was that I never
saw the end coming. It was like every stereotype and cliche was thrown
out the window and real life was just allowed to run its course. And yet,
real life is usually so messy and doesn't make a good story like this. That's
the true magic of this book, that it could feel so real, while also being silly
and serious and having a driving story that propels you through it.

6 Comments | Was this review helpful? Yes   No   Report Abuse

⭐⭐☆☆☆ **All Sizzle**

By Reese Bissle on Feb 22

Verified Purchase

Nothing encapsulates the failures of this book more than the fact that it
includes reviews of itself at the end. Is that meta-cleverness supposed to
make me feel something? All throughout the book, those fireworks are on
display, but they don't satiate my desire for emotional depth. Now there's
some of that to be sure, but it gets lots in the text messages, the youtube
comments, the emoji for Christ's sake! And ending the book mid-sentence,
just cutting out--I mean c'mon, you're not Thomas Pynchon. Honestly, I
think all the cleverness is compensating for some deep worry the authors
have that the book is hollow. That, or they're so worried about being
criticized for writing characters and material that doesn't "belong to them,"
which I couldn't care less about--just saying, so they armor up with layers
of self-reference. I wish they would just own it. There's a really good book
in here somewhere.

1 Comments | Was this review helpful? Yes   No   Report Abuse

☆☆☆☆☆ **Deliver Us Book**

By FE Jonson on Feb 22

Verified Purchase

Was advertised as a new book and was, indeed, a new, unread book. Thank you.

1 Comments | Was this review helpful?　Yes　No　Report Abuse

★☆☆☆☆ **Unexpectedly Boring**

By Tristan Frate on Feb 22

Verified Purchase

Given the premise of this book, I expected much more. This was an opportunity to really get into some of the issues of racial identity in our country but it was never cleary why Amazon drones in Detroit woulud somehow become about racism. This is a far reach for me. I was so bored by a third of the way through that I could no longer push myself to read it. There was no wish to show the plight of the black man in our society, only to show off sophmoric enthusiasm about technology and smart people. I will say that they got the Amazon fulfillment center right, though. I used to work in one. Still, why would that be a subject anyone would want to read about?

6 Comments | Was this review helpful?　Yes　No　Report Abuse

★★★★☆ **Not Ruin Porn**

By Ben Traub on Feb 22

Verified Purchase

When I saw it was two Seattleites writing this book set in Detroit, I was immediately skeptical. I was expecting another exploitive bit of ruin porn glorifying all the negative (and often false) visions of my fair city. Everyone loves to reference the wild dogs, more wild dogs than people they say, which is a total myth that was debunked long ago. But these guys did their homework. Some minor quibbles. They didn't get all the details right. But they did get the strange transitional place Detroit is in, with some areas shiny and new while the rest of the city continues to deal with terrible issues, like the water shut-offs. Mainly, though, it's the spirit of the city, the people, that comes across well. We never gave up. Never lost hope. Call that delusional if you want. I call it Detroit.

3 Comments | Was this review helpful?　Yes　No　Report Abuse

 **Written by Committee**

By Emily St. John Mandel (Amazon Author) on Feb 22

Verified Purchase

Dissapointed by their last novel but wanted to give this a try. There are some clever parts, such as the social media "excerpts," but it lacks a unified voice, due to there being more than one author. It felt soulless This is the kind of book where a character flashes his "weaponized pearly whites." The pacing is off, the plot drags until the very end, and the larded up prose is exhausting. Sparks of brilliance though.

2 Comments | Was this review helpful? | Yes | No | Report Abuse

⭐⭐⭐☆☆ **Russian Dolls of the Race Debate**

By Marcy Sleeper on Feb 22

Verified Purchase

I don't know whether to give this book 1 star or 5 stars, so I'm giving it three. It's so hard to figure out whether I should be angry or not. I mean, two middle-class white men from Seattle writing from the perspective of black people in Detroit...is that literary black-face? But then they have black character Goldman Stackz wearing white-face, impersonating some version of Jeff Bezos who is appropriating black music but rapping anti-black racist lyrics--all to call attention to white supremacy. It's like they want us to laugh and be angry at the same time. I think I feel the same way about Deliver Us as the characters in the book feel about the #BLACKMONEYWHITEPOCKETS video. I'm not sure if it transcends parody or anger. It reminds me of this Ralph Ellison quote:

"The need to control and transcend mere anger has been our lot throughout our history and for many years failing to do so, as the saying goes, got you dead. Nor are things essentially different today, for no matter the headlines of our slogans, an unthinking indulgence in anger can lead to a socially meaningless self-immolation and to intellectual suicide."

Also, the characters were unlikable, and the plot seemed a bit too... convenient.

5 Comments | Was this review helpful? | Yes | No | Report Abuse

☆★☆☆☆ **Amateur Controversy**
By Morgan A. Chalmers on Feb 22

Rather than take on the challenge of educating the public on race relations, Kovite and Robinson's book is merely 349 pages of contrived "controversy" about everything grom gentrification to blackface to tech companies to rape, and attempts to place 100% of the blame on ignorant or "unworthy" people of color. The book is filled with gross generalizations, characters who are walking stereotypes, and cutesy vapid high-fives for privileged tech bros. Maybe they should stick to all-white sci-fi and leave the race commentary to ACTUAL people of color who understand the other side of America. I won't hold my breath.

8 Comments | Was this review helpful? | Yes | | No | Report Abuse

☆★☆☆☆ **No Fly**
By Sara Ellingwood on Feb 22

A dystopian novel about a "certain corporation" taking control of the skies. The main character (no surprise) is white and upper class, with three token black supporting characters. There isn't a lot of insight into race in this book and the authors don't have a lot of explanation either. Why people would steal a drone to harass people is beyond me. Really disappointing. I'm glad the two authors are men because I wouldn't want women to be this stupid.

6 Comments | Was this review helpful? | Yes | | No | Report Abuse

Shout Outs

First and foremost, we'd like to thank White Male Privilege for allowing us to write this book. We couldn't have done it without you. That's both a joke and not a joke, and recognizing the latter is what led us to write about social inequalities that we believe all Americans, regardless of race or class background, must engage with if we're going to make any real progress. That means stepping in, getting dirty, trying to empathize with others' perspectives, and fucking up. We know we haven't done a perfect job, we expect mounds of criticism, and we're sure we've pissed off plenty of people. But just imagine how bad it would be without the many readers who helped us improve this book! To our first, most brutal, and most jovial reader, Phil Klay: Thank you! We also received thoughtful critiques from Clare Needham, Melissa Falcon Field, Renatta Emerson, Richard Armstrong, Jack Ballard, Jessica Rose, and Jake Pederson. And of course, Amanda Knox and Molly Kovite not only read each and every draft, but were reading and critiquing over our shoulders the entire way through.

Preemptive thanks to Jeff Bezos for not suing us! And thanks to the anonymous Amazon employees, both high and low (you know who you are), who gave us crucial insight into the inner workings of this hated and beloved and undisputedly innovative behemoth born in Seattle.

Special thanks to the people of Detroit. We wrote this book for you and that's why we're personally donating as many copies as we can afford to Detroit schools, libraries, bookstores, community centers, bus stops, and street corners.

To the friends we made in Detroit who corrected our misconceptions, shared their stories, and welcomed us to their city: Amanda Brewington, Susan Murphy at Pages Bookshop, graffiti artists Malt and Fel3000ft, Alleah Webb of Drifter Coffee, Eli Gold, Donna Jackson, Gina Balibrera at Literati Bookstore, Pastor Stephens and Brother Dillword at Pure Word Missionary Baptist, the officers of the DPD who took us on an eight-hour ride-along, Kristen Boucher, Patty Whoo, and Ann Turner, who invited us to a BBQ at her house to meet dozens of DPS teachers, Janice Plonka Bays, Bruce Schwartz at Quicken Loans, who gave us a campus tour, Harry Arnold at DetroitDrone, Renee M. Dooley, Greg at Brother Nature Farms, and to the family and friends of activist Charity Hicks, who welcomed us into their memorial service.

And especially, with deep bows and fist bumps, to Melissa Weckler and Ray and Grace, who not only showed us the heart of Detroit, connected us to many of the people above, but who also read our first draft and offered us invaluable feedback. This book wouldn't be possible without you.

We began research for this book while staying with Sally Jane Kerschen-Sheppard at the Blue Field Writers House in Detroit. She was a gracious host. We began the draft at Yaddo—thanks to Eliana Richardson and Candace Wait. Also, to the many friends we made at Yaddo, who heard some early pages of this book: Isabelle Fonseca, Matt Weiner, Eliza Griffiths, Rachel Glaser, Nete Heiges, Matt Taber, Pilar Gallego, James Godwin, Eric Lane, Lisa Endriss, and Patty Volk.

To Krav Maga Seattle, for the hours of training that wormed their way into this book, to Elizabeth Demonico, who shared the most dickish messages she'd received on Tinder, and to our families, for reading, for making us who we are, and for putting up with us daily.

Thanks to Eno Laget for the brilliant cover. Thanks to Blessing Yen for her design expertise. Thanks to James Kaelan, our razor sharp editor at Alephactory Press. And thanks to our agent, Eric Simonoff, and his brilliant team at WME, Kate Barry, Eve Atterman, and Jazmine Goguen: we're lucky to have you representing us.

Shout out to Danny Brown, Angel Haze, Eminem, Guilty Simpson, Black Milk, P-Funk, Prince, Berry Gordy, and all the Detroit music that served as our soundtrack while writing this book.

References

This novel could not exist without the wealth of information, ideas, and perspectives in the following books:

On Detroit:
Lost Detroit: Stories Behind the Motor City's Majestic Ruins (Austin and Doerr)
Detroit City is the Place to Be (Binelli)
313: Life in the Motor City (Carlisle)
Detroit: An American Autopsy (LeDuff)
Detroit: A Biography (Martelle)
Techno Rebels (Sicko)
The Origins of the Urban Crisis: Race and Inequality in Postwar Detroit (Sugrue)
Mapping Detroit: Land, Community, and Shaping a City (Thomas and Bekkering)

On Amazon:
The Everything Store (Stone)
The Amazon Way: 14 Leadership Principles Behind the World's Most Disruptive Company (Rossman)

On Race:
Between the World and Me (Coates)
Losing the Race (McWhorter)

About the Authors

Christopher Robinson is a novelist, poet, futurist, and arm-chair philosopher. He is a recipient of fellowships from the *MacDowell Colony*, *Yaddo*, the *Millay Colony*, and *Bread Loaf*, and he holds an MA in poetry from Boston University and an MFA from Hunter College. He lives in Seattle with his partner, Amanda Knox, who pushes him daily to be more empathic.

Follow him on Twitter: **@manunderbridge.**

Gavin Kovite is a novelist, classical bassist, lawyer, teacher, and veteran. He was an infantry platoon leader in Baghdad from 2004-2005. He attended NYU Law, then served as an Army lawyer for four years. He is now a high school teacher, but remains in the Army Reserves. His writing has appeared in literary magazines and in *Fire and Forget*, an anthology of war fiction. He lives in Seattle with his wife, Molly.

Follow him on Twitter: **@gavinkovite.**

Together, Robinson and Kovite have authored one previous novel, *War of the Encyclopaedists* (Scribner, May 2015). Learn more at www.RobinsonKovite.com.

CPSIA information can be obtained
at www.ICGtesting.com
Printed in the USA
LVOW11*1127280318
571442LV00001B/1/P